At least the dead fell behind a little, unable to match their suicidal dash. Petronius could see that there were three chariots' full of them, one two-horse affair like theirs and two more that were pulled by four. If they reached anywhere wide enough to let the horses have their head, the larger chariots would easily overtake them. But these narrow streets had dangers of their own.

Petronius pulled desperately on the rein with one hand as he clung to Nero's collar with his other. The horses were slow to obey. Maybe they'd been waiting all these years for a chance to truly let loose. Or maybe they could smell the stench of decay behind them. As they galloped into a small, statue-lined square, Petronius could see a desperate white froth around their mouths and knew they couldn't keep up this pace for long.

He yanked again, harder, and this time the horses obeyed – far too enthusiastically. They reared as they drew to a complete and sudden halt, neighing their fury. Behind them, the other chariots raced on, too surprised to stop in time. The dead were closing in, milky eyes glaring malevolently and mouths stretched wide in grins that anticipated victory.

An Abaddon Books™ Publication
www.abaddonbooks.com
abaddon@rebellion.co.uk

First published in 2008 by Abaddon Books™, Rebellion Intellectual
Property Limited, Riverside House, Osney Mead, Oxford, OX2 OES,
UK.

Distributed in the US by National Book Network, 4501 Forbes
Boulevard, Suite 200, Lanham, MD, 20706, USA.

10 9 8 7 6 5 4 3 2 1

Editor: Jonathan Oliver
Cover: Mark Harrison
Design: Simon Parr & Luke Preece
Marketing and PR: Keith Richardson
Creative Director and CEO: Jason Kingsley
Chief Technical Officer: Chris Kingsley

ISBN: 978-1-905437-85-6

Printed in Denmark by Norhaven A/S

TOMES OF THE DEAD

ANNO MORTIS

Rebecca Levene

Abaddon
Books

WWW.ABADDONBOOKS.COM

Dedicated to Helena, David, Sam, Elliot and Kate
Derbyshire – for being top-notch friends, and jolly
good coves all round.

PROLOGUE

Boda hadn't known there were so many people in the world. The tiers of the amphitheatre rose into the sky, each packed with humanity. And all of them here to watch her die. She hadn't known there was so much hate inside her, either, but she felt it now: for these people, this place, this city.

They'd given her a short sword, stumpy and useless compared to the heavy blade she'd carried since she was a girl. A small round shield had been strapped to her arm. They'd told her she was lucky, that these were the easiest weapons for her first match. But she'd seen in their eyes that they didn't expect her to survive it.

The walls of the arena were white marble, too high to climb. If they hadn't been, she would have taken her sword to the throats of the overfed rabble who looked on the fighters beneath them and saw only a morning's entertainment.

Far above her in the crowd, a man in a white toga rose to his feet. Ripples of silence spread out around him, and Boda guessed that this must be their leader, the Caesar. He raised his arms, and around her the other gladiators did the same.

Boda kept hers by her side. The man beside her, an ebony-skinned giant, gestured for her to join the salute. Boda ignored him. She owed no fealty to her people's conquerors.

A trickle of sweat worked its way between her shoulder blades, beneath the leather straps of her armour. It was so unbearably hot in this country. She searched in her mind for a cool memory to counter the relentless sun, but when she tried to imagine the woodland of her home, the green pine trees faded until they were as white as the marble pillars that held up this city, and the snow turned into the sand beneath her feet.

There was a shuffling, an aura of barely contained excitement, and Boda guessed that the fight was about to begin. She already knew her opponent. She'd trained with him many times in the three months she'd been captive here. He spoke little Latin, a prisoner of war like herself, though from distant Judea. His hair was dark, his skin too, a man the colour of oak.

He was carrying a net slung over his left arm and a trident in his right. His eyes appraised her, but weren't afraid. He'd bested her every time they fought, using his superior weight to overpower her when his technique failed him.

He was a fool. All those weeks she'd been holding back, learning her opponent's techniques, strengths, weaknesses, while revealing nothing of her own. Her people didn't fight as if it was a game. They prayed to Tiu, then bathed their swords in their enemies' blood.

But there wasn't time to pray now. The signal to begin had been given, and already Boda could hear the metal clash of weapons around her and the copper stink of blood.

Petronius had always hated the games. All that bloodshed, and for what? He far preferred the theatre, but lately his father had forbidden his attendance there. His father had said it was unmanly. Unmanly! As if there was anything to a man's credit in watching other people fight and die for his amusement. Petronius knew very well that his father, a prosperous merchant, had never once raised a sword in anger. But he'd be the first to call for blood when a gladiator lost his match.

Below them, the pairs of fighters had engaged with a clash of steel. Petronius's eyes scanned over them, uninterested, until they hooked and caught on one figure.

Her blonde hair and ice-pale skin marked her as a member of the barbarian tribes from the far north. She was tall, too – as tall as him, and he towered over many other Romans. From this distance, he couldn't tell if she was beautiful, but he decided to assume that she was. It would make the fight more engrossing.

If it lasted. At the moment, she was doing little more than defending herself, ducking to slide under the swing of the net, almost losing her footing as she dodged back from a fierce trident thrust. Many dull afternoons spent attending the games had taught him that the gladiator known as the retiarius, who looked so under-equipped against sword and shield, was actually a formidable opponent. And he'd seen this particular fighter before. He was a ten-times champion, undefeated in the arena.

Another thrust of the trident, a bright red line on the barbarian woman's thigh, and Petronius looked away. Such a terrible waste. If only her captors had sold her to him, and not to the gladiator school, he could have found a much more pleasant use for her. One he'd wager she would have enjoyed far more.

His father's slave girls certainly never had any complaints. Although, to be fair, they would have been whipped if they had.

Narcissus knew he had to pretend to watch the games. His master Claudius had brought him here to reward him for his hard work. There were other slaves in the arena, but they were standing far above, hidden from their betters behind a wall. The least he could do was pretend to enjoy the privilege of being here.

He tried. It was certainly dynamic. Below him, the pair who had first caught his eyes, the barbarian and the Judean, were already dripping red droplets of blood onto the yellow sand. She was slighter than him, but nimble on her feet, and the bigger, darker man had been underestimating her, allowing her to use the same move twice to slip in beneath his guard before he realised his mistake. Now he looked angry, and Narcissus doubted he'd hold back from a killing blow if he got the chance.

The crowd loved it. They roared their approval every time a blow was struck, the sound doubling and redoubling itself as it echoed from the high stone walls. Narcissus felt overwhelmed by it, and the sour-sweat smell of the 50,000 plebeians all around them.

He'd seen gladiators die before. He'd seen slaves beaten, or crucified, or just left to rot slowly away from diseases it wasn't worth paying the doctor to treat. And every time, he thought: *that could be me.* One day soon, it might be.

Despite himself, his eyes were drawn away from the match, back into the stands to the seated figure above him.

Caligula held all their lives in his fine-boned hands. He seemed to sense Narcissus' regard, and for a moment he was trapped like an insect in the frozen blue ice of the emperor's gaze. Then Caligula looked away, eyelids drooping languidly, as if even getting angry with an uppity slave took more effort than he could spare.

Narcissus let out a long, shuddering sigh of relief. Caesar's curly blond hair was lank and greasy, plastered close to his puffy face, and the dark circles around his eyes were as livid as bruises. He'd heard rumours about

Caligula, that the young ruler had started suffering nightmares that woke him screaming in the middle of the night. But then, Narcissus thought bitterly, a man who'd done the things Caligula had didn't deserve an untroubled sleep.

He switched his gaze to his own master, sitting on the cold stone beside him. Claudius was hunched in on himself, as if he was trying to make his frail body even less visible. His neck was bent at an unnatural angle, holding his face out of Caligula's line of sight. Narcissus wanted to tell him that it was futile, that the less he wanted his nephew to notice him, the more likely it was that Caligula would single him out for the torment that seemed to be his main delight these days.

Not that standing up to Caesar would help, either. Caligula had been known to kill men simply for kneeling too slowly in his presence. Claudius had been kept alive when all around were slaughtered only because he amused Caligula.

Claudius also seemed to feel Narcissus' eyes on him. He jerked a startled look in his slave's direction, then smiled warmly. "En-en-en-joying yourself?" he stuttered.

A thin trickle of saliva seeped out of the corner of his mouth along with the words, and Narcissus quickly reached up to wipe it away before anyone else could notice.

"Yes, dominus," he said. "I'm grateful you brought me here."

That, at least, was true.

Caligula watched with disgust as Claudius chattered to that thin-faced, awkward Greek slave of his. The soft-hearted fool treated the boy more like a son than a possession. Caligula had often thought of having the slave killed, or maybe just disfigured in some way. He imagined the look on Claudius's face as he watched his favourite branded or flogged. But in truth, it was more fun to keep as a threat held over his uncle's head. Not that he needed threats to keep the old stutterer in line.

There was a sudden roar from the crowd around him, deep-throated with satiated blood lust. No doubt one of the matches below had ended in a kill. Caligula didn't bother to look himself – these games bored him now. He'd considered abolishing them altogether, but that blustering bore Seneca had persuaded him that the lower ranks of Rome would take ill to losing their entertainment.

Not that he feared the people. Hadn't they lined the streets to cheer him when he'd returned in triumph from his conquest of the sea itself? He'd showered them with seashells, the spoils of the ocean taken on his daring campaign, and they'd cheered till they were hoarse. He knew that they adored him.

And if they ever ceased to love him, well... When a legion rebelled, decimation was the prescribed punishment, the death of every tenth man.

Caligula amused himself by imagining which of the crowd around him he'd kill in a decimation. Claudius's beloved slave, of course. And there, three rows above, that broad-hipped woman in the blue tunica was far too ugly to live. Her beautiful young daughter would be spared, at least until she'd served her purpose, but the bearded man behind her would have to go. Caligula wondered if he'd scream as his throat was slit, and smiled to imagine it.

The smile slid away into nothing as the crushing boredom descended once again. It seemed nothing could amuse him for long these days. Ever since he'd realised that he was a god, the petty concerns of these mortals had left him yawning. He turned to ask Drusilla if she felt the same –

– and realised, as he always realised, with a sickening jolt of grief, that she wasn't there. That his sister hadn't been there for two years now, and would never be there again. Because no prayer, no offering, no sacrifice of his had been able to bring back the only person he'd ever loved from the shadowy realms of death. And what was the use, really, of being a god, if you couldn't do the one thing you desperately wanted?

Caligula leaned back, closing his eyes so that those around him couldn't see the hot tears gathering beneath their lids.

Seneca watched the procession of emotions chase each other across his emperor's face. He was thinking about that wretched sister of his again, Seneca could tell. Every time he thought of her, he'd spend a few hours – or sometimes a few days – in the depths of the blackest despair, before suddenly switching to a quite lunatic happiness, gorging himself on the pleasures of the flesh until he sickened of them and sank back into despair once again.

Seneca had seen the same cycle play through a hundred times by now. He'd never paid half the attention to his studies in rhetoric that he paid to studying Caesar, though he was regarded as one of the greatest rhetoricians of the age. But then, his ability to move crowds could bring him fame and wealth. His life depended on his ability to read Caligula's capricious moods.

Now Caligula's petulant features were slowly melting into the slackness of sleep, and Seneca looked away at last and back to the fighting below. He knew that, as a man of learning and philosophy, he shouldn't take quite as much pleasure in these things as he did. But this was life in the raw, stripped down to its bare essentials – kill, or be killed.

Just such a decision was being made at this moment in the arena below. It was the barbarian woman he'd noticed before. She was a beauty, he supposed, if you cared for that unhealthily white skin and hair the colour of straw. But he'd marked her for death the instant she stepped out, matched against the undefeated Josephus.

An error in judgement, as it turned out. She'd beaten the bigger Judean down to his knees, his trident thrown to the sand behind him and his own net tangled hopelessly about his feet.

The barbarian woman raised her short sword high, poised for a killing blow. The crowd around Seneca drew in its breath, a hissing susurration as if from the throat of one vast creature, ready to call for clemency. But she didn't give them time. Her sword flashed in the sun as it fell, and then her pale skin and hair were streaked with scarlet, pumping up in great gouts from the fallen man's throat.

The roar of the crowd that followed was a strange noise, half disapproval, half joy in the brutal slaughter. The barbarian made no acknowledgement of it, kneeling calmly to wipe her sword on her fallen opponent's tunic.

Beside him, Seneca felt his companion stirring. He turned to look at her, but beneath the hood of her cloak, only the cherry-red pout of her lips was visible. They were smiling.

"A fresh body," she said. "Young and virile. It will serve our purposes admirably."

Seneca nodded. Everything was already arranged at the gladiator school, so getting his hands on the corpse shouldn't prove to be a problem. And then...

Then Caligula would see who held the real power in Rome.

PART ONE
Et In Arcadia Ego

CHAPTER ONE

At first, Boda thought the other gladiators were staring at her because she'd stripped herself to bathe in the fountain in the school's central courtyard. The Romans were like her own people, comfortable in their skins and untroubled by others'. But some of the men here, the easterners, treated women's bodies as if they were something filthy from which the world needed to be carefully shielded.

To spite them, she turned round as the cool water splashed over her, washing the last vestiges of blood away, and gave the other gladiators a good view of her small, high breasts.

A few of the men did seem transfixed by them, eyes swinging in time with her pink nipples. But the bulk of them kept their gazes on her face, glaring with an anger so fierce is seemed to charge the air around her, like a lightning storm.

"You killed him," said Evius, the bald Greek whose head was as round and smooth as an egg.

"Yes," she said. "Sorry to disappoint you." The Latin words still felt sharp and awkward in her mouth, but she'd learnt the language well enough to make herself understood. She'd known it even before she was taken prisoner, a useful skill when there were captives to be interrogated or enemy camps to be infiltrated.

Evius made a grab for her arm, but she twisted out of his reach, reaching for a sword that no longer hung at her side.

He saw and smiled unpleasantly. "You didn't need to kill him," he said. "He was popular, he fought well – the crowd would have spared him."

Around her, Boda saw the others nodding and murmuring their agreement. "It was him or me," she said, "and I chose me."

"It could have been neither!" That was Josephus's fellow Judean, Adam ben Meir. "We're professionals, not barbarians – well, most of us, anyway. It doesn't have to be a fight to the death. The idea is to put on a good show, not get anyone else killed."

For the first time, Boda felt unsure of herself. She hadn't bothered to talk to the other gladiators in her weeks of training. None were of her tribe, and she didn't make a habit of befriending enemies. Could it be that she'd misunderstood?

"I had to defend myself," she said. "He was trying to kill me."

"It was an act! A show! But the next time, barbarian... The next time you lift your sword in the arena – watch your back."

He spun on his heel and left the atrium before Boda could respond. But the threat remained, hanging heavy in the air behind him.

Narcissus trailed at Claudius's heels as they made their way back to the palace. A red press of uniforms surrounded them, the Praetorian Guard whose sole duty lay in the defence of Caesar's life. Their leader, Marcus, walked behind Caligula himself, leather-sheathed sword thwacking against his muscular thigh with every stride.

Wherever they passed, the people of Rome stopped and stared and cheered and Caligula smiled beneficently at them, accepting their tribute as his due.

Narcissus wondered how the people would have

behaved if the Praetorian Guard hadn't been there. He grinned helplessly at the thought, looking down before anyone could catch him at it. His eyes, as they often did, found themselves fixed on the wooden tablet which hung around his neck and marked him as a slave.

The sun had passed its zenith now, and the streets they walked through were so narrow that the shadow of the buildings enveloped them entirely. Narcissus was grateful for a respite from the oppressive heat. All of Rome had been sweating under it for days now, with no sign of a break. He supposed he should be grateful he hadn't been sold to one of the bakers whose shops lined the street they were currently traversing. The smell of the bread wafted out from the ovens, where the owners' slaves toiled through the long day and into the night, their sweat mingling with the raw dough.

Ahead of him, Claudius stumbled suddenly, tripping over a loose flagstone. His arms flailed, trying to regain his balance.

Taken off guard, Narcissus made a wild grab for him. His fingers hooked into the back of his toga and pulled – and the cloth came away in his hand, leaving Claudius flat on his face on the ground wearing nothing but his loincloth. He blushed a red so virulent it looked diseased.

There was a peel of high, cruel laughter from ahead. Caligula. He'd turned just in time to catch Claudius's disrobing. After a second, given permission to mock their betters by the Emperor himself, the soldiers of the Praetorian Guard also started laughing.

Claudius tried to scramble to his feet, then seemed to realise that this would expose even more of him to ridicule, and sat back down again.

Finally regaining his wits, Narcissus leapt forward, holding out the folded white cloth of the toga to wrap back round his master. Claudius reached out a hand to grab it, avoiding Narcissus's eyes. The worst thing, Narcissus thought, was that Claudius wouldn't beat him for this. His master wasn't angry, he was upset that Narcissus had seen him so publicly humiliated.

"Oh, there's no need for that," Caligula drawled. "I'm sure my uncle will appreciate the breeze without one." And he held out his hand too, demanding the toga.

And this, Narcissus thought, was the moment. This was his chance to prove himself a man, no matter that he was one who could be bought and sold. This was when he could repay Claudius for all his kindness over the years.

He imagined, for a moment, the gratitude in Claudius's eyes. The pride, as Narcissus ignored the demands of his emperor and handed the toga to his master instead.

And then, even more vividly, he pictured Caligula waving at the Praetorian Guard in that uncaring way of his. He saw them falling on him with the pommels of their swords until they'd beaten him into unconsciousness. Dragging his limp body to the Esquiline Gate. He felt the terrible agony as the nails were driven through his wrists, and the cross raised.

He took two steps forward, and handed the toga to Caligula.

The Emperor smiled. He shot one sly, triumphant look at Claudius, still sprawled on the paving slabs where he'd fallen, then slung an arm around Narcissus's neck.

"What's your name, slave?" he asked.

The words stuck behind the lump of shame in his throat. He forced them out with a cough. "Narcissus, dominus."

"Narcissus. Well, not really as beautiful as the myths say, but..." He ran his hand down the slope of Narcissus's shoulder, down his back to cup his buttock beneath his thin tunic. "You'll do."

Narcissus lowered his eyes submissively, afraid of what Caligula might read in them. "I am at my Emperor's command."

"Of course you are!" Caligula said, suddenly pulling away. He turned back to Claudius, who had finally dragged himself to his feet. "Uncle, I want your slave. Give him to me."

Narcissus knew that Claudius was very good at keeping his real feelings from his face. It was how he'd survived so long in the court of the mad Emperor, virtually the only member of his family who had. But he couldn't disguise his expression of dismay now. "He's been with me si-si-sixteen years!" he said. "I bought him when he was just a b-b-boy!"

Caligula shrugged. "Then he must be more than ready for a change of scene. Really, uncle, it's terribly selfish of you to want to keep an energetic young man like this all to yourself."

"B-b-but— "

"I'll go," Narcissus blurted out. He hung his head, because what did it say about him, that his poor, crippled master had the courage to stand up to Caligula for his sake, and Narcissus had none? "I'll gladly go with you, dominus."

Caligula beamed and Narcissus looked only at him and never at Claudius, so he wouldn't have to see the betrayal in his master's eyes.

Boda took her flatbread to a quiet corner to brood. Now that battle was no longer heating her blood, she could think more clearly. She closed her eyes and watched a memory unfold behind her eyelids, the moment when the

Roman soldiers had found her, miles from her tribe and without hope of help.

There had been four of them, two so young they'd barely started shaving and all of them shivering in the northern cold. But their swords were sharp and clean and there had been only a moment of hesitation before they were all pointed at her.

One she could have taken. Maybe two. But four? For a second she'd considered charging forward anyway, dying a glorious death. It would have been the honourable thing to do, and her tribe would have sung songs and drunk mead to her memory.

Honour and glory. In that instant, Boda learnt a shameful thing about herself. She cared more about life than either of them.

Her sword had left a deep imprint in the snow as she dropped it. She remembered seeing the yellow petals of a newly sprouted daffodil, crushed beneath the tip.

And she realised now that, in that moment, she'd stopped thinking, because her thoughts were too painful. She'd let instinct alone and long years of training carry her through the terrible journey back to Rome, the pain of branding, the humiliation of sale at a slave auction and the long, bruising training at the gladiator school.

Instinct had told her that the other gladiators were enemies, only to be fought, and she hadn't questioned it. And now a man was dead because she had never thought that he too was a slave. She'd never seen that these people were her brothers, not her adversaries.

The people of Rome were not all of one tribe, and it was wrong to treat them so. Who was she, without honour or kin, to look down on others who had made choices no worse than hers?

And there was something else, now that she was

thinking again, now that she'd stopped drifting through the world like a spirit, as if she really had died in the dark and ancient woodland of her home.

Why had no one told her that the games were a performance, no more real than the spear-shaking dance that initiated the youths of her people into adulthood? Why had Quintus, the trainer of the gladiator school, not told her? His employers had paid much gold for her and all the others; he should be the most eager of all to save the lives of their possessions.

She saw him now, a fat, silver-haired old man who always stank of violets. He glanced quickly at her, then away and his pace increased, little mincing steps turning into a half trot as he moved away from her.

She sprang to her feet, intercepting him before he could enter the private quarters where the gladiators weren't allowed.

"Quintus – a question."

He turned with an oily smile. "For you, my barbarian beauty, anything."

"The games today. The others – they told me I wasn't supposed to kill Josephus. Is that true?"

"You're a warrior, my petal, my thorny white rose. Fierceness is what the crowd expects of you." He turned away, obviously hoping she'd be satisfied with that.

She took two long paces to put herself back in front of him. "Fierceness, yes. But is it supposed to be real, or a show?"

He waved an expansive arm in the air. "How are such things to be distinguished? All life is a performance, or so they say."

"Real, or not?" she persisted grimly.

He sighed and his eyes darted to left and right, as if checking to see whether anyone was close enough to overhear. They weren't. "There is perhaps an element, the merest hint of showmanship, my dove..."

"Then why in Odin's name didn't you tell me?"

His eyes shifted again. Not looking for anything this time, just avoiding hers. And she knew that whatever he said next would be a lie.

He was saved from voicing it by a commotion, over by the door to the school. "How painful it is to leave you mid-conversation," he said. "But alas, that terrible task-master duty calls."

He slid from her side quicker than a man his size should have been able to move, and headed towards the source of the sound.

Boda considered letting him go. She'd discovered that he was hiding something. Anything beyond that he was unlikely to reveal. But there was something about the noise from the doorway – not any words she could make out, just a tone that was hauntingly familiar – and she found herself following Quintus.

"What's this?" he said. "A fox in the hencoop? Someone come to disturb the peace and tranquillity I've worked so hard to foster?"

"Just a beggar," said Aulus, the youngest and meekest of Quintus's household slaves.

"Then give him some bread and send him on his way."

"I've tried, dominus! He says he won't go without bread and wine."

"Does he now?" Quintus turned back to the door, an unpleasant expression on his face.

Boda moved beside him, getting a clear view of the beggar for the first time.

"Absolutely," the beggar said. "And make the wine something decent – none of that Spanish crap!"

He was tall, red-haired and pale-skinned, with a fine

dusting of freckles over the sharp spike of his nose. Boda felt a flare of something warm and hopeful in her belly. She had never met him before, but she knew his face all the same. This was a man of the Cimbri, of her people. She could hear it in his voice, the accent as he spoke Latin a mirror of her own.

She knew he recognised her too. His gaze appraised her and seemed pleased with what it found. "Greetings, clanswoman," he said in her own language.

She lowered her head, to acknowledge him and to hide her face. She didn't want Quintus to read whatever might be written there. She knew that it was too open, a vulnerability she didn't want to show.

Quintus must have guessed some of it. "One of your own?" he said. "How fortuitous, my virgin huntress. Then you may find him the stalest bread and the dregs of last night's wine, and send him on his way." He smiled thinly and left, clearly glad to be rid of them both.

"I am Vali," the beggar said. His eyes, she saw, were a startling red-brown, unusual for her people. They stared into her own blue ones with amused frankness.

"I am Boda, daughter of Berthold," she said. "A captive here."

"Will you show me to the kitchen, then, and the food I've been promised?"

She nodded. "I'm sure I can find something a little better than stale bread for a hungry man." There was a hungry look about him – in the thin, sharp angles of his face.

"And in return," he said. "I have something to show you."

She paused to shoot him a puzzled look. He was wearing nothing but a tunic, too light to hide anything beneath it.

"Something here," he told her. "A secret darkness in this place."

He walked ahead before she could ask him what he meant. Straight towards the kitchen, as if he already knew where it was.

Petronius sprawled on the bed, wondering if life could get better. A slave girl under one arm, a slave boy under the other, and food and wine enough to sate the entire Ninth Legion. Best of all, he could feel himself beginning to recover from their previous exertions. More pleasure, he felt, was definitely imminent.

Which was why he was particularly displeased when his father strode through the doorway, throwing the two slaves such savagely disapproving looks that they instantly slunk from the room.

"What?" Petronius said. "We were only just getting started!"

His father glared. "You've been in here two hours."

"Exactly."

"You're a disgrace."

"That's not what they were saying half an hour ago."

It was a familiar argument, and one they'd had so often before that Petronius felt his father hardly needed him there to supply his half of the exchange. Except this time, the other man veered wildly off script.

"It's over," his father said. "Enough. You're a man, or –" a pause for him to slowly eye Petronius up and down "– so the calendar tells us. Fifteen years old, and no achievement to your name bar the impregnation of five slaves and the debauching of Jupiter knows how many others."

"That's what they're for," Petronius protested. But he rose to his feet, clutching the bed sheet around him. He felt, though he wasn't quite sure why, that he was about to get some news which needed to be received standing up. His curling black hair was a tangled mess, and he raked a hand through to tidy it, then gave his father the most meltingly innocent look his big brown eyes would allow.

"You're no use to me, you're a disgrace to the family name," his father continued, clearly unmoved. "And it's my fault. I've indulged you. I've allowed you to laze around the house, doing nothing more productive than scribbling a few words when the fancy takes you and claiming you're planning to be a playwright. A playwright! No, it won't do. It's time you started a profession suitable for a man of your station."

A beam of light crept through one of the house's high windows as his father spoke, casting his shadow onto the wall behind him like a harbinger of death.

Petronius shivered involuntarily. "Writing is an honourable profession. Phaedrus is a highly respected man."

His father sniffed. "By the plebeians, maybe."

Petronius forbore to point out that their own family had been plebeian themselves a mere two generations ago. He didn't think now was a good time to be antagonising his father. "I'm not suitable for anything else," he tried instead. "You've said so yourself – who would put up with a no-good wastrel such as myself?"

"A very good question," his father said ominously. "Happily, today I found the answer. Seneca is in need of an apprentice of good family, and despite having heard every sordid tale of your behaviour buzzing through Rome, he declares himself happy to take you on. No doubt it's because he's a Stoic – they're said to crave hardship and unpleasantness."

"Seneca?" Petronius said. "What can that dusty old bore possibly teach me?"

His father smiled for the first time since entering the room. "Rhetoric. I've thought long and hard, and there's only one career in which you can possibly excel – politics. With your propensity for lying and lechery, the Senate should feel like a home from home."

Petronius let himself fall backwards onto the bed and closed his eyes. He was hoping that when he opened them again this would all prove to have been a dream.

Caligula talked to Narcissus all the way back to the palace. It was the longest twenty minutes of his life.

The rest of the Emperor's hangers-on held back, and Narcissus sensed that they were glad of the chance to leave the conversation to someone else. Caligula's mood seemed good at the moment – almost too good, as he laughed raucously at his own jokes and commanded his guards to throw coins to the prettiest of the women they passed. But Narcissus knew that Caligula's moods were as changeable, and as deadly, as a maritime wind. One wrong word and he'd find himself wrecked on the rocks of Caesar's displeasure.

He tried to confine himself to yes or no answers, but he soon realised that even this was angering Caligula. The tenth time he smiled and agreed, the Emperor pouted and pulled away from him. "You're no fun," he said. "I thought you wanted to be my friend."

There was no possible reply to that. Narcissus bowed his head and hoped that would be enough.

It wasn't. "If I wanted silence," Caligula said, "I'd have cut out your tongue."

"I'm sorry, dominus," Narcissus whispered. But he could see that this only angered Caligula more. What did he want? Impertinence, perhaps, a witty retort – but it was far too great a risk.

"He's d-d-dazzled by you, nephew," a voice spoke up behind them.

Claudius, protecting him still. Narcissus was too ashamed to turn round and face him.

Their procession finally swept through the entrance to the palace, purple-painted marble pillars looming on either side. Caligula frowned at Narcissus in the sudden shade. "Are you? Dazzled by me, that is?"

"Yes, dominus." Narcissus said. And then, through a mouth numb with fear, "I've admired you so long from afar. To be suddenly so close to a living god is too much for a humble slave like myself."

"Well," Caligula said. "Understandable, I suppose. But disappointing. As you're such a hopeless conversationalist, I suppose I shall have to find another use for you."

"I live to serve," Narcissus said, and this time it seemed to be the right thing.

Caligula nodded. "Naturally. And I think I have just the job for you." There was a cruel twist to his lips as he spoke. "The importation records for the Empire are in a most desperate state. I had a slave looking over them, but her handwriting was just dreadful. So I cut it off. Her hand, that is. And then I couldn't have her bleeding all over the parchment, so since then there's been no one to sort it out."

"But dominus," Narcissus croaked. "I've no training in accounting. My master—" He caught Caligula's frown just in time. "My former master had me tutored in music, to play the lyre and the flute at his dinners."

"A musician – how wonderful! I play myself, you know. It's a career I could have pursued professionally, if I didn't have a higher obligation."

"The whole Empire speaks of your skill," Narcissus said.

Caligula eyed him coldly. His expression said that he knew he was being patronised, and Narcissus reminded himself that the Emperor wasn't stupid, just mad.

"That's as may be," Caligula said. "But as you can see, I need an accountant, not a flautist. You're a clever man – or so my uncle's always boasting. I'm sure you'll pick it up in no time. And if you don't..."

Caligula's eyes were already drifting away, searching the palace for some other entertainment. "But we don't need to worry about that, do we? I'm quite sure you won't disappoint me."

Petronius had thought he might be given some time to prepare himself. But once his father had made up his mind, he'd always been quick to put his plans into action. It was what made him so successful as a businessman. And it was the reason that, a mere half hour after he'd learned his fate, Petronius found himself at the door of the most tedious man in Rome.

Seneca looked at him sourly after his father had effected the introduction and then hurriedly left, presumably before Seneca could change his mind.

Petronius didn't know what the other man found so displeasing in his appearance. He'd often been told that he was a well-developed young man – and not just by the slaves – while Seneca himself was quite an unappealing sight. With his stringy, greying hair and gnarled limbs, he had the look of a man who'd suffered some debilitating illness as a child, and been slowly decaying into middle age ever since.

"So you're the young reprobate Anthony wants to palm off on me, are you?" he said, in a thin, reedy voice.

"I am Petronius son of Antonius of the Octavii, yes."

Seneca looked even less impressed. "Jumped-up plebeians, the lot of you."

Since this was exactly what Petronius himself had been thinking a short while ago, he elected not to respond.

"Well," Seneca said, "I suppose you'd better come in." He stood aside, ushering Petronius into the room beyond.

Dusk was beginning to fall over the city, but that didn't fully account for the gloom Petronius found within. Most Romans of Seneca's station filled their houses with light, a central atrium for greenery and direct sunlight, and windows elsewhere with bright painted plaster and mosaics for colour and life.

Not here. There were no windows in evidence, and the walls and floor were painted the same stark, gloomy red. The colour of dried blood, Petronius thought, and shivered. The whole place felt old, as if it was a relic from a more ancient city on whose bones Rome had been built.

Seneca led him through at a slow pace, slow enough for him to inspect the clutter of furniture and objects which filled every room. "You've spent time in Egypt?" Petronius said.

Seneca turned to stare at him, brown eyes bright and unfriendly. "Yes. How did you know?"

Petronius laughed. When that just made the other man frown, he gestured around him. A figurine of a cat sat on top of a wooden chest, half-decayed but still inscribed along its length with the little squares and pictures of the Egyptian hieroglyphs. A pile of papyrus teetered in one corner, while the other was taken up with the life-size statue of a cow-headed woman, a half-moon balanced on her crown.

"Yes, I see," Seneca said. "I'm surprised you recognise it."

"I have had some education."

"Little enough, your father tells me. But no matter. With me –" He gestured Petronius through to another room, its door half-hidden behind a thick blue cloth. "You may begin to study those things which really matter."

Here, at last, was a window. High in the far wall, it cast a wan light down on the stacks and stacks of scrolls which sat on every available surface. In the centre of it all was a rickety wooden chair tucked beneath a small desk. The desk too was piled high. Seneca swept an impatient arm across it, pushing the scrolls onto the floor and a cloud of dust into the air.

"I did my own studies here, you know. This room made me the man I am."

"I can certainly believe that."

Seneca ignored – or perhaps didn't notice – his sarcasm. "Your first task will be to copy some of my more famous speeches. Many of my friends have been begging me for their own editions, and you'll learn a great deal in the process."

Petronius eased himself into the chair, sending up another cloud of dust from beneath his buttocks. "About what, precisely?"

"How to address your betters, for a start!" Seneca snapped. He rifled through one of the many piles of scrolls, pulling three out to hand to Petronius. They stank of mildew and old leather. "You may start with these. And I hope your hand is fair – if they're not readable, you'll simply have to start again."

The door slammed behind him as he left, the impact toppling one heap of paper to slide sibilantly to the floor. Petronius sighed and knelt to put them back in some kind of order. But his hand froze, hovering in mid air, when he saw that these too were covered in hieroglyphics.

Seneca had scoffed at him, at the idea that he might have attended to any of his education. And it was true that when the Greek slave his father had bought to tutor him had droned on about the history of the Roman republic, or the conquest of the barbarian tribes on its borders, he had closed his ears. But words, language, stories – these were things he cared passionately about. And when he cared, he applied himself. By the time he was thirteen, he could understand nearly every tongue spoken in the Empire.

He had never told his father, of course. If he'd known, the old man would have sent him off to manage a field office somewhere dreadful like Gaul and that would have been unbearable. A writer of Rome must live at its beating heart. So he'd kept the knowledge to himself, studying by the light of a candle after the rest of the household had retired to their beds.

He could speak all the languages of Rome. And he could read hieroglyphs, too.

He placed the fallen scroll on his desk and ran a finger along the first line, mentally translating it. 'And Osiris says, my hiding place is opened, it is opened. And the spirit falls into darkness, but I shall not die a second time in the land of eternal fire.'

He leaned back, rocking his chair on its legs. This was intriguing. Certainly far more interesting than Seneca's speeches. If he wasn't mistaken, those were lines from the Egyptian *Book of the Dead*. He'd tracked down a fragment once, in the shop of a shady Syrian who dealt in rare artefacts of questionable provenance.

Even those fragments had cost him a small fortune, gold coins he's pilfered from his father when he was too drunk to notice. The Syrian had claimed he was lucky to find anything at all. *The Book of the Dead* had been banned in Egypt two centuries ago, all the known copies burned.

So what exactly was Seneca doing in possession of one?

Vali took the bread and olives that Boda gave him without a word. But his red-brown eyes watched her the whole time he ate, thoughtful and assessing. She felt her pulse quicken, though she wasn't quite sure why.

"How did you come here, clansman?" she asked, when the silence had stretched on too long.

"I'm a wanderer." He shrugged, as if that was explanation enough.

"You've wandered very far from home."

"The world is wide and my time short. I've travelled as far as I can."

"And who are your parents?" she asked. "Your cousins? Where is your people's hearth-home?"

His head tilted to one side as he quirked a crooked smile. "You don't trust me, clanswoman. You're right to be suspicious. This place is full of lies – but not mine."

He was speaking in riddles, like a bard. Could that be what he was? It might explain his presence here. The most famous storytellers among the Cimbri had been known to travel thousands of miles in search of a rare poem or a lost tale.

"You spoke of a secret hidden here," she said to him. "What did you mean?"

He finished the last of the bread before he answered, chewing each mouthful deliberately before washing it down with a mouthful of wine. His lips were stained dark red with it, and when his tongue flicked out to lick them clean it looked very pink in contrast. "There are secrets," he said. "But are you sure you want to know them? Ignorance is safer."

She thought about Josephus, dead by her sword because no one had told her the truth. "I don't care about safety. I want to know."

"Even if it might lead to your death?"

"Even then."

"Good." He smiled, as if she'd passed some sort of test, and his long legs uncurled from beneath him as he rose to his feet. A white litter of crumbs fell to the floor around him and she saw a small brown rat dart from beneath the table to seize them.

"It's through here," he said, moving quickly towards the back of the school, where the weapons and armour were stored between fights.

There were half a dozen other gladiators in the room and they all turned to stare as Boda walked past. Their gaze felt like a physical blow, filled with hostility. She wanted to tell them that she hadn't known Josephus was meant to live, that if they wanted to blame someone they should blame Quintus. But it was her sword that had been the instrument, and even by the laws of her own people the blood guilt was hers.

At the far door, Vali paused, his fingers brushing over the iron keyhole. "The key?" he said, and Boda saw that it was locked. That was new. Only last week she'd been in the place herself, trying out different helmets for the match in the Arena.

She shook her head. "Quintus must have it."

The other gladiators were still watching. If she tried to kick down the door, they'd stop her. She could already hear them murmuring, no doubt wondering why she was giving this beggar a tour of the place. It was probably only a matter of minutes before Quintus himself was summoned. Vali hadn't said so, but she was quite sure that the secret he spoke of concerned the old man.

"We don't have much time," she told him.

He looked skyward for a second, either praying or thinking. Then he shrugged, and turned the door handle.

The door swung open, creaking a little on its rusted hinges. He slipped through, holding it open only a crack for her to follow. When he pushed it shut again, she heard a click that sounded like a lock turning.

She grabbed his arm. "How—"

He put his finger over her lips. His skin was dry, and hotter than she expected, as if he had a fever.

"There's not much time," he whispered. "You can ask your questions when I've shown you what you're here to see."

She could hear nothing except the gentle sound of her own breathing and the harsher rasp of Vali's. The sun had set outside, and the room's two windows were dark and blank. But there was a flicker of golden light, illuminating the neat racks of swords and the shelf after shelf of breastplates and helmets and greaves. The light seemed to be coming from behind them, in the far corner of the storeroom. Candles, she realised, smelling the honey-scented wax in the air. But why leave them burning in an empty room?

Vali nodded at her, as if he knew what she was thinking.

She crept forward, bare feet cold on the marble floor. Vali's footsteps slapped softly beside her. If there had been anyone else in the room, they would have heard him. But there wasn't. There was no one else living inside.

Josephus had been laid on a slab of stone at the far end, wedged into a corner beside a row of tridents. The candles were arranged around him, two of them already burned out and one guttering near extinction.

His body had been mutilated. Her sword had pierced his heart, but it had left a neat hole when she withdrew it. Now his chest had been cut open entirely, the ribs peeled back to emerge from the red flesh beneath like a row of jagged white teeth. She could smell rotting meat and shit combined, but there were no flies buzzing around this feast, though she could see them thick on the window above. It was as if something about the corpse repelled them.

Boda felt bile rise into her throat, acrid and burning, but she forced herself to move closer. She peered into the wide cavity of the chest, and saw that the wound in his heart had been repaired, the jagged edges sown together with small black stitches. The heart should have nestled between the two lobes of his lungs, but those were gone, nothing but a bloody vacancy in their place. The folds of the intestine were also missing and the great purple disc of his liver.

His face was mostly intact, but his nose was bloodied and broken. A thin white gruel dripped from one of his nostrils and Boda realised with a nauseous shock that it was what remained of his brains.

Set on each corner of the slab on which he lay were four earthenware jars. Up close, she could see that their lids were fashioned in the form of heads: man, monkey, fox and something that might have been a hawk. The smell of shit came most strongly from this last, and after a moment's hesitation, she lifted its lid.

Josephus's intestines lay coiled inside, like a slick brown serpent.

She dropped the lid, hardly noticing as it smashed on the floor beside her foot. Vali shifted beside her and she wrenched her eyes away from the corpse to look into his grave face.

The sound of the key turning in the lock was startlingly loud in the silence.

Boda spun to face the door. The rack of tridents was beside her, and she snatched one to defend herself, though the foreign weapon had always felt clumsy in her hand.

There was a slight hesitation before the door opened, as if the person on the other side was equally nervous about what he might find inside. Boda placed herself in front of Josephus's body, though she wasn't sure what she could defend him from, except further desecration.

Finally, the door flew open. The light was far brighter behind it, blinding her for a moment so that all she could see was the dark silhouette of a man. A spear of cold fear shot down her spine and she tightened her grasp on the trident, fingers suddenly slippery with sweat. Then the figure stepped forward. Two steps and the softer light of the candles washed over his face.

It was Quintus. For just a second his expression was closed and hard. Then his eyes met hers and his face sagged into its usual weak, ingratiating lines.

"Boda, my lioness, what are you doing here?"

"We were looking for a fresh sword," she said, knowing that a quick lie was always more convincing than a slow one. "My old one is nicked from the fight."

"We?" Quintus said.

Boda turned to Vali – only to realise that he was no longer standing beside her. She jerked a look behind her, thinking he might have tried to hide, but the room was empty save for her and Quintus.

Then a waft of air blew into her face, from a window that she was sure had previously been shut, and she saw the edge of a booted foot slide across the sill and out of sight. But the window was high above the floor. How could he possibly have reached it?

"Boda, sweetness," Quintus said. "Are you quite all right?"

"Yes," she said, turning back to him. And then: "No! Quintus, what have you done to Josephus?"

"I? It was you who dispatched him to a better place, my treasure."

She stepped to one side, so there'd be no question that he saw the body.

His eyes widened in shock. But there was something theatrical about it – too rehearsed to be quite real. "For the love of Mars, what has happened here?"

"Yes," Boda said icily, "what has happened here?"

He studied her for a moment, no doubt gauging the probability that she'd believe a denial. He must have realised that she wouldn't. His eyes returned to their normal size and his mouth to its customary greasy smirk.

"I'm sorry that you had to see this, truly," he said. "Josephus begged me to do this for him, in the event of his death. It's the death ritual of his people, you see. Without it, he told me he'd be condemned to wander the near shore of the afterlife forever."

Boda looked back at the body, lying with candles all around it, nearly all extinguished now, and the four jars at the four corners of the slab. There was a ritual look to it, that was true, but a deeply unholy one. "His people?" she said.

"The Egyptians."

"But Josephus was of Judea," she said. "A Jew."

Quintus shrugged with a look of careful unconcern. "Once, maybe. But he converted to the worship of Osiris. You know those Jews, a flighty lot, changing gods as easily as the rest of us change tunics."

He looked at her, face bland and composed and eyes so unreadable it was as if he had shutters behind them. She could see there was nothing further to be gained from doubting his word, and much to be lost. By Roman law, she was property, with no more rights than a table. If she became too troublesome, he need only dispose of her.

She bowed her head. "I apologise for questioning you, Quintus. It... disturbed me to see a body treated this way, that's all."

"Understandable, my northern star." He smiled and slipped an arm around her shoulders to guide her from the room. She stiffened, but managed to stop herself from shrugging it off.

Outside the room, he noticed her watching him as he carefully locked the door and pocketed the key. "To spare anyone else the shock you've had," he said.

She nodded, as if she understood, and he turned and walked away. She watched him go, wondering how much he guessed of what she believed. And what exactly he might do about it.

CHAPTER TWO

The next day began as the previous one had ended –
with Petronius banished to the musty room at the back of
the house with nothing but a stack of scrolls for company.
Seneca left him with a slice of flatbread, a pot of honey
and the suggestion that he might like to try working a
little harder than yesterday.

By the time the old man returned, Petronius had
uncovered five other pages from the *Book of the Dead*, as
well as three papyruses so ancient even he could barely
decipher them. He heard the old man approach a few
seconds before the door opened, and hurriedly re-seated
himself at his desk, pulling a scroll open in front of him
at random.

He remained bent over it, pen poised, as the door
opened.

"Young man," Seneca said.

Petronius raised his head, blinking. "Oh, I'm sorry. I
was so engrossed I didn't hear you enter. I've never read
prose of such fluency before."

Seneca smiled. "Really? Well, I have been told my
talent is quite unique."

It said something about Seneca, Petronius thought, that
he was ready to believe so egregious a lie. Some people's
opinion of themselves was so high that no flattery seemed
too outrageous.

"I stand in awe," Petronius said, carefully shifting his
elbow to cover the blank scroll on which he was supposed
to have been writing.

Seneca nodded, taking this as his due. "I came to tell you
that I have a meeting to attend. The rest of the morning is
yours, though your father has instructed me that you're

not to leave this house except in my company."

Of course he had – the old bastard. Still, Seneca must have some household slaves working for him. Petronius would simply have to make his own entertainment. He managed a smile. "Don't worry, sir. Despite what my father may have told you, I value nothing more than quiet study and contemplation."

That, he quickly realised, was a lie too far. The old man frowned at him disbelievingly, then shrugged. "Your may spend the day in your sleeping quarters, or in the public areas. My own rooms, of course, are out of bounds." And with a curt bow, he was gone.

He left the door open behind him, and Petronius remained in his seat, listening to his retreating footsteps until he was quite sure the other man had gone.

His bones clicked as he stood, stiff after so long crouched on the floor. He looked down longingly at the scrolls he'd discovered, but he couldn't risk taking them. If Seneca discovered they were gone, Petronius might find himself out of an apprenticeship – with no guarantee that his own family would take him back.

No matter. He imagined he'd be spending quite some time in that room. Plenty of opportunities to uncover any other treasures that might be hidden there. He could make copies for himself when he had more time – or, if he was careful enough, leave the copies and take the originals for himself. Now he had an opportunity to explore the rest of the house without the old bore around, he should make the most of it. His quarters were to the left, the common areas lying between there and the door. That must mean that Seneca's own quarters were on the right. He'd start there.

His head was down, deep in thought, and he didn't see the slave until he'd walked right into him.

The man was so massive, he had to slope his shoulders to fit beneath the stuccoed ceiling. His arms were as thick as Petronius's thighs, knotted with muscles beneath the bronze skin.

"Where are you going?" the slave said. His voice was so deep it felt more like vibration than sound.

"Looking around," Petronius told him. "Seneca said I could have the run of the place."

The man nodded his head, like a rock teetering on the edge of a cliff before an avalanche. He was standing foursquare in front of the doorway leading to Seneca's quarters, blocking it entirely. It would have taken a small siege engine to move him. "The dining room is behind you," he said. "Food can be prepared, if you wish it."

"Of course," Petronius said.

He remained where he was, and so did the slave. They stared at each in silence for a few moments.

"Well," Petronius said eventually. "Perhaps a prayer before I eat. I'm a deeply religious man, as I imagine Seneca has told you."

The slave didn't respond. He shifted a little, moving his weight from one plate-like foot to the other.

"So where," Petronius persevered, "might I find the lararium?"

For the first time, something resembling an expression crossed the other man's face. He frowned. "There is no shrine to your gods here."

"My gods?" Petronius said. The lararium held household gods, not the great deities of Rome. "Well, no, of course, but as the newest member of this household, I'd like to pay my respects."

"No shrine here," the slave repeated, face mask-like once again.

"Then," Petronius said, "perhaps I'll head out to find a

suitable temple. My day doesn't feel complete without a prayer."

He expected the slave to try and stop that too, but he just looked away, as if the conversation no longer concerned him. His massive arms remained folded in front of his smooth chest, and it occurred to Petronius that he looked like a statue of a god himself. One of those frightening Eastern ones who was terribly keen on sin and purity.

He gave the slave one last smile and backed away, unwilling to take his eyes off him. When he felt the door against his shoulder he slid round it and away, letting out a breath he hadn't known he'd been holding.

This stay with Seneca was proving to be considerably more interesting than he'd imagined. And considerably more nerve-wracking.

Caligula had been right: the Empire's records were a mess. Narcissus thought about Hercules, challenged to clean out the Augean stables in just one day, and decided that he'd had the easier task. The Emperor had left Narcissus in a room with a thousand sheets of parchment and one abacus. He flicked the beads from side to side, the click-click-click a distraction from the roaring of panic in his mind. He didn't know how to do this. He didn't even know how to start.

"It's pointless, you know," said a voice from the shadows.

Narcissus yelped and spun round so fast that he fell off his chair. Paper wafted in the air all around him as a figure appeared through the storm of white, brushing the sheets impatiently aside. It was a woman, a young one, face as pale and blank as the paper which surrounded her.

"Who –?" Narcissus said.

She held an arm out to him, and after a moment's hesitation he grasped it to lever himself off the floor. Only when he was on his feet again did he realise that he'd been holding a wrist – that there was no hand at the end of it.

"I'm your predecessor," she said.

She was quite pretty, he realised, her curly hair a shade darker than honey and her cheekbones high and sharp. But her skin had the unhealthy pallor of someone who didn't see the outside world enough, and there was a feverish brightness to her eyes.

"Your hand," Narcissus said.

She snatched the stump behind her back. "He took it."

"Caligula?"

She nodded, twisting her face away so that he couldn't read her expression. It brought the mutilated arm back into his line of sight, but he was careful not to look at it again.

"The Emperor told me about you," he said. "What he'd done."

She moved with startling quickness, slipping past him to perch cross-legged on the table in front of him. "I showed him. I showed him what was wrong, but he wouldn't listen. They told him I was lying, and he listened to them instead."

"He said..." Narcissus cleared his throat and looked away, embarrassed. "He said he didn't like the way you wrote."

She laughed at that, a high, jarring giggle that didn't sound entirely sane. "He didn't like *what* I wrote."

Narcissus nodded. He could well believe it. Caligula had

a talent for seeing those things he chose, and overlooking the ones he didn't. How else could he believe that the people still loved him?

"And you?" she said. "Down here in the darkness with all the numbers. The rows and rows of numbers all lined up, like soldiers on parade. What is it you did that displeased him so?" The mounds of paper in the room muffled the sound of her voice, smudging it like ink on a page.

Narcissus picked up his chair from the floor, setting it in front of her before gingerly sitting down. She immediately shuffled backwards, her eyes wide and fixed fearfully on his.

He held out a hand to her, palm up, as he would have done if she'd been a skittish horse in need of gentling. "I'm not going to hurt you."

"Aren't you?" She frowned. "But you're here to replace me. If he has you, he doesn't need me. If he doesn't need me..."

Narcissus imagined her, all these weeks in this room, in the dark. Waiting for Caligula to finish the job he started with her hand. To break her apart, piece by piece, until she wanted to die.

"I won't let that happen," he said. "I promise you."

"Oh, you promise." And now she looked entirely sane and far too knowing. "You've been promoted, have you, *slave?*"

"No. But I can help you, if you help me. I need you. I was never taught to calculate. I can't do the thing Caligula's ordered me to do – which is why he asked me to do it, of course."

She reached out suddenly, moving as quick as a striking snake to grasp his hand. He tensed then relaxed, letting her pull it towards her. She cradled it in hers, turning it from side to side, as if it was some rare and delicate artefact. Her fingertips trailed along the lengths of his fingers and over the ball of his thumb, a sensation that was half ticklish, half something else.

"Soft hands," she said. "But calluses, here, here and here." She touched the very tips of his fingers. "You're a musician."

"Yes," he said. "I understand songs – not numbers."

"Numbers are easy," she said. "Eight hundred and twenty-three thousand, five hundred and forty-three."

Narcissus paused, waiting for more, but that seemed to be it. She tilted her head to the side, waiting expectantly.

"That's... a very large amount," he said.

She let out a *tssk* of frustration, jumping from the table with the same snake-quick speed she'd shown before. She leaned towards him, bringing her mouth so close to his ear he felt the whisper of her breath in his hair. "The days of the week multiplied by themselves, of course. Numbers are easy – it's people who are difficult."

He pulled away so he could look her in the eye. "Then will you help me? So the same thing doesn't happen to me as happened to you?"

She shook her head, backing away until she was in the far corner of the room, half hidden behind a stack of ledgers. "Maybe that's what I want," she said. "Maybe I'd enjoy watching someone else suffer the way I did."

He could feel himself shaking as he studied her. She was what he might become, if Caligula had his way. "No," he said. "I don't think you would."

After a moment she sighed and nodded. He noticed that she was wearing a beautiful chiton, blue trimmed with gold lace, but it was torn and stained. He wondered who she'd stolen it from. Or had Caligula given it to her, back when she'd still been in his favour?

"What's your name?" he asked.

She smiled, a bright and carefree expression that made her look suddenly very beautiful. "I'm Julia. And you're Narcissus. Do you find your reflection as pleasing as he did?"

He felt himself blushing. "My mother named me for my father. She was sold away from him before I was born."

"Greek, yes. I will help you. Or, anyway, I'll tell you. Whether that will help, only the gods can know. Come – over here."

She led him to a shelf halfway along one wall, the wood buckling under the weight of the years of ledgers lined along it. She picked the furthest of these, its paper still pale and new, and pulled it to the floor, crouching in front of it on her heels. Narcissus knelt beside her, reading over her narrow shoulder.

"My work," she said, gesturing at the whole row of books. "Twenty-five years of records. Tiberius kept none while he reigned, there was nothing but disorder when I started. And here – look what I found."

She'd flipped to the back few pages of the ledger. Narcissus studied them, the lists of goods and money and what might have been ships' names beside row after row of figures, some large, some small – all incomprehensible. The only conclusion he could draw was that Caligula had a point about her handwriting.

"I'm sorry," he said. "I don't know what I'm supposed to be looking for."

"Here – just here!" She jabbed her finger down on one line: *The Khert-Neter*. "Every week this ship travels from Egypt to Ostia, empty, and every week it returns home with a hold full of oil."

Narcissus kept looking at the figures as if, given enough time, they might explain themselves. But nothing made sense and he began to wonder if this imagined finding was nothing more than a delusion. "So? Hundreds of ships trade with Rome every week. It's the lifeblood of the Empire."

"Idiot!" she said. "As foolish as him! Listen. They travel the sea every week, three days' journey across wave and through storm and all to bring a hold full of air?"

And, finally, Narcissus thought he understood. "Yes, yes. I see. Why not carry something on the way there as well as the way back? They're halving their profits – it doesn't make sense."

"Exactly," she said. "He understands." She rocked back on her heels, looking up at the ceiling with her eyes half lidded. "And when a thing makes no sense, what do we conclude?"

Narcissus could feel the excitement building in him now. "That it's not what's really going on. That ship wasn't empty – it was carrying something on every trip. But whatever it was, they didn't want it entered in the Empire's records. Smugglers, I suppose."

"Maybe. Possible, yes."

"And you told Caligula about this?"

Her eyes closed completely for a moment and she shuddered. "Yes. But the ship belongs to Seneca – an honoured man. A free man, a citizen. He told the Emperor I lied."

"And the Emperor believed him and not you," Narcissus said bitterly. And, of course, if he made the same accusation now, the outcome would be the same. Worse, probably. He knew that Caligula didn't care about him – he enjoyed tormenting his uncle. The more he made Narcissus suffer, the more it would torment Claudius, so he'd make that suffering as terrible as he could contrive.

She must have read something in his face, because she

nodded sadly. "Proof. We need evidence – something more concrete than this."

He looked back down at the ledger. "Am I reading this right? Does the ship follow the same schedule every week?"

She nodded. "Into Ostia on Mercury's Day. Loaded and leaving again that same night."

He jumped to his feet, wishing this room had windows so he could judge the position of the sun. "It's Mercury's Day today, isn't it? The ship might be in port now."

"It arrives at midday, leaves at midnight," she said. "There's still time."

And something in the tilt of her smile, or the way her eyes wouldn't quite meet his, told him that this had been her intention all along: for him to finish the job she'd started. He was being used, but then he'd intended to use her, so he supposed it was only fair. And saving her might be the only way to save himself.

"Fine," he said. "I'll go to the docks. And hope that Caligula doesn't come looking for me in the meantime."

Training was brutal for Boda that morning, the other gladiators taking every opportunity to bruise and wound her. By the time lunch approached she was exhausted and aching and only a few lucky blocks away from losing an eye. But the dusty training ground felt solid beneath her feet, and in the light of day the horror of last night seemed more tolerable, the memory already losing its vividness, like a painting that had been left out too long in the sun.

And yet she couldn't quite forget. Every time she looked up after a fight, wiping away the sweat that dripped into her eyes, there was Quintus. He lurked in the shadows, a measuring look on his face as he watched, and she knew that whatever business had begun between them last night wasn't finished.

When midday approached, a messenger came for him. A slave, young and round-cheeked, he drew the older man aside and whispered in his ear. She was resting when it happened, pouring a handful of water over her head to try and cool off in the endless heat.

Quintus's eyes flicked to her, as they often had during the morning, but this time they didn't flick away again. "Boda, my somnolent Siren, are you worn out already? Truly, your stamina must improve if you're to last another bout in the Arena. Vibius there – give our barbarian queen a work-out."

Vibius eyed her balefully as he picked out the sharpest of the wooden practice swords and gestured her towards him.

Quintus smiled and executed a small, mocking bow – then turned to follow the messenger slave towards the entrance.

Trapping her here so she couldn't follow him, she thought. Which was foolish. It might not have occurred to her that he was worth following, if he hadn't gone out of his way to ensure she couldn't.

She threw her short sword to the ground. "Sorry, Vibius, I have something more important to attend to."

The jeers and catcalls of the other gladiators followed her as she left the training ground, but she didn't let it bother her. If she could prove that Quintus had lied to her, that – for some reason – he'd deliberately arranged to have Josephus killed, then maybe she could restore her honour in their eyes. Maybe she could restore it in her own.

Outside, the streets were crowded with slaves and citizens too poor to make others work for them in the noon heat. Quintus was already far ahead and she let him stay there, sticking to the shadows as she trailed him past the austere Temple of Serapis and towards the heart of Rome.

He stopped several times, forcing her to hang back too, but she didn't think the people he spoke to were the reason for this trip. His expression was too unguarded, and theirs too open. They were probably just spectators from the games, she thought bitterly, congratulating him for putting on such a fine and bloody show.

She'd seldom been outside the gladiator school since she was brought to the city and she was struck once again, as she had been on her arrival, by the sheer size of the place. Even the simple tenement houses were bigger than the chief's mead hall in her own village, and towering above them were great edifices of marble, their purpose unknown to her but their message clear: here sat the wealth and power of the world.

What was wrong with these people, to want to live so close together, without trees or grass to remind them of their roots in the ground? This was a city of strangers, where every day unknown faces passed on the street. No wonder they were so cold, so in love with blood for its own sake. In a place such as this, one could forget how to be human.

She was so lost in her own thoughts she almost failed to notice when Quintus finally reached his destination. And when she saw where it was, her spirits sank. The bath house. She'd wasted an hour and more following him to no purpose.

Except, no. Instead of going straight inside, Quintus paused, turning to survey the street around him. Boda hurriedly ducked her head, hiding her face from sight and hoping that her yellow hair wouldn't draw his eye.

It didn't seem to. When she looked up again, Quintus had moved. She could just make out the back of his head, thinning hair dripping with sweat as he entered the bathhouse between two tall white columns.

A man who didn't want to be observed had something to hide. She waited a few more moments to be sure he didn't leave, then crossed the street to follow him inside.

Petronius lay back, eyes closed, as the attendant scraped the oil from his shoulders. She was red haired, with a pert nose and the largest breasts he'd ever seen, and he was having to concentrate quite hard on not getting an erection.

When he'd left Seneca's house, he'd fully intended to carry on his investigations, perhaps ask around his father's friends to see what rumours might be circulating about the man. Rome was a city of sins, but they seldom remained private ones for long.

He'd headed towards the Forum, where his father's cronies were usually to be found, tallying the latest price of the goods they imported from all over the Empire. But then his route had taken him past the bath house, and just the sight of the steam wafting through the window of the sudatorium reminded him that he hadn't washed himself in nearly two days.

Before he realised he'd made the decision; he found himself inside, stripping off his toga in the apodyterium and handing over the two denarii that bought him a personal attendant for the duration of his visit. And, really, if Seneca was going to keep him cooped up inside for days at a time, he had to take advantage of opportunities like this while he could, didn't he?

Still, his conscience had continued pricking him until he'd plunged into the scaldingly hot water of the caldarium. After that, his worries seemed to float away on the steam.

Only to return with a sharp stab of guilt when he heard a familiar, grating voice not three paces from where he was lying. His eyes flicked open, then quickly shut again as soon as they lighted on the man's face.

Seneca. Petronius didn't think the other man had seen him, but he wasn't risking another look to see. He mock-casually raised an arm, throwing it across his face to shield it from view and hoping the movement itself didn't attract the old man's attention.

There were three bath houses within far easier reach of his home – why in Saturn's name did the miserable fool have to come and visit this one?

After a second of lying statue-still, heart like a galloping horse in his chest, it occurred to Petronius that this was a very good question. Just what was Seneca doing so far from home?

He opened one eye a crack, peering out from beneath the shelter of his elbow. Seneca was still dressed, the cloth of his toga sweat-soaked and clinging to his spindly limbs. He wasn't lying down and it was clear he wasn't here to bathe. A few of the other occupants shot him puzzled looks – no one ever came into the heat of the caldarium dressed.

Seneca ignored them, stooping down to whisper in the ear of a man lying on the bench beside Petronius. The man, plump and red like a ripe plum, listened in silence for a few seconds. Then he rose to his feet and the pair of them hurried from the room. Petronius only hesitated a second before following them, snagging an unattended tunic to pull on as he passed.

After the hot bath, most people headed for the lukewarm tepidarium before going outside to brave the frigidarium. Seneca and his companion were certainly walking in that direction, past the massage room and into the central atrium with its burst of sunlight and mosaic-covered walls. But at the end of the atrium they turned left instead of right, towards a small side room that Petronius had only ever seen used by slaves before.

At the doorway they paused – and then turned back, eyes sweeping the room behind them. Petronius spun round so quickly he made himself dizzy. He rested an arm against a pillar for support, slowly easing himself round until his back was pressed to the far side and there was no way that Seneca could see him.

When his breathing had returned to normal, he leaned his head back against the cool marble and cursed. That had been far too close.

It was only when he looked around that he realised he wasn't the only one hiding there.

The woman was being more subtle about it than he was, leaning forward on her elbows as if she was taking a rest, but the darting glances she kept shooting past the pillar gave her away. She caught him looking at her and met his eyes for a moment, her own a bright, light blue beneath her barbarian-pale hair. Her face was pleasingly rounded but somehow not soft. There was something familiar about it, though he couldn't place her. Then she turned away, clearly dismissing him as irrelevant.

"Well," Petronius said. "I know what I'm doing skulking behind this pillar. How about you?"

Her mouth pulled into a tight, tense line as she turned to look at him, but otherwise her expression remained impressively blank. "Apologies dominus," she said in heavily accented Latin. "I'm afraid I don't know what you're talking about."

"I'm definitely up to no good," he told her. "So I can only assume you are too. The question is whether our nefarious activities happen to coincide."

She stared at him silently for a long moment, and he was just about to say it again using shorter words when she smiled slightly and shook her head. "You speak as if I trust you – a strange assumption."

"I can always find your master and tell him what you've been up to," Petronius said, and instantly regretted it when he saw the flare of anger in her eyes. The muscles in her right arm tensed from shoulder to hand, as if grasping for a sword that didn't hang at her side – and he realised suddenly where he'd seen her before.

"You're a gladiator!" he said. And then, that memory jogging loose another one, "And that man with Seneca is... I can't remember his name, but he trains half the fighters in the Arena."

She looked at him for a long, cold moment. Then her hand unclenched and she nodded sharply. "Quintus, yes."

"You're following him – from the school, I suppose."

Another nod, then her head tilted to the side as she studied him. She really was very pretty, in an exotic sort of way. "And you were following him too?"

"No. I know the man he's with – Seneca."

As if by mutual agreement, they drew apart again to dart their heads round opposite sides of the pillar – just in time to see Quintus and Seneca disappearing through the doorway, accompanied by a middle-aged man and woman whom Petronius was sure he'd never seen before.

"We must follow them," she said.

Petronius frowned. "Are you sure that's safe?"

He only caught the edge of her smile as she turned away. "Probably not." And then she was walking calmly across the atrium towards the door, not waiting to see if he'd follow.

After a second's hesitation, he did. There was no point coming all this way, only to balk at the last hurdle. And besides, if he didn't follow her, he might never see her again – and that would be a terrible shame.

The Port of Rome lay on the right bank of the Tiber, in the long shadow of the Theatre of Marcellus. Narcissus's breath was burning in his lungs by the time he reached it, and his clothes were plastered to his body with sweat. The crowded streets of the city didn't allow a man to run, but he'd pushed through them as fast as he could, desperate to complete his mission and return to the palace before Caligula noticed he was missing.

Narcissus felt a tight, hard knot of fear in his stomach, knowing there was every chance the Emperor had already noticed. He couldn't let himself think about it, though. He had no choice. Better to risk possible punishment now than face certain torture later if he didn't find what he was looking for.

The great seagoing ships didn't travel this far up the river, its bed too shallow to allow them passage. But barges brought their wares to the gates of the city, labouring day and night to supply the needs of the million people who called it their home. He could see three of them now, floating amid the debris of crates and rotten vegetables strewn across the ruffled green surface of the water.

If the *Khert-Neter* was bringing a cargo from Egypt as

well as sending one to it, the goods would pass through here. Illegal or not, there was no other route. By land the journey from Ostia to Rome was fifteen miles, a weary ride for any pack mule and far more conspicuous than simply bribing a port official to look the other way while the barge was unloaded.

The waterfront was a filthy place, the slaves who worked it treated little better than the field slaves who broke their backs tilling the rural estates of many Roman notables. Narcissus could see a group of them now, bowed under the weight of a huge crate as they hauled it from barge to shore. One slip and they'd all be crushed beneath it, but the citizen who commanded them didn't seem to care, flicking his whip against their calves as he shouted at them to move faster.

If the port master was being bribed, there would be no point asking him about the missing cargo. And the freemen here all worked for him, so Narcissus doubted he'd get anything from them, either. That left the slaves. He watched them working, waiting for a pause, a break for them to recuperate when he could question them without interruption.

It was only after half an hour that he realised there wasn't going to be one. The anger he felt surprised him. He'd known all his life the way things were, that some were born free and others into servitude and the gods said this was just, though no one had ever been able to explain why. But cosseted by Claudius in the Imperial Palace, it had been easy to ignore what that really meant. Here, there was no denying it.

Five more minutes and he snapped.

He strode to the nearest overseer, wrenched the whip from his hand and threw it to the ground. "Enough."

The overseer's cold gaze took in his simple tunic, the

wooden tag on his neck that marked him as a slave. He raised his arm to strike Narcissus in the face.

Another arm caught it. A stringy, wire-haired man pulled the overseer back, holding on tight until he could see the fight had gone out of him. "This is Claudius's man," he said. "Have a care."

The overseer's eyes widened and he turned to Narcissus, suddenly abject rather than arrogant. "I didn't know. If you'd said you were here..." He held up his hands, backing away. "Apologies."

It was the first time in Narcissus's life he'd ever inspired fear. He wasn't sure he liked it, but it had saved him a beating, or worse. "Thank you," he said to the newcomer.

The man inclined his head. "Sextus. You won't remember me, but I'm an old friend of your master's. It's my ship they're offloading right now – and putting my cargo at risk by working the men doing it into the ground. I've had two crates of fine Syrian glassware shattered by these oafs, and not a hint of compensation."

"Shattered glass," Narcissus said. "Of course."

Sextus looked at him through narrowed eyes. "And men maimed or killed to no purpose. A waste all round."

Narcissus felt himself relax a little. "Indeed, dominus."

"Even watching this is thirsty work. A drink with me in the shade, perhaps?" He slung an arm over Narcissus's shoulder without waiting for an answer, leading him to a low table in the shadow of the docks.

The wine was welcome after the long walk, and Narcissus gulped it gratefully. When he looked up again, Sextus's eyes were sharp on him. "So, what interest of Claudius's brings you to these parts?"

Narcissus looked away. "I'm not here for Claudius, dominus. I'm on the Emperor's business."

"Ah." Sextus leaned forward, steepling his fingers on the table in front of him. "The *Khert-Neter*, perhaps?"

Narcissus knew the answer was written on his face. The other man smiled and clapped a companionable hand on his shoulder. "It's no secret round here, boy. We all drop some gold into the harbour master's hand now and again, to see our cargoes unloaded first or fastest. But every week, when that ship comes in..."

"We think..." Narcissus hesitated, but Sextus had given him no reason not to trust him. "It's been suggested they might be smuggling something in to Rome."

"Bringing a cargo they don't want examined, that's for sure." Sextus nodded to his right, to the far side of the docks where a lone warehouse sat separate from the rest. "They put it in there, and that's the last we see of it. Don't ask me what it is; I doubt there's a man on this dock who knows. And whoever runs that ship has enough gold to ensure it stays that way."

Narcissus studied the warehouse. It looked newly built, the wooden slats still pale where the axe had shaped them, untarnished nails holding them together. "In there?"

"Yes." Sextus tipped another splash of wine into Narcissus's goblet. "The owners of the *Khert-Neter* are powerful men, influential. And that warehouse is tucked away out of sight, hard to find unless you're looking for it. If I hadn't been here, you might never have discovered it. If you returned to the Emperor and reported that you had found nothing, no one would ever question you."

Narcissus wondered for a moment if he was being threatened, but he saw only kindness in the other man's face. "Thank you, dominus. I understand. Unfortunately, I have to know."

"Your choice," the other man said, but he didn't look as if he thought it was a wise one.

The door was locked. Well, of course it was. Boda shot a look at the young man she'd met behind the pillar – who'd introduced himself as Petronius of the Octavii – but he was frowning in obvious bafflement. She didn't think he could have seen more than sixteen summers, his body gawky and angular as if he hadn't quite grown into it yet, but the potential for beauty was there in the soft, half-formed lines of his face.

"Well, I suppose that puts a stop to our plans," he said. He scratched a hand back through his mop of dark, curling hair.

She shook her head disbelievingly at him. "If the door needs a key, we'll find it."

"How?"

"You!" She grabbed a passing slave, pulling him round to face them. "My master wants entry here."

The slave's eyes flicked between her and Petronius nervously, finally settling on him. "But there's nothing there, dominus," he stammered. "It's a store cupboard for towels."

"And a fresh towel is precisely what I need." Petronius's smile was charming, and he obviously knew it.

"I can fetch you one –"

"Open it," Boda said coldly. "Or my master will be displeased."

The slave studied Petronius, as if trying to work out what form his displeasure might take. Then he looked at Boda and swallowed hard, perhaps realising that her own was likely to be more immediate and painful.

"At once." He bowed and scurried off.

"Well," Petronius said when they were alone. "Now we've alerted everyone to what we're doing, it only remains for us to be denied entry and our mission will be complete."

"Tell them you belong inside, and they'll believe you," she said.

"Why?"

She sighed. "Because you're a free man, and they are slaves, and they've been raised their whole lives to obey."

He looked dubious, but she was right. A minute later another man approached, older and less nervous, and pressed a small iron key into Petronius's hand. "Apologies, dominus," he said. "I thought all were inside today."

He backed away, bowing, as Petronius bent to put the key in the lock. But when he drew level with Boda, he paused. "Don't go in," he whispered too low for Petronius to hear.

She spun to face him, but he wasn't looking at her. He shook his head, a warning. "Listen to me, woman. Our kind go through that door, and they never come out again." And then he was gone, quick strides carrying him to the far side of the atrium.

"What was that about?" Petronius asked, peering back over his shoulder.

"Nothing." She shook her head. "Nothing important."

Petronius shrugged and turned back to the door. It swung open silently, revealing a dim cavity beyond. He gestured her before him, but she shook her head and after a moment he strode through. She took one last look behind her, searching for the other slave in the crowd, but he was long gone. Then she sighed and walked in after Petronius.

Only to find herself pressed up against his back, a mere two paces from the door. It slammed shut behind them, plunging them into darkness.

"Why have you stopped?" she said.

Petronius sighed. "Because we are, in fact, in a cupboard. With a lot of towels."

She reached forward, ignored his yelp as her hand collided with his hip, and eased herself round his slender body. He was right – in front of him there was a shelf and her questing fingers found soft folds of material stacked on top of it.

But Quintus had come through here, and those other people. This couldn't be what it appeared. She braced her feet against the floor, then pushed forward against the shelf with all her strength.

For a moment, her feet slid backwards on the marble floor and the shelf remained stubbornly as it was. Then her heel caught in the gap between two slabs and she stopped moving backwards as her arms started to move forward. The shelves groaned as they slid back, splinters of wood shaved from the sides by the walls.

When she'd finished, the cupboard was five paces deeper and the trapdoor in the floor beneath was fully exposed. Boda pulled on the metal ring set in its centre, and it swung open with little effort. A waft of dank and unwholesome air swirled through the gap. Beneath, the darkness was almost absolute, only the faint orange hint of torches somewhere in the distance.

Petronius swallowed hard. "After you," he said.

There were guards on the warehouse, but only two of them, fine-boned Egyptians in short white kilts. Every five minutes their patrol route took them to opposite ends of the building, the entrance unwatched between them. Narcissus waited till the second time it happened, then darted though the doorway, sending up a silent prayer of thanks that it was unlocked.

Inside, the overriding smell was of wood sap and saltwater, strong but not unpleasant. There weren't as many crates as he'd expected, only ten or so scattered over the floor, with smudged footprints in the sawdust between them. He circled them cautiously, looking for anything hidden between them, but there was nothing there. All the way from Egypt, and they'd only brought ten crates. It didn't look like a major smuggling operation at all.

At first, he barely noticed the sound. But gradually it began to intrude on his consciousness, a dry, high-pitched chittering. He tilted his head, trying to identify the source, but it seemed to be coming from all around him. It was, he realised with an unpleasant shock, coming from inside the crates.

There was something alive in there.

A thin, cold sweat broke out on his chest and arms. His body rebelled at the thought of getting any closer to the source of that sound and he found himself backing away until he was leaning against the wooden wall of the warehouse.

But this was ridiculous. Finding out what was in those crates was exactly why he'd risked so much to come here. And Julia had been right. There was something coming into Rome from Egypt that wasn't being recorded. Something living.

It took a fierce effort of will to force himself forwards. His feet dragged through the sawdust, leaving long thin scuff marks behind him. He realised that he'd balled his hands into fists, and concentrated on unclenching them, one finger at a time.

By the time he'd finished, he was standing beside the first crate. The sound was louder close to, a clicking and a scratching that grew more frantic as he approached, as if whatever lived inside could sense him. He licked suddenly dry lips, wishing he'd drunk more of Sextus's wine before he came here.

The crate would be very easy to open. It was held shut with nothing but twine and a couple of small rocks on top to weight down the lid. He removed one of these, paused, removed the other – and now he could see the crate shaking. Vibrating, as if whatever was inside was flinging itself against the walls in a desperate attempt to escape.

He waited a lot longer before starting to untangle the twine. It was only the sound of voices outside that startled him into action, and his fingers fumbled as he worked, shaking too hard to get a firm grip. He bit down on his lip, trying to get himself under control, and finally the knot began to work lose.

He was pulling the last twist of twine free when the lid of the crate rose under its own power. He gasped and stumbled back, an instant later moving forward again, throwing himself against the lid to keep it closed.

Too late. The crate gave one final shudder and the lid fell to the floor with a crash.

For a second, Narcissus thought there was nothing inside but earth, little round balls of it, packed so tight the crate bulged at the sides. Then the first ball moved, stretching translucent brown wings behind it. The chittering grew in volume, louder and louder, and now Narcissus understood that it was the sound of legs rubbing against each other, against ridged carapaces, scratching against the walls of the crate.

The first beetle launched into the air towards him, and a moment later a thousand more followed behind.

CHAPTER THREE

The beetles were everywhere, small dry legs pattering over his stomach and back and neck, crawling through his hair and under his clothes. They stank of the worst kind of filth. Narcissus froze into horrified immobility. And then, before he'd consciously decided to do it, he ran.

He could see nothing, one hand over his eyes to protect them from the razor-sharp jaws of the beetles, and he hit the far wall with an impact that jarred from his elbows to his backbone. His fingers scrabbled, desperately searching for a door that wasn't there. Splinters of wood lodged painfully beneath his nails and he realised with a sick shock that he was making exactly the same sound the beetles had made inside the crate. Mindless creatures fighting to escape.

Sweat was running down his back. He felt some of the beetles slipping, legs floundering for purchase in the moisture. It was the most horrible sensation he'd ever experienced. After that he couldn't think at all. He just ran, into another wall, then another, stumbling to his knees halfway across the floor only to push himself upright as a torrent of insects headed towards him.

It was sheer chance that led him to the door, and for a second he didn't realise what it was. He'd almost pushed off again, driven by the overwhelming urge to run, run, run when he realised that it was metal beneath his fingers, not wood. Hinges.

He felt the bodies of beetles squashed to a pulpy liquid beneath his hand as he fumbled, trying to find the handle, trying to get out. But all he found was more wood and eventually he was forced to take his hand away from his eyes.

When he opened them, it was like a vision of Hades. The beetles were everywhere, blunt and brown and clinging. His own body crawled with them, five or ten thick so that he could barely see the skin beneath. He let out a muffled whimper of horror, unable to open his mouth for fear of letting the creatures in. But there, finally, he could see it, and he yanked the handle down with the last of his strength and tumbled out into daylight.

All around him the beetles took flight, a black seething cloud heading high into the sky. A moment later they were gone, over the warehouse and away.

He drew in a deep, shuddering breath of relief and fell to his knees, lifting his face to the sun and shutting his eyes.

When he opened them, he saw the two guards. They were staring at him with expressions of shock slowly transmuting into rage.

He didn't think there was any strength left in him. But he used what little he had to drive himself to his feet and stumble away, back towards the docks. He could feel runnels of liquid coursing down his cheeks and arms and he knew that not all of it was sweat. The creatures had bitten and scratched him, a thousand wounds that suddenly started to tell him how much they hurt.

He had no breath left to cry for help, even if he'd been certain it would come. He could hear the guards at his heels. He didn't dare waste the time to snatch a look behind him, but he knew they'd been armed. He imagined their swords, poised above their heads for a killing blow, and his heart somehow found the strength to pump a little harder and his legs to run a little faster.

A second later and he was in the maze of port buildings. He dodged right and left, jumping over abandoned barrels and sometimes weaving in and out of the buildings themselves, his breath like fire in his lungs. He didn't know where he was going – nearer the city, further away – only that he had to escape.

Another warehouse loomed straight ahead of him, and he wrenched open the door and flung himself inside. He was so intent on his pursuers behind that he didn't notice the man in front until he'd run straight into him. They fell to the floor together in a tangle of limbs and Narcissus struck out without thinking, the primitive part of him that cared only about living overriding all civilisation.

The other man caught his fist in his palm, wincing at the impact. "Easy," he said. "I can help."

Narcissus tried to wrench his hand free, and after a moment the other man let him. "Who are you?" he gasped.

The other man laughed. "Does it matter?" He was red-haired, a barbarian, with a sharp nose and a mobile, mocking mouth.

Narcissus scrambled to his feet and the other man followed, moving with a grace that Narcissus couldn't emulate. "It matters to me," he said.

The man bowed. "Then I am Vali, a stranger here. And you are about to be caught, unless you do precisely as I say."

Narcissus opened his mouth to argue – then closed it again as he heard the sound of the warehouse door opening and guttural shouting in Egyptian. More than two voices now; the guards must have found reinforcements.

He turned to Vali, though he didn't know how he could help. The man wasn't even armed.

Vali smiled. "Some fights can't be won – only avoided." And then he stepped aside, and Narcissus saw that there was a crate behind him, half-filled with jars of olive oil.

"I threw the rest out earlier. Plenty of room for both of us in here."

There wasn't time to argue. Narcissus scrambled in, bleeding arms and legs jarring painfully against the awkwardly shaped glass, worse when the other man climbed in after, pulling the lid shut behind him.

A second later he heard the Egyptians, moving through the building as they shouted incomprehensibly to each other in their own language. He held his breath, too afraid of being heard to ask Vali the hundred questions clamouring for answers, but they circled in his mind as he crouched and shivered. And the loudest of them was: if Vali had already prepared their hiding place in advance, how had he known that they'd be needing it?

The steps beneath the baths led a very long way down. Boda descended without any sign of fear, but Petronius could feel a sour lump of it in his stomach, and threatening to head north. He paused a moment to swallow it back, then scrambled to catch up. The only thing worse than being down here would be being down here alone.

Boda waited for him at the bottom, squatting on her haunches with a look of supreme unconcern. They were in a natural cavern, chill and wet. It was too dark to make out much detail, but he saw the shadows of paintings on the wall, relics of a civilisation older than Rome's.

"What is this place?" he whispered.

Boda shrugged. "I don't know. But whoever built the bath house must have known about it."

That was a sobering thought. The bath house had been here as long as Petronius could remember. He vaguely remembered his father telling him that it had been

constructed as part of the public works Emperor Augustus
had commissioned in the city. Thirty years ago? Fifty?
Whatever Seneca was involved in, it didn't seem likely
that it was just smuggling banned books from Egypt.

Boda pointed to the far side of the cavern, where a
tunnel could just be seen, snaking up. "The light's coming
from that direction."

Petronius was prepared to take her word for it. She
seemed to know what she was doing. In fact, she didn't
really seem to need him there at all. For a brief moment
he entertained the thought of turning round, climbing
back up the wooden ladder and leaving her to it.

He'd never been this afraid before. He'd thought he had
– he thought he was frightened last year when his father
very nearly caught him in bed with his business partner's
wife. This, though, was the real thing. His father would
just have given him a beating. He had no idea what would
happen if he was caught snooping around here, but he
didn't think it would be good. His body could rot down
here a very long time before anyone found it.

Some of what he was thinking must have showed in his
face. Boda was staring at him narrow-eyed and impatient.
"Are you coming?" she snapped. "Or are you going?"

And then again, he thought, Seneca could have come
down here for some innocent – or at least safe – reason.
Sexual recreation, perhaps. At the end of that tunnel he
might be confronted with nothing more than the sight
of the old man balls-deep in a woman, which would
certainly be unpleasant, but definitely not fatal.

"I'm coming," he said.

She took his arm, guiding him over the uneven floor of
the cavern. His sandals slapped on the wet rock, echoes
of the sound bouncing from the walls. She frowned and
motioned to her own feet, showing him how she slid

them forward without lifting them. He copied her, and as
the fear receded he realised that he was starting to enjoy
himself. He was having an adventure, something he could
tell Flavius the next time he boasted about his convoy
being chased by Gauls all the way to the Rubicon.

She released his arm when they came to the tunnel, too
narrow for them to walk side by side. There was a sound
from up ahead, a muffled babble of voices that implied
more people than the four they'd seen enter, a lot more.
Still, their chatter should cover any sound that he and
Boda made.

"So," he whispered, "what brings a lovely girl like you
to a place like this?"

She turned to frown at him, then said: "Quintus is
hiding something, I know it."

"Well, obviously." Her body blocked the dim light that
shone back through the tunnel, and he trailed a hand
against the wall to guide himself through the darkness.
"What exactly do you think he's hiding?"

"A reason why he'd arrange for one of his own
gladiators to be killed. And why he'd mutilate the body
afterwards."

"Oh." He stopped, suddenly very sure that turning back
was a good idea. Dead bodies, mutilated ones – these
weren't the sort of adventure he had in mind.

He turned to go, and found her hand clawing at his
arm to stop him. He opened his mouth to protest and
her other hand clapped over it. Her eyes bored into his,
demanding something. Silence, he supposed. When he
blinked acknowledgement she released him, dropped to
her knees and gesture to him to do the same.

Without her body to block it, he saw what lay ahead.
The tunnel opened into another chamber, broader than
the first, its walls carved flat and smooth. He couldn't

see Seneca, but that wasn't very surprising. There were at least fifty people here and Petronius recognised a large number of them, the great and the good of Rome. They were chatting, laughing and drinking wine from crystal goblets, as if this was just another social gathering, an informal dinner party for close friends.

But it wasn't. He counted twelve coffins, leaning against the walls at regularly spaced intervals. The guests ignored them, but Petronius was unable to look away, however much he might have wanted to.

The coffins were open. Inside each, he could see bandage-wrapped corpses, and even from his hiding place in the tunnel he could smell the stench of death that wafted from them. All that, though, all that might have been bearable, if the corpses hadn't been moving.

Publia tried not to look inside the coffins. She could see the movement out of the corner of her eye, the white flicker as bandaged arms and legs twitched, but she did her best to ignore it, as everyone else seemed to be doing. It wouldn't do to look like naïve yokels gaping in shock at these big city ways.

Which was precisely what her husband was doing. "Antoninus!" she hissed, stamping on his foot to stop him gawping quite so openly.

He turned to her, face blank with shock. "They're alive. They're dead – but they're alive."

"Of course." She laughed gaily, in case anyone more important was listening. "I'm sure this sort of thing goes on in Rome all the time."

"Does it?" He looked a little sick, though it had been his idea to join the Cult of Isis in the first place, and his business partner who'd proposed them for membership. Antoninus had seen it as a way of expanding his network of contacts, perhaps securing a few more lucrative contracts for his slave-importation business.

Publia had understood that it could be much more than that. The Cult could be their route to social acceptance, to a class above the one they'd been born to. She couldn't say that she liked everything they stood for. She'd been brought up traditionally, to honour Jupiter and Juno, the divine parents of them all, and steer clear of foreign gods, who were seldom to be trusted. But all around her she could see evidence of the power of the Egyptian deities – and more importantly, of the power of those who worshipped them. If she and Antoninus played it right, her four-year-old son might not grow up to be a merchant like his father. He could be a senator, or even a consul. They just had to ingratiate themselves with the right people.

There was one of them now: Seneca, who was said to have the ear of the Emperor himself. He didn't look like much, skinny and stooped, but Publia put on her best smile as she approached him. "An honour, sir – I can't tell you how thrilled myself and my husband are to be here."

Seneca looked at her and Antoninus a long moment, clearly trying to remember who they were. Then something seemed to click in his memory and he smiled back. "The slave traders, of course. You're most welcome."

"I've long venerated Isis," Publia said, gesturing to the cow-headed statue behind the altar. "It's such a relief to find others of a like mind."

"Indeed. And for us it was like a blessing from the goddess herself to find a supplicant with such a plentiful supply of slaves."

"I'm sure it was," Antoninus said dryly, and Publia

stood on his toe again. She knew he'd bitterly resented the five slaves they'd been told they needed to offer to the goddess to secure their membership. And a final one tomorrow night, before their initiation would be complete. Expensive in terms of gold but cheap when you thought what it might buy them.

"We were glad to dedicate them to the service of Isis," Publia said. "I hope they've proven useful – we did send you our very best."

"Oh yes." A slight smile twitched at the corner of Seneca's mouth. "They were exactly what we required." His eyes wandered the room, sweeping over the twitching bodies in their coffins, and his smile widened.

Publia followed his gaze. There were slaves mingling with the crowd, pouring the wine and handing round small snacks, oysters and stuffed dates, but she didn't think any of them were the ones Antoninus had supplied. She distinctly remembered that one of them had been a Nubian – she'd been fascinated by the deep blue black of his skin – and no one here looked like they hailed from south of the Mediterranean.

"And now your initiation is almost complete," Seneca said.

Publia paused, her eye caught by a flicker of movement to her left, in the entrance tunnel. Was it her imagination, or were there two figures crouching there?

Seneca raised an enquiring eyebrow.

"I think," she said, "that we have some uninvited guests."

It took Boda a second too long to realise they'd been spotted. She'd been watching Quintus as he circulated through the crowd, trying to figure out his place among them. Respected, she decided, but not honoured. He bowed too low and smiled too ingratiatingly to be among equals.

And then she saw the smile drop from his face, and his eyes darted towards her – just for a moment – before darting away again. He knew she was there and he'd been told not to show it.

"Move," she said to Petronius. "Get up – we've been seen."

He froze as a flash of terror crossed his face, already pale from what they'd witnessed. She knew she was faster and stronger than him. She could outrun him and leave him to slow their pursuers. He was a citizen of Rome, one of those who'd enslaved her, and she owed him nothing.

But she still found herself dragging his arm to get him moving, then pushing him in front of her. Maybe it was because he was still so young. Or maybe it was because no one should be left to those things they'd seen, the twitching corpses in their wooden boxes.

They were behind her now. She could smell the death-stench of them and hear the rustle of their bandages as they ran. Petronius stumbled on the uneven floor, falling to his knees, and she had to waste precious seconds hauling him to his feet. She felt the brush of skeletal fingers against her back, and despite herself she cried out in fear, a base animal reaction to a thing that should not be.

The creature behind her answered, its voice a dry rattle. She heard its teeth snapping together, the clash of bone on bone, and she knew that if Petronius fell she wouldn't stop for him again.

But the boy kept his feet and fear drove them both through the tunnel and into the cavern beyond. Petronius was chanting a Latin prayer between desperate pants of breath. She realised she was doing the same, begging Tiu to spare her this death – to grant her any death but this.

When they reached the ladder and began a desperate climb, she looked down at their pursuers for the first time. The bandages had begun to loosen in the flight through the tunnel. She could see skin beneath at shoulder and waist and hip, grey-green and rotting. A hand reached up to grab her ankle, putrid flesh falling away as it grasped to reveal the white bone beneath.

She kicked out. The toe of her sandal caught the thing beneath its chin and the head snapped back, spewing corpse fluid through its jagged teeth. Another kick and it fell back the twenty feet to the floor below, leaving its hand still clamped to her leg.

The hand twitched and started to inch its way up her calf, and this time Boda couldn't control the scream that bubbled out of her throat. She scraped her other foot along her leg, peeling skin and not caring because a second kick dislodged the hand to fall and shatter on the rock below. Droplets of blood from the raw scrape on her leg splattered on top of it, falling faster as she pulled herself up the ladder, sending the blood racing through her veins.

And then, finally, she was at the top, pressed against Petronius as he shoved at the trapdoor. One of the walking dead was only eight rungs below and closing fast. The rest clustered at the foot of the ladder. When the corpse that was pursuing them pulled them down, the others would be waiting. She couldn't see their eyes beneath the bandages, just the blank white of their faces as they looked up. And still Petronius was pushing against the closed door.

"Hurry!" she shouted.

"I'm trying!" he gasped. But then he gave one final shove and the trapdoor swung open with a hollow thud.

She lifted her arms from the ladder to push him through, ignoring his grunt of protest. Her own feet wobbled and slipped on the slick wood of the rungs and for a terrible moment she thought she was going to fall, into the waiting arms of the dead below. Then Petronius's hand reached through, grasping her wrist and jerking up hard enough to tear the ligaments in her shoulder.

She stifled the cry of pain and used the last of her strength to leap up, fingers scrabbling for purchase on the marble floor around the trapdoor. They slipped, slipped again, and then held in a crack between slabs. And finally she was able to lever herself up and through and she didn't even pause for breath, just slammed the trapdoor shut behind her.

A second later the door bounced on its hinges as the thing below pushed up with inhuman strength. Petronius flung himself on it, an act of bravery that seemed to take him by surprise. His eyes widened in horror as he realised what he'd done.

And it wasn't enough. A decaying hand crept round the edge of the wood to fumble at his arm. He shuddered and drew back.

Boda stepped over him, ignoring his yelp of pain as his fingers were caught beneath the heel of her sandal. The shelves were even heavier than she remembered and she was at the last of her strength. One tug, two, and they remained stubbornly in place. Then another body was pressed up behind her, two big male hands over her own, and finally the shelves were moving, grating over the stone floor with a nerve-jangling screech.

Boda had one last, brief glimpse of the undead creature. The bandage had ripped from half its face and she could see the flesh beneath, hanging in decaying strips from the hinge of its jaw. Its eyes, the milky-white of blindness, glared malevolently at her. Then the weight of the shelves slammed the trapdoor shut.

Claudius tried not to worry. He knew that his nephew could read every emotion on his face. The more concerned he seemed for Narcissus, the more Caligula would torment him.

But he'd been down to the records room twice now, and there was no sign of the young man. The other slave there, the head-touched one whom Caligula had maimed, claimed that Narcissus had been sent on an errand and would be back any minute. Claudius had been prepared to believe that the first time. Now... He pictured Narcissus's thin, not-quite handsome face, his cautious smile, and his stomach clenched.

"You look troubled, uncle," Caligula said.

Claudius's head jerked to the doorway, sending a fine spray of spittle from his open mouth. He'd thought the Emperor would be kept busy entertaining himself with his latest lover, the sixteen-year-old wife of Senator Flavius. He thought he'd have longer.

"No t-t-trouble," Claudius said. "Merely moved by the t-t-travails of Troy." He set aside the scroll of the *Iliad* he'd been trying to read to distract himself from his fears.

The light had fled the atrium this late in the day, and his nephew's face was in shadows. A lone sparrow twittered in the silence, the water of the fountain behind it wetting its drab wings.

"Well," Caligula said. "I must say, your man Narcissus

is proving a disappointment. You always spoke so highly of him, but I set him a task and he's shirking already. You don't happen to know where's he's hidden himself, do you?"

The Emperor's expression was bland, but Claudius had long practise at reading the malice lurking in the depths of his light eyes.

He nodded. "I sent him to the market, nephew. W-w-was that wrong?" He kept his face open and guileless as Caligula studied it and, after a second, the other man let out an annoyed huff of breath and turned away.

"He's my slave now, uncle – *mine!* In future, you must ask my permission to use him."

"Of course." Claudius bowed his head in submission, and when he looked up again, his nephew had gone. But the lie would only satisfy him for an hour or so. If Narcissus didn't return before the sun set, there would be nothing Claudius could do to protect him.

Petronius and Boda didn't stop running until they reached the Forum. Lost in the crowd there, and in the fading light of day, they finally felt something like safety.

Petronius leaned against a marble wall, beside a red-and-blue-painted statue of Minerva, and gasped for breath. Beside the goddess, someone had set the stuffed body of a snowy owl. A faint smell of badly preserved flesh drifted from the offering, and he had to swallow hard to keep the contents of his stomach down.

He could hear Boda's ragged breathing beside him, keeping pace with his own. When he turned to look at her, he realised that she was laughing. A part of him wanted to join in, a desperate release of tension, but he was very much afraid that what started as laughter might dissolve into tears.

"So," she said. "We can at least be certain that something is going on."

"That was..." Petronius didn't know how to complete the sentence. Terrifying? Impossible?

"Raising the dead is forbidden among my people. Is it different here?"

Petronius did laugh at that, a jagged bark quickly cut off. "Of course it's forbidden here. It doesn't happen here! That must have been... I've heard about these cults, the shows they put on to impress initiates. It's all smoke and mirrors – a con trick!"

"A con trick?" She stared at him incredulously.

He nodded, convincing himself as he failed to convince her. "Yes – of course. Keep the light low, dress up a few followers in bandages and there you have it. Something to scare the plebs."

"And us," she said dryly. "This was no trick. The things that attacked us were the bodies of the slain. I saw the flesh falling from their bones!"

"No," he said. "No. The peasants still believe that sort of superstitious nonsense. But we're educated people, or at least I am. I've found out Seneca's secret, and it's nothing that matters. The mystery cults have never been banned. If he wants to take part in their theatrics, it's his business. I had no right to follow him, and I won't do it again."

Now she simply looked disgusted. Petronius started to turn away from the contempt in her blue eyes.

She didn't let him, grabbing his chin and forcing him to face her. It was a whipping offence for a slave to treat a citizen that way, but he didn't say anything. A twist of her wrist would snap his neck like kindling. He'd seen it happen in the Arena often enough.

She must have read something in his face, because she abruptly released him. "That's not good enough. The man outside the door, the one who gave us the key, he told me that slaves disappear in those caves. They go in but they don't come out. Don't you wonder what happens to them?"

Petronius shrugged, drawing a deep breath to steady his voice. "They're just slaves."

He had a minute of long cold silence to regret saying it. Then she nodded. "Of course. Roman, I understand." She looked at him a moment longer, then spun on her heel and stalked into the crowd.

Petronius watched her go, her blonde hair a beacon that drew his eyes as she moved away. He thought about chasing after her, but he knew that he wouldn't. She was beautiful but dangerous, and the world was full of men and women who were only the former. And in the end she was just a barbarian and a slave. Her problems weren't his, and he'd be a fool to make them so.

Narcissus didn't know how long they lay inside the crate. Long enough for the arm trapped beneath him to go entirely numb, and for the pervasive smell of olive oil to transmute from pleasant to unbearable. At one point, he felt the crate being shifted, rattling the jars together and pushing his face so hard against the wood it left the imprint of the grain on his cheek.

His heart clenched tight in his chest, but the lid never lifted and as the rattling went on and on, he realised that the crate was being moved, not searched. Five more minutes and it was set down again, somewhere so dark that not even a sliver of light penetrated between the wooden slats.

He was painfully aware of the second body pressed up against his, an elbow in his ribs and a knee digging into the soft flesh of his thigh. He could hear the other man's breathing, slow and steady, but he didn't say a word and Narcissus didn't either. He pictured the Egyptian guards in their white kilts, standing by the crates and waiting for them to give themselves away.

Time lost all meaning in the darkness. A day could have passed or only an hour, but the waiting finally became too much, and the risk of getting caught here less than the risk of being found missing from the Palace. He didn't give himself time to worry about it, just braced his feet against the slick glass of the bottles and pushed up.

The lid instantly lifted, far faster than he'd anticipated. He made a desperate grab for the wood before it could fall. His fingers clutched and missed but the lid stopped anyway and he saw that another hand, paler and finer than his own, was slowly easing it to the ground.

Vali smiled at him, a wide grin under his sharp nose.

"Where are we?" Narcissus whispered. The room they were in looked like part of a warehouse, with wooden walls and a sawdust-covered floor stacked with similar crates, but it wasn't the same one they'd entered. Had the crate been shifted to another part of the docks?

"Listen," Vali said.

Narcissus tilted his head, straining for the sound of pursuit. Nothing at first, and then footsteps, coming from above. "Do they know we're here?" he mouthed.

Vali shook his head. "Listen," he said again.

The feet were still pacing, more than one pair of them, but Narcissus tried to hear beyond them. Nothing. It was quiet here, no voices, only the soft sound of the wind, rising and falling outside the walls. Except, no, there was something too regular about that noise, a push and pull that the wind never had. And something else, too, a gentle slapping that sounded like water.

And as soon as he became aware of that, he became aware of the motion too. The floor, the whole building, was swaying from side to side. He'd only failed to notice it because it had been going on so long – since the crates had been moved.

It took him five minutes of frantic searching to find a knothole in the wall big enough to see through. He pressed his eye to it, blinking against the stinging salt spray.

The horizon was miles distant, a dividing line between blues, one dark and troubled, the other light and clear. The ship was already a long way out to sea, not a speck of land in sight.

CHAPTER FOUR

When Quintus told Boda she was to fight in the Arena that day, she knew he'd seen her in the Cult's hideaway. She could read it in his face, the calculating look in his watery eyes. And she knew it because she wasn't supposed to be fighting. No gladiator was expected to do battle on two consecutive days. There could be only one reason he was sending her out there. This time he meant for her to die.

Her shoulder still pained her from when Petronius had yanked her to safety. The tendon was inflamed and she barely had the strength to lift a sword. Not that that would matter. She wasn't to use a sword this time – Quintus had decreed that she was to fight as a Retiarii, with trident and net.

She'd never practised with those weapons. Quintus knew it, and so did the other gladiators. She saw them watching her as she stretched her muscles in the training ground. There was no warmth in their eyes and she knew that they'd give her no quarter. Quintus had whispered to them too, no doubt giving them permission to go for the killing stroke. He needn't have bothered. They hadn't forgiven her for Josephus's death, and this was their chance for revenge.

When she stepped into the Arena the sun was at its peak and the same crowd thronged the stands. Boda hated them even more, because they'd come to watch her die, and she was afraid that today they'd get their wish. The ache in her shoulder throbbed in time with her strides, and the trident felt clumsy and too heavy in her hands.

The gladiators weren't the first spectacle that day. A

group of prisoners from Gaul had been set against a pride of lions, and the carnage of that unequal battle lay all around: a severed hand already black with flies, gobs of blood and torn hair. Boda remembered Josephus's body, torn open on a slab, and wondered if hers would end the same way.

The crowd roared when their fight began. She'd been paired against Adam ben Meir, a close friend of Josephus's and the most skilled of them with a sword. He swung it now, too swift to parry with the longer trident, and it cut across her ribs. She saw the blood a moment before she felt the pain. Another slash of his sword and a line of fire opened high on her chest.

If she let him rule the fight, she was finished. Though it pulled agonisingly at her torn shoulder, she flung the net low at his feet, as she'd seen the other gladiators do.

He was already moving, leaping over the net and inside the reach of her trident. She used it as a stave instead, knocking aside his sword arm when he drove it towards her leg. In the second it bought her she rolled out and away. But her feet tangled in her own net, and when she regained them she'd lost her hold on it. Now she had nothing but the trident to defend herself with.

There was a shriek from the crowd, half fear, half pleasure. They knew that she was finished. She knew it too, but she refused to give in. This time she would face her death with honour.

Another slash of Adam's sword, and this time her forearm took the blow. The flesh parted in a neat line, exposing the thin yellow layer of fat beneath before blood bloomed red and covered it all.

It was her weapon hand. Her trident drooped and nearly dropped and she shifted it to the other hand. But this arm was weaker still and she could do little more than jab and retreat, never hoping to strike a killing blow.

Adam knew that he had her. The crowd groaned as he toyed with her, driving her first right, then left, knowing he could finish it at any time. A few more contemptuous strokes of his sword, and cuts opened on her thighs and stomach. His eyes glared into hers, with battle-rage and something else, something more personal. He wanted her to suffer before she died.

She knew that in a minute more she'd be too weak to fight, her wounds leaking her life away drop by drop. There was only one chance. She darted forward with the trident, a reckless but unexpected move that forced Adam back. In the second it bought her she retreated herself, ten places clear of him and maybe far enough for what she intended. Her shoulder screamed in agony as she drew her arm back, but the heat of battle overcame the pain.

Adam knew what she was doing. He charged forward, snarling. No more games – he meant to kill her now. And then her arm moved forward and she threw the trident as hard as her abused body would allow.

For just a second, she thought she'd succeeded. Adam's eyes widened in shock, and the trident caught his sword on the down-slash and knocked it aside. Then it was through his guard and the metal tines were heading for his chest. And in an acrobatic move she wouldn't have expected from a man so large he twisted to the side, and the trident passed beneath his arm and behind him.

He smiled as he raised his sword and walked slowly towards her. Boda raised her head. It was over now, and in a way that was a relief. If death was inevitable, then fear became pointless.

"This is for Josephus," he hissed when he stood in front of her.

She nodded, accepting that, then bared her throat to him.

Narcissus sat on a crate, head cradled between his hands. This was worse than he could have imagined. Caligula must know he was gone by now, and if he didn't he soon would. Even if the ship turned straight round, he'd never get back to the palace in time. And if he simply left the ship at the end of its journey, kept on travelling, he'd be condemning himself to spend the rest of his life on the run. Crucifixion was the punishment for runaway slaves.

"I'm sorry," Vali said, sitting on the crate beside him.

Narcissus tilted his head, looking at the other man through one eye. He remembered that it had been his idea to hide in the crate. "It doesn't matter. If they'd caught me they would have killed me anyway."

"Probably." Vali stretched, then rose to his feet. "Since we're here, I suppose we may as well explore."

Narcissus remained seated. Now the first panic was over, the questions returned. "Who are you, anyway? Why did you help me? If that's what you were doing."

Vali tilted his head, considering, and Narcissus was quite sure he was deciding how much of the truth to tell him. Then he shrugged. "I heard of your investigation, and it matched my own."

"You're looking into smuggling?"

Vali shook his head. "No. Well, yes, but only as a by-product. I'm interested in the Cult of Isis."

"The Cult?" Narcissus had heard of them, of course.

Claudius had attended a meeting once, but he hadn't gone again. Decadent and meaningless, he'd said. "They're Egyptian, I know – but shipping in crate-loads of beetles? Why?"

"They were scarab beetles," Vali said. "Carriers of death."

Narcissus stared at him, but that appeared to be as much of an answer as he was going to get. "And how did you know I was looking into this? I didn't tell anyone." But as soon as he said it he pictured her sitting in the dark, with her pretty face and broken mind. "Did Julia tell you?"

Vali smiled and shrugged. "She is one of mine."

That was a non-answer, too, but the bland, unreadable expression on the other man's face told Narcissus he'd have to be satisfied with it. He sighed and rose to his feet, pacing the length of the storage room. "None of that matters now, anyway. Neither of us can do what we want until we get off this boat and back to Rome." He tried the handle of the door at the far end of the room and smiled to find it turning, unlocked.

Vali moved up beside him, placing a hand on top of his to still it. "Why would we want to leave here? This boat is taking us exactly where we want to go. We're on the *Khert-Neter* itself, didn't you realise?"

Boda shut her eyes, waiting for the killing blow. She knew it would hurt, but not for long.

After a minute, as the noise of the crowd grew, she opened her eyes. Adam wasn't looking at her. He was frowning up into the stands, his sword slack at his side. She couldn't work out what had caught his attention at first. And then she saw him, high above and to the left, a lone figure on his feet and shouting, his fist raised in the air.

She couldn't make out what he was saying, but after a while the crowd took up his words and then she could hear them chanting: "Let her live, let her live, let her live!"

Something unfolded in her chest, sharp and painful. She thought it might be hope.

Adam looked back at her, his sword raised once again. She knew he was wondering if he could chance a killing blow before the demand to spare her became too loud to ignore. But the words were so clear now he couldn't deny them, and in the Emperor's box, she saw an upraised arm.

Adam flung his sword into the sand and walked away.

The spectators roared their approval. Boda found that she didn't know what to do. She tried to locate the original figure, the one who'd begun the cry to save her, but the whole crowd was on its feet now and he was lost in the multitude of white togas and brown faces.

So she just bowed, and hurried to the great gateway that led out of the Arena. The other fights were finished – none of them fatally – and the gladiators crowded around her. They stank of sweat and blood and she knew that she did too. But she was alive, when she hadn't thought she would be, and that warmed her stomach like beer.

There was a ceremony after, gold and a laurel wreath to the victor. Boda smiled and drifted through it, ignoring the hate-filled looks the other fighters gave her. But the expression on Quintus's face when they returned to the school was more troubling.

She knew he'd been in the crowd. He already knew his plan had failed, but in the hour since his rage had built.

The instant she stepped through the door he struck her across the face.

She gasped and reeled back, more shocked than hurt. The old man had little strength in him.

"Useless bitch!" he said. "You call that a fight!"

She lifted her chin. "As much of one as you allowed me."

"You disgraced me! You made my school a laughing stock!" There were little flecks of spittle at the corner of his mouth. He wiped them away with a quick hand and struggled to compose himself. The fury in his eyes faded to be replaced by a more calculating light. A more dangerous one.

"You must be punished, of course," he said. "Two hundred lashes should suffice."

Two hundred lashes was near enough a death sentence – and a far worse way to die than sword-stuck in the Arena. Even some of the other gladiators murmured their protest.

Quintus ignored them. She guessed he'd have preferred to dispose of her more subtly. A death in the Arena would have aroused no comment while this might spark some questions. But she wouldn't be around to answer them, and that was what mattered to him. He gestured at two of his household slaves and they moved forward to seize her hands. She tensed her arms but didn't try to shake them off.

"Wait," Quintus said, as they began to drag her to the whipping post in the centre of the training ground. He leaned in, his mouth so close to her ear that she could feel the moist brush of his lips. "I'm sorry, my petal. Truly. But you've seen too much."

When he pulled back, she saw that his eyes were misty with tears, and she realised that he meant it. It was almost funny.

"Stop!" a new voice said. She thought it must be one of the other gladiators, their conscience pricked, and didn't bother to look up. There was nothing they could do. But the man spoke again and the men dragging her away stumbled to an uncertain halt.

It was Petronius. His deceptively guileless brown eyes darted towards her, and he sent her a brief, tight smile. Then he looked back at Quintus. "I can't have you whipping her."

Quintus looked baffled and Boda guessed that Petronius hadn't been spotted at the Cult meeting. Quintus didn't understand why the young man would want to intervene.

"It can be distressing, young sir," Quintus said. "But disobedient slaves must be punished."

Petronius nodded. "By their masters."

"Indeed." Quintus licked his lips, nervous, because although Petronius was agreeing, he wasn't going away. Instead, he walked to Boda and put a hand on her arm, drawing her gently away from the men holding her.

"Even when the crowd has chosen to spare them for their valiant display?" Petronius said. And something in his voice, some intonation, sparked Boda's memory. It had been Petronius who called for mercy in the Arena. He was the one who'd saved her life.

"Even then," Quintus said.

"Well, clearly you're a hard master. I, however, am more lenient. And as this slave is now my property, I choose to spare her this punishment."

Quintus's eyes bulged from his face. "Your property?"

Petronius smiled brilliantly, at Quintus and then at her. "That's right. I bought her from the school half an hour ago."

Narcissus didn't want to explore the ship. Now he knew where they were, he didn't want to leave the safety of their crate for the remainder of the voyage. But Vali clearly intended to poke around, and Narcissus felt safer with him than he did on his own. So when Vali pressed his ear against the door, listening in silence, then pulled it sharply open, Narcissus found himself following behind.

The other man seemed to have some idea of where they were going. The below-decks area was cramped and crowded, a maze of storerooms filled with crates, all seeping a rich olive oil smell into the air. Vali wove a course through that, five minutes later, took them to what appeared to be the ship's armoury. One wall held a rack of swords, polished and sharp, the other rows of round leather shields.

Vali took one sword for himself, pushing the scabbard through the belt of his tunic. He looked back at Narcissus, holding out another.

Narcissus shook his head. "I've never handled one. I don't know how."

Vali continued to hold out the sword. "Perhaps now would be a good time to learn."

But Narcissus stepped back, hands by his side. "I'd be more of a danger to myself than any enemies," he insisted.

The other man smiled at that and returned the sword to its rack. "As you wish."

Narcissus could hear footsteps again, above them on the deck. No more than four sets, and he was beginning to wonder if that was all there were. "What now?" he whispered. "Do we try to overpower them?"

Vali raised an eyebrow. "Can you sail a ship?"

Narcissus shook his head.

"Then it would probably be inadvisable."

He was right, but Narcissus couldn't stand the thought of being cooped up below decks for the entire journey, constantly wondering if they were about to be discovered. Fears, he was beginning to discover, were less frightful if you turned and confronted them head on.

"The sun's set," he said. "It should be dark enough to sneak on deck unseen. We could try to overhear what the sailors are saying."

Vali looked amused. "And do you speak Egyptian?"

"No!" Narcissus snapped. "But if you have a better plan, feel free to share it."

Vali's smile widened. "I do speak Egyptian, and I think your plan is absolutely fine."

It took them a while to locate the steps leading up; the narrow treads glistening white with caked salt. The crystals crunched gently beneath their feet and Narcissus winced at every step, but Vali didn't hesitate.

The moon was only a silver sliver in the far corner of the sky. A million stars shone bright around it, but none shed enough light to reveal Narcissus and Vali to the others on deck as they crept through the hatch.

Narcissus could hear the sailors, muttering softly near the sharp prow of the ship. He wanted to ask Vali what they were saying, but didn't dare risk it. Sound carried too clearly on the open water.

Vali laid a soft hand on his arm, then gestured forward.

The wind sighed through the rigging, a haunting, mournful sound. A haze of sea-spray hovered all around, and the deck beneath was spongy and slick. Narcissus trod carefully, securing one foot before he moved the next. The sailors were visible now, dark silhouettes against the distant moon, though their faces were hidden beneath deep cowls. He kept his eyes fixed on them, alert for any sign that they'd been spotted.

And because he was looking at the sailors, he didn't notice the tangle of ropes strung across the ship. They whipped his legs out from under him so fast he didn't have time to put out his hands to break his fall. His head met the deck with a meaty thud and he couldn't stop himself from calling out.

The sailors were on them before he'd regained his feet, moving faster than he could have guessed. A wicked-toothed knife jabbed towards his ribs and he rolled desperately. The blade sliced through his tunic and into the skin beneath, but the point hit wood and stuck there and he managed to scramble clear.

There were four of them, as he'd thought. Black-cloaked in the darkness, only the silver of their blades shone bright, and deep within their cowls the sparkle of eyes.

He dragged himself backwards and away from them. Splinters of wood drove beneath his skin and he tried to regain his feet but his legs were wobbly with fear and as the hooded figures approached, he fell to his knees again. There was nowhere to escape to, anyway – nothing but sea all around.

He understood for the first time why people spoke about dying with dignity. He longed for the sword he'd refused earlier. He didn't want it to end like this, with him cowering in front of his killers.

And then Vali attacked. His sword carved graceful arcs through the air, a moonlit blur of movement. His aim was true and the metal bit deep into the chest of the nearest sailor.

It didn't even slow him. The man turned, jabbing his own blade forward in a less elegant but equally deadly thrust.

Vali leapt back, but now there were hidden ropes behind him. He stumbled, his sword arm flailing wildly as he fell. His blade missed flesh and instead caught and hooked in the hood of the nearest sailor. The material parted and fluttered to the ground.

At first, Narcissus thought it was a trick of the moonlight, the long blackness at the front of the man's face, the hint of curved teeth within. But then the man shifted slightly, the remainder of the hood fell away, and there was no more hiding what lay beneath.

The sailor had the head of a jackal on the shoulders of a man.

CHAPTER FIVE

Narcissus cringed back, crying out in fear. The jackal head swung towards him, jaws parting in a wide grin. A long pink tongue snaked out to lick the purple lips.

"You have seen us, mortal," the creature said. Its voice was slurred, as if that mouth wasn't made for human speech.

"I'm sorry," Narcissus babbled. "I'm sorry. I meant no blasphemy."

"These creatures aren't gods," Vali whispered.

Narcissus felt his bowels loosen. If these creatures weren't gods, then they must be something darker, the enemies of divinity – because they surely weren't human.

The creature let out a laugh that was almost a howl. "You are right to fear us, child of man. None who see us live to speak of it."

It knelt in front of him, reaching out to clasp his chin. Its hands were human, black and thin, but their touch burned like fire. Narcissus flinched and the creature's grip tightened.

"No escape," it said. "You will lie in these deep waters for all eternity and time will turn your bones to rock."

"Or," Vali said, "you might like to think about this for a minute." He sounded strained but unafraid.

The sailor released its grip on Narcissus and swung to face the other man. "In such a hurry to die? We care not which throat we slit first." It loomed over Vali, spittle dripping from its open mouth onto his cheek.

Vali brushed it away and Narcissus could see that it had left the skin red and blistered beneath. "But does it matter to you," he said, "why we're here? Or how we found you?

If you kill us now you'll never know."

The sailor reared back while his comrades clustered closer, whispering in a guttural language that Narcissus didn't think was Egyptian or any other human tongue.

The one who seemed to be their leader turned back to Vali. "And will you answer those questions?" it said.

Vali smiled. "Will you kill us as soon as I have?"

The creature didn't answer, but its fangs shone white in the moonlight as it smiled.

"In that case, no."

Narcissus wanted to scream that he would answer, that he'd tell them anything they wanted to know. But Vali was right. Silence was their only hope and he bit his tongue to still it, hard enough to draw blood.

"So be it then," the sailor said. "It is as well. Only answers found in pain are to be trusted. You will tell us what we want to know, when even death seems sweeter than what we offer you."

"You intend to torture me, then?" Vali said. Narcissus couldn't see his face, but his voice sounded calm, almost as if this was what he had expected.

"Not you," the sailor said. "Your mouth is full of lies."

As one, the jackal heads of the sailors swung to face Narcissus.

It was dark as Boda and Petronius walked from the school to his home. Boda had never been out at this time of day before, and she was shocked to find the streets crowded with wagons, their wooden wheels the cause of the deep ruts in the road's surface which had baffled her before. The noise was unimaginable, ten times the volume of the yearly fair at which her people traded their cattle with other tribes.

"What is this?" she shouted to Petronius above the din.

He looked puzzled and she gestured around her as they squeezed against a wall to let a heavily laden wagon through. The horse paused to shit as it passed, the pungent smell quickly buried in the cacophony of other odours.

"What occasion is it tonight?" she asked. "Why do they all gather?"

His expression cleared. "Oh, it's like this every night. An edict forbids wheeled vehicles by day."

"Every night?" Boda could hardly believe it. She knew that trade was the lifeblood of the Empire, but to see it like this! How could so many people want so many things?

Petronius nodded and Boda looked away from him to study their route, trying to memorise it. She was used to fighting on her own ground, where she knew the place of every tree and twig. Here she'd be fighting blind, and if – when – Quintus came after her, she needed to be prepared.

After a long space of silence, Petronius turned to her. "So, are you really not going to thank me?"

Boda's muscles tensed. "I don't know how much gold you spent, but don't expect repayment in another coin."

Petronius laughed. "I'll take that as a no. I did save your life, you know."

"Yes," she said. "Why?"

He shrugged and looked away. "Maybe I think the world would be poorer without you in it. Or maybe I'm just desperate for company."

She laughed at that, though she still wanted to know the real answer. Guilt? Perhaps, though he hadn't struck her as a person who heard the voice of his conscience very loudly.

"I did spend a lot of gold," he said. "But it wasn't, in fact, mine."

"Your father's?"

"Seneca's."

She frowned. "Wasn't he the man you were following when I met you? He was one of the cultists."

He nodded.

"Was it wise to steal from him?"

"Probably not. It's probably not very wise to take you back to his house, either, but I don't have much choice. There's nowhere else I can go. I'll try to sneak you in when he's not looking, hide you in my quarters."

"I've heard more impressive plans," she told him. But there wasn't much heat in it. He had, as he said, saved her life.

When they reached it, the house was grand but dark, the white marble blank and unwelcoming. It took her a second to realise why. There were no windows facing out, only a metal-studded wooden door leading in.

Petronius read her expression. "I know, and it's no better on the inside. Wait here for a minute."

He disappeared through the doorway, only to reappear again a few seconds later.

"Empty," he said. "Even that ten-foot-tall slave of his is missing. Hurry now, while we can."

He'd been right about the interior. A few candles flickered in sconces high on the wall, but they did little to dispel the general gloom. There was a musty smell to the place, and she wondered if it was ever cleaned. It would be a hard job to shift the dust from the piles of books and statues and trinkets which covered every surface and crowded every corner. It looked more like a warehouse than a home.

"This way," Petronius whispered.

He led her to the left, through a low doorway and into another wing of the building. Where the other parts of the house had been full to overflowing, these rooms were so stark they barely looked lived in. The first held a low table with just one cushion on the floor beside it, and she glimpsed a narrow wooden bed through an archway ahead.

Petronius caught her expression and shrugged apologetically. "I think the old man's trying to teach me a lesson about the worthlessness of material things."

"A lesson he clearly hasn't learned himself," she said.

He choked off a laugh as they both heard the hollow sound of the main door closing. A second later there were voices, one quavering and male and the other low and sweet and female.

"He's back," Petronius whispered.

The sailors were quick, but Vali was quicker. He flung himself on Narcissus, toppling him to his back and out of their reach.

For a moment the two men were face to face. A trick of the moonlight shaded Vali's red-brown eyes to scarlet, the exact colour of fresh blood. For a split second, Narcissus was more afraid of him than of the jackal-headed sailors. Then he felt Vali pressing something small and cold against his palm. He looked down to see that it was a simple silver coin.

He would have dropped it, but Vali squeezed his hand, closing his fist tight. "You'll need it," he said. And then the sailors had hold of him, and they pulled him away and Narcissus had no one left to defend him.

He slipped the coin inside his mouth in the brief moment before the sailors came for him. He couldn't imagine what good it would do. No bribe so small would turn them away from their course. But he needed a talisman to ward off what was to come.

When the sailors descended, he fought. He knew it was futile, but the panic consuming him was beyond rationality. He bit and thrashed and clawed with his nails and it was all for nothing. Each of the sailors took a limb, pulling with inhuman strength, and when he was spread-eagled between them, they carried him to the prow of the ship. Face up to the sky, Narcissus could see nothing but the ghostly white of the sails as they slid in front of the waning moon.

They tied him to something flat and wooden, the ropes tight enough to cut off the circulation in his hands. He clung on to that small pain, hoping it would drown out the greater to come. He could feel hysterical laughter bubbling inside him, at the thought that he'd once feared Caligula's wrath. That escaping it had brought him to this.

The laughter died as the stars above him were blotted out by the dark dog-shape of the sailor's head. "You may speak now, and spare yourself this," it said. "Who sent you to us, boy?"

The words were in his throat, pushing to come up. It would be so easy to speak. But he remembered what Vali had said and he didn't think he was ready to die. Not yet, not before his twenty-second birthday.

"I won't tell you," he whispered.

They didn't ask again. He'd been expecting blows and that was what they gave him. The first drove into his stomach, leaving him so empty of air that he couldn't scream when the others followed, against his chest and groin and on his face. His left eye swelled shut and he could feel the blood trickling from a cut on his forehead where his skin had split like a ripe peach.

The agony was so intense that he was certain it must end soon. It didn't seem possible that anything could hurt this much for this long. But it didn't end, and when he had enough breath to scream he did. He screamed his throat raw and still they carried on.

When they finally stopped, he was too dazed to realise it. His mouth was still open in a voiceless cry. The pain didn't abate, every part of his body joining in the chorus. But gradually sense returned and he knew that there were no new injuries being inflicted.

"We ask again," the sailor said, voice so calm it was as if the preceding torment had never happened. "Who was it who sent you here?"

Narcissus had no voice left to answer and the sailor took his silence as a refusal. He saw the dark space inside the creature's maw as it snarled.

"They sent you to this," it said. "You owe them no loyalty."

Narcissus agreed. He wanted to tell them, but only a dry croak emerged. He shook his head to clear it, and the creature thought he was refusing it again.

"Very well," it whispered. "Then the torment will be increased."

Narcissus saw a flash of silver as it brought its knife to his hand, and though he hadn't known he could feel any more terror he felt it now, at the thought that he was about to lose a part of himself. He remembered Julia, hiding the stump of her hand behind her back. Was that his future? Would his mind crack, as hers had?

The blade slid over his forearm, leaving a slick trail of blood behind. It pressed into the bone of his wrist for a moment, a sharp agony, then slid down the length of his hand to his fingertip. A pause – and then it drove inches deep beneath his fingernail.

His body convulsed and his back arced from the board, straining against the binding ropes. For one second the stars blazed so bright they blinded him, pinpoints of white fire in the darkness. And then everything was black.

Petronius and Boda stood face to face, ears pressed against the door as they listened to the conversation beyond. He'd begged her to hide in the relative safety of his bedroom, but she'd ignored him, and he couldn't risk further conversation to make his point.

She was utterly infuriating. What did these barbarians teach their women? He'd never met another like her, and certainly not one who was a slave. She'd asked him earlier why he saved her life, and the truth was he didn't know. Oh, he'd felt guilty about leaving her to her fate, but not guilty enough to steal a purse full of Seneca's gold to rescue her. And she was pretty, but Rome was full of beautiful women who could be had a lot more cheaply.

Now, though, he was glad he'd brought her here. Seneca and his female guest were talking in low, guarded tones, but they'd chosen to seat themselves right next to the door to Petronius's quarters, so that almost every word was clear. And the more he heard, the less he liked.

"It's all prepared, then?" Seneca said. He sounded almost meek, a tone of voice Petronius had never heard from him. Whoever this woman was, she seemed to make the old man nervous.

"Everything's in place."

Seneca grunted. "We've cut it fine this time. One night

to spare till the dark of the moon."

"True. But this is the thirteenth, the most important. Everything must be perfect – the goddess demands it."

Petronius heard a grating sound, as a chair scraped back against the floor. When Seneca spoke again, his voice was more distant. "And you're satisfied with the body?"

"Indeed," the woman said. "The body is ideal – young and strong. And the man died a violent death. The power of it will fortify the spells."

"Excellent," Seneca said. "Quintus may be ill-educated and vulgar, but he's proven his value to us."

Boda gasped, a voiceless puff of air Petronius felt against his face.

Outside there was a sudden silence. It stretched on so long that Petronius begun to wonder if Seneca and his companion had left, though he was sure he would have heard that.

A moment later, the door was wrenched open and he and Boda fell forward into the main room. She kept her feet, but Petronius stumbled to his knees. From there he looked up at Seneca's furious face.

"So," the woman said. She was Egyptian, he could see that now, though there was no trace of it in her voice. Her face was perfectly round and very smooth but still not quite young. She could have been any age from fifteen to fifty. She smiled when she saw him looking, a delicate pout of her rosebud lips. "You heard us speaking, I suppose?"

He nodded. There was no use denying it.

"And do you know who I am? Who we are?" She was looking at Boda now.

The gladiator glared back, blue eyes as dark as midnight in the ill-lit room. "Worshippers of the gods of Egypt," she said. "And you are their priestess."

The woman looked momentarily startled. Then she smiled – a dazzling expression that transformed her face from serenity to almost unearthly beauty. "Indeed. I am Sopdet, high priestess of the Cult of Isis, and when you spied on our meeting last night you trespassed on secrets which only the initiated may know."

"We didn't hear anything!" Petronius said. Sopdet gave a small satisfied nod, and he realised he'd been played. Until he'd spoken, she hadn't been entirely certain that he'd been at the cult meeting.

"I tried to keep you out of this, boy," Seneca said. "What concern was this of yours?"

It was a good question, so Petronius just shrugged and looked away.

Sopdet put a restraining hand on Seneca's arm. "This boy – he's of good family, is he not?"

Seneca sniffed, but nodded grudgingly. "Good enough."

"Precisely," she said. "Good enough for him to be eligible to join the Cult. And if he were an initiate himself, the secrets of the Cult would be open to him. No need to punish him for his intrusion then." Her face was friendly as she looked at Petronius, her expression almost conspiratorial.

He felt a flood of sweet relief coursing through him. He had no particular desire to prance around in subterranean caverns with bandage-wrapped lunatics, but it was definitely preferable to the alternative.

Seneca frowned. "And what of his joining fee?"

Sopdet's eyes swung to Boda and her expression shifted, only a subtle movement of muscle beneath skin, but suddenly her face didn't look friendly at all. "This slave will do very nicely," she said. "The dark of the moon is in three nights' time. Let her be sacrificed then."

When Narcissus woke he was by a river. It was dark all around and that made sense, because it was still night, but then he realised it was the darkness of an underground world. The river ran through a cavern, more vast than any he'd ever seen.

The air was full of a gentle hissing sound. After a moment he understood that it was voices, thousands of them. He strained to make out the words but they remained, tantalisingly, always at the edge of his consciousness. And whoever whispered was hidden from him, though his eyes strained into the outer reaches of the enormous, dim cave.

There was only one person visible. An old man stood by the banks of the river. He was ankle deep in the brown-green mud, an unclean smell oozing into the air around him. The slapping of small waves against wood grew louder as Narcissus approached, and he saw that there was a boat in the river. It looked half-decayed, and a foot of water sloshed inside, but it was the only way to cross.

The old man wore a cowl, like the sailors. Narcissus thought he might be human, though. He caught glimpses of a thin white nose and the gaunt curve of a cheek in the darkness. Sometimes it looked like a skull beneath the hood.

Narcissus needed to cross the river. He wasn't sure why, but he knew it was important. If he stayed on this side, he was in danger. Something awful was following him, a person or maybe just a sensation. An agony he had to escape.

The old man looked up as he approached, though his face remained hidden.

"How much to take me over?" Narcissus asked.

He'd expected a dry croak, but when the old man's voice came it was high and light. It sounded like birdsong. "One piece of silver, son."

Narcissus felt for the pouch that usually hung at his neck, but there was nothing there. His money was gone. Only... what was that sharp metallic taste in his mouth? He probed his tongue between gum and upper lip and felt the edge of something solid. When he spat it out he saw that it was a small silver coin.

"Will this do?" he asked.

The old man took it from him, bone-thin fingers ghosting over his as he picked it up. "This will get you there – and back."

Narcissus looked behind him. Something seemed to be resolving itself out of the darkness. It almost looked like the deck of a ship. There was a body on it, tied down and bleeding. Whoever it was must be suffering terribly. "That's all right," he said. "I'm not sure I want to come back."

"You will," the old man said. A yellow slice of teeth smiled beneath his hood. "Everyone wants to return while they still can."

Narcissus nodded, and stepped into the rickety boat...

...And on the deck of the *Khert-Neter*, the jackal-headed sailors prodded and struck his unconscious body, but nothing they tried could wake him.

PART TWO
Morituri Te Salutamus

CHAPTER SIX

Petronius woke, sweating and frantic, from a dream he'd already forgotten. There was no light in his room, so he didn't know what time of day it was, but he suspected it was late. A painful stab of guilt told him he should have been up with the sun, searching the streets of the city for Boda. But he'd been doing that for the last two days, and to no avail. Wherever Seneca and Sopdet had hidden her, he was pretty sure it wasn't within the walls of Rome.

He didn't know why he felt responsible for her. She had, after all, got herself into this mess all on her own, and if it hadn't been for him, she'd be crow-meat already. But the thought of her dying was unbearable to him. And now time had almost run out. Tonight would be the dark of the moon.

He'd managed to track down a few cultists, but they'd said nothing, only reported back to Seneca everything Petronius had asked them. After that he'd tried to talk to his father. The old man hadn't listened past the point where Petronius described following Seneca to the secret meeting. Then he'd offered a beating if his son ever did anything so disrespectful again. And it turned out he'd been a fool to buy Boda with Seneca's money. That made her Seneca's possession, to do with as he wished. No one would help him, and no one but him could help Boda. However futile it seemed, he had to keep trying.

He rose from the bed, joints creaking, and splashed some cold water onto his face, but didn't bother to shave. His dark, curling hair hung limp with grease. He hadn't been to the baths since Boda was taken. What was the point?

There was no one in the main room when he entered. The door to Seneca's quarters stood at the far end, enticingly unguarded for the first time in three days. Could this finally be his chance?

He sidled up to the entrance, glancing behind him for any sign of the old man's huge, silent slave. No one. Not quite believing his luck, he put his hand on the doorknob and turned.

The door was yanked out of his hand as Seneca pulled it inward. He paused when he saw Petronius, eyebrows raised. "Something I can do for you?"

Petronius felt a sudden flare of rage. The old man was treating this like a joke. As if he found the death of a woman nothing to get too worked up about. "You know what you can do," he said. "Release Boda."

Seneca shook his head. "Really, boy. I don't understand why this concerns you so much. She is, after all, only a slave – and a barbarian one at that."

Petronius opened his mouth to give a heated response. A second later, he closed it again. A slave, yes. How could he have forgotten?

"You're right, of course," he said, bowing. "I shan't trouble you again."

The old man smiled cynically. Petronius could tell he didn't believe a word of it. "Won't you? Well, just be sure to be here before sundown tonight. I wouldn't want you to miss the ceremony." And he slammed the door in Petronius's face before he could say anything further.

Petronius didn't mind. The sooner he got out of there, the sooner he could start searching for someone who really could help. Someone who not only knew Boda's location, but might have some motivation for revealing it. He couldn't suppress a wry smile. No doubt it would amuse Boda to hear that it had taken him three days to realise the best person to ask about the fate of a slave was another slave.

Narcissus woke to a wavering blue-green light. He was aware of pain, but it was faded and dull, and when he rolled to his feet he felt only a residual discomfort.

"Awake at last," Vali said. The other man was sitting cross-legged on a small crate. When Narcissus looked around him, he realised he was back in the ship's hold.

"What happened?" he said. His voice was a dry croak, rusty with disuse.

"You passed out when they started torturing you, and they didn't seem able to revive you. So they left you in here to deliver to their mistress when we reach our destination."

Torture. Yes, Narcissus remembered that. He examined the blue-brown bloom of bruises on his arms, and when he lifted his tunic he saw that his stomach was covered in them, barely an inch of pink skin showing through. His eyes were caught by the index finger of his right hand, the red blood clot where his nail had once been.

He let his tunic drop and looked back at Vali. "So why didn't they torture you?"

Vali hesitated, then lifted his own tunic, exposing a white, lightly muscled chest. Tattooed in its centre was a five-pointed star. "A hex of protection," he said. "They couldn't harm me."

Narcissus thought about the silver coin which seemed to have bought him these three days' respite from torment. He'd heard that the northern tribes had powerful sorcerers among them. "And have we reached our destination?" he asked.

Vali nodded to the far wall, and Narcissus saw that he'd somehow managed to carve a large chunk out of the ship's hull. The sea surged in choppy little wavelets only a few feet beneath. And closer than the horizon, a broad low land began. Narcissus held to the side of the gap, leaning out to enjoy the warm sun and refreshing sea-spray.

"It's Egypt," Vali said, which wasn't much of a surprise. "Alexandria."

"And what will happen to us when we arrive?"

Vali shrugged, leaning into the space beside him, arm to arm. His flesh where it touched Narcissus was surprisingly hot, as if he'd already basked in the sun for hours. In daylight, his face looked even paler, a fine dusting of freckles visible over his high cheekbones and sharp nose.

"Will I be able to... go wherever it was I went if I need to?" Narcissus asked him. "Can I hide there if they torture me again?"

Vali continued to look out, frowning slightly against the glare. "You're assuming their leader will try the same technique. I would guess that, violent persuasion having failed, they will try something else."

"What sort of thing."

Vali's mouth turned down. "You've seen what those sailors are. They're not of this world. And their mistress... Who's to say what she might be capable of?"

Narcissus felt an icy chill, even in the baking midday air. "Then what do you suggest?" He didn't know when the other man had become their leader. Probably right from the moment they'd met. A lifetime as the pampered house slave of a Roman patrician hadn't prepared Narcissus for command in a crisis.

"I think," Vali said, "that it would be best if we didn't

arrive in Alexandria in the company of our captors."

Narcissus looked out at the mile of sea between the ship and the shore. He thought he understood what Vali was suggesting, but the idea was impossible. "I can't swim."

Vali's red-brown eyes remained hooded as he slung a friendly arm around Narcissus's shoulders. "I expected as much. Fortunately, I can. Tell me – do you trust me?"

"No." Narcissus said. "Not entirely."

Vali smiled. "That's very wise."

It took a second for Narcissus to realise that the arm on his shoulder was no longer loose. It was pushing him, and somehow Vali's leg was tangled with his own, tripping him as he tried to regain his balance.

He fell forward, into space and sunlight. A second later, the sea rushed up to grab him. There was a moment when his head was still above the surface and it seemed that he might float. Then a wave curled over him and he was lost beneath the water.

It took Petronius an agonising three hours to track the man down. Boda had said a slave working in the bathhouse warned her against exploring the hidden chamber, but there must be a hundred slaves employed to clean and pamper the citizens who washed there, and he could hardly go around asking each of them what they knew about the Cult of Isis. He bathed instead, spending just long enough in each pool to study the slaves who serviced it.

In the end, he recognised the man. His beard was short and square in the Syrian style, but it was his eyes that gave him away, sliding shiftily away when Petronius glanced at him.

Petronius followed him outside the next time he took some towels out to dry, then pinned him against the wall by his shoulders. The man didn't fight back. A citizen could treat a slave as he wished.

"You know about the Cult," Petronius said.

The man opened his mouth in what was obviously going to be a denial. Petronius cut him off. "I know you do – you said something to my friend about them."

"Your friend?" The man relaxed a little.

Petronius hesitated, then released him. "Yes. You told her it was dangerous for slaves to get involved, and you were right."

The man nodded. "Been taken, has she, your woman?"

"And not to their meeting place here – I've already checked."

There was a painfully long silence as the man considered. Petronius didn't try to force him. The slave had cared enough to risk exposure when he warned Boda before. Petronius had to hope that the man would risk it again.

Finally the Syrian licked his lips, looked right and left, then said in a low whisper: "Here is where they meet. They hold their ceremonies elsewhere."

Petronius felt a rush of hope. "And is that where they're keeping her?"

He shook his head. "I don't know. But every month they gather there, in the catacombs outside the city. Every month on this day."

Once when he was three and his mother still took care of him, Narcissus had fallen in a river. He remembered the terror he'd felt then and he felt it again now. It was a panic so unreasoning that he could do nothing to save himself, just flail helplessly. He screamed and his open mouth let the salt water flood in. He gasped in fear and it was in his lungs, and a blackness began to press against the edges of his mind.

There was sound, something beyond the murmuring of the waves, but though he knew it was speech, he couldn't resolve it into words. Something was holding him and he kicked out against that too, but it kept its grip and then his head was above water and he was choking up a froth of seawater and vomit. It trickled noisomely down his chin and the sharp smell of the bile stung his nose and cleared his head.

"For the love of the gods, stop wriggling about!" Vali shouted.

His voice was right by Narcissus's ear, and after a moment longer of futile struggle, Narcissus realised that it was Vali who was holding him up. It was Vali's arm around his neck. Vali's grip loosened as Narcissus's legs kicked out in a spasm of panic that seemed outside the control of his conscious mind.

"Calm down!" Vali said. "Just relax."

With a supreme effort, he forced himself to stop struggling, tensing every muscle until it submitted.

Now that he wasn't moving, he felt the whisper of air over his ear as Vali sighed. "Go limp – as if you're unconscious. I can't swim with you otherwise."

That was even harder, but as the minutes passed and the water didn't rise to cover his head, he slowly let the tension drift out of him. His legs floated behind him, and his head lay back, pillowed on the water and Vali's chest.

It was a long way. Narcissus was astonished that the other man had the strength. He had nothing to look at but the perfect blue sky above, blurred now and then as one of the larger waves washed over them. The water stung his eyes and in the barely-healed cuts on his face and chest, but this was almost comfortable. There was something easy for him in giving total control of himself to another. It was what he'd been trained to do all his life.

After an uncounted space of time, he felt the drag of sand beneath his feet.

"We're there," Vali said breathlessly, and released him.

He floundered a moment, panic returning full force, but when he found his feet the water only came to his chest. They were some distance from the docks, on the outer edge of a city that rivalled Rome for size, but was full of angles and colours that marked it as the product of another land and culture. On an island near its entrance stood a huge tower, a light as bright as the sun blinking at its peak. It must be the famous Pharos of Alexandria, a warning to shipping that approached the east's greatest port.

When Narcissus reached the shore above the waterline he fell to his knees. Though he'd been doing none of the work on their swim he was wrung-out with exhaustion. He could only imagine how Vali must be feeling.

The other man remained standing, though he leaned over with hands on knees, gasping to regain his breath. As soon as he had, he reached down to draw Narcissus to his feet. "We can't stay here," he said. "I think the sailors saw us leave the ship. They'll be looking for us."

And as if Vali's words had summoned them, Narcissus heard the shouts of their pursuers, and the scrape of swords drawn from scabbards. They were very close.

Vali released his arm and ran, away from the sea and the shore. Narcissus staggered after, trusting the other man to find his way, though he looked no more Egyptian than Narcissus was.

Their pursuers spotted them almost straight away. They let out an ululating cry – high and unearthly – and followed on their heels.

Petronius had only been to the catacombs once before, to witness the internment of his father's father. Then he'd been in the company of a crowd of mourners, brightly dressed and loud, if not exactly cheerful. Now he was all alone, and he hesitated at the entrance to the tombs and wondered if he really had the courage to go in.

He'd brought a torch, a spare in the bag slung over his arm. He lit it now, its flame a translucent wavering in the air. The sun wasn't yet close enough to the horizon for its rays to turn the red-orange of a dying day.

Petronius drew a breath, then walked forward into the dark mouth of the cave. He kept his eyes on the flame, which seemed to brighten and brighten as the light around it faded. Finally he was in darkness with only the yellow flicker of the torch to show him where he trod.

For the first hundred paces he saw nothing around him but earth and rock walls, gradually narrowing as he descended. Side tunnels snaked off at irregular intervals, but he ignored them. The whole vast place was a maze with no map. If he stuck to the straightest route, he stood the least chance of getting lost.

He wished that, like Perseus in the Labyrinth, he'd thought to bring a thread to mark his path. Too late now – the catacombs lay outside the walls of Rome. If he went back he'd never find Boda before the moon rose.

Deeper down, beyond the reach of any daylight, he

saw the first urns, tucked into alcoves low in the walls. The fashion had been – still was, in the more traditional families – to burn the dead before they were buried. He thought of all the generations of Rome, reduced to the same black ash.

The bodies were worse. He came to them deeper inside. The freshest were first, stinking of rotting flesh. The light of his torch shone briefly into one of the shallowest crevices and he saw the corpse of a little girl inside, so recent that he could still make out the structure of her face, though the flesh was beginning to green and hang away from it. She'd been a pretty little thing.

After that he kept his eyes on the path. He was looking for other footprints, the hint that a large group of people had passed here recently. It was futile. Too many funerary parties had come this way, obscuring the marks left by anyone engaged in less respectable activities.

The tunnel was barely head-height this deep in, and soon there was no obvious main path to take. He stood for a moment, looking at the three-way fork that faced him, then decided to take the right-hand turning. If he did the same at every junction, he should be able to reverse his steps without getting lost.

The bodies were fewer here, and older. He'd heard that the catacombs had been in use since the founding of the Republic. These bones were brown with age and it was hard to imagine that they'd ever walked and talked and fucked. It was damp here, too. Rank moisture dripped onto his bare neck and when he brushed it off it left a green streak on his hand.

Then he came to a turning that led to a tunnel which narrowed and narrowed. At first he stooped and then he crawled forward on his hands and knees until finally he realised that he could go no further. For a moment of clenching fear he thought he was stuck tight. But he wriggled and drove himself backwards with his hands, and eventually he made his way back to the original turning.

He took the middle turning this time, but soon he found another blocked path and then another. By the fourth time he'd reversed himself and headed down a different path he realised that he had no idea which way would lead him back out.

There were no dead ends in Alexandria, no gently curving roads and nowhere to hide. The entire city seemed to be laid out on a perfect grid, parallel streets meeting at right-angled crossroads. And there was nowhere to escape to, no refuge outside the city limits. At either side lay water, the sea on one and a great inland lake on the other.

Narcissus and Vali were fleeing down the broadest avenue, a hundred paces wide and lined with marble palaces that would have put most Roman villas to shame. Only the crowds shielded them from their pursuers. Filling every street, they moved at the sluggish pace of those who'd rather not be out in the midday sun. No amount of shouting induced them to move aside.

Narcissus dodged between black-robed old matrons and naked street children and heard cursing behind them as their pursuers tried a more direct route through. The salt water soaking his clothes and hair never dried, just slowly gave way to a sheen of sweat in the unbearable heat.

At the next crossroads he snatched a quick look back and saw that the men chasing after them weren't the jackal-headed sailors from the boat. No doubt they'd have been too conspicuous, even here. Alexandria held the same mix of peoples as Rome herself, only the shades of their skin a little darker. But all of them were human.

The shouting behind continued and now the strangers on the street began to notice. The city was full of Greeks like Narcissus, but Vali's pale skin and flaming red hair stood out like a beacon. The men behind them wore the clothing of local guards and spoke the Egyptian tongue. It was clear whose side the crowd would take and hands began to reach out for Narcissus, snatching at his tunic as feet sought to trip and stop him.

He fell to his knees and cried out in pain as the impact jarred every bruise on his body. Ten paces ahead, Vali heard the sound and turned. He ran back, dragged Narcissus to his feet and pulled him on. Another hand reached out to grab them, dirty nails on the end of blunt brown fingers. Narcissus kneed its owner between his legs and the arm dropped away.

Their pursuers were only a few paces behind them now. But the mood of the crowd was starting to turn ugly. People pushed aside fell into others, and those others turned and shouted and shoved back. It was close to a riot and thankfully it was happening behind them – slowing their pursuers and not them.

A few more paces and they found themselves in a market. Stalls stood everywhere, piled high with produce from all of Africa. Narcissus dodged the first and brushed against the second. A hail of apples tumbled into the street, bouncing between his feet.

The next stall they came to, Vali deliberately kicked. One supporting leg came away, and a cascade of oranges joined the green apples. Seconds later they were trodden underfoot, releasing a strong smell of citrus and cider into the air. The stall keeper shouted and swore but was more worried about rescuing his wares than chasing after the culprits.

Vali kicked over the next stall and the next, while Narcissus did the same to his left, sending dates and peaches to join the other fruit on the pavement. A display of small red and black pots smashed to pieces in their midst.

Now a full riot was in progress. Narcissus could see Egyptian soldiers rushing to quell it, but he and Vali were clear now, and there was no one close to point to them as the cause of it all.

The crowds thickened as the broad avenue opened out into an even wider space where it met a road of the same massive breadth. A huge structure stood in its centre, caked with gold. The sun glittered from every angle of its intricate carvings, reflecting distantly on the great buildings that ringed the square.

Vali stopped abruptly in front of Narcissus, and when he tried to run on the other man laid a hand on his shoulder to pull him back. "They've lost us," he said. "Try not to draw any attention."

Vali himself ambled easily on, looking around as if casually shopping for food. Narcissus tried to do the same, though he imagined his performance was rather less convincing. His heart was pounding so hard he could hear the pulse in his ears, and the lingering terror of his torture aboard the ship tensed his muscles whenever he thought of it.

Vali kept an arm slung over his shoulder companionably as he guided them both to the centre of the vast crossroads and the gold-inlaid building that stood there.

"The Sema, the tomb of Alexander," Vali said. "We'll be safe if we hide in there."

"Really?" It seemed to Narcissus like the most obvious landmark and therefore the first place they might look.

"It's sacred to them," Vali explained. "No Egyptian will enter a resting place of the dead. Only your Roman rulers come, to gawp at the remains of the greatest general who ever lived."

A moment later, as they entered the cool of the building, Narcissus could see why. The interior was empty and echoing, vaulted spaces leading to a high, thin spire. The tomb stood in its centre and he found himself drawn helplessly towards it. The whole thing was made of crystal, its facets sparking back a thousand glints of light until Narcissus had to shade his eyes as he looked at it.

"A hero of your people, I believe," Vali said.

Alexander was there, entombed in the shining centre of the crystal. His body had been preserved in the Egyptian way and someone must have painted colour on his lips and cheeks. His eyes were shut, but it seemed possible that they might open at any moment.

Beside the fallen hero, Narcissus caught his own dim reflection in the crystal. His face was too thin and too serious, but then it always had been.

"Good," Vali said. "We'll leave it for a few minutes, then head back out and try to track down our sailors and their friends. It shouldn't be too difficult with the ruckus we've caused out there."

Narcissus stared at him. "Track them down? But we've only just escaped!"

"Exactly," Vali said. "So now the pursued can become the pursuers." He tilted his head to the side, studying Narcissus quizzically. "This was the whole point of coming to Alexandria, you know. We have to find out what they're up to."

The cage was too small to either stand or sit. After three days inside it, every joint in Boda's body was a screaming agony, and she feared she'd never be able to walk again.

The worst thing, though, was the darkness. It was so absolute that she couldn't see her finger when she held it an inch from her nose.

She thought that her last visitor had been a day ago, though it was hard to tell time here, with nothing to mark it. A group of cultists had come to bring her food and water during a brief interval of torchlight. After they'd gone she'd had nothing but sound for company.

The tombs were alive with it. There was dripping near and far, water seeping through the ceiling to the rock below. And she could hear a perpetual soft sighing that she eventually decided was an echo of the wind in the tunnels far above. The skittering sound of nails against rock must be the rats, hurrying to their latest feast of dead flesh.

And there were other sounds, harder to place and therefore more frightening. What was that sudden dry snap, over to her left? Was it a human voice she could hear humming that tune somewhere in the distance, or was it something else?

Boda was unused to such unreasoning fear. She'd been training as a warrior since she was big enough to hold a sword, and killed her first man before she saw her first moon as a woman. She'd screamed and cowered when the men danced round the fire at midsummer and midwinter, wearing the masks of the tribal gods, but she'd known it was only in sport. She knew the stories of Asgard, the home of the gods, and Hel, where the evil went when they died. She knew that the world was filled with demons;

she'd just never expected to meet any.

She never thought she'd see the dead walking. She didn't know if they walked here, but she imagined them, lurking in the darkness her eyes couldn't penetrate. And now she heard footsteps, echoing through the caverns. She told herself they were just a product of her mind, giving flesh to the spectres of her imagination.

But the footsteps grew louder and nearer and soon they brought with them a glimmer of light. Her captors, then. Were they coming to feed her again? Or was this finally it, the moment when they would spill her blood in a sacrifice to gods who were not her own?

As the light grew nearer she could see the slab over which she hung suspended. A body lay on top, wrapped in fresh bandages. Four animal-headed jars surrounded it. She couldn't say how, but she knew that Josephus's mutilated corpse lay beneath the white cloth. Around him, the ancient rock was splattered with the black of old blood.

The torchlight grew nearer and brighter, and the bloodstains brightened to a rusty scarlet. She couldn't take her eyes from them, even as she heard the newcomer walking towards her.

"Boda!" he said.

It was Petronius. She was shocked into silence. It had not occurred to her, even in a second of desperate hope, that the Roman would come for her.

Now he was here, of course, he was looking characteristically clueless. "How do I get you out of there?" he asked helplessly.

The cage locked from the outside. She'd tried to force it in the days she'd been here, but it was solid iron and impossible to shift. No doubt her captors had taken the key with them. "Try breaking the lock with a stone," she said.

He fumbled on the floor for a loose rock, then juggled his torch uncertainly when he found one.

"There's a sconce on the wall behind me," she told him, trying to keep the impatience out of her voice.

"Oh, yes, right." He fumbled for a second before finding it, and the quivering yellow light settled into a steady, comforting glow. She realised that he was shaking and terrified.

"Thank you," she said, meaning it.

He grinned at that, suddenly looking very young. "I knew if I put myself in enough danger for you, you'd say it eventually."

He had to balance himself on the slab beneath her to reach the lock. He braced his feet to either side of Josephus's corpse, averting his eyes from the body. It took him three strikes with the rock before the lock broke.

Then the side of the cage fell open, hitting Petronius on the head and knocking him to the cavern floor. Boda tumbled after, landing beside Josephus on the stone slab. She groaned in pain as cramped joints slowly unknotted. Petronius groaned too, rubbing his hip and thigh as he stumbled to his feet. Metallic echoes of the lock breaking washed back into the chamber.

They masked the sound of approaching feet. Boda didn't realise they were no longer alone until the light in the cavern brightened unexpectedly and she heard a coughing laugh.

"So," Seneca said. "It seems you couldn't wait to get started."

Behind him, the other cultists began streaming in. They were dressed in their festival best, chatting and smiling, but a dark current moved beneath the social surface.

"I won't let you get away with this!" Petronius said. His throat bobbed as he swallowed nervously.

Seneca smiled. "My dear boy, there's absolutely nothing you can do to stop it."

CHAPTER SEVEN

The sailors had gone to ground in the Royal Library. It took Narcissus and Vali an hour to trace them there, by which time the sun had set and the insect-rich African night had descended. The chirping of crickets was louder than the daytime crowds had been.

Every monument in Alexandria seemed to be built on a grand scale, but the library dwarfed them all. Narcissus had heard of it – everyone had – but he'd always pictured it as just one building. It wasn't. There were scores of interconnecting structures arranged around courtyards both open and closed. The place was almost a city in its own right.

The fifty-foot high wooden doors stood open even at night, the warm glow of torchlight spilling out from within. He expected trouble when they entered, but the bored-looking guards didn't even glance their way, just stayed crouched on the marble floor over their dice. Red-kilted librarians were everywhere inside. Deep-set black eyes peered suspiciously out of the palest Egyptian faces Narcissus had yet seen, but nobody moved to stop them.

"This place is huge," Narcissus said.

Vali nodded. He asked a librarian if there was a map they could follow, but the man sneered that any true scholar would know his way around. He strode off before they could ask him anything further. And the endless rooms of the library stretched away to either side, doorways framed within other doorways like reflections within paired mirrors.

Narcissus looked around him in despair. "We'll never find them here."

Vali nodded gravely. "You're right. We may as well give

up now."

Narcissus glanced at him from the corner of his eye. "You're mocking me, aren't you?"

"Yes." Vali strode forward, deeper inside. To his left, a doorway led to a circular lecture hall, ranks of stone seats surrounding a central podium. There was a lecture in progress now, a stooped professor holding court over three hundred or more students. Narcissus only caught a few words as they passed, but he thought the man was talking about the work of Archimedes. It was here, of course, that the mathematician had laid down the principles for calculating the surface of a sphere, and invented the device used throughout the empire to pump water.

"So you know where we're going?" he asked as they walked on.

Vali shook his head, and Narcissus repressed the urge to hit him.

"This is just aimless wandering, then? A pleasant walk on a quiet evening?" He'd never spoken to a freeman in such a tone before, but the barbarian was infuriating.

Vali stopped at last, turning to face Narcissus. "We don't know where they are," he said, "but we know something. We know that they like to carry out their business in secret."

Narcissus looked around him, at the shelves stacked high with scrolls and the never-ending progression of rooms. All the knowledge of the world was here. "Yes, but there could be a million places to hide and we'd never find them."

"True, but remember this is a library. There are books here that are meant to be read – and some that aren't."

Narcissus began to see what Vali might mean. "You think they're hiding among the banned works?"

Vali shrugged. "These are people who covet the forbidden. And only a select few are allowed to read the texts that are held to have the power to corrupt."

"A select few that doesn't include us," Narcissus pointed out.

The other man smiled crookedly, and the smile somehow transformed his face. Maybe it was just a trick of the light, but his skin seemed to darken, and his hair too, and Narcissus couldn't believe he hadn't noticed before how long his tunic was. Long and black. Only his eyes remained the same, the colour of banked flames.

He winked at Narcissus, then turned into the path of an elderly man walking head-down towards the library's exit. "Teacher," he said. "May I beg the favour of a word?"

The old man stopped and stared. He was dressed in the same long black tunic that Vali now wore, and over it a fringed shawl that draped his head and shoulders. "Of course, my brother. What is it you would ask?"

His accent was lilting and round and Narcissus realised that he was a Jew. There were said to be many here in Alexandria, a community second in size only to the Greeks.

"It's knowledge, I seek," Vali said. "I've heard that treasures are held here, lost books of the Torah. I seek the Martyrdom of Isaiah, and the Fourth Book of the Maccabees, which speaks of reason's triumph over the body. But the librarians will tell me nothing."

The old man's face lit up at this, the gleam of enthusiasm in his eyes. "You've heard the truth. They are indeed here, if you know where to look. But –" and a flicker of suspicion played over his face. "Their words are not for everyone. The unwary may be led off Hashem's true path. Is your virtue strong enough to withstand that which is inside them?"

Vali bowed his head. Narcissus strongly suspected it was to hide a smile. "If Hashem is willing, I will keep to the Law and gain only knowledge, not sin."

It seemed to be the right thing to say. The man nodded approvingly, and slipped a small silver key into Vali's hand. He told him to come to the Room of Anatomy when he wished to return it.

When the man had gone, Vali turned back to Narcissus. His face looked the same as ever, pale and freckled, and how could Narcissus have thought that his tunic was long and black? It was quite clearly knee-length and a light brown.

"So," Vali said, flipping the silver key from hand to hand. "Now we know where to look."

Petronius didn't think Seneca could have devised a better way to torment him. He could see Boda the entire time. They hadn't put her back in the cage, just closed a metal collar around her neck and chained her to the wall. She glowered at the people around her, but they stayed out of her reach, and Petronius could see that her neck was already chafed raw from her futile efforts to escape.

He thought he could have borne it if they'd just got on with it. But the fifty or more people crowded into the small cavern didn't seem to want to do anything more than sip at goblets of wine and exchange small talk. A particularly irritating woman to his left was coaching her husband on what to say if Senator Trebonius should deign to speak to them. Her voice was shrill and affected and it grated on his nerves like a serrated knife.

Seneca was looking at him with a smug smile he very

much wanted to wipe off his face.

"Why don't you just get on with it!" Petronius hissed. "Do you think killing her is some kind of entertainment?"

"No. Unlike that vulgar spectacle in the Arena, this is not for pleasure. It's an act of worship."

"For some jumped-up African god!"

"Not a god," Seneca said coldly. "A goddess. And you should be wary of offending her. You've already seen the evidence of her power."

He nodded to the side of the room, where the bandage-wrapped corpses once again twitched in their coffins. Petronius had stopped pretending to himself that it was all some kind of trick. He felt a trickle of cold sweat down his back, because Seneca was right. Any goddess who could do that was indeed to be feared.

Seneca bowed sardonically and moved away as a white-haired slave sidled nearer, offering Petronius a plate of delicacies. He raised his hand to slap him aside, then let it fall again. Boda would hate to see him do that. And none of this was the slave's fault.

"You're a new face here, aren't you?" someone said behind him. It was the woman he'd heard before, with the annoying voice and meek husband.

He nodded and looked away, hoping that would end it.

It didn't, of course. "I'm Publia," she said, extending a hand, "and this is my husband Antoninus."

"I'm Petronius of the Octavii," he said stiffly.

"And this is your first time, is it?" Her tone had shifted to become a little patronising, a result of his family name, no doubt. Not prestigious enough for sycophancy, but too rich to offend.

He sighed. "This is my first meeting as a member of the Cult."

"How exciting for you," she gushed. "I remember our first time. Don't you, Antoninus?"

Her husband nodded glumly. He had grey-sprinkled hair and the sort of long, morose face that always looked faintly equine.

"I was terrified, of course." She giggled, and he wanted to tell her that she didn't know what terror was. That perhaps she might like to ask the woman who was about to be sacrificed for her amusement. He looked at Boda, blonde hair awry and cheek bloody and bruised where they'd subdued her, and felt a boiling anger like none he'd ever experienced.

"And they were all like this, were they?" he asked, biting back on his fury. He nodded at the coffins – and then at Boda. "They all ended the same way?"

She must have detected something in his tone, because her expression grew more serious. "Yes. The goddess demands a heavy price of her worshippers."

"Of her worshippers?" Petronius said incredulously. His hands balled into fists and he thought that it would be worth it, worth any consequence, to wipe that sanctimonious look off her face.

"Don't listen to her," Antoninus said suddenly. "We've been to several meetings, but never a ceremony before. This is our first time, too."

"So you don't actually know what's going to happen tonight?"

Antoninus shook his head as Publia said sententiously: "The mysteries of Isis reveal themselves to mortals only gradually."

Petronius felt marginally less like hitting her this time. His eyes met Boda's across the room and he felt the first faint stirring of hope. If these people didn't know what the ceremony involved, then perhaps they might object to it. Perhaps they'd help him to stop it.

"Listen," he said. "I do know what—"

"Brothers and sisters in Isis," Seneca's voice cut across him. All around, the cultists turned to look at the old man as he approached the stone altar where the bandage-wrapped corpse lay. Petronius realised for the first time that it was the only one that wasn't moving.

"I'd like to welcome our newest initiate," Seneca said, smiling sardonically at Petronius. Then he looked back at the crowd, watching him with rapt attention. "And I'd like you all to take your places. Tonight's ceremony is about to begin."

When Narcissus and Vali found the room the elderly Jew had directed them to, it seemed like a dead end. The only door was the one through which they'd entered, and all four walls were lined with shelves, each stacked high with scrolls.

"The stories of the gods of Egypt," Vali said, reading a sign written in both Greek and hieroglyphs.

Narcissus glanced along the shelves. There were labels beneath the scrolls, and he saw that they were arranged according to era. The very oldest drew him, so brown and frail it seemed the slightest breath of air would crumble them.

"These are an ancient people," he said.

Vali nodded. "A civilisation older than your own, and gods more powerful and strange." He picked up a scroll and unrolled it. The papyrus crackled but it didn't crack.

Narcissus studied it in fascination. The old writing was interspersed with illustrations, animal-headed beings who strode through a world of sand. He saw a picture of the sun, carried on a barge down a great river.

"Can you read it?" he asked.

Vali made a non-committal sound and replaced the scroll on the shelf.

Narcissus turned away, scanning the room. "This can't be the place he meant, can it?" There was nothing to stop common entrance here, no lock that fitted the silver key.

"The entrance must be hidden." Vali said.

Narcissus searched the floor first. An ornate mosaic covered the whole thing, satyrs at each corner and a depiction of Dionysus springing full-grown from Zeus's thigh in its centre. The lines of a trapdoor could easily have been lost in the pattern, but Narcissus stamped on every square yard of it, and nothing rang hollow.

It was only when he reached up to straighten a crooked scroll – the instinct for tidiness of a house slave – that he realised what the trick was. The scroll didn't move, stuck fast to the shelf beneath. He ran his hand along the edge of the wood until he came to the gap that he knew he'd find, and when he looked above it, the keyhole was there.

"This is it!" he said excitedly. "The old man was right."

Vali fitted the key in the lock, and the whole wall swung out, shelves and fake scrolls attached.

There was light within. Torches lined a short flight of steps leading down to another, larger room. When Narcissus and Vali followed them down, they found themselves in a hall so large the far end was lost in darkness.

There were more books, thousands of them, some more ancient than those above. Down here they were separated by nation rather than age. Within that category Narcissus saw that they'd been subdivided further, each different heresy with a section of its own.

"Imprisoned knowledge," Vali said. "Locked up for its sins." His words echoed loudly from the vaulted ceiling, and Narcissus looked around nervously, though there was no one to hear.

Vali scanned the shelves, drawing out volumes here and there and reading them with raised eyebrows.

"Anything interesting?" Narcissus asked.

Vali smiled. "Well, the old man was right. They do have a copy of the *Fourth Book of the Maccabees*."

"And does it, in fact, explain how reason triumphed over the body?"

Vali laughed and put the book back. "Possibly." He moved deeper inside the room, where the shelves lay parallel to the walls, row after row of them that left little space to slide between.

"This one's more along the lines we want," Vali said, drawing out a thick scroll, bound with a black silk ribbon. It was ancient, but unlike the others it didn't seem to be made of papyrus. The scroll was parchment, old and grey, and it gave off a putrid smell as it was unrolled.

The first image Narcissus saw was a jackal-headed man, holding a flail in the crook of his arm. "One of the sailors!" he said.

Vali nodded. "Or their master."

"What is that book?"

"*The Book of the Dead*, banned but not forgotten these many years."

He unrolled the scroll further, and Narcissus flinched when he saw the picture of a beetle. There was a red-gold sphere clasped between its mandibles, and he realised after a moment that it was a symbol of the dying sun.

"A scarab," Vali said. "Born spontaneously from the dung in which it lives. The Egyptians believe it's a messenger of reincarnation."

He rolled the scroll on, and Narcissus was glad when the creature was lost to sight. The next image was of a lizard, its long strong body emerging from a river. A mouth full of razor-sharp teeth grinned out of the page.

Vali frowned. "Crocodile. The Nile is infested with them. They're said to guard the gateway to the underworld."

"Really?" Narcissus tried to keep the excitement out of his voice. "Crocodiles like those ones, you mean?"

They were at the far end of the room, another fifty paces on. The marble they'd been carved from was the same mottled green as a living creature's skin, and as Narcissus approached he got a true sense of the scale of them. Their heads, filled with the same brutal teeth as their picture, were at the same height as his. Their eyes glittered black in the light of the torches.

They stood face to face against the wall, a gap wide enough to admit two men between them. But there was nothing there, just blank white marble. No entrance, and this time no hidden keyhole either.

Vali moved to join him, rolling *The Book of the Dead* back into a cylinder and tucking it beneath his tunic. "You think this is a doorway?" he said.

It seemed absurd to be so certain, but Narcissus was. "Everything we know so far links back to *The Book of the Dead*. Wouldn't it make sense if this did too? And –" he looked around the vast room "– where else do you think the sailors could have gone?"

Vali shrugged. "I was only guessing that we'd find them here."

"It was a good guess," Narcissus insisted. The floor was plain marble, a scuffed white, but he checked every inch of it for a trapdoor anyway. There was nothing. And the wall between the crocodile statues was a total blank. He clenched his fist in frustration.

"Maybe it only opens from the inside," Vali suggested. "A way to stop unwanted intruders."

"Yes," Narcissus said. "But then how does anyone on the outside let them know they want to get in?"

Vali shook his head, but Narcissus knew the answer to his own question. He raised his fist and knocked on the wall between the two statues.

The sound rang loud and musical, as if a gong had been stuck. Narcissus flinched and backed away from the wall. But the sound went on and on, ringing through the whole room. Then, as abruptly as it had started, the ringing stopped.

At first, the line that appeared in the plaster between the statues was barely visible. Then, gradually, it widened and darkened until it was clearly the outline of a door. A polished gold handle protruded from the wall where no handle had been before.

Narcissus froze, afraid now to finish what he'd begun. Vali looked at him a long moment, then shrugged, reached forward and turned the handle.

The door swung silently open. Ice-cold air wafted out, raising goosebumps on Narcissus's bare arms. There was a noise inside, too quiet to place. Was it the murmuring of water, or voices? And were those skittering footsteps human or something else?

"You were right," Vali said.

Narcissus nodded, but he wished he hadn't been. Everything in him rebelled at the thought of stepping through that doorway. He thought suddenly of the ancient ferryman on the river of his dream. This library room was nothing like that bleak cavern, but he sensed a kinship between them he couldn't explain.

Anything could be waiting beyond those doors. And the jackal-headed sailors who'd tortured him didn't seem like the most frightening possibility.

"Do you want me to go first?" Vali asked.

It was the hint of pity in his voice which spurred Narcissus to find his courage. "No," he said. "Side by side."

Vali nodded and they stepped forward together, between the watchful black eyes of the crocodiles.

The moment their feet crossed the threshold, all four eyes blinked.

Petronius found himself squeezed between Seneca's large, silent slave and another man with darker skin and an even more forbidding face. Each held one of his hands tight behind his back, where the other cultists couldn't see. He was sure if he tried to protest he'd be silenced, maybe even removed. Better to keep quiet and stay and hope desperately that he'd have one final opportunity to rescue Boda.

She'd been moved again. They'd tied her arms and legs to a light metal frame, then hung it from the ceiling above the bandage-wrapped body. He'd seen a similar arrangement at the Temple of Mithras once. Only then it had been a bull, hung above the worshippers so that when its throat was slit they could bathe in its blood. The thought brought a sour lump of bile into his throat.

At least the ceremony preceding the sacrifice seemed to be a long one. Long and dull as most religious observances were. The priestess Sopdet officiated as the corpses surrounded her, swaying in time to her atonal chanting.

Some of the cultists had joined the chant, eyes shut in either ecstasy or boredom. The sound reverberated from the walls and echoed back, low and distorted.

Seneca knelt in front of Sopdet, head lowered and hands raised, a curved bone dagger resting on top of them. He was shaking, but Petronius thought it was with excitement, not fear.

Boda was shaking too, rattling the frame from which she hung. Her eyes were wide and her pupils huge. They'd made her drink something before the ceremony began, holding her nose until she swallowed. Petronius thought it might have been an hallucinogenic. Maybe that was better. If his life had been about to end this way, he'd have preferred to be out of his head while it happened.

Without warning, the chanting stopped. The circle of corpses shuffled back until they surrounded not just Sopdet but the stone altar and Boda's body above it. The priestess moved to each of them in turn, daubing a spot of red on their brows and chests. Petronius thought it might be her own blood.

When the circle was complete she returned to Seneca and took the bone knife from his hands. Her eyes caught Petronius's for one second. Then she raised the knife and walked towards Boda.

For things so large, the marble crocodiles moved with lightning speed. Narcissus heard stone rasping against stone as their jaws snapped just behind his ear, and he tucked his head down and fled.

Vali ran at his side, though he sensed that the other man could have outpaced him if he'd chosen. A vague gratitude floated somewhere in his mind, subsumed by the overriding panic. His muscles burned with the poison of over-exertion. Today felt like one endless flight, and he was losing the energy for it. After a while, he'd discovered, even abject fear becomes boring. He longed for an end to it – even if it cost him his life.

He didn't have time to examine the place they were fleeing through. But he caught flashes of it from the corner of his eye, mismatched and baffling.

The first time he looked, he thought he saw sand, a vast undulating sea of it glittering white in the moonlight. But he blinked and looked again and no, they were inside as he'd thought. Though that marble pillar, twined with vine leaves, seemed to stretch too high to fit anywhere inside the library.

A left turn down a corridor that somehow was also a woodland path, and the crocodiles were still behind them. Their breath was pure and odourless as no living beasts' would have been. Sometimes Narcissus felt them far above him, as if they'd grown since he'd last seen them. Other times they were low to the ground, snapping at his heels.

Only the sound of their claws remained constant, nails scratching across marble.

There were other noises here, too. That murmuring might have been the river they ran beside now, though when the water disappeared the sound remained. It was growing louder, and Narcissus began to think he could make out words. He strained to hear them, but they remained elusive, like a half-remembered song.

He could feel himself slowing. It wouldn't be long before he could run no further. He decided that he'd turn and face the creatures. He might buy Vali some time, and it would be the closest to a dignified death he could contrive.

He braced himself, ready to surrender. They seemed to be indoors again, running down a mosaic-lined corridor that might actually be hidden beneath the Library of Alexandria. But in the moment before he stopped and turned, he saw something else – something that didn't belong.

It lay fifty paces ahead of him, a perfect circle of rock, its rim carved with hieroglyphs, and a milling crowd of people visible through its centre. But when Narcissus looked to either side of the ring there was nothing but bare rock. It was a doorway in space.

Hope filled Narcissus with energy. He pushed leaden legs for one last burst and saw that Vali was doing the same beside him. The crocodiles fell a little behind, the harsh susurration of their breath like the sound of wind across rock.

When they were ten paces away, Narcissus could see what lay through the round portal. It was another chamber, a cave by the look of it, deep underground. Figures wrapped in bandages circled a woman holding a knife. And there was another woman, hung upside down above a stone altar.

Narcissus realised with a sick shock that he was watching a human sacrifice. He flung himself at the portal, not sure if he was trying to save the woman or himself.

The air between this place and that was as hard as stone. He bounced from it, face already swelling where he'd struck. Vali grabbed him as he tumbled, arresting his fall before it took him into the mouths of the waiting crocodiles. The other man's face was grim.

There was nothing to stop the animated statues now. They slowed, as if taking the time to relish their victory, and the nearest yawned wide, displaying every glistening tooth in its long mouth. There was a thick black tongue inside, and then the darkness of its throat.

It was big enough to swallow them whole. Narcissus

supposed he should be grateful. It would be better than being torn apart piece by piece.

But there was something else behind the crocodiles, something that made even them pause. It seemed to float in the air, a suggestion of a face that might almost have been a trick of the light. As it came nearer it grew more substantial, resolving into the form of a young woman with pale hair and something trailing from her back that might have been wings. She screamed soundlessly as she approached.

"Grab hold of it!" Vali said.

Narcissus didn't know why he obeyed. The spirit horrified him. But he found his arm clutching at one of hers. Her skin was clammy and cold but he held fast and then he was being dragged after her, towards the portal.

Boda sensed that the ceremony was over. Her head felt so light she wondered if it might float away. She could see Petronius, helpless between two full-grown slaves. She knew he would have helped her if he could.

Then Sopdet stepped closer, bone knife raised. The blade shone white, but Boda could see flecks of red on its edge from the last time it had been used. It was sharp, at least. Her blood would drain quickly and then she'd know nothing.

The priestess's eyes locked with hers. There was no more fellow feeling in them than Boda felt for her father's cattle. She was just a beast to this woman. Boda turned her gaze on the cultists instead. Let them see the light die in her eyes and know whose life they'd taken.

There was a collective indrawn breath from the crowd, a poised moment as the knife hung at the apex of its arc

– and then the breath turned to screaming as something entirely unexpected happened.

The air behind the priestess shifted and changed. Where Boda had seen Seneca behind her, still on his knees, now she saw two other men, standing somewhere else. She realised with a jolt that one of them was Vali. The other was young and thin-faced and looked as terrified as she felt.

There was something between them, too insubstantial to make out, though the two men seemed to have hold of it.

The men knocked Sopdet to the floor as they fell through air and on to the sacrificial slab, squashing Josephus's body beneath them. And behind them came something else, lizard-like creatures larger than any Boda had ever seen.

The cultists were already fleeing, but Boda was unable to escape, and she hung right in their path.

CHAPTER EIGHT

At the last minute, the great beast turned its head, and snapped its jaws at Sopdet. The priestess scrambled back. She didn't look so elegant now, with her mouth stretched tight with fear and her dress torn where the crocodile's teeth had caught it.

Petronius heard somebody whimper and was rather surprised to discover it wasn't him. He saw the faces of the slaves holding him, frozen in fear, then they released his arms and fled. Seneca fell to the floor beside him, huddled into a ball. The keychain hanging from a belt at his waist jangled as he shook. Petronius snatched it, kicking Seneca when the old man tried to stop him. It felt good.

The two men still lying on the altar grunted when he trod on them. He ignored them, fumbling through the keys as he tried to find the one which would unlock Boda's chains. The crocodiles glared balefully at him. Their scales scraped across the floor as they slunk nearer. Most of the cultists had fled, but the living corpses remained. They too were closing in, blank white faces watching what he did.

To his surprise, one of the men on the altar – the red-haired barbarian – rose to help him. "I think it's this one," he said, picking out the slenderest key. He was right. The lock clicked open and Boda tumbled from her chains, bowling Petronius and the other two men to the floor beneath her. The giant crocodiles' jaws snapped shut on empty air.

Behind them Petronius saw Sopdet. She still held the bone knife in her right hand and there was murder in her eyes. The circle of corpses closed around them.

Boda flung herself at the nearest with a roar of rage, but she staggered as she moved, weakened and disoriented by her hours chained. The corpse fell back a step, then steadied. Its arms closed around her and she let out a choked gasped as the breath was squeezed out of her.

But she'd had the right idea. Petronius closed his eyes so he wouldn't have to see what he was doing and flung himself forward. His strength was greater than hers and both Boda and the corpse fell to the floor beneath him. A hideous green fluid oozed between the bandages but its arms fell away and Boda was free.

They ran. The others followed, though Petronius was no sort of leader. He had no idea of the route out of the crypt, and even if he had, he wouldn't have been able to follow it. At every turning, bandage-wrapped corpses or fear-crazed cultists loomed to block their way. And within a minute they were running in darkness. Petronius hadn't thought to grab a torch as he fled and nor, it seemed, had any of the others.

He could hear them behind him, breath panting as hard as his own. But one false step and they'd be lost to him. He reached back and grabbed a hand. Thin and damp, it probably belonged to the younger of the two men who had somehow saved Boda's life. Petronius pulled and after a moment's resistance the man's hand tightened on his and he followed after.

Running was impossible in the darkness. When Petronius tried it he rebounded hard from a wall he hadn't seen, then tripped over a shelf in the rock beneath his feet. After that he slowed, sliding his feet forward and holding out his left hand to feel the way. The catacombs were huge and he knew that he could wander them this way for hours or days, until he died of hunger and thirst in the never-ending night. He tried not to think about that, or about the fact that his groping hand sometimes touched bone rather than stone.

At least, moving slowly and near silently, they stood some chance of hearing their pursuers before they stumbled over them. For a while the voices were all around them, crying out in fear and sometimes screaming. There was a softer, darker sound too, of stone scraping against stone. Petronius thought it might be the crocodiles that had fallen through the gateway to nowhere along with the two men. He knew that the creatures weren't flesh and blood. He was choosing not to think about that, either.

After an unmeasured time, words floated forward out of the darkness. "Head upwards. That's bound to take us out of here." There was the trace of a harsh, foreign accent in the voice. It must belong to the barbarian.

"What a brilliant idea," Petronius hissed irritably. "Obviously, that hadn't occurred to me."

"No, he's right," another voice said, the second stranger. "There's a slope to the floor, I can feel it."

"You lead the way then, if you think you can do better."

Petronius hadn't meant it seriously, but after a moment he felt the other man fumbling along his arm, pressing close as he inched along his body to overtake him. For a moment the man's breath was in Petronius's face, hot and moist, then his other hand was clasped and pulled as the man started moving forward again. For a moment Petronius's trailing hand was empty, then another reached forward to take it. It was harder and more callused but small and fine-boned.

"Boda?" Petronius said.

He heard her breath huff out in what might have been a laugh. "I should have listened to you back at the baths," she said.

"And miss out on all the fun?" the barbarian said behind her. Unlike them, he wasn't whispering, and his voice echoed too loud through the tunnel. Petronius cringed and kept his peace, hoping that none of their many pursuers had heard.

The minutes stretched on, but gradually Petronius realised that the man leading them had been right. They were going up. Around them, the tunnel was broadening, changing the quality of sound so that their footsteps seemed to ring a little louder while their breath faded into nothing. Petronius remembered the wider tunnels near the entrance and felt a relief so intense it left him faint.

Soon a glimmer of light seeped in. It must be night still, and moonless, but after the absolute darkness of the catacombs the faintest illumination shone bright. Twenty more paces and they were out, the sky spread broad and star-speckled above them.

Though Petronius would have lingered to enjoy the freedom, the barbarian hurried them on. "We don't know how close behind they are," he said. But after a few more minutes he stopped and looked around. "Where are we, anyway?"

The question was directed at Boda but she shook her head. Petronius guessed that she'd been unconscious or blindfolded when they brought her to the catacombs. "The walls of Rome lie that way," he told the barbarian. "No more than fifteen minutes' walk."

The man nodded and they carried on in silence. The thought of people and noise and light drew Petronius. And there was safety in a crowd, too. The cultists hid what they did. He doubted they'd dare attack in a public place.

Soldiers guarded the gates of the city. They eyed Boda and the barbarian man askance, but Petronius lifted his chin and told them he'd been visiting his family's tomb, and after a moment's hesitation they let him through. He heard them mutter something about the catacombs being crowded tonight and wondered how many cultists had made it back to Rome before them.

The younger man looked about him in wonder as they walked down the Appian Way towards the heart of the city. He wasn't much older than Petronius, but his long, bony face looked like it had seen a great deal more unpleasantness. He had the sort of ugliness that could be almost attractive, in the right circumstances.

"Your first time in Rome?" Petronius asked him.

The man laughed, a disbelieving gulp. "I live here. I was here three days ago. I just didn't expect to be returning so soon."

Narcissus took them to a tavern he'd sometimes been allowed to visit with Claudius's other household slaves. It was dark and dingy, the torches inside filling it with a choking smoke – a place for plebs, not patricians. The owner recognised him and cleared a table by the door.

After they sat down, they stared at each other for a minute in silence. Narcissus found his eyes drawn to the barbarian woman. She looked ill-used, face blood-stained and limbs bruised. She sat as if it pained her but held her back straight and proud. Beside her, her friend slouched. His face was still soft with youth, but his large brown eyes and full mouth had the arrogant cast of a high-born Roman. Narcissus wondered if the woman was his lover.

The youth saw him looking and raised an eyebrow. "I'm Petronius of the Octavii," he said. "And this is Boda, my—" He caught her eye and swallowed whatever he'd been about to say. "Boda, a woman of the northern tribes."

"That's Vali, also of my people," Boda said. "He was the one who first told me about the Cult."

Narcissus glanced between them, shocked. It hadn't occurred to him that they knew each other. Was it a coincidence, or had Vali planned to rescue her all along? He looked at the other man, but his face was unreadable as he nodded a greeting to the barbarian woman. Narcissus was sharply reminded of how little he actually knew about him. Do you trust me? Vali had asked, and Narcissus was fairly sure that he didn't.

"And your name and clan?" Boda asked. "You're not Roman, are you?"

"I'm Greek," Narcissus said. "I'm Narcissus, a slave of the Emperor Caligula and Vali's travelling companion. Though you seem to know more about him than I do."

Petronius studied Narcissus and Vali closely. "You saved Boda's life, so I suppose I should thank you. But on the other hand, I don't think you actually meant to. What were you doing in the catacombs?"

"And how did you get there?" Boda asked.

Narcissus shrugged, helpless to answer. His head was still spinning from everything that had happened, and he saw flashes behind his eyelids of the strange place they'd travelled through to return to Rome.

"We've been to Alexandria," Vali told her. "In the hold of the Cult's ship."

Petronius frowned. "They own a ship? Smuggling, I suppose, but what could they want?"

"Beetles," Narcissus said. And then, remembering what Vali had told him, "Scarab beetles, which the Egyptians believe carry messages from the dead."

"Everything comes back to that, doesn't it?" Boda said. "Everything we know about the Cult. We know they animate the bodies of the dead. And we know they sacrifice the living – maybe to help them raise the dead. I think if you hadn't saved me, my blood would have revived Josephus's corpse."

Petronius shuddered, then nodded. "We know that they venerate Isis, of course, and maybe the other gods of Egypt."

"We know they have powerful friends," Narcissus added. "The previous slave who investigated their ship was – she was stopped and punished."

"Yes," Petronius said. "Seneca's a member, and many others of high family."

"But what do they want?" Narcissus said. "Why sacrifice the living? Why bring back the dead?"

Boda shrugged. "Perhaps their goddess demands it. I've heard that foreign gods can be cruel."

Petronius smiled a little. "Whereas your own, of course, are masters of rationality and kindness."

She glared at him a moment, then looked away. "War isn't kind, but Tiu and Odin reward those who fight it with courage and honour."

"Isis isn't cruel either," Narcissus said. "Some of Claudius's other slaves used to make offerings at her temple. They told me she's the sister-wife of Osiris, ruler of the Egyptian gods, and she's said to take a special care of the poor and downtrodden. If she's demanding these sacrifices it isn't because she enjoys blood for its own sake. There must be some other reason."

"But her husband is lord of the underworld, who sits in judgement on the dead. Perhaps he's the one who wants this," Vali said.

"And just how," said Petronius, "does a barbarian like you know so much about the gods of Egypt?"

It was a good question. Suddenly Vali had three sets of

eyes trained on him, none of them entirely friendly.

He shifted uncomfortably. "I could just as easily ask each of you what your interest is in this."

"You know what my interest is," Boda said. "You were the one who showed me where to find Josephus's body."

"And I was auditing the Empire's records," Narcissus said. "I travelled to the docks to track the missing cargo, and you rescued me there."

Their gaze switched to Petronius, who shrugged. "I was bored. And Seneca was clearly up to something much more interesting than sitting on my arse copying out his quite extraordinarily dull speeches." He looked back at Vali. "So that's us explained. How about you?"

The other man lowered his eyes and smiled crookedly. "I could tell you the truth, but you wouldn't believe me."

"I think we would," Petronius said. "How much more improbable could it be than walking corpses and gateways to nowhere?"

Vali gazed at him a long moment. The lone torch by their table cast the shadow of his nose sharply across his cheek. "Sopdet is my sister," he said finally.

Petronius snorted. "You're right – I don't believe you. You're about as Egyptian as I am."

He was right. With his pale skin and fiery hair, Vali was clearly a man of the far, cold north. And yet... Narcissus remembered the way the other man's face had seemed to shift and change in the library of Alexandria, and suddenly it didn't seem quite so unlikely.

But Vali just shrugged and raised his palms, as if he'd been caught out in a lie. "Very well. Then this is the truth. I'm the Cult's enemy. And I'll do anything that's needed to stop them."

Boda's tilted her head as she looked at him. "Stop them doing what?"

"Opening the gates of death."

"They've done that already," Petronius said. "We've all seen it."

"They have," Vali said. "But only very briefly, just long enough to revive one body."

"You think they want to do it for longer? To let more dead spirits through?" Boda asked.

Vali shook his head, expression grim. "No. I believe they want to open them permanently – to erase the barrier between life and death for ever."

Petronius clicked his fingers suddenly, face lighting up. "When we overheard Sopdet and Seneca talking, she said something about tonight's ceremony being important – special somehow." He turned to Boda. "Do you remember?"

She frowned. "I think so. She said that the sacrifice..." She laughed humourlessly. "That *my* sacrifice would be the thirteenth."

"That's right," Petronius said. "It sounded as if, whatever they're trying to do, tonight would have completed it."

Boda nodded. "And it had to be done at the dark of the moon, they said that too."

"That means they can try again in a month, doesn't it?" Narcissus said. "And even if we aren't sure what they want, we can be pretty certain we want to stop it."

"How?" Petronius said. "The great and the good of Rome are members of the Cult. Why should anyone listen to us?"

"Why indeed?" said another voice, one Narcissus instantly recognised. If he hadn't been so caught up in his own conversation, he might have noticed that all the others around them had stalled.

"Narcissus," Caligula said. "What a surprise to see you here."

The Emperor was surrounded by his Praetorian Guard. Their scarlet cloaks looked black in the dim light. Narcissus knew them all by name but none of them would meet his eyes as he fell to his knees in front of his master.

Caligula slid into his empty chair. "I must say, this was the last place I expected to find you. Runaway slaves usually have the good sense to, as the name implies, run away."

Narcissus tried to swallow past the dry lump in his throat. "I wasn't trying to escape, dominus."

Caligula's face tightened with displeasure but Narcissus ploughed on. It wasn't as if he could make this any worse. "I found a discrepancy in the audit, and I went to the docks to investigate."

"Yes," Caligula said, "so Julia told me when I put her to the torture."

Narcissus squeezed his eyes shut to banish the images this conjured. When he opened them again, Caligula was staring at him.

"And what happened at the docks?" the Emperor asked. "It must have been truly fascinating, to keep you so long from your duty."

"I was trapped on board a ship. It put to sea before I could escape. But I found what I was looking for, dominus – evidence that the Cult of Isis have been smuggling scarab beetles into Rome to use in their ceremonies to raise the dead."

Caligula rocked back in his chair, eyebrow raised. "I'm amazed. My uncle never told me you were such an accomplished storyteller."

There was a muffled sound as Boda tried to speak and Petronius clapped a hand over her mouth. She mumbled indignantly behind it as Caligula turned to look at her.

"You have something to say?" he asked.

Petronius shook his head. "Nothing, Caesar. My slave merely intended to denounce this villain. Had we known we were drinking with a runaway slave we would, of course, have reported him to the authorities. I feel sullied."

Caligula studied him for a long time. Then he smiled. "I'm pleased to hear it. Cowardice has always been something I cultivate in my subjects. It causes so many fewer problems than bravery. You, your slave and your barbarian friend may go."

It was a dismissal, and Narcissus's three companions didn't lose any time in obeying it. He watched them disappear through the door of the bar and knew that his last hope went with them.

"And you," Caligula said, "will come with me. It's been far too long since I've seen a crucifixion and I'm looking forward to yours immensely."

CHAPTER NINE

Boda walked in silent fury through the bustling night-time streets. She kept her mouth clamped tight shut. She knew if she opened it something would emerge which was likely to get her killed. Petronius still owned her, she needed to remember that. The fact that he'd fought briefly by her side didn't make him her friend.

"I know what you're thinking," he said. "If you'd spoken he would have killed us all."

She couldn't control herself. "And preserving your life is, of course, your first concern."

"Yes," he bit out. "My life – and yours too."

"And Narcissus's life," Vali said, and she jerked a startled look at him. She'd forgotten he was there. He drew to a halt, pulling them beneath the awning of a baker's, shut for the night. "Caligula won't give him an easy or a quick death – there's no fun in it for him."

Petronius flinched, but Vali put a comforting hand on his shoulder. "Which means you've bought us time to try and save him."

"Oh," Petronius said. "Of course – naturally, that was my intention."

Boda shot him a disparaging look and he blushed and dropped his eyes. "How can we save him?" she said. "That man was the Caesar, wasn't he? God-king of the Romans. There's no power in this city greater than his."

Petronius shook his head, smiling beneath his curling black hair. "You've got it back to front. Caligula's weak, not strong. All my father's friends said so, when they thought there was no one near to overhear. He's terrified he'll be killed and replaced like Julius Caesar was. Any other power – any rival power – is a huge danger to him."

Vali was smiling too, the expression less joyful and more sly on his angular face. "You think he'd see the Cult as a threat."

"The Cult is a threat, isn't it? If the dead rise, what becomes of Rome or its rulers?"

Boda understood. There had been a king of a neighbouring tribe who ordered killed every boy child whose height or strength exceeded his. In the end, his wife had put a knife in his back before he could murder his own son. "But we need proof," she said. "The Emperor won't take our word."

"Even with proof, he might not listen to us," Petronius said, suddenly despondent. "He's a lunatic."

"But there is someone he listens to," Vali said. "His uncle, Claudius, who was Narcissus's master before him. If we brought our story to him, he might convince his nephew we're telling the truth."

Petronius shrugged. "It's worth a try, isn't it? It's not as if Narcissus has anything else to lose."

They led Narcissus outside the walls of Rome again, through the Esquiline Gate. The soldiers on guard saluted as they passed, fists thumping against the leather of their cuirasses. The sound rang loud in his head.

Outside the gates, the rows of crosses began. Only slaves and foreigners were crucified. The punishment was considered too humiliating, too agonising for a citizen to endure. He could hear the sobs of some of those hanging above his head. They were begging for a mercy they knew they wouldn't be granted. Narcissus was sure he'd be begging too, before the end. The line of crosses stretched into the distance. Even Tiberius hadn't killed so many and he'd been notorious for his love of slaughter.

Caligula kept snatching glances at him. The Emperor was relishing his fear. His mouth was twisted in a smile of cruel pleasure.

Narcissus's steps began to drag. He tried to keep walking, to keep his dignity, but his body rebelled against him. It didn't want to die, and especially not this way. In the end, the Praetorian guards to either side dragged him by his arms. He wished they'd look him in the eye. He wished that Vali were there, even if there was nothing he could do to help, or Petronius, or Boda. It would have been good to see a friendly face.

When they reached their destination, a cross lay on the ground waiting for him. The wood was newly cut and he could smell the sweet sap as they laid him against it.

Caligula stood beside his head. When they brought the nails he held out his hand. "Give them to me," he said. "I want to do it."

The soldier hesitated, glancing uneasily between Caesar and his commander.

Marcus, the captain of the Praetorian Guard, stepped forward and bowed. "It wouldn't be wise, my lord. The placing of the nails needs to be exact. If they don't fit between the bones of the wrist they're likely to come loose."

Caligula pouted, but he dropped his hand. "Go ahead then. I'll just watch." He knelt on the ground beside Narcissus's head, his purple toga trailing in the dust.

Narcissus shut his eyes as Marcus crouched beside him. A moment later rough fingers pinched his eyelid and pulled it open. He gasped and tried to blink but it was held fast.

"Oh no you don't," Caligula said. "I want you to watch.

I command it."

For a wild moment, Narcissus thought of asking what Caligula could threaten to oblige his obedience. What more could the Emperor do to him? But he didn't ask the question because he feared the answer.

Marcus gripped his tongue between his teeth as he positioned the nail against Narcissus's wrist. His eyes flicked up a moment and Narcissus flinched at the sympathy in them. Then he screamed as the nail was hammered home.

He thought he'd known what pain was on the Cult's ship, but it didn't compare to this. Each strike of the hammer rang up the nerves of his arm to resonate in his mind. And the pain went on and on, even when the nail had been driven home. The slightest shift, the slightest movement, grated the metal against the nerve and launched a fresh spear of agony.

His left arm was stretched out and then the other nail was hammered in. Now he could think of nothing but the pain. His mind seemed to expand to encompass it. He could see Caligula saying something. The Emperor's lips moved and there was a hum of sound, but it meant nothing.

Then they began to lift the cross. As Narcissus rose, his weight pulled down on his arms and the pain increased still further. He hoped he'd pass out, like he had on the ship. But he'd lost Vali's coin when he swam to Alexandria and there was no escape into darkness here.

His cross had been placed on a hill. When they'd pulled him upright, the soldiers grunting at the strain, he had a view over the whole of Rome. The city's streets were arteries of light, and the clamour of traffic reached even this far outside the walls. A million people lay in front of him, but he would die alone.

Only Vali's fast-talking and Petronius's charm saw them through the gates of the Imperial Palace. After ten minutes of confused wandering, they found Claudius deep inside, sitting in a room lit by the faint pre-dawn light of the unseen sun. The old man looked up as they entered, eyes watery and wary.

Petronius had heard his father talk disparagingly about Caesar's uncle. They said he was a simpleton. "My lord," he said, bowing, "may we beg an audience with you?"

"With me? D-d-do I know you, young man?" The words sounded like they were sticking on something in his throat, and a thin line of drool trickled down Claudius's chin as he spoke.

Vali stepped forward. "We've come to ask for your help. We're friends of your slave, Narcissus."

"Narcissus? Are you here from m-m-my nephew?"

"Your nephew is the Caesar, isn't he?" Boda said.

"He is. And you're a gladiator, if I'm n-n-not mistaken."

Boda moved forward to kneel at his feet. "You're not. We're told you treated Narcissus kindly. That you cared for him. Is that true?"

Claudius's eyes narrowed as he studied her, and suddenly he didn't look like such a fool. "I love him like a s-s-son. And you've come with bad news. I can see it in your faces."

"Narcissus is being crucified," Vali said.

Claudius flinched and so did Petronius. These barbarians had no tact. But Claudius only rested his head in his hands for moment. "Thank you for t-t-telling me," he said when he looked up.

"But listen." Vali grasped Claudius's arm. "He's not dead yet. He could last a day or more – there's time to save him."

"From my nephew's cruelty?" Claudius shook his head. "There's no stopping it. I'm sorry – m-m-more sorry than you can know."

"There is a way," Boda said. "Or are you simply afraid of what Caligula might do to you too?"

For the first time, something like anger twisted the old man's face. His cheek twitched, pulling his mouth to the side and widening the stream of saliva seeping from it. "Of c-c-course I'm afraid of him. I've s-s-seen what he's capable of. I know it b-b-better than any man alive."

Vali didn't release his arm. "But will you risk his wrath for Narcissus's sake?"

This was the question and Petronius tensed as Claudius considered it. He didn't care about Narcissus, of course. He barely knew him. But he found that he cared about Boda's good opinion. He cared about it far too much, and he suspected that if the Greek slave died he'd lose it for ever.

Finally, Claudius bowed his head. "I've lived too long already, and s-s-seen too much. Yes, I'll do what I can for my b-b-boy. But how do you think I can help him?"

This was where Petronius came in. He'd been considering it carefully on the walk over. "It's all about the Cult of Isis," he told Claudius.

Claudius nodded. "There have been rumours about them for a long time. And they've grown very strong this last year."

"Yes, that's because they're..." Petronius remembered how Caligula had reacted to hearing the same story. "Well, they're up to no good, and that's what Narcissus was investigating. All of us were. The trouble is, when Caligula found us we had no proof. But I think I know where we can get it."

"You do?" Boda frowned sceptically at him.

He gave her a triumphant smile. "Seneca's something big in the Cult – its high priest, it seemed, judging by that ceremony. He's bound to have more information about them. And the last we saw him, he was trapped in the catacombs being chased around by –" He caught Claudius's puzzled expression "– something he couldn't escape from in a hurry. And that enormous slave of his was at the ceremony too. While they're down there, his house stands empty."

"While they're down there," Boda said. "We found a way out – why shouldn't they?"

"No reason at all," Petronius said. "But that's the only idea I've got. Do you have a better one?"

It was clear from her face that she didn't.

Caligula had stopped enjoying himself about half an hour ago. He always forgot how long it took people to die of crucifixion. That was part of the fun, of course, but a warm bed and the terrified son of one of his enemies in the Senate were waiting for him, and as dawn approached the air was chilling unpleasantly.

He thought about his sister Drusilla, who loved this time of day. She used to say that beginnings were better than endings. Caligula had always taken exception to that. He'd liked the end of things, which made them complete and whole. But then she'd died and he'd thought that maybe he'd been wrong all along. There were some things that should never end.

He looked up at Narcissus on the cross. He was writhing, lifting himself up on his toes to take the strain off his arms, then falling back down when his strength failed him until the pulled-down position of his chest stopped his breath and he had to try to stand upright once again. Caligula sighed. There was clearly plenty of life in the boy yet.

He turned to Marcus. "I'm bored. This is failing to entertain me."

"Should I bring him down then? Has the punishment sufficed?"

"Don't be absurd!" Caligula snapped. "He disobeyed me. He needs to die. I just want him to get on with it. Isn't there something we can do to speed the process along?"

Marcus bowed his head. Caligula suspected that he liked the slave and didn't approve of what Caligula was doing to him. That was a shame. Caligula had always thought highly of the guard captain, and he didn't particularly relish the thought of killing him. Still, disloyalty couldn't be tolerated. Bad enough when he was just a man, but now that he was a god, it amounted to blasphemy, didn't it?

When Marcus looked up, though, his expression was blank. "A spear in the side would hasten things, Caesar. Or if you broke his legs he'd be unlikely to last out the hour."

Caligula squinted up at Narcissus. The young man was looking down at him, eyes wide in his pale, innocent face. It looked like he'd heard. Would he beg for his life – or for death?

"Well?" Caligula asked him. "Which would you prefer? I imagine a spear in the side would be quicker. Though stomach wounds can be awfully painful, I'm told."

Narcissus opened his mouth, but only a rasping croak emerged. His lips were chapped and bleeding. He moistened them with a swollen tongue, then spoke again. "Whatever you wish, dominus. I live to please you." He let out a dry rattle that might have been a laugh.

Caligula almost spared him for that. Except was the slave actually mocking him? It seemed hard to credit, but Caligula thought he probably was. A slow death, then. "Break his legs," he told Marcus. "One at a time."

Marcus nodded, then signalled a legionary to bring over his shield. He'd use the edge of it to shatter the bone. Narcissus turned his face away as Marcus drew the shield back.

"Stop," a voice shouted. "S-s-stop this, nephew."

Marcus dropped the shield, looking almost as glad of the reprieve as Narcissus.

Caligula scowled at Claudius and the small group of people behind him. The same three who'd been with Narcissus in that bar.

Claudius was shaking and twitching. He always twitched when he was nervous. But he raised his head defiantly when Caligula approached. "You h-h-have to listen," he said. "This isn't a game any m-m-more."

Caligula looked him up and down, his frail, twisted body and thinning hair. Was his uncle really defying him? And over a slave? "You think this is a game? He ran away! He shamed you!"

"That's not what happened," Claudius said. "Nephew, if you've ever t-t-trusted me, t-t-trust me now. We're facing a terrible threat. Only you have the p-p-power to stop it." His face was drawn and serious and Caligula suddenly realised, with a strange jolt, that it wasn't him his uncle was afraid of.

He swallowed. "A threat? From where?"

Claudius gestured at one of the three behind him, the red-haired barbarian, and he stepped forward to hold out a stack of documents. "The Cult of Isis," he said. "Caesar, we bring evidence that they mean to do an unspeakable thing."

"To me?" Caligula said, voice high with fear.

The barbarian shook his head. "To your Empire."

"Oh, that." Caligula frowned.

"And through it, to y-y-you, nephew," Claudius said quickly. "If you don't p-p-prevent it, it's the end of all of us."

Caligula looked in his eyes. Usually so watery and weak, they were hard and determined. He couldn't see the shadow of dishonesty in them. He fell to his knees, cradling his head in his hands as he rocked back and forward. "Oh, Jupiter. Mighty Jupiter, save me. Save me, I beg you."

Claudius knelt beside him, resting a warm hand on his shoulder. "Don't fear, n-n-nephew. There's time to s-s-stop this. A full month."

Caligula's paralysis lifted as quickly as it had descended. He was Caesar. He was a god! He could deal with this, as he'd dealt with all threats to his rule and person – ruthlessly. He leapt to his feet. "Then we'd better get started. Oh, and take your slave off that cross. He might be useful."

The sun was rising when Seneca finally emerged from the catacombs, Sopdet beside him. The shattered remains of the marble crocodiles lay in the darkness behind them. She'd found the spells to destroy them eventually, but not before several cultists had been killed and the whole ceremony ruined. Seneca had never felt so weary – or so furious.

Sopdet caught his expression and rested a finger on his arm to draw him to a stop. Her own round face was smooth and calm but he sensed that she was angry too. Everything had been leading up to the sacrifice tonight. *Everything!*

"That boy..." he said. "When I next see him, I'll kill him. I don't care how rich his father is."

"It wasn't the boy who ruined it," she pointed out. "It was those two men, who came through the gateway from the other world."

"Who were they?" Seneca asked. "The younger one I've seen before, I think. A slave at the palace. But the red-haired barbarian..."

She frowned. He'd known her for twenty years, since he'd lived in Egypt as a youth. The Cult had been nothing then, a mere social club for bored Romans in a foreign land. He'd seen her lead it from obscurity to unrivalled power at the heart of the Empire. And in all that time, he'd never seen her age a day, and he'd never known her look as uncertain as she did now.

"Did you recognise him?" he asked.

"I thought perhaps I did, but it was too dark to be sure..." She shook her head. "It doesn't matter. They stopped us once; we won't let it happen again. That fool Publia will need to persuade her husband to part with a new slave. The gladiator's body was damaged but there's time to mummify another. We can ask Quintus to provide us one by midday. A terrible accident in training, or some such."

Seneca felt a rising excitement banishing his tiredness. "So we can do it again? The ceremony can be completed?"

She smiled. "Yes. The dark of the moon lasts three nights. We've missed the first, but tonight another sacrifice will honour the goddess. And nothing will prevent us from opening the gate."

CHAPTER TEN

Narcissus was burning up with fever. The wounds in his wrists had festered where the nails had driven dirt deep into his flesh. He knew that he was being supported as he walked, Boda under his left arm and Vali under his right, but he felt as if he were floating. Sometimes he thought he was walking beside the bank of that dark river once again. Sometimes he wondered if it was all a fever dream, and in reality he was still dying on the cross.

The city was painted in shades of grey. A dark hole loomed in front of him and he flinched back from it. The pressure on his arms increased, forcing him through, and when he blinked against the new light he realised that it was just the gateway to the Imperial Palace. He was home.

He was laid on a bed, and something cool was placed against his forehead. Liquid dripped into his eyes and down his cheek and he tried to catch it on his tongue. His throat felt like it was coated with sand. Someone seemed to sense what he wanted, because he felt an earthenware cup pressed against his lips and gulped the water down greedily.

He realised that it was Claudius ministering to him. His face swam in and out of focus, sometimes looking so old he seemed seconds away from death, other times like the anxious young man he must once have been.

"Dominus," Narcissus said. "You saved me."

Claudius smiled, but even in his delirium, Narcissus could see that there was something a little false about it. He was still dying, then. Oh well. "You tried," he said. "You faced Caesar for me."

Claudius swept a strand of sweaty hair away from

Narcissus's forehead. Even the light touch of his fingers was painful against burning skin, but Narcissus didn't flinch away. He was grateful for any contact.

"It was a very brave thing you did," Claudius said. "Stowing away on that boat."

When Narcissus smiled, his lips cracked and bled. "It wasn't deliberate. I was just hiding."

Claudius's hand kept stroking his hair. "You've saved Rome, all the same. You've paid for your freedom a thousand times over. I always meant to free you, you know. I only kept you as a slave because I thought you'd be safer that way. Protected from Caligula's malice by your insignificance." His voice drifted into silence and Narcissus's mind floated away with it, somewhere dark and filled with a terror that lingered when he startled awake and opened his eyes. He must have made some noise, because Claudius was leaning over him again. Or maybe he'd never left.

"Don't be afraid," Claudius said. "They tell me this is the crisis. When it's over, the wounds will heal and you'll be well."

Narcissus wondered why his master was speaking so clearly, without the trace of a stutter. But the thought faltered, burning up in the blazing heat of his fever, and he didn't ask the question.

"I'm sorry," Narcissus said. He meant to tell Claudius that he regretted allowing Caligula to laugh at him after the games in the Arena. That if he'd stood his ground then, and defended his master, none of this would have happened. But his memories were all jumbled, the short years of his life merging together. "I lied," he said in a childish voice. "I told you that Nerva stole the honey, but he didn't. It was me."

"I know," Claudius said in a strangely tight voice.

"That's why I didn't whip him for it. You were always a terrible liar, even when you were only seven."

Tears were trickling down Claudius's face, and Narcissus didn't know why. Why was he sad? It was a beautiful sunny day and tomorrow they'd be travelling to the villa in the country with the swing he loved to play on. Dominus had promised him. "What's the matter?" Narcissus asked. "Why are you crying?"

Claudius took his hand and kissed the palm. "Because I love you. I love you and I don't want to let you go."

Narcissus nodded and closed his eyes, trusting his master absolutely. A darkness was waiting for him, deep and restful, and he let himself sink into it.

Petronius had been drinking since dawn, huddled alone in a corner of the same dingy tavern where Caligula had found them. He caught his reflection in a silver platter and saw that his lips were stained dark red with wine. There was a lot more of it inside him. His head was spinning in a way which he knew would remain pleasant for another hour or so, then swiftly become unbearably nauseating, before finally triggering a relentless, pounding headache. As his father had often complained, he had extensive experience with inebriation.

His father. He, of course, was the reason that Petronius had been drinking so long and so hard. Because Petronius had realised, some time during the euphoria of convincing Caligula that they were actually telling the truth, that he'd completely destroyed any possibility of going back to Seneca's. That left him really only one option: being welcomed back into the bosom of his family.

He didn't anticipate an effusive welcome. For one mad

moment he'd contemplated asking Caligula to vouch for him. To explain that, just this once, he really had been acting entirely selflessly. However, one look in the Emperor's over-bright, half-crazed eyes had convinced him that would be a bad idea. He'd wanted Boda with him, too, to provide moral support – or, if necessary, muscle. But did he really want her to know how little his family thought of him? No. So he'd left her being questioned by Caligula with her barbarian clansman and headed off alone. He'd only stopped for a quick drink to fortify his nerves.

That had been half a day ago, when the sun was just rising. It was setting now. If he didn't go soon, the doors of his home would be bolted against everyone. He sighed and heaved himself to his feet. The room staggered, or maybe he did, and he grabbed the edge of the table for support.

It took him two tries to find the door, by which time he had a bloody nose from walking into the wall and a bruised arse from bouncing back onto it. That was good, he decided. If he looked like he'd been roughed up, his father might treat his stories of rogue cults and raised dead more seriously.

"What do you think you're doing here?" his father said coldly, and Petronius blinked. Hadn't he just left the tavern a second ago? He swayed and put a hand out to steady himself, grabbing his father's toga rather than the doorframe by mistake. His father looked down at Petronius's hand as if it was a cockroach which had just landed on him.

"I've come to..." Petronius trailed off, temporarily forgetting what it was he had come to do. "I've come to be welcomed back into the loving arms of my family!" he shouted, pleased to have remembered.

His father brushed his hand away and stepped back. "You're no member of this family, boy. Seneca told me how you disgraced yourself."

"He did?"

"Caught in bed with Seneca's own niece – for shame! How can your mother and I show our faces in public after that?"

Petronius frowned, confused. It certainly sounded like the kind of thing he would have done. But he was fairly sure he hadn't. "I don't think that's true," he said.

His father made a disparaging noise.

"I mean, I know that's not true! That's really, really, not even the tiniest, slightest bit true." Inspiration suddenly struck. "Think about it. Why on earth would I do something so stupid?"

"Because you always do?" his father suggested.

"Yes, but... But I didn't! I did nothing wrong there. It's Seneca who's the villain!"

"Really."

He realised that his father had started to swing the door shut and stuck out his foot to stop it. He yelped as it slammed into his toes. "No, honestly, you have to believe me. Seneca's running this Cult, you see. The Cult of Ishtar. No – the Cult of Isis! He's sacrificing virgins. I saw him do it. Well, try to do it. And he's raising the dead."

Now his father looked disgusted. "That's the best you can do, is it? I'd hoped your time with Seneca might at least have improved your powers of invention."

"I'm not lying!" Petronius said desperately. But his voice echoed too loudly in his own head, resonating against his skull and down into his stomach where it threatened to send his dinner back up. He swallowed with difficulty, feeling a cold sweat start on his face.

"You've shamed me and you've disgraced your family,"

his father said. "But no more. From now on, you're no longer Petronius of the Octavii. You're Petronius the wastrel, the orphan – the man without family or name!" He kicked Petronius's foot aside, and slammed the door in his face.

Petronius stared at the closed door for a few minutes. Then he knelt down and was violently sick on the doorstep.

Once it became obvious that Narcissus was too ill to speak, Caligula summoned Boda and Vali for questioning. Boda had heard much about the Emperor's madness and lust for blood. They said he'd bedded his own sister, and made his horse a consul of Rome. She'd been prepared for his erratic mood and knife-edge temper – but not for the sharpness of his mind.

He kept them with him for hours, going over their accounts again and again to wring every drop of information from them – and, she suspected, to test them for any inconsistencies. There were none in hers, she knew that. She had nothing to hide and told him the unvarnished truth.

When it came to Vali, she wasn't so sure. His narrative remained unchanged with each retelling, but there was something too perfect about it. It had the neat structure of a story, not he messiness of real life. He claimed he was a bard of the Cimbri, that he'd heard tales of the Egyptian gods and come to Rome to learn more. He said he'd been searching for new stories to tell and instead found a conspiracy to uncover.

Caligula believed it. Why wouldn't he? He knew nothing of her people or their ways. But she did, and no bard she knew would have acted as Vali did. And he'd also told them that Sopdet was his sister. Both couldn't be true, but each explanation was equally plausible. Or implausible.

She saw Vali's sly, relieved smile as they left the Emperor and knew that she was right to suspect him. His smile widened when he caught her expression and she also knew that he would never tell her the truth.

"A fine performance," she said dryly.

He bowed mockingly, red-brown eyes glinting in the sunlight. "I live to entertain. And now the Emperor will act against the Cult."

Boda frowned. "If he's to be trusted – or relied on."

"You think we should continue our own investigations, then?"

"I think we'd be fools not to."

They searched for Narcissus, but a guard on his door told them he was too sick to receive visitors. Boda had seen the waxy pallor of his face when they brought him down from the cross and could well believe it. She wasn't sure he'd last the day. Vali looked like he thought so too. His mouth turned down but he didn't say anything, just led them in search of Petronius instead.

He was absent too – still not back from visiting his family.

"We won't see him again till the whole thing's over," Boda said dismissively. "Now he's passed the responsibility on to someone else he can get on with what he does best – drinking and whoring."

Vali shook his head as they settled onto cushions in a small back room of the palace. "I wouldn't be so sure about that." Boda could see his eyes studying her from beneath lowered lids. His hair looked darker in the shaded room and the angles of his face sharper. There was something curious about it – she couldn't decide if he was very handsome or profoundly ugly.

"The boy is in love with you, after all," he said.

She snorted. "In lust with me, you mean."

"No, I don't think so. He risked his life for you, or so you said."

Yes, he had, and it made her uncomfortable. She didn't want to be indebted to any Roman, much less the one who owned her. And she definitely didn't want to like Petronius. But she found that she did, his irresponsible laughter and quick wit. He was nothing like any of the men of her own people. Except, she realised, for Vali. There was mischief in both their eyes.

There was mischief in his eyes as he looked at her now. "A love requited, perhaps?"

"Don't be ridiculous, he's a decade younger than me!"

The shadows disguised Vali's expression, but she thought perhaps he looked pleased.

"Besides," she said. "Love is a bad reason for heroism."

"Is it?" Vali titled his head, puzzled. "And what would be a good one?"

She shrugged. "Loyalty. Honour."

Vali laughed. "Loyalty is reciprocal – it demands something in return. And honour is for the self alone. Love is the best motivation of all, the only one that's purely for another."

There seemed to be some message in his words, but Boda couldn't decipher it. Vali's riddling talk infuriated her. He was the first man of her own people she'd met since being taken captive, and he ought to have been the first with whom she felt the bond of shared knowledge and beliefs. Instead, he baffled her. She understood Petronius better.

"It's no matter," he said, almost in answer to her

unspoken thoughts. "The boy will return, and in the meantime, I have something we should look at."

He pulled a scroll from beneath his tunic. An old, unpleasant smell fluttered out with it. "The Egyptian *Book of the Dead*," he told her. "We found it in the Library of Alexandria."

"And you believe it has some clue to the Cult's purpose?"

"I believe it's their holy book – the thing which guides them."

She shuffled nearer to peer at the parchment over his shoulder and its musty odour was swamped by the sharp, almost spicy scent of Vali's body. He smelt like burnt cinnamon.

She shook her head and glanced back down at the scroll as he unrolled it. Images flashed quickly by – a beetle, animal-headed men, the moon between the horns of a cow – but he didn't pause over them and she guessed he must have studied that section already and found nothing useful. He seemed able to decipher the strange script of the Egyptians, though her own people had no written language and she herself could barely make out the letters of the Roman alphabet. Yet another of his mysteries.

Finally, he paused. She could see what had caught his eye, a drawing of twelve bandaged-wrapped figures circling a thirteenth corpse laid out on an altar. A screaming woman hung above them all. It was her own intended sacrifice in every detail, and she couldn't repress a shudder at the memory.

"Last night's ceremony," Vali said. "'And the blood that is spilled shall waken the thirteenth, for the thirteen months of the greater year. And as the year is completed so shall the gate be opened, when the moon rises where it is not seen.'"

"But does it say what the gate is?" Boda asked.

Vali unrolled the scroll further, scanning it, until he read: "'The souls of the dead shall fly out, and the mortified flesh will rise, and the river that is life will flow backwards, taking from the sea and giving to the land a harvest of destruction, and the life before shall be as the life after.'"

"Well, that's as clear as mud," she said.

He laughed. "I think it's as I said, a permanent portal between the underworld and this world."

"Even if it isn't," she conceded, "it certainly doesn't sound good. But if it has to be done when the moon's hidden, they have to wait another month. The difficult thing will be tracking down all the cultists. If we leave any out there, they can still perform the rite. It doesn't stipulate the number of worshippers who have to be present, does it?"

He shook his head. "Just the number of corpses." He continued to shuffle forward through the scroll as he spoke, sometimes hesitating over a word or image before moving quickly on.

When he stopped, frozen into immobility, Boda immediately understood why. She didn't need to read the Egyptian script to understand the drawing in front of them. A circle of circles, it was clearly a chart of the phases of the moon.

Three of them were entirely black.

"Allfather!" Boda hissed. "This says – does this really say that the dark of the moon lasts for three nights?"

She could see Vali's eyes flick from side to side as he scanned the text beneath. When he'd finished he didn't need to say anything; she could read the answer in his face.

"When does the moon rise tonight?" she asked, voice harsh with panic. It was already dark outside, the first stars struggling to shine through the lights of the city.

"I'm not sure," he said. "Last night it was a few hours after sunset."

"And will it be the same tonight?"

He spread his hands hopelessly. "It might be. We have to hope it is."

"If Caligula sends a regiment of his soldiers, there's time for them to stop it."

"We'll have to hope so," he repeated.

But Caligula was nowhere to be found. Eventually they tracked down a slave who knew his location: a large house on the far side of Rome. The slave didn't think Caesar would want to be disturbed. Boda didn't care what Caesar wanted, but the house was too far away. The moon might rise unseen while they searched for it.

This time they didn't listen to the guard outside Narcissus's room, pushing past him to get inside.

Claudius glanced up sharply as they entered. Boda could see the faint glimmer of tear tracks on his cheeks.

"Is he...?" she said. The figure on the bed looked very still, arms and torso bare where he must have tossed the sheets aside in a fever sweat.

Claudius lowered his eyes again. "Gone," he said.

Boda bowed her head for a second. "I'm sorry. But we've made a terrible mistake."

"Have you?" Claudius's voice was flat and dull, as if he wasn't really listening to his own words.

She turned to Vali, hoping he could rouse the old man, but he was staring at Narcissus, an unreadable expression on his face. She dropped to her knees beside Claudius and grasped his arm. "The moon is dark again tonight," she told him. "The Cult can hold their ceremony. They might be holding it right now!"

Claudius laughed, a horrible, joyless sound. "So the w-w-world will d-d-die on the night my Narcissus has."

She tightened her fingers on his arm. "But there might still be time! If you order the Praetorian Guard to the catacombs, we could stop them."

"If I did..." He pried her fingers away without looking at her. "And why sh-sh-should I? Why sh-sh-should I save my n-n-nephew's city when my boy is no longer in it?"

His eyes finally met hers, bleak and hard.

"Please," she said. "Everyone will die – *everyone* – if we don't stop this."

"Let them," he said. "Let tonight be the end of it all."

Petronius returned to consciousness with a cry of pain as someone trod on his hand. They'd moved on by the time he was able to pry his gummy eyes open and he remained lying on his back for a moment, trying to piece together the shattered fragments of his mind.

He'd had another argument with his father, he remembered that. No – he'd had a terminal argument with his father. Which meant – yes. He rolled over on his side and looked around him. He was lying in the gutter, somewhere in one of Rome's less salubrious neighbourhoods. He thought he must have continued drinking after his father disinherited him, but the memory was as blurred as rain on glass.

He wanted to carry on lying there. It wasn't comfortable, but it was flat, and it wasn't as if he had anywhere else to lay his head. He had no home, and no apprenticeship. His head felt like an elephant had urinated in it, but his thinking was a little clearer. He knew he had no choice left but to throw himself on Caligula's mercy.

He didn't anticipate that going any better than the encounter with his father. In fact, he suspected it might go considerably worse. At least his father wouldn't actually kill him.

Two more people walked past him, stepping over rather than on his body this time. They were too well dressed to be out at this time of night in this neighbourhood, he thought, as their trailing togas swept over his face.

With a groan of effort and pain, he rolled onto his stomach, then heaved himself up to his knees. He knew those men. They were cultists. And so were those three women scurrying past on the other side of the road. Now he thought about it, he suspected the man who'd trodden on his hand had been a cultist too.

His heart started pounding and he felt a wave of nausea that had nothing to do with the wine he'd been drinking. He didn't think they'd seen his face. He was just a drunk in the street and they hadn't paid him any attention. He had to make sure it stayed that way.

Head lowered, he staggered across the road, into the shadow of a statue of Tiberius Caesar. A few eyes flicked over him but none of them paused. He still looked like a hopeless drunk. He *was* a hopeless drunk, he thought angrily. If he'd had his wits about him he might have noticed this far sooner.

The cultists were being clever about it, he could see that now. They came in twos and threes, leaving a gap between each group. No one who didn't know who they were could possibly suspect anything.

But Petronius did know. He just didn't know what he could do about it.

Boda wasn't sure why she was doing this. She and Vali couldn't defeat the cultists alone, and they hadn't been able to persuade a single soldier to accompany them from the palace. She would have welcomed even Petronius's presence. He, at least, might have some idea of where the Cult's chamber lay inside the catacombs. In his absence, she and Vali were trusting to blind luck.

Vali was leading, the torch in his hand casting long shadows behind them on the grey, uneven rock. His footsteps were nearly silent, hers a little louder. She was glad of even that low noise. It made this place seem real, not the half-dream it had been when she'd last been here, still shaking off the effects of the drug they'd made her drink.

The dead lay all around. Some of the bones had crumbled to dust, but many skeletons were intact, curled inside their niches in the wall. The Cimbri burnt their dead. She thought that better – a quicker route to the other side than this slow rotting away.

They hadn't seen anyone else approaching the catacombs when they came. Even deep inside as they were she could hear no breathing except their own.

"This is a good sign," she whispered to Vali.

"Is it?" His head was bowed as he walked in front of her, the tunnel too low to accommodate his full height.

She nodded, even though he couldn't see it. "I don't think any cultists are here yet. We might be able to sabotage the ceremony before they arrive. If we burn the body they won't be able to reanimate it, will they?"

His narrow shoulders shrugged. "Maybe not. Or maybe it's over, and we're already too late."

They stumbled on. From time to time the torchlight revealed their own footprints in the dust ahead of them, and they knew that they'd doubled back on themselves. And all the time Boda felt a prickle of fear between her shoulders, as if some primordial instinct sensed the hidden moon nearing the horizon – or already over it.

Then, finally, they stumbled on a chamber that Boda recognised. She'd stared at that rock formation – the one that looked like a rider on a bucking horse – for long minutes while they chained her arms and legs to the grating.

She grabbed Vali's arm, pulling him to a stop. "This is the place they prepared me for the ceremony. The chamber's very near here."

He looked around, frowning, and she knew what was worrying him. It worried her too. There was no sign of any cultists, no glimmer of light from the surrounding tunnels. And the grating itself and the chains with which they'd bound her were gone.

Five minutes later, when they found the central chamber, that was empty too. There were bloodstains on the slab of rock that served as an altar, but no body. Boda could see marks through the dust on the cavern floor where Josephus's corpse had been dragged away.

Vali and Boda looked at each other with the same horrified understanding. The cultists were gone from here, and they weren't coming back. Tonight's ceremony would take place somewhere else.

CHAPTER ELEVEN

Petronius hovered on his toes, wracked with indecision. Two more cultists were passing him now, the first he'd seen for several minutes, and possibly the last. If he let them go, he might lose them altogether. But if he followed them, they'd be bound to spot him. They still needed a sacrifice, and they'd lost Boda. He didn't want to volunteer himself as a replacement.

The second of the pair paused to adjust the shoulder of her white peplos, then disappeared round the corner. Petronius hesitated only a second more, then hurried in her wake. He'd been introduced to the Cult as just another member. There was no reason for them to suspect him – only Seneca and Sopdet knew his part in Boda's escape. As long as he didn't run into them, he should be safe.

Still, he hung back, keeping to the shadows as he slunk after them. He didn't have far to follow. In fact, he guessed their destination several streets before they reached it. The Temple of Isis. Its ornate marble façade loomed ahead, crowned with a silver dome.

He hovered at the edge of the wide square which held the Temple. A tradesman's horse, forced to a halt by the crowds of wagons which crowded the roads at this time of night, pushed its nose into his palm. He stroked its long, silky face absentmindedly.

He didn't know what the cultists were doing, but he could guess. They intended to complete tonight what they'd started the night before. Why else risk a meeting when they must know that the authorities had been warned against them?

Last night the ceremony had seemed to drag on for ever, but he thought that it had actually lasted less than an hour. It might be shorter tonight. There might be no ceremony at all, just a quick knife across the throat of some poor unfortunate and it would all be over. Petronius had almost no time to find help.

The palace was on the other side of Rome. It would take him half an hour to reach it – out of the question. He'd have to persuade someone nearer at hand to intervene. There were a few soldiers outside a building on the far side of the square. He could see their blood-red cloaks and the glimmer of their armour and weapons in the torchlight. They'd be members of the Praetorian Guard, of course. No other legion was allowed to bear arms within the walls of Rome.

He was already crossing the square towards them, shouldering the crowd of pedestrians aside, when he realised what that meant. The Praetorian Guard protected Caesar. If they were outside that building, Caligula was almost certainly inside.

The soldiers didn't want to let him through the door. When he tried to push past, he felt the point of a sword piercing his tunic to prick a drop of blood from his stomach.

"Please," he said. "Caesar knows me and he'll want to hear what I have to say. Just send to ask him."

The guards – one short and dark, the other tall and fair – exchanged a look.

"Caesar's busy right now," the shorter one said. "Not to be disturbed."

Petronius felt a rising tide of exasperation and fury swamping his good sense. He pushed the guard's sword aside with a violent jerk. "Listen to me, you idiots—"

"Now, now," the taller guard said. "There's no need to be insulting." He grasped the front of Petronius's tunic and pulled him high on his toes until they were face to face. The soldier's breath smelled of fish, and there was a half-moon of pimples round each corner of his mouth.

"Oh, leave him be," the second guard said. "Send him in and let Caesar deal with him – however he chooses."

The tall guard smirked as he dropped Petronius, who teetered for a moment on his heels before regaining his balance. He ostentatiously smoothed down his tunic. "I can pass then?"

The short guard scratched a hand through the rough stubble on his chin. "Go ahead – it's your life, citizen."

The other man held the door open with a mocking bow. Petronius hurried through, his heart pounding. Caligula had listened to them earlier, but there was no guarantee he'd do it now. The unpredictability of his moods was notorious. And Petronius had no evidence of wrongdoing tonight, only instinct. He just had to hope that would be enough.

"They're meeting somewhere else," Boda said. And as soon as she said it, it was completely obvious. The cultists would have been fools to return to a known location to hold their ceremony. She and Vali were fools for assuming it.

Vali's face looked very pale in the torchlight and she could see the strain in the lines around his mouth. "Where then?"

She shrugged. "Back in Rome? The chamber under the baths, maybe? Not here, anyway."

"We can still find them," he said. And though neither of them really believed it, they started moving again, retracing their steps back. They had to try. What else was there to do?

But they had no more idea how to leave the cavern than they'd known how to find it. Following their own tracks was impossible. Nearly a hundred cultists had fled from here yesterday, setting off in every direction and leaving footprint on top of footprint throughout the surrounding tunnels.

"Up," she said, because that had worked before. Vali nodded and reached out to clasp her hand. His was warm and she could feel his pulse beating a comforting rhythm through his palm. Then he pulled and they started to run, heading down the broadest of the tunnels that led from the sacrificial chamber.

The air down here was stale. Within a few paces she felt as if she'd already sucked all the nourishment out of it. Her lungs burned as they strove for more and her legs wobbled but she forced herself to keep moving. Vali's torch cast an uncertain light ahead of them, flickering and nearly dying as they moved.

Its flame was little more than a spark when the pit opened in the rock floor in front of them. Neither of them saw it in time. A stride ahead of her, Vali fell in first, and his grip on her hand dragged her in after.

The bottom was a very long way down and when she hit it, she hit it hard. There was a brief bright flash of red behind her eyes, then darkness.

Caligula was naked, and so were the three women who were with him. The youngest sat astride him, brown hair flowing down her shoulders as her head was thrown back in – Petronius suspected – feigned ecstasy.

The second squatted athwart his face and looked like she might genuinely be enjoying herself. It was probably the most fun she'd had in years – her hair was bone-white and her cheeks seamed with wrinkles. They crinkled further as her lips spread wide in a rictus of pleasure.

The third woman, a portly matron, lay sprawled alongside Caligula's lean body. She wasn't participating, just gasping for breath as if she'd recently been exerting herself.

There was something curious about the women's faces, and after a moment Petronius realised what it was. They all had the same upturned nose and rounded cheeks, the exact same shade of hazel eyes. They looked like the same woman pictured at different stages of her life. They were clearly a family, mother, daughter, and grandmother.

The mother opened her eyes and saw him staring. She screamed and sat up, clutching her hands to her breasts. The daughter jerked round at the sound, pivoting on Caligula's cock, and the grandmother fell backwards against the headboard, uncovering his face.

He looked murderously angry. "Get out!" he said. "Get out, and I'll kill you when I've finished!"

Petronius took a step back. He wanted to take more. He wanted to get out of there as fast as he could, and most of all he didn't want the image of the four of them seared on his mind for whatever remained of his life.

His hand trembled as he covered his eyes, but he didn't retreat. "I'm sorry, Caesar. I didn't mean to interrupt, but this couldn't wait."

Petronius heard the bed creaking and risked a peak between his fingers. Caligula had sat up, drawing the sheet around him. "Wait," he said. "You're one of them – a friend of those barbarians who told me about the Cult." He frowned. "Is something wrong?"

"Yes!" Petronius's voice was breathy with relief. "Yes, something's *very* wrong. They're gathering, Caesar.

Tonight – in the Temple of Isis."

Caligula's petulant mouth turned down. "But you told me they wouldn't meet for another month. You lied to me!"

Petronius bowed his head. "I'm sorry. We didn't mean to – we didn't know. But tonight I was walking through the streets and I saw them, and I thought..." He swallowed as he looked into Caligula's pale, unreadable eyes. "I thought there was only one man in Rome with the power and wisdom to deal with this."

Rage twisted Caligula's mouth and Petronius stumbled against the wall as he backed away from it. He could feel his heart beating in his throat. Then, like a storm cloud in a high wind, the expression passed swiftly across the Emperor's face to be replaced with one of mild irritation. He flung the covers away from him and, buck-naked, strode across the room and through the door.

He paused on the other side and glanced back over his shoulder at Petronius. "Well, come on then. We haven't got time to waste!"

Boda knew that she'd only been unconscious for a few seconds. She could still feel the reverberation of the impact through her bones. She struggled to sit up, squashing something soft beneath her. It let out a groan and she realised that it was Vali. He must have cushioned her fall.

"Are you all right?" she asked.

"I'd be better if you took your knee out of my crotch," he told her.

Clearly not hurt too badly, then. She rolled away, onto her back. There was still light and she realised that the torch had fallen to the ground beside them, weakly aflame. It illuminated the sheer rock walls of the pit, stretching three times the height of a man above them. The small square of darkness at the top looked very distant.

Vali grunted as he sat up beside her and propped the torch against the wall. She saw that there was a smear of dirt on his left cheek, and his hair was sticking up at wild angles, glinting red in the torchlight. He caught her expression and asked: "What?"

She shrugged, smiling. "You're not always perfectly in control, then."

He laughed. "Very seldom, in fact."

She climbed to her feet, wincing as muscle and bone protested. She didn't think anything was broken, but she'd barely recovered from her long imprisonment in the cage, and now she felt as slow and inflexible as a woman of seventy. She sighed and let her fingers trail over the wall, searching for finger-holds.

Nothing. "Do we have rope?" she asked Vali, but she knew the answer before he shook his head.

He was sitting cross-legged, staring down at the ground rather than at her. She saw him prod it tentatively with a finger.

"I don't think we're going to be able to dig our way out," she told him.

"They're bones," he said. "Look."

He was right. When she knelt beside him she saw that the five white lumps she'd mistaken for pebbles were the fingers of a skeletal hand. And there beside them, half buried in the dirt, was the dome of a skull. There were still scraps of skin attached to it and strands of brittle black hair.

He picked up the torch and swept it over the floor and she could see suddenly why it was so uneven. The bodies must have been piled on top of each other, who knew how deep? There was only a thin layer of grit and dust on top of them, barely hiding the withered arms and sunken chests. There was nowhere to stand that wasn't on the dead.

She could hear her own breath, harsh and rasping. She'd never been afraid of death. She'd seen enough of it, over the years. But when she looked down at the piled bodies beneath her she remembered the corpses the cult had raised and her stomach heaved. The torchlight flickering over the bones seemed to make them dance. She was afraid to take her eyes off them in case they actually did.

She looked up again at the walls of the pit. Even if she climbed on Vali's shoulders, she'd barely reach halfway to freedom. And she'd never been much of a climber. She preferred to feel the earth beneath her feet. Unable to help herself, her gaze dropped back down to the carpet of bones. In a few months, their own might be among them.

In the end, Caligula was only able to muster twenty of the Praetorian Guard. The rest were at the palace or off duty, and there was no time to gather them.

When they marched across the square to the gates of the temple, people stopped to stare. They were mute, but their faces spoke volumes. Petronius wondered if Caligula knew how much his subjects hated him. Or did he only care about their fear?

The cultists guarding the entrance to the temple were afraid. Petronius could see that they wanted to bar Caligula's way. They'd no doubt been told to stop all comers, but whoever had given them their orders couldn't have anticipated that Caesar himself would demand entrance.

"Let me through," he said imperiously, and they glanced at each other and stepped aside.

The gates were guarded by silver statues of the goddess, horned head looking down at them. Petronius looked up at her face as they passed. Narcissus had said she was considered kind, but he didn't think whoever sculpted these statues had thought so. Her face was beautiful but remote, as if no human troubles could touch her.

The interior of the temple was dark, despite the torches which lined the walls. Petronius saw that there was a vast round hole in the ceiling, a few stars glittering distantly through it. He guessed it was meant to let in the moonlight, when the moon could be seen.

More cultists rushed towards them as they marched on. Their sandals slapped against the marble floor and they brought the smell of incense with them, and a faint copper whiff of blood. Petronius felt his gut clench. Were they too late? Had the sacrifice already happened?

"Caesar," the first cultist said. "You come at an inauspicious time."

Petronius recognised the vacuous woman he'd spoken to at the last Cult meeting. She was pale and sweating and he could hear her yellow robe rustling as she trembled. She must know the risk she took speaking to Caligula this way.

He ignored her, continuing to stride forward and forcing her to trot along beside him. "There's a ceremony in progress," she gabbled as she ran. "Initiates only."

He did stop at that, his glare freezing her tongue. "Are you denying your Emperor entry? Do you really think that's wise?"

He pushed past her as she stammered an answer, and then they were at the heart of the temple. Another statue of the goddess towered in front of them, far larger than those at the door. Its face was nearly lost in shadow high above, but Petronius didn't think it looked any kinder than the others.

When they'd first entered, the low hum of Sopdet's chanting had drifted through the temple. That had stopped, but as they drew nearer to the gathered cultists, another sound grew louder. Petronius thought it was the cultists chattering until he saw that they were silent, turned from their circle to watch Caligula's approach. The ring of corpses surrounding them stood so still they might actually have been dead. Only their bandages fluttered in the slight breeze.

The sound was coming from a stack of crates behind them. As his eyes adjusted to the light, Petronius could make out something moving inside them, brown and restless like a muddy puddle in the rain. Two more paces and he flinched as he realised that the crates were entirely full of beetles.

Caligula noticed them too. He shuddered and turned to Sopdet. Petronius saw with relief that the knife in her hand was still clean and white. Above her head, a black slave writhed on the grill to which he was chained. The body beneath him on the altar was motionless.

Sopdet lowered the knife as Caligula approached.

"So it's true then," Caligula said. Around him, the Praetorian Guard drew their swords, scarlet cloaks swirling back to free their arms.

Sopdet bowed her head in submission, but when she raised it again, her eyes were unapologetic. Petronius saw that the cultists, pale and frightened, were watching her rather than Caligula – as if the high priestess represented the greater source of danger.

"Caesar, this isn't what you think," she said.

Caligula glanced around him. The Temple was bare, no ornamentation or treasure except the vast statue of the goddess and the bare stone of the altar on which a freshly wrapped corpse lay. Beyond the light of their torches, the room faded into darkness. Anything could have been hiding in it, and the soldiers shifted uneasily, moving until both Petronius and their Emperor were ringed by a circle of steel.

At the outer edges of the light, the twelve corpses suddenly moved, taking shuffling steps forward as if they intended to fight the soldiers for their mistress. Petronius saw the men's eyes narrow – then widen as they realised what the bandage-wrapped figures were. The stench of death hung heavy around them.

Caligula noticed them too. His fingers fluttered nervously, then tightened into a fist. When he looked back at Sopdet he seemed both more frightened and more determined.

"But you are raising the dead, I can see it."

She held out her hands, palm up, letting the bone knife clatter to the marble floor. "We have opened a gateway to the other world, yes."

Petronius pushed forward till he was standing level with Caligula. "And you plan to keep it open, don't you? To break down the barrier between life and death?"

The thousands of beetles hissed, as if in agreement, and Sopdet nodded. Behind her, several members of the Cult gasped. They hadn't known and – judging by Seneca's worried frown – they hadn't been intended to know.

"I don't think I can allow that," Caligula said. "I know offering you a trial would be the decent thing to do, but let's be honest –" his eyes swept the crowd of cultists cowering away from him "– there are for too many important people here for a trial to be politic. So I'll just put you all to the sword now, and make up an excuse afterwards."

He gestured at the Praetorian Guard, a negligent flick of his wrist. There was a moment's hesitation – there were Senators among the crowd, and two of the richest men in Rome – but only a moment. The soldiers could see the corpses rotting beneath their bandages. They understood why these people had to be disposed of.

Some of the cultists screamed. Petronius saw a man with a big, sweaty face and hairy arms cower behind a petite woman who was probably his wife. Another dropped to his knees and then his side, curling his arms round his head as if that might somehow protect him. He smelt the sharp stench of urine as one or more of them lost control of their bladders. And these were the people who had planned to end the world? Petronius almost felt sorry for them. But he saw the slave struggling, suspended above the altar, and he remembered Boda's face when she'd thought she was about to die, and his pity curdled into contempt.

Only Sopdet seemed unafraid. Her face was as beautiful and serene as the statue's she stood under. "Kill us," she said, "and you'll never see her again this side of Hades."

Petronius had no idea what she meant, but he could see that Caligula did. His face twisted, though it was impossible to tell if it was with anger or pain. "Stop," he whispered.

The Praetorian Guard hesitated, looking round. They didn't know if the order had been for them, or for the priestess.

Petronius didn't think Caligula knew either. In the taut silence he left, Sopdet took a step forward. She was barefoot, her feet startlingly brown against the white marble beneath them.

"Think, Caesar," she said. "If the gates are open, all may return. We have only to call them through. There will be no more mourning, or grief. Mother and daughter, husband and wife, brother and sister – need never be parted."

Caligula licked his lips, a nervous flick of his tongue. Petronius realised with a jolt of terror that the Emperor was actually moved by these arguments.

Petronius clasped Caligula's arm, hard enough for his nails to bite into flesh, not caring that he could be killed for it. They'd all be dead anyway, if Caesar gave in. "Don't listen to her," he said. "The gate between life and death is barred for a reason."

Caligula turned to look at him, a wild, almost pleading look in his eyes. "Is it? And why do people die, tell me that?" His voice thickened. "Why did she die when I loved her so much? What's the point of being Caesar if I can't open the gates of death when I want?"

Petronius shook him a little. Some of the soldiers shuffled their feet, a few pointed their swords at him. But nobody moved. Everything balanced on this one man's decision – this one, selfish, cruel, half-crazy man.

"The gods forbid it," Petronius said. "They'll punish you."

Caligula wrenched his arm free. Petronius could see the red half-moons where his nails had bitten in, and Caligula rubbed them absently as he spoke. "I am a god, you fool."

"Indeed you are," Sopdet said, and Petronius could hear in the feline satisfaction of her voice that she knew she'd won. "And Isis is a goddess, the mother of the sun, and this is what she commands."

"Then let it be done," Caligula said. "Let the gates of death be opened."

Sopdet moved as quickly as a striking snake, stooping to pick up the bone knife from the floor, then jumping to balance on the edge of the altar. The knife swept out, a white blur through the air, and its keen edge ripped through the slave's throat.

At the same moment, something opened in the darkness behind the altar – a deeper darkness like the gateway to nowhere Petronius had seen in the catacombs, the one Vali and Narcissus had tumbled through at the most opportune moment.

There was no similar reprieve now. Something flew through the dark gate, but it wasn't human. It was barely there, like the sketch of a man in the air, strokes of pale light picking out his nose and wild hair and silently screaming mouth.

The slave above the altar screamed too, a horrible bubbling sound. His limbs jerked and spasmed against their chains and his eyes rolled back in his head as the cut in his throat gaped like another mouth, wide and red.

Some of the blood sprayed on Sopdet's face, dotting it with red freckles. Petronius saw her raise her other hand to wipe herself fastidiously clean while the rest of the blood jetted down. When it struck the body lying below, it stained the bandages scarlet.

Petronius didn't realise he was running until he was right there, heaving at the corpse's arm, trying something – anything – to stop this before it was too late.

But it already was. The red of the blood soaked into and then somehow through the bandages, leaving them pure white again, and the apparition from the gate followed, seeping into the bandaged corpse. For a moment a face was overlaid on the blank bandages, snarling and savage.

Then that too disappeared.

The corpse began to twitch, limbs jerking in a horrible echo of the slave's death throes.

Sopdet smiled mockingly at Petronius as he backed away. Even Caligula looked horrified, finally realising what he'd allowed. Sopdet seemed to sense his doubt. "Wait," she told him. "Just wait."

The corpse juddered one last time, arching its back until only its head and heels touched the altar before falling back down. Then its arms flexed and stiffened, reaching out to lever it upright. Its legs swung round, landing on the floor with a muffled thump.

Sopdet flung her head back, letting out a scream of triumph that was high and strange, hardly human. Even the cultists flinched away from it, but the corpse moved on, joining the ring of twelve that now circled them all.

Behind them, Petronius saw that the gateway to another world – to the underworld – was closing. The darkness within darkness narrowed, until only a man's arm could have fitted through.

"In the name of Osiris, brother-husband of Isis!" Sopdet called.

There was an echo, a buzzing sound that came both from the walking corpses and the insect-filled crates.

The gateway in the air stopped narrowing. And now there was a light behind it, sickly and green. It glowed on the cultists' pale faces and on the blood-streaked knife Sopdet still held in her hand.

"In the name of Horus, god-child of Isis!" she shouted, louder still.

The corpses stretched out their arms and the air crackled between them. At first it was no more than a sensation, something that prickled the hairs on the back of Petronius's neck like the build-up to a storm. Then it broke. Streaks of blue-green lightning shot out from the corpses' arms, linking them together and encircling the living in an impenetrable, brilliant barrier of light.

Petronius fell to his knees, Caligula beside him. The Emperor looked terrified. If the crackle of supernatural energy hadn't been so loud, Petronius thought he would have heard him sobbing. And so he should – he could have stopped this, if he'd chosen to.

Behind Sopdet, the gate widened, the green light behind it brightening until it rivalled the lightning pouring from the corpses' hands.

"In the name of Isis," she roared, "widow of Osiris, mother of Horus, guardian of life and death!"

There was a crack as loud and sudden as thunder, and the gateway seemed to freeze in place. At its rim, the green light swirled and congealed, hardening into a gritty grey marble. It was a true gateway now, and the landscape beyond could finally be seen, a vast dark cavern, sprinkled with sharp rocks. In the distance, a broad and sluggish river flowed.

There was something there, gathering. Petronius couldn't quite make them out, the forms tickling at his mind, like the half-remembered words of a song. Though they became no clearer as they drew nearer, flying at a terrible speed towards the gate, he realised what they were – spirits, like the one that had animated the corpse.

He would have run if he could, if there'd been any possible escape. But the ring of corpses still circled them, though the lightning that linked them was fading, sparking away to nothing.

The insubstantial spirits of the dead flew through the gateway into the living world. Petronius thought they'd come for him – that they'd possess his body as they'd animated the corpse on the altar. But they stopped behind Sopdet, hovering for a moment in which their faces became clearer, blank and hopeless, and then they plunged down and fell into the beetle-filled crates.

Behind them, the landscape of death was lost once again behind a sick, green light.

Sopdet lowered her arms, groaning, as if it was her own energy which had been used to power the ceremony, and was now drained. And, suddenly and unexpectedly, the circle of corpses slumped to the floor.

Petronius watched, expecting a trick. Expecting them to rise again, stronger and more lethal than before. But instead they seemed to deflate, the bandages slowly sinking in on themselves until there was nothing more inside them, only a fine grey dust.

There was a collective sigh from the cultists and the soldiers of the Praetorian Guard, part relief, part fearful anticipation of what might come next.

"Is that it?" Caligula asked, voice quavering. "Is it over?"

The captain of the guards shook his head. He was one of the few soldiers still standing, sword in hand. Most had dropped to their knees beside their Emperor. A few were sobbing. One was clinging to a young female cultist, his eyes darting from place to place, alert for the next threat, the next terrible, inexplicable occurrence.

And for a moment, nothing at all happened. The loudest noise was the chittering of the beetles in the crates where the spirits of the dead had vanished, almost lost beneath the clash of metal against leather as the soldiers struggled to their feet. But gradually, the sound began to change.

The hissing of wing casings rubbing against each other transmuted into the whisper of voices, thousands upon thousands of them. Petronius couldn't make out the words, but the tone was clear – cold and angry. Leaning on the altar, gasping for breath, Sopdet looked up and smiled.

Petronius took a step back, then another, almost tripping over Caligula, crouched on the floor behind him. He kept his eyes on the crates, guessing what was coming, dreading it and powerless to stop it.

Finally, like a cloud of darkness, the beetles rose into the air. A stench of shit and death rose with them and there was a blaze of green light from the gate behind. It lined their wings and sparked from their twitching antennae. And in the light Petronius could see faces, one face hovering over each beetle, and then narrowing, disappearing, somehow being sucked inside it.

The beetles, he finally understood, were carriers – transporting the spirits of the dead through the living world. The buzzing cloud, thousands strong, hovered above their heads one final moment as the light within it died. And then the beetles stretched their wings and flew from the temple out into the streets of Rome.

PART THREE
Deficit Omne Quod Nasciture

CHAPTER TWELVE

When Boda first heard the sound, she thought it was voices. They sounded angry and hateful, but after two hours in the pit she didn't care.

"Help!" she shouted. "Please – we're in here!"

"I don't think they can hear you," Vali said. He had spent the last hour sitting cross-legged on the ground, seemingly untroubled by their situation. Now she saw his face drain of colour, and a sheen of sweat stood out on his pale forehead.

"Down here!" she yelled, making a trumpet with her hands to amplify the noise.

Vali stood up, his long legs creaking as they unfolded. He grasped her shoulder hard, and shook. It startled her enough to silence her momentarily. He'd never laid hands on her before.

"Don't attract their attention," he hissed.

"Why not? We can't get out of here on our own. Even if it's cultists, we'll have a chance to fight them once they've rescued us. Down here we've got no chance at all."

"It's not cultists," he said. His voice sounded weary, almost defeated. "It's nothing human – nothing living."

And as soon as he said it, she knew that he was right. Why had she thought that those were voices? Now she could hear that it was the chittering of insects, thousands of them. The beating of their wings echoed down the tunnels until it was impossible to tell what direction they were coming from.

Then they were there, a dark cloud hovering over the mouth of the pit. Boda didn't know why they frightened her so much. They were just insects – what could they do? But she remembered the beetles in *The Book of the Dead*, and guessed these were part of the Cult's plans.

"We're too late, aren't we?" she said. "It's already happened."

Vali just nodded as the cloud of beetles flew on, a smaller group detaching and swooping down towards them.

Boda crouched, covering her eyes. The wings brushed her cheeks as they passed, but they didn't settle on her. She waited a second for something more, something worse. When it didn't come she slowly uncovered her eyes.

Vali was still standing, looking down at the ground. Boda followed his gaze and saw the beetles burrowing – into the pile of corpses.

A moment later, the corpses stirred. The earth covering them shook and slid aside, and the brown finger-bones of a dead hand curled around her ankle and pulled.

A few of the beetles remained, hovering around the altar as the cultists slowly rose to their feet. Most were white and shaking, but a few were beginning to smile. Caligula dismissed them from his mind. They were merely Sopdet's tools, as she had become his. They could be rewarded or punished later as he saw fit.

Sopdet looked at him, half smiling. "It's done," she said. "Thank you, Caesar."

The Praetorian Guard were beginning to collect themselves, forming up in ragged ranks on either side of him. They hadn't exactly covered themselves in glory during the last hour or so, and their faces suggested they knew it. He'd have to punish some to educate the others, and from the grim set of their mouths several of them knew that too.

"It's not done," he told Sopdet. "You have what you want. Whereas I..."

She nodded. "Your sister, yes. I can sense her, waiting on the other side of the gateway. She's been waiting for you there from the moment she died. I can summon her through, but we need a body to house her. Although the spirits can animate anything that was once flesh, I imagine you might want a fresh corpse for her."

Now that it was almost here – now that it was finally possible – he found himself shaking with excitement. Or was it fear? He couldn't tell. For a moment he thought about telling Sopdet that he'd changed his mind, that he wanted to wait a little longer. But what if the opportunity never came again?

The cultists were an unpromising looking bunch. There were more men than women and the few women were more notable for their wealth and power than their youth and beauty. "You," he said, pointing to the prettiest and youngest of them. "Come here."

She hesitated.

"Your Emperor commands you," he said, and the soldiers to either side of him drew their swords.

A man approached with her, probably her husband. She bowed, so low that her thick brown hair brushed the floor. "I am Publia of the Julii, and this is my husband, Antoninus. Your loyal servants." When she rose from the bow her eyes met his, desperate and pleading.

Her husband gripped her arm. His long, melancholy face was pinched tight with fear. "Please, Caesar," he said. "We have slaves – young ones, pretty ones. I can bring them here in less than an hour."

Claudius turned to Sopdet. "Tell me, once a spirit is

embodied, can it move? Or is that it – stuck forever in the new body?"

She smiled. "Once inside a scarab, the spirit is a free agent in the living world. It can move at will."

"Good," Caligula said, and then to Antoninus. "Yes, bring your slaves. I'll choose the appropriate vessel for myself."

The man sagged with relief as Caligula turned to his soldiers. "In the meantime, kill that woman for me. But do try not to damage her too much – a knife through the back would probably be neatest."

Antoninus let out a choked cry of protest. He flung himself towards Publia, but it was already too late. She opened her mouth on what might have been a scream. Only a soft cough came, and then a flood of red-purple blood.

Caligula looked down at her corpse, as the last of the life twitched out of it. To one side, his soldiers were holding back a sobbing Antoninus, but that didn't interest him. Publia's blood was gently steaming as it pooled around her. He watched and watched, waiting for his sister to appear. Nothing.

"You lied to me!" he screamed at Sopdet. "You said that she'd come back!"

The cultists surrounding her backed away, but Sopdet herself seemed unmoved. "Patience, Caesar," she said. "She's found her carrier – look."

And there she was at last – *at last.* He could see the outline of her in the air, sketched in pale blue fire. She was screaming and his heart clenched. Did it hurt, coming back? But it didn't matter. She'd be here soon, whole again, and then he could ask her himself.

Drusilla's spirit hovered for a moment, high above them. Then one of the cult's beetles flew to meet it and her form twisted and narrowed and slipped inside, between its wide mandibles.

The beetle's wings whirred as it flew down towards Publia's body. Her mouth was still open, only a trickle of blood seeping from one corner. The beetle's legs pattered through the pool of fluid, leaving little red pinpricks on her cheek. Then it was inside her mouth. For a moment its back legs were visible, waving at them. There was a sudden stronger smell of blood and something meatier, the sound of chewing, and the legs disappeared.

The smell of bile joined the stench as Antoninus fell to his knees and vomited, dry-retching when there was nothing left inside him to bring up.

The chewing inside Publia's head went on for a few more seconds, and Caligula tapped his foot impatiently. Then, finally, she sat up.

One of the cultists screamed, and a soldier dropped his sword. Even Caligula found himself jumping back. For a moment Publia's eyes were blank and staring, as if no more than a beetle's intelligence lived behind them. Her head swivelled, stiff on her neck, until her unseeing gaze settled on him.

"Drusilla?" he said. His voice was a dry croak.

Publia's dead body smiled. "Hello again, brother."

Vali saved her, stamping on the skeletal hand and grinding its bones to dust. But there were more, hundreds more, a pit filled with them, and one by one they were all waking.

"We've got to get out of here!" he said.

Boda laughed, high and hysterical.

He shook her, rattling her teeth. They made the sound

of bone on bone, just like the bodies beneath them. She shivered convulsively and he shook again, shook her until she put her hands on his arms and pushed him away.

"We can climb," he said. "The rock's soft – look." He dug his fingers in, above his head, and the stone flaked away until there was enough room to fit the tips of his fingers inside, but no more. "Your feet too!" he said, and she saw him kick a hole in the pit wall a foot above the floor, then hook his foot in it, using the finger-hold to heave himself up.

But the corpses were pulling themselves up too. She saw one, skull bobbing on its narrow neck as its legs struggled free of the earth. She lashed out in terror, kicking the dome of the skull, and it broke off and flew to imbed itself in the wall behind.

For the first time, something like reason triumphed over blind panic. They weren't invulnerable. They were just bone, and she'd hacked enough of that, even if it had been wrapped in flesh at the time.

She drew her sword from its scabbard and swept it around her. Vali was four feet up now, above the blade's path, and she was able to spin in place, clearing the pit of everything that had emerged.

There were more, though, and still more beneath them. Another skeletal hand grabbed her foot, then another, and though she stamped them into fragments she knew they'd overcome her eventually. There were far too many of them.

"Boda!" Vali shouted. "Climb!"

She hesitated a moment, sword in hand. To climb she'd have to sheath it, and the thought of facing the legions of dead without a weapon was horrifying. But in the end, she had no choice. She slashed with the blade one last time, low and wide, giving herself a second's grace. Then she dug her fingers into the stone above her and pulled.

Her legs flailed gracelessly against the wall. She hadn't thought to make a hole for them first and without any leverage there was no force behind her kicks. As she struggled something brushed against her leg. She looked down and saw an arm, brown and rotten, reaching towards her. It was blind, the head still buried beneath the ground. But she could see the skull's dome rising from the earth and soon it would see her.

One more wild kick and her foot stuck in something. She realised that it was a hole Vali had dug on his way up. In the panic of battle she hadn't thought to literally follow in his footsteps, but she thought of it now. She could see him hanging, fifteen feet above her and slightly to her left. The pale oval of his face looked down on her as she reached her left arm out, running her palm over the wall until she found the dent he'd left.

His fingers were broader than hers and the hole threatened to be too big, spilling her back to the pit's floor still far too close below. She grimaced and dug her nails in, then stretched her leg out and found a foothold before her handhold gave.

Bone fingers closed on her calf. Every instinct screamed at her to kick out at them. She bit her lip and forced herself to stay still, only her right hand grappling above her for another hold.

But she couldn't stop herself from looking down. The floor of the pit was full of the dead. And escape lay twenty feet above her. She fumbled for another handhold, closing her eyes so she wouldn't have to see what waited for her below.

Caligula held out his hand, drawing Publia's corpse to its feet. Its face smiled but the expression looked wrong, as if whatever lived inside it now didn't quite know how to move its features naturally. The Emperor didn't seem to care. He leaned forward and pressed his lips against the corpse's, ignoring the blood that smeared across his mouth and cheek.

To one side, held fast between too beefy soldiers, Antoninus yelled a wordless, helpless protest.

Petronius didn't think he'd have a better opportunity to escape. He toed his sandals off, leaving bare feet to pad soundlessly across the temple floor. Untended, most of the torches had burnt to cinders in their sconces, and he found himself walking through darkness. He curled his arms around himself, shivering, and quickened his pace. The great arched doors were ahead of him, within reach now. But they didn't represent any sort of sanctuary. He'd seen the beetles fly through them. Who knew what they'd woken outside?

He was almost at the door when he heard Caligula's voice shouting something that was probably "Stop!"

Petronius hunched his shoulders, pretending not to hear. Ten paces to the door, and now he could hear the beat of approaching footsteps running towards him. Two, maybe three people. There was a jingling too and the slap of leather against skin. Soldiers. A shiver of fear ran down his back, but he forced himself not to look. If he didn't look, he could pretend he hadn't heard. And now the door was only five paces away.

He was almost through it when the soldiers caught him. They took his arms, holding them behind his back as if they expected resistance, but he didn't struggle. What would be the point?

"Leaving us so soon?" one of the soldiers asked. It was

the same man Petronius had seen earlier clinging to one of the cultists, sobbing.

"When the party's over..." Petronius said, trying for insouciance. His voice only shook a little.

There were more footsteps drawing near. The soldiers turned him round between them, an ungainly manoeuvre, and he saw that Caligula was approaching, Sopdet and the cultists trailing behind.

Publia's body walked by his side. The thing that lived inside it already seemed to have better control. The stride was easy, only the arms a little too stiff at the body's sides. "Is this the one?" she asked Caligula. Her voice was mushy, as if her tongue kept getting in the way.

"Indeed he is," Caligula told her and then, to his soldiers: "Bring him."

The march through the streets of Rome back to the palace felt like a dream. It was past midnight now, and the streets were less busy. The crazy clatter of horses' hooves and wagon-wheels on flagstones had faded, leaving individual sounds easier to distinguish.

At the far side of the square, a couple were arguing. Her voice was high pitched, teetering on the brink of a sob. His was deep and abrupt, curt words interposed here and there into her long diatribe. Petronius couldn't hear what they were saying, but he could imagine it. *You're still seeing her when you promised me not to! That's a lie. You treat me like a vassal, like a slave! I love you. You never have.*

Nearer to them two traders were locked in their own argument, quieter but every bit as fierce. *I wouldn't pay ten denarii for this crap. Five is the most I'll give. You're a thief and the son of thieves. Seven then, but my children will starve.*

This was Rome, a city Petronius had known his whole life, but it seemed like an alien place tonight. When he looked at the squabbling couple, the haggling merchants, he imagined them dead. He could see the bones beneath their skin. How long before they looked like Publia, walking along at Claudius's side with some other woman peering out from behind her eyes?

Another ten minutes and they were passing the Senate House, white and austere. It stood empty now, and Petronius imagined it fallen, the tall columns cracked in two and the roof caved in, rain dripping through and plants growing out.

The next street was lined with domi, the houses of the rich. The doors were bolted, slaves posted outside as guards. A flickering yellow candlelight shone from within and there was the sound of laughter and music. Petronius had spent many similar evenings and knew this one would stretch on for hours yet, the guests drinking and eating and later fucking – if a guest or a slave had caught their eye – and they had no idea, none at all, of the devastation that was to come.

As they walked on, the cultists began to slip away, one by one. The first glanced behind him, expecting Caligula to order him back, but the order didn't come. The Emperor had eyes for no one but his resurrected sister. A flood of them left after that, scurrying away to their holes, like rats. Only Sopdet remained, smiling that tranquil, unreadable smile, as if she was enjoying some private joke.

The soldiers had dropped Petronius's arms long ago. But when he too tried to slip away they grabbed him, and the taller sour-faced man tutted.

And there, finally, was the palace. The building had stood since Augustus's time, renovated and enlarged by Tiberius, gilded by Caligula. Statues of each Emperor lined the path that led to it. The sculptor hadn't flattered. The Emperors were clearly people. There was Julius's furrowed brow and thin lips, and Augustus's weak chin. And there was Tiberius, as frightening in marble as he'd been in the flesh. His eyes were round white nothings, but Petronius thought he could see the rage in them. He wondered what the old Caesar would have thought of what his nephew had done. Would he have understood? Maybe he would. Maybe they all would. There was something wonderful, Petronius imagined, in knowing that you were the last Emperor of Rome. That yours was the last golden age.

The palace was a domus writ large. In place of one atrium there were a score, filled with bright-flowering plants from every corner of the Empire. Petronius almost smiled as they passed the lararium, where the household gods lived. Caligula had ordered his own image set up there, above all the others. His empty eyes seemed to follow Petronius as they moved on.

The Praetorian Guard had started to melt away, too, taking their usual places around the palace. Or maybe sneaking home to their wives and children. Perhaps warning them what would come, when the beetles found the graves that lined every road outside Rome. When the dead came back for the living.

Finally, they reached the great triclinium, where Caligula's infamous banquets were held. Now only Sopdet, the Emperor and his sister, and Petronius's two guards remained. And the slaves lining the walls, waiting on the Emperor's pleasure. It shamed Petronius how nearly invisible to him they'd become. But Boda had taught him to see that they were people too. He was trying very hard not to think about what was happening to her, wherever she was.

The Emperor looked at Petronius, as the soldiers forced him to his knees. Caligula's hand was twined with Publia's. Drusilla's now, Petronius supposed. Publia's face had worn an expression that hovered between haughty and ingratiating, ready to switch at a moment's notice depending on the company. Drusilla was entirely different. There was a self-indulgence about her mouth that a woman in Publia's position couldn't have afforded. Publia's plump lips pouted a shape they'd never made before.

"So he was the one who brought you there, brother," she said.

Caligula nodded. "But not to bring you back. He wanted to stop the ceremony. Isn't that right?"

Petronius thought about lying. The Emperor was crazy, he might believe him if he claimed that this had been his plan all along. "That's right, Caesar," he said. "I didn't want this to happen."

"You see!" Caligula said.

But Drusilla was still studying Petronius. She ran her fingertip up the bridge of his nose and then along the curve of his cheek beneath his eye. He forced himself not to flinch away from the ice-cold touch.

"He isn't frightened," Drusilla said.

Caligula's mouth drooped. "Isn't he? That's disappointing."

"It makes him more of a threat, Caesar," Sopdet said.

Petronius laughed, he couldn't help himself. The only things he'd ever threatened were his family's good name and his female acquaintances' virtue.

Caligula scowled at the priestess. It occurred to Petronius that the Egyptian didn't know him terribly well, although she'd managed to manipulate him earlier. She didn't understand his perversity, how little he liked being told what to do.

"The boy's intentions were good," Caligula told her. "He had the interests of Rome and his Emperor at heart. Didn't you?"

"Yes, Caesar," he said. "Only that."

"We should let him live," Drusilla said. She moved her hand to cup Petronius's chin, turning his face up to her. "He's a handsome thing. I could enjoy him."

An expression of mingled shock and pain crossed Caligula's face.

Drusilla laughed, and released Petronius to embrace her brother. She rubbed her face against his, like a cat begging for food. There was no real warmth in it, only self-interest, but Caligula's expression softened.

"How about it?" he asked Petronius. "Do you deserve to live?"

Sopdet glared and Drusilla smiled, cruelly amused. Would he talk his way out of this, or fail and die? It was clear she'd be entertained either way.

"No one deserves to live," Petronius said. "Life is a gift – from our gods and from our Emperor."

Caligula laughed delightedly. "A poet in the making! Indeed, life is a gift, and one I intend to grant you. After all, if it weren't for you, Drusilla wouldn't be here – even if it wasn't quite what you intended."

Drusilla jumped up and down like an excited child, clapping her hands in glee. Only Sopdet glowered her displeasure, but she had the sense to keep it to herself.

"Caesar, your generosity undoes me," Petronius said. He didn't have to fake the tears in his eyes. He wasn't sure how much more he could take. "And now I beg leave to return to my family."

"Return?" Caligula said. "Don't be absurd – the day's just beginning." He snapped his fingers, bringing a slave scurrying to his side. "Send an invitation to all the top families in Rome. Tell them refusal is not an option. We're celebrating the return of my beloved sister, and there will be more food, more drink and more copulation than this palace has ever seen."

He turned back to Petronius, drawing him to his feet and slinging an arm around his shoulders. "And you," he said, "shall be the guest of honour. What fun we're going to have!"

The dead remained in the pit when Boda and Vali finally struggled out of it. They were too weak or stupid to scale the walls, but it didn't matter. The catacombs were full of corpses. In every nook they passed a body was uncurling, strips of rotting flesh falling as bones jerked into new life.

Boda drew her sword and swung wildly. She soon discovered that a blow to the arm or leg wasn't enough. The severed limb dropped and the dead carried on. Only a blow to the head, smashing the skull, finished them off. Her arm ached with the effort of heaving it. Vali ran beside her, wielding his small belt knife, but it wasn't much use. The blade passed through putrid flesh and between bones and did no harm at all. And the dead loomed in front of them, at every turn in every tunnel, skulls swaying on their bony necks.

They found the exit from the catacombs by sheer luck. The entrance loomed, a midnight blue within the black and then they were through and the dead were shambling after, too slow to catch them.

When they'd left them out of sight behind, Boda and Vali finally stopped. He reached out to touch her arm and when she saw the red on his finger she realised she was bleeding. The pain immediately hit, as if it had been waiting for her to notice it.

"It's nothing," she told him. "Just a scratch."

His face was more sombre than she'd ever seen it. "We failed."

"Yes. So what do we do?"

"We failed," he repeated.

Now she wanted to shake him. "We failed to stop the seed being planted. That doesn't mean we can't uproot the plant that grows."

"You really think so?"

"I have to. Or would you rather stand back and let this happen?"

"It's Rome," he said, eyebrows dipping as he frowned. "Why should you care if it's destroyed?"

"Is it just Rome?" she said. "Do you think it will end here?"

He sighed. "No. The dead will spread like a plague over the whole world."

"Then we have to stop them."

He didn't argue, but he didn't look convinced either. She could see the doubt in his face more clearly now. The sun must be nearing the horizon. The light grew and their view widened from just a few paces in either direction to ten and then twenty, and then all the way to the walls of Rome on one side and the farmland ringing it on the other.

"Odin protect us," Boda whispered.

Ahead of them, the Appian Way was lined with graves. She hadn't seen them on her journey to the catacombs but they were obvious now, a line of white pillars marching into the distance. Beside each one, the earth was churning. Some corpses had already pulled themselves free. They were fresher than the bodies in the catacombs, more whole. In the dawning light they could see Boda and Vali too. Their heads swung, nostrils flaring as they sniffed the wind.

To their left ran the Esquiline Way, lined with crosses. Some of those nailed to them were still living. During the long nights they'd been slumped and motionless, waiting for the end. Now they were twisting against the metal that held them, though it must have been agonising.

On the crosses beside them, men and women who'd already surrendered to death opened their eyes. They struggled too, harder and more determinedly. From their blank faces, Boda guessed that they felt no pain. The heads of the nails in their wrists and feet were broad. They ripped flesh and chipped bone but then the corpses were free and they fell to the ground beneath them. Blood flowed but didn't spurt with no heart to pump it.

The bodies lay crumpled as the living crucified around them screamed, and Boda hoped for a futile moment that they were too broken to move. Then bleeding hands pressed beneath the corpses to push them to their feet. A hundred heads swung towards Boda and Vali.

And nearer still there was a heap of earth taller and broader than the Senate House itself. That was stirring too. Unlike the silent human corpses, whatever lay under here was growling and hissing and braying.

Then the first animal emerged. It was a lion, killed in the Arena as everything in that charnel pit had been. A tiger followed and then a grey barrel of a monster with a single horn whose name Boda didn't know.

In her short time as a gladiator, Boda had seen thousands of animals killed. They'd all been buried here, and now they were all rising. The lions snarled round mouthfuls of sharp white teeth while the grey creature put down its head to charge.

Vali grabbed her arm, pulling her back, though nowhere was safe. The dead were everywhere. "Tell me, Boda," he said. "How can we stop this?"

CHAPTER THIRTEEN

The guests started to arrive as the sun rose, bleary-eyed and desperately trying to seem happy. It was a lunatic time to hold a feast but their Emperor had never been known for his sanity. Petronius watched them bowing and laughing and pretending they were honoured to be there.

Caligula looked happier than Petronius had ever seen him. While he talked to his guests his fingers were constantly brushing Drusilla – her arm, her waist, her face – as if he was afraid she'd disappear. The guests heard Caesar calling another woman by his dead sister's name and smiled politely, no doubt taking it for another manifestation of his madness.

The Emperor insisted on seating Petronius at his right hand, with Drusilla on his left. From there he had a fine view down the table as it was heaped high with food. When he tasted it, Petronius discovered that the suckling pig centrepiece was actually cunningly disguised fish meat. And the enormous pie no one quite dared to cut into was said to contain live sparrows. The slaves in the kitchens had outdone themselves. Amazing how motivating abject terror could be.

The Cult had been summoned to attend, too. Unlike the rest of the guests, none of them could meet Drusilla's eye. And they had even less appetite than everyone else, desultorily picking at morsels of chicken disguised as lamb or wood pigeon stuffed with humming bird whenever Caligula looked their way.

Sopdet was seated beside Drusilla. She didn't even pretend to eat, just watched the gathering with haughty eyes. Petronius smiled smugly when she looked at him.

His continual existence was a pretty small victory in the scheme of things, but he was very pleased with it.

Seneca had been seated beside Petronius. He turned and smiled at the old man. "Enjoying yourself?"

Seneca returned a smile that looked more like a grimace. "Immensely."

"Tell me," said Petronius, "because I've been wondering. Just what did you think would happen when the Cult got its way?"

Seneca paused, a wizened chicken foot halfway to his mouth. He chewed it whole before answering. "You're too young to understand."

"Funny, I don't feel as young as I was yesterday. And I want to know."

"Very well then. I wanted exactly what's happened, a breaking down of the barriers between life and death."

"But why?" Petronius leaned forward, genuinely interested. The other cultists seemed to have been in it for the prestige, the social lubrication. Many of them had seemed entirely ignorant of the actual purpose of the ceremonies. But Seneca – Seneca had known.

The old man shook his head. "When I say you're too young, it's not an insult to your intelligence or understanding." Petronius raised a disbelieving eyebrow and Seneca almost smiled. "Don't misunderstand me, I think very little of your intelligence. But what I meant was that you can't have felt the approach of your own death, felt it colouring every moment of your life. And I doubt you've lost anyone who mattered to you, not yet."

Petronius thought of his twin sisters, who'd died shortly after their birth. Or his elder brother killed in bread riots during the last emperor's reign. None of them had really meant anything to him. But he looked across at Caligula, gazing into his dead sister's eyes. "You're wrong, I do understand that. But death is long and life is short. Why not wait until you're reunited?"

"When you're grieving, every second seems like a year. A year stretches into eternity."

"Then slit your wrists and join them that way. Why should the world be changed to fit your needs?"

Seneca was scowling at him now. "I've seen the other side, boy. I know what waits for us there. When I was young I was very sick, did you know that?"

Petronius looked at the other man, the way his stick-thin limbs seemed to struggle to support even his own frail body. "I can believe it."

Seneca smiled bitterly. "My parents thought I'd die – and I did. For two whole minutes illness took me out of this world and into the next, until the doctors brought me back. And I saw..." The focus of his eyes shifted outward as his thoughts turned inward. "You've heard the legends, but like every educated man today you probably don't believe them. You laugh them off as superstition and metaphor. Idiots, all of you. The afterlife is exactly as the legends say, a bleak darkness where the sun never shines and the rivers that run are icy cold and empty of life. And the people... they've forgotten what it is to feel, or think. They're shades indeed, mere shadows of who they once were, waiting for judgement from a god who has no patience with human foibles or needs. At the age of seven, I swore I'd never return there – and Sopdet offered me a way to ensure that I never did."

Petronius was left momentarily silent by the old man's passion. His narrow, sagging cheeks were flushed and there was a light in his eyes Petronius had never seen before. And he almost agreed with him. Almost. "But this is no kind of escape," he said. "Without the barrier between them, won't this world become like that one?"

Seneca shook his head, but for the first time he looked a little doubtful. "Sopdet promised me that it's this world which will change the other."

"Did she?" Petronius looked across the half-eaten heaps of food to find that Sopdet was watching them closely. "And did you ever ask her why she wanted this? Or did you just assume her motives were the same as yours?"

Seneca's mouth thinned, and it was obvious he didn't have an answer.

Boda was used to fighting other men, and the vacant look in the corpses' eyes made them easier to hack and dismember. Her arm was smeared with blood up to the elbow from the recently dead and she was splattered with fouler fluids from those who'd been lying in the ground longer.

But her people had taught her to respect animals, and the tiger was the most astonishing creature she'd ever seen. Powerful muscles moved liquidly beneath its fur and it could only have been dead a day. Despite her knowledge that it meant her harm, she couldn't bring herself to strike it. And then it leapt, lethal and beautiful.

Without thinking, she raised her sword, the point positioned precisely to skewer its heart. The sword sunk in to the hilt but the tiger didn't even slow. Its body landed on hers, knocking her to her back beneath it. Close to, she could smell the earth caked in its fur and the first hint of putrefaction.

The creature's jaws snapped shut, inches from her face. She braced her arm beneath its neck and pushed desperately, but it was no good. The tiger was stronger than her, and it had the leverage. When its jaws closed a second time its teeth grazed her nose, scraping the skin and flesh from its tip. Then its front leg slashed out, claws digging deep grooves in her arm. She gasped and her hand loosened, an involuntary reflex she couldn't control.

Instantly, the tiger lunged. She twisted her body and jerked her head to the side and this time its teeth caught her ear. They closed and pulled and she felt the lobe tear away. The agony was instant and almost overwhelming. But the second the tiger took to chew its morsel gave her a chance.

Her sword arm was hopelessly pinned beneath its left leg. She dropped the blade and rolled to one side, away from its terrible jaws. It tried to stop her, legs scrabbling to keep their hold on the ground, but the force it could exert sideways was weaker than the pressure of its massive weight bearing down. The leg gave and she was free.

Her own sword sliced her back as she rolled over it and her first grab took the blade and not the hilt, opening a deep cut in her palm. The hilt was slippery with her own blood when she finally grasped it, but she held on tight and swung. This time she was aiming for the neck, and her blade bit deep and stuck fast in the tiger's spine.

The tiger writhed on the end of her blade like a fish on a hook. She braced her feet on the ground and held tight. The metal rang as its teeth snapped against it but the blade held. A stalemate.

A quick glance to the left showed her that Vali had his own troubles. He faced the wickedly hooked tusks of a great black boar as a skeletal monkey gibbered on his shoulders and tore at his hair. There'd be no help for her there.

The tiger was still twisting and turning and she realised

that it would never tire or stop. But she would. Her hand could barely keep its grip on the hilt of her sword and the blade was already beginning to loosen, working free of the bone.

She only had one chance. The next time the tiger's head swung round she pulled against the motion rather than moving with it, allowing the creature's own strength to wrench the metal out of its neck. The flesh and bone gave grudgingly and for a moment she thought the sword would stick fast. She was unbalanced and vulnerable – easy prey without a weapon to wield. She gritted her teeth and gave one final, desperate tug, straining her injured shoulder almost beyond endurance. And suddenly her sword was swinging free.

She scrambled desperately backwards, almost falling to her knees in her haste. The neck was still her only sensible target, beheading the tiger the only way to stop it. But she was weaker now than when she'd first tried that move, and her blade blunter.

The creature span to face her, lips curled back as it snarled. In a second it would pounce. With a fierce yell, she circled her sword above her head – one circuit, then two – before bringing it down with all her strength.

The blade sliced through flesh and bone and then flesh again to emerge the other side, nicked but whole.

The tiger's head flew a short distance through the air and landed neatly on its neck. Its eyes blinked and glared furiously at Boda as its jaw snapped on nothing. She stamped on its head, again and again until the bones of its skull cracked and splintered and the grey spongy mess of its brain oozed between her toes. When she finally took her foot away, the eyes were blank and the jaws still.

She took one deep, gasping breath, then turned to Vali.

His short knife was buried deep in the boar's eye. Blood oozed around it and he was using it to hold the creature away from him. She wondered if he'd seen her own fight and decided to follow the same strategy. But with only a short belt knife he had no hope of administering the coup de grace.

Her shoulder ached fiercely and her arm burned with fatigue but she lifted her sword and brought it down behind the boar's ears. After three more strikes the creature's neck parted, and one quick thrust took the monkey's head from its shoulders, leaving the bones of its body to slither down Vali's back. There were deep scratch marks around his eyes where it had tried to gouge them out.

"You need a bigger sword," she said.

He gasped a surprised laugh. "Maybe we can ask them for one."

He gestured to their right and she realised for the first time that there were other living people nearby. Abandoned horses and wagons suggested they were merchants or farmers, bringing their wares to market. But some of them had swords and were fighting back against the dead. Boda could see small clusters of them scattered over the approach to the city's walls.

It was obvious the dead were winning. The living were hopelessly outnumbered.

"We have to get inside the city," Vali said. "The walls will keep the dead outside."

Boda nodded, looking at the struggling bands of living people. Some of them included children, huddled at the centre of the groups. "Yes, we need to get to Rome. And we need to bring them with us."

Petronius was eating a concoction of strawberries and honeycomb when the messenger came from the city walls.

The man bent over to whisper in Caligula's ear, but he was panting for breath, and fear made his voice so loud that everyone at the table could hear it. "There's news, Caesar. Grave news..."

Caligula raised an eyebrow. "Grave enough to interrupt my dinner? To tear me away from celebrating my beloved sister's return?" His hand reached out for Drusilla but met empty air. She was leaning away from him and across Sopdet, whispering in the ear of the man beside her. The young, good-looking man with merry eyes and a full head of honey-coloured curls. Caligula's lips thinned and the messenger flinched back when he turned his angry eyes on him.

"Well?" Caligula said. "What is this news?"

The messenger looked like he wanted to turn tail and run, but he didn't, and Petronius shivered. News serious enough to risk the Emperor's wrath must be very grave indeed.

"It's... outside the walls of Rome, Caesar. There are..." He dropped his head. "The dead have risen from their graves. They're marching on the city."

Sopdet smiled gently. The cultists' eyes darted around the room, frightened or ashamed. There were a few gasps from the other guests, but mostly laugher and catcalls. Suggestions that the messenger was drunk, that he'd lost his mind.

Caligula laughed too. "The dead rising? How absurd."

The messenger's hands balled into fists. "I've seen them with my own eyes, Caesar. They're slaughtering everyone they can find. And the walls are barely defended. If they fall... You must send the Praetorian Guard to reinforce the soldiers there."

"I *must* send them? Whose command *must* the Emperor of Rome obey?"

"It's... it's... Caesar, it's..." The messenger stuttered into silence.

Caligula turned his back, flicking a finger at one of the soldiers who guarded the door. "Kill him."

The legionary stepped forward, sword drawn.

"Outside, you fool!" Caligula snapped. "We don't want to put people off their dinners. And while you're there, fetch that wretched uncle of mine. He's mourned long enough – the boy was only a slave, and a Greek at that."

The door closed behind them and it was only because he was listening for it that Petronius heard the messenger's muffled scream, quickly ended. The other dinner guests continued to gorge themselves. Caligula poured more wine for his sister. And Sopdet's eyes met his, spiteful and triumphant.

The first group Boda and Vali found was completely unarmed. There had been at least twenty of them to begin with, but ten were dead now. The rest stood in a tight ring, arms held out to ward off the dead. In the middle of their circle crouched a boy and a girl, with fine light hair and open, trusting eyes. They couldn't have been older than five.

The dead weren't armed either. Unlike Boda's people, it seemed Romans didn't bury their warriors with their swords by their sides. It should have been an even match, but the walking corpses could shrug off any injury.

She saw one man kick out, the toe of his boot catching

a shambling corpse between its legs. The blow was hard enough to lift it off its feet for an instant, but when it came down it leapt forward, its own arm lashing out to catch the man across the face. His head snapped back and he dropped to the ground, stunned. The circle of the living closed tight to fill the gap he'd left – and he lay helpless outside it.

Boda had to look away as the dead descended. But she smelt the blood they spilled, and the contents of his stomach as they ripped it open. She raised her sword and prepared to charge.

Vali's fingers clawed into her arm. "We can't help them. You'll just get yourself killed."

"We've got a chance," she said. "The dead are weak."

It was true these were less recent corpses, only dry skin covering old bones. When a woman kicked another in the chest, the ribs caved in, revealing hollow nothingness inside. Her sword would make quick work of them.

Vali didn't release her. "It's not just them. Look."

Behind the living, the undead animals were preparing to charge. She saw another tiger leading them, and a row of wolves behind.

"Then we save who we can," she said.

The merchants smiled as she approached, sword swinging. It cut through two corpses in one stroke and they crumpled to the ground, dead hands still grasping. Boda stamped on them as she pushed past a merchant and into the centre of the ring.

"What –" the man said.

She didn't have time to explain. Maybe these were his children. Maybe he'd understand.

Vali had followed her, though he was cursing her idiocy. Close by and getting closer, she could hear the roars and growls of the dead animals. She picked up the girl first and swung her little body high to settle it on Vali's shoulders. The boy she put on her own. His weight was almost intolerable on her injured shoulder but she made herself run, out of the ring of the living and away from the attacking beasts.

The shouts of the merchants followed them. She wanted to believe that some of them were thanks, but she couldn't worry about it. The girl was sobbing, wriggling on Vali's shoulders as she tried to look behind at her parents. Boda held fast to the little boy's legs, forcing him to face forward. She could hear the screams behind her and she didn't want him to see what was causing them.

If the animals had charged on, they would have been finished. But the creatures stopped to feast on the merchants and Boda and Vali managed to run clear, legs labouring under the weight on their shoulders.

The little girl fisted her hands in Vali's red hair and Boda saw him grimacing as he ran. A corpse lurched in front of him, teeth bared in a grin too wide for any living face. His small knife flash out and widened the smile still further, splitting the skull at the weak point of its jaw.

The corpse staggered to the side then made another grab for him – until Boda's blade took it through the stomach, sending its upper torso crashing to the ground and its legs running aimlessly in the other direction. She grabbed Vali's hand after that, keeping him within her sword's defensive range.

Ahead of them she could see another group of the living, larger and better armed than the previous ones. They even had shields, which they'd used to form themselves into a defensive turtle, the weakest members of the group crouched beneath as they shuffled agonisingly slowly towards the city walls. It was the same formation the legionaries had used when they defeated Boda's people in the western forest. Maybe there were soldiers in that group. They certainly looked like the best hope. But Boda and Vali would have to fight their way through fifty paces and hundreds of the dead to reach them.

Caligula couldn't stop looking at Drusilla. It was amazing how quickly he'd come to accept that it really was his sister looking at him through another woman's eyes. But he knew Drusilla better than he knew anyone in the world. He was familiar with every expression that flicked across her face – the small polite smile that showed she was unbearably bored, the droop of her eyelids when she was planning some mischief, the arch of her eyebrows when she saw something she liked. He knew the way her hand would land, light but not innocent, on the arm of a man she was interested in. He'd always known what the spark of desire looked like in her face.

He knew her so well, how could he have forgotten how miserable she made him? She knew she was doing it, too. As she flirted with that son-of-a-whore Nerva, she kept shooting glances at Caligula out of the corner of her eye, gauging his reaction. Working out just how much she was hurting him. She'd always done this, *always*.

Another messenger came in, blathering something about the dead rising outside Rome. Caligula didn't bother taking his eyes off Drusilla, just clicked his fingers for a guard to dispose of him.

"Caesar," a voice drifted from further down the table. Caligula couldn't remember the man's name, but he was something big in the wine trade. "Perhaps, Caesar, we should listen to him."

There was a murmur – no, more than a murmur, a chorus

– of agreement. Caligula finally wrenched his attention away from his sister to look at his other guests. They were staring back at him with expressions ranging from fearful to angry, with every shade of alarm in between.

"What is this?" he said. "Are you questioning my judgement?"

The soldier left the door open this time, and the scream of the dying messenger was very loud in the near-silent room. The only other sound was the chink of silver against ceramic as one grey-haired, barrel-chested guest continued eating, oblivious. Outside, the pile of bodies had grown quite high. Flies were beginning to buzz around them.

"Please, Caesar," the wine importer said. "Killing the messenger won't change the message. You need to do something."

Instead of gasps of shock at this treachery, there were nods of agreement from the other guests. Even some of the cultists were joining in – and they were the ones who'd caused the problem in the first place.

"I don't like that man," Drusilla said. "Get rid of him for me." She leaned back in Caligula's direction and trailed her fingernail from his shoulder to his wrist. Exactly the same trick he'd seen her using on Nerva earlier.

Caligula shrugged her hand off petulantly. Her face fell, a tear forming in the corner of her eye, and he instantly felt like a scoundrel. How did she do that to him?

"You heard her," he said to the nearest soldier. "Kill him." He looked around at the other guests, not cowed even by this, and thought that an object lesson in obedience wouldn't be out of order. "And you can leave his body where it is. Even dead he'll be better company than half the people here."

This time, the soldier didn't jump to obey him instantly.

His hand hovered over the hilt of his sword as he looked across at his captain. But Marcus's face was as impassive as a statue, and he nodded without hesitation.

The man – what was his name, anyway? – rose to his feet as the soldier approached. "Don't do this, citizen. You know that I'm right. You should be at the walls fighting the enemies of Rome, not in here—" His last word tailed off into a choked gurgle as the sword took him through the gut.

The soldier pulled it free, resting a hand against the man's shoulder to ease the blade out as his knees gave from under him and he collapsed back onto the cushions. Caligula smiled to see his neighbours flinch away from his corpse. His blood pooled around him, viscous and red.

That should keep them quiet. And most of them did look cowed. Except that man there, Trajan. He had his face lowered, but Caligula caught a glint of his eyes glaring with hatred from beneath thick black brows. "Him too," he told the soldier. "And her – to the left there. Her nose has been distracting me since she got here. It's enormous."

The soldier's face was pale, but he didn't look for confirmation from Marcus before obeying this time. Trajan glared at him defiantly as the blade slid through his heart. The woman tried to flee, feet hopelessly tangling in the cushions. She held out her hands in mute pleading to the soldier, and Caligula saw him turn his face away as he killed her too.

He thought that would be an end of it, but now there was shouting all around the table. Some of the other guests were standing up, and one of them was waving a belt knife around. He didn't even have to tell the soldiers to finish that one off.

But as the chaos grew rather than abated, Caligula realised with a quiver of fear what he'd done wrong. He shouldn't have ordered that woman killed, even though she did have a quite absurdly large nose. Her killing had been too random – not the obvious result of questioning their Emperor – and now they all felt threatened. And they outnumbered the Praetorian Guard four to one.

Drusilla knew it too. Her strange new face was pale and when Nerva touched her arm she shook him off impatiently. "Do something!" she said to Caligula. "This is all your fault!"

The room was in uproar. Only Sopdet and Seneca were still sitting in place, and the youth Petronius. "You!" Caligula said to him. "How do I stop this?"

The boy looked round at the near riot, the soldiers in danger of being overwhelmed by the frantic guests. A huge, black, over-muscled man who had once been a gladiator appeared to be their ringleader. He'd managed to overpower one of the guards and take his sword, and was now laying about him with frightening efficiency. Caligula had a bad feeling he was the husband of the woman with the huge nose.

"Well!" Caligula snapped. "What can I do?"

"Not start this in the first place?" Petronius suggested. His eyes were wild, and Caligula realised he was close to hysterics.

Drusilla reached across to slap Petronius's face. "Don't be a fool! They saw my brother seat you at his right hand. Do you think you'll be spared if they win?"

The youth seemed to pull himself together a little. The hand rubbing his cheek shook as he nodded. "Let them go, then."

"They're traitors!" Caligula hissed. "They need to die."

"But we need to live!" Petronius shouted. "Didn't

Julius himself say that you should never leave an enemy without an escape route? No one wants to fight a man with nothing to lose."

"He's right," Drusilla said, and smiled at Petronius with far too much warmth.

Caligula wanted to ignore his advice just for that, but then he saw the black ex-gladiator gut a soldier with his own sword. "Marcus!" he shouted. "Let them out!"

The guests heard. Some of them looked like they wanted to continue fighting. They knew they had the upper hand. But enough of them were soft and frightened and they stampeded for the door as soon as the guards moved aside from it.

For one terrifying instant, the Nubian gladiator stood in front of Caligula, sword raised for a killing blow. His mouth opened in a roar of rage – and instead of words, a torrent of blood poured out of it. Marcus had skewered him through his undefended back.

After that, the remaining guests turned tail and fled. They left behind a room littered with corpses. Some had fallen onto the table, heads buried in bowls of syllabub or resting on raspberry flans. The smell of fruit and cream and cinnamon almost overwhelmed the stench of blood. Four of the Praetorian Guard were dead, too, and several more injured.

Claudius, with his usual genius for ill-timing, chose that moment to finally join them. His eyes scanned the destruction with horror, lingering over the mutilated body of a fourteen-year-old girl. When they looked at Caligula, horror had been replaced with accusation. "What h-h-happened here, nephew?"

Caligula shrugged but couldn't meet his gaze. "There was a rebellion. They disobeyed me."

Some of the soldiers shuffled, and he heard a cough as

if someone was about to speak, but nobody did.

Claudius leaned down to close the young woman's staring eyes. "A rebellion?"

"A very entertaining one," Sopdet said. She'd remained seated throughout the whole thing, untouched by any of the combatants. Now she rose gracefully to her feet. "I thank you for your hospitality, Caesar, but myself and Seneca have other things to attend to."

Caligula scowled. "You think you're going to leave? You're the one who caused all this!"

"I think you'll find," Seneca said, "that it was your own inability to control your temper which sparked it off. It really is quite extraordinary – the mightiest Empire in the world ruled by a man with the self-control of a three-year-old."

Caligula was shocked into temporary silence. No one had ever spoken to him in that way. Even the people he had ordered put to the sword were too afraid for the families they left behind. "How dare you?" he finally said, voice trembling with rage. "You'll die for this."

Sopdet rested a hand on Seneca's shoulder as she stood beside him. "Really? Do you really think creating more corpses is a good idea?"

"Why not?" Caligula raged. "You're all ingrates – treacherous scum. Why shouldn't I kill you all?"

"Because," Sopdet said, "you're simply adding to the forces on my side."

Caligula stared uncomprehendingly at her as she snapped her fingers. But when the beetles flew through the doorway in answer to her summons, he knew exactly what it meant.

"Stop them!" he yelled.

The soldiers leapt to obey, swords flailing uselessly at the tiny, flying targets. Untroubled, the beetles buzzed past the metal and settled on the corpses.

Caligula dived at the nearest one, trying to brush the insect away from the dead gladiator's mouth. But he couldn't get a purchase on its slick carapace and then it was in the man's mouth and burrowing through to his brain. A moment later, the corpse's eyes opened, staring straight into Caligula's.

He screamed and jumped back, pressing himself against Drusilla. She whimpered and buried her face in his shoulder as all around the room the corpses of the recently dead woke.

The Praetorian Guard moved, ready to attack – and their own dead rose to face them. The soldiers' faces drained of colour and their swords drooped in their arms as they looked into their comrades' dead white faces.

"Your rule is over, Caesar," Sopdet said. "Soon there will be no one left alive within the Servian walls. And then the armies of the dead will march from Rome, until this whole world is a second kingdom of death."

They were almost within arm's reach of safety when the horse attacked. At first Boda thought it was a stray, panicked by the fighting around it. Then, as it turned to face her, she saw the red gleam in its eye. Its hoof pawed the ground and its lips pulled back, baring yellow teeth. She saw that the flesh of its belly had fallen away, leaving the white arch of its ribs exposed as its entrails dangled in the dirt below.

The little boy on Boda's shoulders yelled and the horse reared, hooves lashing out towards Vali as flecks of spittle flew from its mouth.

Vali crouched, shielding his head. But the move was

pure instinct, an animal reflex that didn't take account of the little girl sitting on his shoulders. The horse's kick caught her head straight on, stoving in her skull in one blow. She didn't even have time to scream, just slumped lifeless on Vali's shoulders.

Boda saw the moment Vali realised what had happened, as the little girl's blood trickled through his hair and into his eyes. He shuddered convulsively, even as his hands still clung tight to the dead girl's legs, holding her above him as the rest of her blood drained out of her.

The horse reared again, directly above Vali's crouched body. Boda couldn't reach the creature's neck, stretched taught with strain above her. Instead she swung her sword at the legs themselves, putting every atom of her remaining strength into the blow.

Her sword swept clean through the joint above the hoof and out, first the right leg then the left. The horse screamed and began to fall, all its weight plummeting towards Vali's head.

Vali didn't move. His face was blank, no fear in it, no expression at all. Boda's heart raced. She'd seen this before – battle shock. It had paralysed him. The horse's legs were inches from his face now, and its balance was gone. Its whole body would fall on him.

She didn't think, just flung herself at Vali, knocking him to the side as she clung on desperately to her own small human burden.

The horse fell to one side of them, landing on the stumps of its forelegs. It screamed its frustration, but without its hooves it couldn't move and though its mouth foamed and snapped at them, they were out of its reach.

They lay, dazed, in a disorderly heap, Vali at the bottom, Boda on him and the little boy resting on her back, gabbling nonsense words that might have been his idea of a prayer. The dead girl's corpse was beneath them all. Boda could see the sloppy mush of flesh and bone that the fall had made of her little body.

When Vali realised what he was lying on, it seemed to snap him out of his stupor. He let out a cry of revulsion and rolled to one side, pulling Boda and the small boy with him. The girl's mangled body lay motionless where it had fallen. Vali couldn't seem to take his eyes off it. He wasn't weeping, but his silent grief and horror were harder to bear.

Then, as they watched, a beetle landed on the girl's lips. By the time Boda realised what it was, it had crawled inside her mouth and out of sight.

Vali whispered something, a wordless denial, but it was already too late. The light which had so recently gone out in the girl's eyes sparked back into life. Her knees were bent at the wrong angle, her chest squashed almost flat, her intestines oozing from its sides, but somehow she stumbled to her feet. And then, teeth bared, she came towards them.

Boda had to force herself to keep her eyes open as her sword separated the girl's head from her neck. Beside her, Vali fell to his knees and was copiously sick.

It was the little boy who pulled them out of their shock. Boda was horrified to realise that she'd forgotten him – forgotten to shield his eyes from what she'd done to his friend. But he wasn't looking at her. He pointed over Boda's shoulder. "Soldiers," he said.

He was right. In the minutes their fight had taken, the group of the living they'd been trying to join had changed their course to envelop them. There were no words exchanged. Boda didn't think she had any words left. But she, Vali and the little boy were absorbed into the centre of the shielded ring as, step by painful step, it edged its way nearer to the safety of Rome's walls.

Boda wanted to join the outer perimeter, the ones defending against the dead. But the leader of the group – Silvius, a former tribunus in the seventh legion – took one look at her bloody-face and stumbling steps and told her she was too weak to fight, a danger to those around her. She didn't argue, just passed her sword to a man better able to use it. She knew he was right. Her sword arm was burning with pain and she barely had the energy to lift her head, let alone her sword.

Besides, she wanted to keep an eye on Vali. She'd known men choose death rather than live with the pain that lined his face. She'd tried to talk to him but he shrugged her off and so, on an impulse she didn't fully understand, she passed him the young boy to hold.

Vali rested his head against the child's. She wasn't sure which of them took comfort from it, but there was nothing more she could do. They marched on, one painful step at a time, until finally they stood before the gates of Rome.

The city wall was patrolled by archers and javelins prickled along its length. The gate itself was barred. Silvius pushed through to the front of the formation, and the others cleared a space around him so the centurion guarding the gate could see that he spoke for the group.

"Open the gates!" Silvius shouted.

The soldiers' faces on the battlements above remained grim and ungiving.

"Open the damned gates!" Silvius screamed. "For the love of Jupiter – there are women and children here!"

"I'm sorry," the centurion said. "It's too dangerous to let you pass." Then he signalled to his soldiers and, as Boda watched in horror, the gates of Rome were barred against them.

CHAPTER FOURTEEN

The dead stood in a ring around them. But Petronius saw that some of them were swaying on their feet, while others stumbled to their knees when they tried to walk. He remembered how Drusilla had seemed to take a few minutes to gain full control of Publia's body, and he knew that right now was their only chance to escape.

"Be ready!" he shouted.

He couldn't see the remnants of the Praetorian Guard. If they were alive, they were outside the ring of undead. Caligula and Drusilla were still clinging and cowering together. Only Claudius looked up, face still clawed by grief. But the old man nodded and Petronius guessed that was as much encouragement as he was going to get.

In the wreckage of the dinner party, one item had survived unscathed – the huge, brown-crusted pie no one had dared cut into. Petronius launched himself across the table towards it, scooping up a knife along the way. The undead reacted but, just as he'd hoped, were too slow and uncoordinated to stop him. His knife bit through the crust, the pastry crumbled – and the terrified flock of living birds baked inside burst free.

For one moment, there was pandemonium. The living screamed. The dead flinched back. And even Sopdet crouched, covering her face, while Seneca turned tail and fled.

It was almost impossible to see through the flutter of wings and the flurry of loose feathers. The sparrows squawked and shat as they flung themselves against walls and windows. Petronius had been terrified of birds since he was a little boy and his aunt and uncle's geese had attacked him on their farm in the country. His flesh cringed at the light touch of wings or the sharp scratch of claws but he made himself ignore it, running straight for Claudius and grabbing his arm.

Caligula turned fearful, panicked eyes towards him. Petronius wasted a precious second in indecision. But then he took the Emperor's arm too. Caligula still ruled the city, and once they were outside the palace they might need his powers to command.

The Emperor in turn seized Drusilla's hand.

"Leave her – she's one of them!" Petronius yelled.

Caligula's expression was mulish as he held on tighter and Petronius couldn't waste the time arguing. The flock of birds was thinning as they stunned themselves to insensibility against the walls, and the dead were beginning to master their new bodies.

Petronius ran for the door, pulling the line of other survivors with him. The dead tried to stop them. Some of them had swords and when one swung for Petronius's head he thought he was finished. But then another blade clashed with it, thrusting it aside. And he realised that the Praetorian Guard had gathered, the few that remained, ringing them as they headed to the door.

He saw a guard go down as three of the dead flung themselves on him. One of them had been a soldier himself, only the jagged, bloody hole in his leather tunic distinguishing him from his living comrade. Petronius thought the living soldier might have fought back if it hadn't been for that. Instead he screamed and shuddered as a blade pierced his own heart – only to rise a few seconds later, a new spirit lighting his eyes.

Another one took a knife to the face, cutting his cheek to the bone. But he managed to keep his feet, only hissing at the pain, and then they were at the door and the dead were penned inside the room.

There was a pause as both sides faced off against each other. For a moment, Sopdet's expression was a study in pure rage. Her eyes burned with it and her cheeks flamed redder than the cloaks of the undead guards around her.

"You bitch!" Caligula said. "You foreign whore! I should never have trusted you!"

Petronius bit his lip very hard to stop himself pointing out this was precisely what he'd tried to warn the Emperor.

Sopdet just smiled, as if Caligula's ranting had strengthened her.

"Laugh, will you?" Caligula hissed. "I've beaten you! You tried to kill me and you've failed!"

"It's true," she said, "that I can't prevent you leaving. But what difference does it make to me, if you're among the first in Rome to die, or the last? For, in time, die you will – every last one of you."

Boda saw the hope drain out of the eyes around her. She understood. Their fight through the horror around them had been sustained by the prospect of an escape from it. Now that had been taken from them, they were close to giving up. Already the dead were throwing themselves against the outer perimeter of the living, and she didn't think it would be long before that cracked like the shell of a nut, and the dead could rip through the soft flesh within.

She reached out to take the little boy from Vali. Vali was slow to release him, and the child wriggled and fussed, but eventually she had him cradled in her arms. She carried him forward to stand beside Silvius, facing the captain of the gate.

"You have to let us in," she said. "If you don't, you're condemning this child to die."

The captain's face reddened with shame. "I'm sorry. But until we know what they are... How can we know that you're not with them?"

"Because they're killing us!" Silvius snapped. "Can't you see?"

As if to underline his words there was a desperate scream behind them as another of the defenders fell, gored by the rotting remains of a black boar.

"But they're... they're dead," the captain said. "How can we stop them? If we open the gates they'll break through and the whole city will be doomed."

The small boy grizzled in Boda's arm and she rocked him, but he didn't take any comfort from it. She couldn't blame him. "Exactly," she said. "The city will be doomed with no warriors to defend it. There are nearly a hundred of them here. Can you afford to do without us?"

The captain's face was hard to read but she thought she saw him begin to soften. Then his eyes shifted and widened as they caught on something behind her. She spun round to see that a defender had hacked a corpse's arm at the shoulder, only for the dismembered hand to catch around his ankle. He tripped and fell, tumbling out of the defensive wall, and the walking corpse was instantly on him, ripping out his throat with its decaying teeth.

When she looked back at the captain, he was pale and shaking. "Nothing can stop those things. *Nothing*."

But Boda remembered the little girl in the moment before she'd risen from the dead. She remembered the beetle, crawling into the girl's mouth. That was what had woken her. Without that, she would have stayed dead.

"It's in their heads!" she shouted, to the captain and

the other defenders. She picked up a fallen sword and charged towards the armies of dead. "We can kill them."

Desperation gave her arm strength, and she took off the corpse's grey, rotting head in one swing. "Look!" she said. And a moment after it fell, the brown body of a scarab beetle crawled from the corpse's nose, its carapace smeared with the white meat of the brain.

"Look!" she said again and stamped down hard on the beetle. When she lifted her sandal there was only a brown mush left beneath it – and neither the beetle nor the body moved again.

"Help us!" she shouted to the guard captain. "Shoot them in the head!"

Petronius blinked at the brightness of the daylight when they emerged from the Palace. The streets of Rome were thronged with people, but the atmosphere had changed in the last few hours. There was fear in the faces around them, and sometimes hostility. The news from the walls must be spreading. And it looked like Caligula was being blamed.

The Praetorian Guard pushed through the crowds, clearing a path for their Emperor where once one would have opened spontaneously. Petronius was glad they'd managed to gather so many of the soldiers, more than two hundred picked up from around the palace or collected from various drinking dens as they passed. The mood of the people was ugly and there was an unhappy muttering as they passed. Caligula clearly sensed the anger. He kept his face down and mouth shut as he walked beside his sister.

Caligula had ordered Marcus to take them to the Temple

of Saturn, though he hadn't bothered to explain why. Petronius guessed the Emperor thought that priests would be the least likely to turn against him. But the route led through some of Rome's poorest districts, and here the hostility was more overt. When they passed a stall selling elderly vegetables, some unseen hand liberated a few and threw them towards the Emperor's party.

An overripe tomato spattered against Petronius's tunic. He spat out the seeds and wiped juice from his eye, but it was impossible to see who'd thrown it. Caligula was hit with a mouldy peach, while a patter of grapes rained down on Drusilla's head.

Petronius expected the Emperor to react with rage, but instead he tucked his head tighter against his chest and quickened his pace. He seemed to have lost his pride – or maybe just his nerve – when Sopdet defied him and won. But Marcus drew his sword from its sheath and the other soldiers did the same and the crowd muttered, drawing back.

Part of their route took them close to the city walls. Here there were fewer people and those that were still around seemed intent on leaving. Petronius saw some families outside their homes, hurriedly packing the contents of their houses into waiting wagons.

"Where are you going, citizen?" Petronius asked the father of one family.

The man turned wide, frightened eyes on him. "Away from the walls. They say they'll be over them soon. We're seeking refuge in the Temple of Jupiter."

Petronius didn't imagine the temple would be safer than anywhere else in the city but he just nodded and moved on. No need to create more panic than there already was.

Closer to the walls, they heard screams and the clash

of weapons.

Marcus turned to Caligula. "Caesar, it seems the messengers spoke the truth."

"So?" Caligula snarled. "You killed them for treason – not perjury."

Marcus nodded, face carefully blank. "But now the people need us. The walls are only lightly defended – my men could make the difference between victory and defeat."

"Your job is to defend me!" Caligula screamed. "Not the good-for-nothing inhabitants of this rat-infested city! Me, do you understand – me!"

Petronius winced as the Emperor's voice echoed down the narrow street. Windows opened above them and someone flung a pitcher of liquid out of one. It missed Caligula and struck two of his guards, stinking of piss. The soldiers roared with anger, but Marcus called them back when they made to enter the house and Caligula smiled his satisfaction.

Only Claudius walked unheeding through it all, mouth and face closed. Petronius dropped back to walk beside him.

It took several minutes for the older man to notice him. When he did he attempted a smile, but it looked ghastly, a mere stretching of lips over teeth.

"I should thank you," Claudius said, "for t-t-trying to save N-n-narcissus."

Petronius shook his head. "You don't need to thank me. What Caligula did to him was wrong."

For the first time, some life came into Claudius's eyes. He darted an anxious look behind him. "Don't speak so loudly. And d-d-don't be fooled by his cowardice. The most dangerous animal is a c-c-cornered one."

Petronius lowered his voice. "But he's not just a danger

to those around him. Rome will fall if he doesn't act. Or if someone else doesn't act in his place..."

As suddenly as they'd filled with life, Claudius's eyes drained of it again. "Rome is not my concern," he said, and moved closer to his nephew to forestall any further conversation.

Petronius bit his lip in frustration. It wasn't just about preserving his own life, though it certainly was about that. But if Caligula continued this selfish, suicidal course, too many people would die.

He sneaked a look at the surrounding guards and found that Marcus was looking right back at him. Something about his expression told Petronius he'd overheard the exchange with Claudius. His heart thumped almost painfully hard against his ribs, but after a moment the guard captain looked away, the expression on his square face inscrutable.

At the tall, golden gates of the Temple of Saturn, the priests bowed and scraped and let them in. But they watched the Emperor from lowered eyes, and some of them whispered in corners, and Petronius would have bet good money that they knew about the trouble outside Rome, and the Emperor's refusal to do anything about it.

A statue of the god sat enthroned at one end of the main chamber. His face was bearded and kindly and his marble hands held marble stalks of corn. Beneath his feet and spread across half the floor of the temple, piles of fruit and vegetables teetered, some stretching almost to the ceiling.

"Excellent," Caligula said, rubbing his hands together. Now that he'd reached safety, he seemed to have regained both his confidence and his arrogance. "The god of the harvest has admirably lived up to his name. There should be food enough here to last us weeks or months, if we need it."

It was true – at this time of Saturn's great harvest festival, the Temple was better supplied with food than anywhere else in Rome. The smell of it all was overpowering, rich and sweet and just a little rotten.

"Bar the gates," Caligula ordered the nearest priest, a shabby young man in a dirty toga.

"But Caesar," the priest protested, "today is the lord Saturn's feast day. The poor must partake of the bounty provided by his grace."

"Listen to me, you jumped-up eunuch. That was an order, not the starting point for a debate. Now bar the gates!" Caligula's face reddened as he spoke, and this time the priest leapt to obey.

At the doorway, Claudius blocked him. "No," he said. "Y-y-your city needs you, nephew. Answer its call."

"Get out of his way, fool!" Caligula snapped, but Drusilla laughed and clapped her hands.

"Look, brother!" she said. "The dribbler's finally found some backbone. In fact –" she ran a teasing finger down Caligula's nose "– rather more backbone than you. I do believe you were actually shaking in front of that ghastly priestess."

"I was not shaking!" Caligula snapped. Petronius saw him struggle to master himself, and continue in a softer voice. "I was afraid for you, my love. As I am now. So stand aside, uncle – those doors will be barred whatever you say. Your only choice is whether you live to appreciate the safety they offer."

Petronius didn't quite know what possessed him. They would be safe inside the Temple. But he found himself stepping forward to take up position beside Claudius, blocking the doorway. "No. We can't cower in here while

Rome burns. It isn't right."

"Oh," Drusilla purred, slinking up to him. "Handsome and brave. This one's a real find."

When she leaned in to Petronius, he had to restrain himself from leaning back. In the heat of the walk from the Palace, her flesh had begun to decay. He could smell its fetid odour, and he saw that the skin of her face was beginning to soften and sag, her lips drooping away from her gums.

"Get your hands off him!" Caligula yelled.

Drusilla turned to him, raising an ironic eyebrow. "Don't be silly, darling, I haven't touched him."

"And you're not going to," Caligula hissed. "I didn't bring you back for anybody else. I brought you back for me!"

"Really?" Drusilla's tone was icy now. "You expect complete fidelity, undying gratitude? I've only been gone two years, brother – can you have so quickly forgotten what kind of woman I am?"

"It seems I have," Caligula said. His voice was high and breathy and Petronius saw that he was shaking with rage. He wanted to step away from the pair of them, but he was terrified of drawing any more attention to himself. If Caligula's anger moved away from his sister, it would almost certainly be turned on Petronius.

"I'd forgotten everything about you," Caligula said. "I'd forgotten how self-centred you are. How selfish. I'd forgotten that you treat me like dirt, when all I've ever done is love you. And I'd forgotten that you have the morals of a two-denarii whore!"

Drusilla slapped him, the blow ringing through the suddenly silent temple. "How dare you! Love me? The only person you love is yourself! And that's just as well – because who else would love a scrawny, under-endowed, worthless little bastard like you? Even father despised you!"

Caligula let out a roar of mingled rage and pain that made Petronius flinch. He lurched to the side, towards one of the soldiers, and before the man could react, snatched his sword from his hand.

The Emperor wasn't much of a swordsman. His swing was wild but Drusilla was unprepared and unprotected. The blade sliced through her neck in one clean sweep. For a moment, only the line of red along her throat betrayed what had happened. Then her body toppled one way and her head tilted and fell the other. Her eyes stared accusingly at Caligula, still bright with rage. Then something behind them died, and a moment later a small brown beetle crawled from her mouth and scuttled across the temple floor. Caligula crushed it beneath the heel of his sandal.

There was a very long silence, finally broken when Caligula dropped his sword to the floor. He fell to his knees beside it, cradling his head in his hands. "Sweet Aphrodite, what have I done?"

It was Marcus who answered, stepping forward to scoop the fallen sword from the floor. "You've killed her, Caesar. Again. You risked everything – your whole Empire – to bring her back. And for what? For this?"

Caligula looked up, eyes streaked with tears. "You can't... you can't talk to your Emperor that way."

"That's true," Marcus said.

Unlike Caligula's, his sword-stroke was quick and efficient. It pierced Caligula through his heart and ripped downwards, opening his belly to spill his guts on the ground.

The Emperor looked down at the wreckage of his chest with disbelieving eyes. "What?" he said. "How?"

Marcus wiped his sword clean on Caligula's purple toga, then sheathed it. "Refusing the Emperor's command is treason. Luckily," he said, "we've just had a change in leadership." He turned to Claudius and saluted. "What are your orders, Caesar?"

With the gates barred against them and the living inside, the dead had retreated from the walls of Rome. The defenders took the opportunity to rest and eat inside the watchtowers; to regroup for a new offensive which everyone was sure would come.

Vali stared at the plate of bread and cheese in front of him, but his stomach rebelled at the thought of putting anything inside it.

"You should eat," Boda said.

She still had the little boy with her, clinging to her hand. Vali could hardly bear to look at him, but she wouldn't let him look away.

"He told me his name's Nero," she said. "He claims he's the Emperor's nephew, so we're keeping him here until Caligula can be found. I need you to look after him while I take my turn on watch."

Vali turned his face away. "You might want to leave him with someone safer."

She hauled him up by the front of his tunic, pushing him so hard against the wall that all the air was forced out of him. "Enough of this," she said. "Enough. You did what you could and the gods willed that you failed. Terrible things happen in battle – haven't you lived long enough to know that?"

How could he tell her he'd lived far longer than she knew, and understood the reality of the world far better than she could imagine? That he didn't know why he held himself responsible for one insignificant little girl's death, when he'd done far worse before and never felt a moment's guilt? That every time he shut his eyes he saw the girl's face, and he thought he probably always would, not because of what had happened but because of what she represented – the moment he became something both less and more than what he'd always been. He laughed, because he couldn't tell her any of that.

She looked puzzled, but she released her grasp on his tunic, letting him slide back down to his feet. She was still very close to him, her breath hot on his face. He felt a stirring of desire, but something else – more complicated and more troubling.

"You're right," he told her. "I've been here too long. This place is starting to change me."

She frowned, misunderstanding. "I thought you were newly arrived in Rome."

He nodded, because that was true, though not what he'd meant.

"I think I understand," she said. "I came to Rome as a captive, yet it seems I'm about to give my life to defend it. Maybe it's changed me too."

He looked away from the walls, towards the great city spread below him. He'd visited before, of course, many times, as he'd visited every city on earth. But that had been different – he'd been different, his full and wonderful self, not this cut-down version he'd been forced to adopt when he fled the punishment that awaited him.

The streets near the walls were empty, but he could see people deeper inside, milling in confusion and panic.

"The trouble is," Boda said. "Rome isn't just one thing, as I'd always imagined. Every nation of the world has a place here, and for all its cruelty there's something in it worth saving."

He turned back to study her face. Her blue eyes were wide and serious but the lines around her mouth came from laughter, not anger. She was a contradiction, as all these people were. And she was right. It was easy to see them as simple, but embroiled in the centre of life rather than observing from its edges, the complications were inescapable.

She rested her hand against his arm, and his heart beat a little faster – a man's reaction to a woman. He struggled to see her through other eyes, the ones that had first chosen her. Had he made the right decision then? He didn't know. He'd lost all clarity.

A second later she abruptly released him. He saw her horrified expression before he saw what had caused it, and felt an icy flush of fear.

"Take Nero," she said. "They'll need me on the battlements."

Outside the walls, the dead had returned. There were far more of them than he'd seen before. The beetles must have flown far, finding every corpse they could animate within reach of the city. Their ragged legions were no match for the iron discipline of the soldiers defending Rome, but they outnumbered them a hundred to one. And there were soldiers among the dead – some in the scraps of uniform that had survived the grave, others in full armour, their faces intact.

Vali heard some names called in horror by those manning the walls and guessed that they recognised comrades among the dead. And then there were shouts of fear from everyone as the defenders saw what the dead had brought with them.

A grey wall of flesh marched behind the human corpses. Their trunks swung in time with their footsteps, so heavy they seemed to shake the earth. Smaller animals crowded around them, but the elephants didn't seem to care where they trod, crushing the bodies of wolves and tigers beneath them as they advanced.

As they came closer, Vali realised that they were drawing something behind them. Nearer still, almost within bowshot, and he saw that they were wooden towers topped with spikes – as tall as the walls of Rome and designed for scaling them.

All around him, men fell to their knees and prayed as the dead prepared to besiege the city.

CHAPTER FIFTEEN

When the dead attacked, discipline disintegrated. The word had been passed down the line and repeated by every centurion to his men. The dead could only be killed by a shot to the head. The men knew this, but in the fear and panic that accompanied the appearance of the elephants and their siege engines, they fired wildly. Hails of arrows flew into the rotting bodies below, most striking harmlessly at arms and legs and torsos. The dead didn't even bother to pluck them out.

Boda wasn't used to the Roman recurve bow she'd been given – she'd have preferred something longer and straighter – but an arrow was an arrow and at least she was aiming in the right place. Her first few shots went wide, but after that she hit her mark, time after time. It wasn't difficult. The walking corpses made little effort to defend themselves. Bodies must be like mules to them, she supposed, mounts that could be flogged to death and then replaced.

Vali was fighting by her side. He'd proved to be an able archer, too valuable to waste as a child-minder. Nero was being cared for by some of the refugees from outside the city while they fought.

She could already see that it was a hopeless battle. The siege engines remained out of bowshot for the minute, allowing the front ranks of the dead to advance unprotected. With nothing to shelter behind they were easy targets. They fell in droves, some still writhing, pinned to the ground by javelins through their chest, others truly motionless after arrows had pierced their heads.

But there were always more of them and they were

fighting back. Some held bows, and though their aim was poor the defenders couldn't afford to lose a single man. Others flung head-sized rocks at the wall with inhuman strength and Boda saw several men brought down by them.

One rock flew towards her with terrifying speed. She flung herself to the ground and it missed her head by less than an inch. The man behind wasn't so lucky. She saw his skull caved in by the impact as he fell, limp, to the ground.

She couldn't spare him any attention. More dead were flocking to the walls and she grimly picked up her bow and prepared to thin their ranks. The focus of her attention narrowed to the corpses below, and there was none left over for the rock headed straight towards her. It caught her a glancing blow on the side of the head, momentarily stunning her. Her knees began to buckle and she saw that she was falling forward, towards the battlements and the lethal drop beneath. Her arms flailed but she couldn't seem to regain her balance and her vision was slowly fading to black.

Vali's arm grabbed hers and yanked her away from the precipice, and the pain in her injured shoulder shocked her back to full consciousness. She turned to thank him – and saw, a second before it struck, the sword that was heading for his back. He gasped in shock as she flung herself on top of him and the sword swung high over his head to clang against the ramparts.

She realised with a cold shock that the man attacking them was the same one who'd been felled by the earlier rock. In the moment of his death he'd left their side and joined their enemies. When she caught his eye he swung his sword again, but the spirit inside him was still clumsy in its new body, and it was an easy matter to evade the blow. One slash of her own weapon severed his head from its body. She tried not to look at the familiar face as she tossed it over the battlements.

And then the next wave came. They'd been hidden behind the main front, rows of undead carrying ladders between them. She could see a group approaching the section of wall she and Vali were guarding. Her bow sang as she picked off first one and then another. Beside her, Vali accounted for two more, but then they were at the wall.

The ladder thumped onto the parapet beside her and a hail of rocks accompanied it. She was forced to take shelter, cowering beneath the overhang as the lethal rain continued above. She could see the top of the ladder, only two paces from her head. It was shaking, and she knew that meant the dead were climbing it. How long before they reached the top?

She drew her sword, using the tip to prod at the top rung of the ladder. The metal pierced the wood but didn't shift it.

"It's too heavy," Vali said. "You'll break your sword."

She grimaced. "But they'll have to stop throwing rocks when their people reach the top."

She was half right. The rocks stopped but the arrows continued. She guessed the dead were unafraid of the damage the arrows could do to their brethren, or judged it trivial compared to the harm it would inflict on the defenders. Her heart raced, knowing it would take only one lucky shot to finish her off. But when she saw a skeletal hand grasp the top of the ladder, she knew she had no choice.

"Now," she mouthed to Vali, and didn't wait for his nod before launching herself to her feet, arms braced to lift the ladder. For a moment she strained alone, fighting hopelessly to push the wood away from the wall. It was crawling with dead, twenty of them at least and more waiting beneath to follow after those. Then Vali put his shoulder to the other side, and suddenly the weight was bearable and the ladder was tipping out and away, some of the dead still clinging, others plummeting to the ground below.

The day wore on, the sun climbing steadily higher to beat down mercilessly on the living and rot the flesh of the dead. Another ladder clanged against the wall and then another, and each time it grew harder to push it away and there were fewer men to do it. The ranks of the defenders were thinning alarmingly fast, and when the sun reached its zenith the attackers launched their final wave.

Boda heard the thump of the elephants' great round feet across the ground and the unearthly trumpeting when they raised their trunks skyward. The siege engines rattled behind them, and when they drew closer she could see that they were filled with the dead. When they reached the walls, it would be over.

She felt Vali standing beside her, shoulder-to-shoulder, and when she turned to look at him she saw that he'd been watching her.

"I'm sorry," she said. "If we'd run away... You said it was hopeless and you were right."

To her surprise, he grinned. Under his sharp nose and red hair, the expression was startlingly vulpine. "No, you were right. The dead aren't indestructible and they haven't broken through yet."

She looked at the siege engines, within arrow-shot now, but utterly impervious to them. "They will. There's nothing that can stop those things." She flung one of the last of their javelins at the approaching wall of flesh. It flew true and hit its target, striking the nearest elephant through its eye and sinking in almost to the grip.

The beast didn't even pause, just continued its lumbering, inexorable march onwards.

"Not the creatures," Vali said. "The engines themselves – and all the dead inside."

"But the walls are too thick too pierce."

His smile broadened. He flicked his fingers, and she couldn't see it but there must have been a flint hidden in his palm, because a flame sparked to life between them. "Fire," he said. "Wood burns – and so do the bodies of the dead. We'll give these Romans a proper northman's funeral."

He grunted in surprise when she flung her arms around him. A moment later, his arms met behind her back and squeezed briefly. His expression was strange when she released him but she didn't waste time puzzling it out.

"Silvius!" she yelled to the nearest battlement commander. "We need fire arrows, rags. Raid the nearby houses for their cooking oil if we need to – anything that burns."

She saw the white flash of his smile before he turned to his men. The soldiers he barked orders to scurried to obey, making a pile of everything usable within reach – a small stock of fire arrows as well as pots of oil made for throwing. But even as Vali fitted the first flaming arrow to his bow and sent it into the nearest siege engine, she knew it wasn't enough.

"We need more!" she called to Silvius. "They can douse single flames – we need to start too many fires for them to extinguish."

He shook his head, expression grave. "I can't spare the men. If I send them for supplies the walls will have fallen by the time they return."

He was right. Beside the siege engines, more ladders were

approaching, and there were fewer and fewer defenders to push them away. Vali's plan had come just too late to save them. She shrugged and flung a pot of flaming oil at the monstrous engine. At least this way they'd go down fighting. They'd take some of the dead with them, and when the end approached she'd throw her own body on the fire so that it could never rise again.

The oil she'd thrown hit the siege engine at the apex of its tower. The flames caught and spread before any of those inside could scale the heights to douse them. She smelt the stench of burning flesh and, for the first time, heard the dead cry out in fear.

"The flames will consume the beetles as well as the flesh that holds them," Vali said beside her. "They dread a final return to the realm of darkness."

He was right. As the flames spread downwards, red and gold and bright even against the midday sun, a sudden brown cloud burst from the heart of them, hovering a moment in the sky above before diffusing to spread over the battlements.

"The rats leave a sinking ship," Vali said.

The tower was close enough to allow Boda to see what had happened to the dead inside. Without the beetles to animate them, the corpses were just corpses. Some of them crumpled and stayed where they were, slumped on the ladders and platforms inside the engine. Others toppled from the side to be crushed beneath the feet of the advancing army, careless of their own casualties.

The whole tower was aflame now, a beacon that belched an evil thick black smoke. The flames licked forward and the elephant too began to burn. The fat fried beneath its skin as the fine grey hairs singed and lit. The creature reared, a terrifying sight, its curved tusks gouging the air. And then it fell back to earth with an impact that shook the ground, and turned and ran. Its path took it sideways into another elephant and another engine that was not yet burning. Both toppled to the ground, and the ones behind were halted, hopelessly mired in the mess.

For one moment, Boda thought it might be enough. She sent another arrow into the engine to her left, and Vali joined her, but the dead quickly pounced to put out the flames and the engine trundled on. It was only forty paces from the walls now, and behind and beside it there were scores more, far too many for the defenders to burn. Soon the dead would come swarming over, and too few of the living remained to stop them.

And then, a sound she hadn't hoped to hear – the marching feet of reinforcements. The siege engine was thirty paces away and drawing closer and she didn't dare a look behind to see how many had come, whether it would be enough. She flung a pot of oil, then another – and when she flung a third a hail of arrows accompanied it, burning through the sky from behind her.

The dead screamed and the nearest engine caught, a thousand embers sparking a conflagration that they'd never put out. It spread too quickly even for the beetles to escape it. She saw a few of them try, but they were sparks of light, already burning, and then the whole structure sank in on itself, a blackened wreck.

Finally, Boda lowered her bow and looked behind her.

There were more men than she could have hoped for – it looked to be as many as a thousand. Some were in the uniform of the Praetorian Guard, others in civilian clothes. Claudius stood at their head, a slight, stooped figure with a new air of command.

Beside him stood Petronius, curling black hair plastered to his scalp with sweat. He grinned at her expression. "So," he said, "did you miss me?"

The dead retreated when they saw the new force arrayed against them. They'd lost at least a third of their siege engines and the walls were now too heavily manned to overpower.

Petronius looked over the field of battle below and marvelled that so few had held the walls for so long. Then he looked at Boda. There was a bloody graze along one side of her head, the red bright against her pale hair. She stank of stale sweat and ash and she looked on the point of collapse. She was absolutely beautiful.

He'd told her what happened at the Temple of Isis, how he'd failed to stop the ceremony. He'd been expecting anger but she'd just nodded and when she saw his expression, told him: "You did everything you could." She was right, but he'd needed to hear someone else say it.

When it was certain the dead weren't merely regrouping for another attack, Claudius gathered a council of war. At Petronius's suggestion he included Boda and Vali as well as Marcus and two Senators – Flavius and Justinian – who'd joined them on the march to the walls.

The little boy Boda had rescued clung to Petronius's leg as if he never intended to let go. She'd said that he was Nero, Caligula's nephew, but no one among Claudius's party seemed to want to claim responsibility for him, including the new Emperor himself, and for want of anyone else to care for him he seemed to have attached himself to Petronius.

"We can arm the citizens," Claudius said. "Many have served in the legions. And those that haven't can still carry equipment, act as look-outs…"

Petronius realised that Claudius hadn't stuttered once since the Praetorian Guard had declared him Emperor. He seemed like a different man, confident and commanding for all his fragile body.

"But what about the dead inside the city?" Boda asked.

Nero whimpered, burying his head against Petronius's thigh. No doubt he'd seen his share of horror on the way to safety. Petronius picked him up and held him securely on his lap.

"There are very few dead inside the walls of Rome – only the ones Caligula killed and those guarding the gateway to the underworld." Petronius told Boda. "Our burials always take place outside the city gates."

She nodded. "Then we can hold the walls with the men we have."

"Don't be a fool," Vali said. "The walls will never hold."

Boda's head jerked to face him. "How can you say that? Less than an hour ago you told me I was right to fight."

"But this isn't an ordinary war," Vali said. "In battles soldiers fall and no one but their families mourns their loss. Here every man we lose is a defector to the other side."

"Yes," Claudius said. "I see. Their ranks swell as ours thin, making time their friend and our enemy."

Vali bowed his head in acknowledgement. "It's a battle we can't win."

Boda glared at him and Petronius had to suppress a smile at the other man's expression. He knew what it felt like to be on the receiving end of that glare. "You're counselling surrender, then?" she asked.

Vali held up his hands, placating. "No. I'm saying we should fight a battle we can win."

"We can't defeat the dead," Petronius said. "But the beetles that carry their spirits are easily crushed. Is that what you mean?"

Vali shook his head and Claudius said: "No. I believe his ambition is greater. You mean that we should try to shut the gateway itself, don't you? Close off the source of the infection rather than fight its symptoms."

"The dead will be guarding the gate," Boda said. "They won't be foolish enough to leave it undefended." But Petronius could see a spark of excitement in her eyes.

"That's the least of our problems," Vali said. "More importantly, the gates of death open outward – and close inward."

It took Petronius a second to understand what he meant. "You mean they can only be closed from the inside?"

The red-haired barbarian nodded, and the group erupted as everyone tried to talk at once. Petronius saw Vali lean back, a half smile on his lips as if the chaos he'd caused amused him.

Boda turned to him. "How do you know this?"

"*The Book of the Dead*," Petronius guessed.

Vali nodded – a little too quickly, as if latching on to a convenient lie.

Boda frowned. "You went there, didn't you? You entered the gateway in Alexandria. If we went back there..."

But Vali shook his head. "That gateway wasn't the same as this, it's not meant to be crossed. You saw the guardians who followed us through – they'll be alert now, and ready to stop another incursion by the living. Besides, Alexandria is the centre of the Cult's power. They're still much weaker here in Rome, especially inside the city, where there are only a few of the dead."

"You think we should return to the Temple then?" Petronius said, and shivered. He still remembered, all too clearly, the terrible light that had shone from the gateway to the other world. The thought of passing through it horrified him.

But Boda nodded grimly. "It seems that we have no other choice."

It was decided that half the Praetorian Guard would remain to protect the walls and half accompany Boda and Vali to the Temple of Isis. Claudius had told Boda and Vali that they needn't go, that they'd already done enough for a city not their own. Boda knew the mission had little chance of succeeding, but she preferred to contemplate death in a near-impossible attack than a futile defence. And Vali had said that the underworld could hold little fear now that its worst denizens had entered the land of the living.

Petronius had also insisted on accompanying them. She could see him ineptly buckling on a sword he barely knew how to use. The little boy, Nero, was trying to help him. He seemed to have taken a liking to the young man, a relief to Boda, who hadn't known what to do with the clinging, demanding infant.

Petronius seemed to sense her eyes on him. He looked up and smiled, but the expression looked strained. He didn't seem such a youth any more. The last few days had aged him in indefinable but definite ways.

Was Vali right that Petronius loved her? It seemed absurd, but when she'd seen Petronius's face as he realised she was still alive, she thought he might be right. And here he was, voluntarily putting himself in danger, when he'd always seemed to devote most of his energies to avoiding it.

She didn't love him – how could she? He was a Roman, and her master. He was ten years her junior and, until last week, had lived a life of unmitigated self-indulgence. The Boda who had first arrived in Rome would have thought him worthless. But she didn't, not now. The world was a more light-hearted place with him in it. And she couldn't bear the thought that he would die for her sake.

His smile widened when she approached him. Nero smiled too, holding out his arms to be hugged. She lifted the little boy, an awkward lump in her arms, but after a moment he wriggled to be free, and she released him to return to Petronius.

"He likes you," she told him.

Petronius shrugged. "Children and animals always do. It's adults who seem to find me objectionable."

"Claudius tells me his mother's in exile," she said. "He was travelling to Rome with his aunt and cousin, but..." She looked at Nero, happily playing at Petronius's feet.

"Yes," Petronius said. "He's seen too much for such a little one."

"He needs looking after."

Petronius nodded, stooping to stroke Nero's wispy blond hair.

"He needs you to look after him," Boda said.

Petronius's eyes snapped up to hers. "What are you saying?"

She rested her hand against his shoulder. "Stay here, Petronius. Keep him out of danger."

His shrugged her away angrily. "Don't treat me like a child. If you think I'll be a liability, just say so."

She sighed. "You're not a liability. If it wasn't for you, I'd be dead three-times over. But I can't... Listen to me, we're accepting death, all of us who enter that gateway. And I know you're prepared to face it too. But I have no one here, nothing in Rome I care about – except you."

His face flushed with pleasure. "Oh. I... I care about

you too."

"Then do this for me," she begged him. "I can enter that gateway and risk my life if there's something left behind that's worth saving."

He looked anguished. "But you're asking me to let you go to your death!" He licked his lips, and she knew that she wouldn't like whatever he said next. "I still own you, if you recall. I could forbid you to go."

She felt a flare of rage, but tamped it down. She didn't want their last words to be bitter ones. "There is a chance we'll succeed, you know."

He just looked at her, and she dropped her eyes.

And then, before he could say anything else, the shout came from the walls. "They're back! The dead have returned!"

Marcus approached, the ranks of the Praetorian Guard waiting behind him. "We should go."

Though Boda knew he was right, she couldn't bring herself to abandon the walls without seeing what danger they were leaving behind. She nodded to Marcus but walked away from him, up the stone stairs that led to the battlements. She heard footsteps behind her and saw that Marcus had followed. It was clear from his face that he felt the same conflict she did. Claudius had ordered him to leave half his men behind to face an unbeatable enemy alone.

When they reached the top, the soldiers on watch saluted hand to heart and stepped aside. They'd been right to raise the alarm. Beyond the battlements, the dead had returned in force. They remained outside bow range, their ragged ranks stretching into the distance as far as the eye could see. There were more of them, Boda was sure of it. The beetles had had more time to fly, she supposed, and find fresh bodies to raise.

As she watched, the front ranks stirred and parted all

along the line. The undead were bringing something new to bear on Rome. After a moment, as the great wooden mechanisms trundled into the open, she realised that they were catapults.

Marcus shrugged. "It's to be expected. The walls were built to withstand it."

She was sure he was right. The walls were thicker than she was tall and no rock, no matter how well aimed, would topple them. But she felt a stirring of unease all the same. The dead weren't fools. Whatever controlled them had proven to be a master tactician. They must know that the catapults would fail – so why had they brought them?

Her disquiet grew as she watched the catapults being braced, hordes of the dead working together to pull the tightly coiled mechanisms back. And then there was a roar, the catapults leapt upright – and the loads cradled inside them flew through the air towards Rome.

Boda could see within seconds that they'd misjudged the trajectory. The rocks were heading high over the walls and would crash harmlessly into the street behind.

Except they weren't rocks. As they flew closer, Boda saw that, impossibly, they seemed to be moving. For one brief, horrible moment as she looked up she saw an eye look back at her. Then the thing was over and down and it landed on the street below with a horrible wet thump. Blood spattered all around it and around the scores of others that had landed close by.

The dead weren't throwing rocks – they'd thrown their own bodies over the walls. The corpses remained broken and motionless on the ground for only a second. And then, one by one, they began to rise.

CHAPTER SIXTEEN

There was chaos. The dead landed everywhere, more and more of them as the catapults did their work. Some of the defenders they killed as they landed, crumpling their bodies beneath them when they hit the ground. And then both corpses would rise to battle the remaining defenders.

A body fell to Boda's left, and she slashed out with her sword, severing its head before it could rise. The torso twitched and its dead eyes glared, and then the beetle crawled out of its mouth and it was still. She stamped down hard, but the creature was ready for her, on the wing before she could crush it. And soon, somewhere else, it would bring another corpse back to life.

Vali was at her back, hacking away with his own short blade. He was less skilled than her, but fearless. She saw him hack off the arm of a lurching corpse, then – as it kept advancing – its left leg. The body hopped another step forward, mouth open in a scream of rage, before losing its balance and toppling to the ground.

Petronius was already cut off from her, a horde of undead separating them. He'd drawn his sword but he couldn't wield it. Nero clung to his neck, his yells audible even over the din of battle, and Petronius couldn't use his weapon without hurting the boy. He shot her one last, desperate look, and then was lost to sight.

"To me!" Marcus shouted, and she saw that he was only ten paces away, gathering the ragged remnants of the Praetorian Guard around him.

The ground between them was thick with the dead. They'd strapped on swords and spears before they flung themselves over the wall. Boda saw a corpse which must have fallen on its own spear. Its hands pulled futilely at the long wooden handle protruding from its stomach, lacking the leverage to pull it out.

Boda stamped down on the spear, pinning the corpse in place as she lopped off its head. But behind it was one who'd landed better, his sword already in his hand. With a sick shock she realised that she recognised him. It was Silvius, the battlement commander who'd led them all to safety behind the walls of Rome.

Unlike many of the other undead, he knew how to fight. And, for the first time, she could see the intelligence shining behind his milky eyes. He didn't just want to kill – he wanted to kill *her*. His sword slashed low and lethal towards her legs.

She jumped clear of the blade only to stumble as she landed, tripping over the bloody remnants of another corpse. She brought her sword up just in time to counter the downward sweep of Silvius's blade. But he'd always been stronger than her and death had made him stronger still. His weight bore against her sword arm and pressed it down, bringing her own blade to within inches of her throat.

His face pressed nearer as if he wanted to be as close as possible to watch her die. His flesh had already started to rot, and a fetid smell washed off him. When he smiled she saw that his teeth were loose in their sockets, his gums brown and decayed. There was no spittle in his dry, dead mouth and his tongue looked as desiccated as an autumn leaf.

Her arm weakened and she let the tension seep out of it, allowing his face to come closer, closer... And when his cracked lips were within inches of hers she lashed her head forward, catching her forehead against his nose.

The blow forced the bone up and in, through what was

left of his brain and the insect that had made a nest for itself inside it. Silvius's body gave one last, convulsive shudder and was still, his mouth gaping open to let his shrivelled tongue hang out.

A hand on hers helped drag Boda to her feet. It was Marcus, and she saw that while she'd been down the troop of Guards had moved to surround and protect her and Vali. There were pitifully few left now, and far too many among the dead attacking them.

"We should go," Marcus said. But she could see the conflict in his eyes. He didn't want to abandon the fight at the walls. He wouldn't forgive himself if the city fell because he wasn't there.

"Just get us a few streets away," she told him. "We can look after ourselves after that."

He shook his head. "I can't. Caesar's orders—"

"Were given before this latest attack!" Boda snapped.

"You'll die!" Marcus yelled, but Boda was pulling away and the dead were already moving in to separate them.

"That's actually the idea," Vali said, and then the Praetorian Guard were lost in the sea of bodies, leaving them to face the dead alone.

Petronius saw Boda for one second, her eyes meeting his across the crowd of bodies. Then the tide of battle took her one way and him the other, and she was lost from sight. The little boy in his arms squirmed and cried and Petronius hugged him closer. Boda had asked him to look after Nero, and that's what he meant to do.

He'd given up on the idea of fighting altogether. After whirling his sword and nearly cutting off his own head – not to mention Nero's – he returned it to his scabbard and concentrated on running away.

He could hear the footsteps of the dead behind him. Why were they following? Did they know who he was? Sopdet knew his face, and she knew he'd opposed her. Was this her revenge?

When he chanced a look behind him, he saw that there were ten or more corpses racing after him. Some were long dead, staggering on flaking leg bones, sword pommels rattling in skeletal hands. But others were whole and strong and they were catching up. Nero's body was nearly a dead weight in Petronius's arms, dragging him down. The only chance he had to live was to drop the little boy.

He couldn't do it. How could he look Boda in the face if he did? He pulled Nero tighter against him instead, and turned left, swerving into a side street that he knew would take him to the Circus Maximus. He couldn't risk losing the time to look behind him again, but he could hear the undead following. It was clearly him they were after – or maybe the child in his arms. Perhaps they were trying to wipe out every drop of Imperial blood, leaving no one to rule Rome but Sopdet and her legions of the dead.

He could feel Nero's snot and tears running down his neck as he forced his legs to pump faster, harder. He forced himself to keep running when his body had already eaten up every morsel of energy inside it, and the breath was burning in his lungs.

The gates of the hippodrome loomed ahead of him, broad enough to admit four horses abreast. Petronius ducked beneath them, flinching for the moment of darkness while they hid the sun.

Then he was inside the great oval, at the bottom of the stands where the spectators sat. They were empty, as he'd expected. News from the walls must have reached here and the people had fled, but they'd left in a hurry. Petronius could see the detritus they'd abandoned: a cup of dates only half-eaten, one with teeth-marks visible in it; a dropped silk wrap, ripped at the hem; a child's doll, scuffed with dust where others had run over it. And below, something far more useful had also been left behind in the confusion – the chariots that would have raced today, if the dead hadn't intervened.

Petronius had nursed a dream of becoming a champion chariot racer for his whole childhood, until his father told him it was no job for a respectable boy. He'd watched every race religiously, bet on the Greens and joined in the riots when they lost. He knew everything there was to know about racing a chariot – without ever having actually done it. But how hard could it be?

The horses seemed to sense the unnaturalness of the dead. They snorted and pawed the ground as he approached and one let out that peculiar high neighing that was almost like a human scream. The dead let out a full-throated roar in response, and Petronius could hear that they were only paces behind, seconds away from catching him. Nero raised his golden-haired head and howled in fear.

But they were lucky. Petronius's gamble – his life-or-death gamble – had paid off. In their hurry to flee, the charioteers had left the horses in harness. The nearest team had begun to chew through the leather that imprisoned them, and the one beyond was hopelessly tangled in it, but the next chariot looked ready to go. As he drew closer, Petronius saw that it belonged to the Green team – and he took that as a good omen.

Nero yelled in shock as Petronius slung him onto the light steering platform, then hopped on beside him. The dead were close, but slowed by the horses, which reared and kicked as they passed. He saw one head crushed beneath a flailing hoof.

Then he had the reins in his hand, and they were off.

The streets of Rome here were eerily deserted. But as Boda ran through them with Vali at her side, she thought that they didn't feel empty. She could sense the people huddled silent and afraid in their boarded-up homes. She could feel their eyes on her, wondering if she was one of the dead. If she would be the death of them.

Her chest was tight with the effort of breathing and after five more minutes with no sign of pursuit, she slowed to a walk. Vali shot her a questioning look but dropped his pace to lope along beside her. The sunlight sparkled in his red hair and amber eyes.

"Can we really stop this?" she asked him.

He flicked her a surprised glance. "You were the one who told me we must."

She shrugged. "Even hopeless battles must be fought, if they're just. And you and I don't face the same death these Romans do. If we meet a warrior's end there'll be no endless darkness for us, but song and mead in the Halls of Valhalla."

He smiled, a sly, unreadable smile. "How dull. Imagine what the company will be like. All those over-muscled thugs bragging about their great deeds while drinking enough to poleaxe an ox. And at the head of the table, Odin himself – in all his dour, one-eyed, humourless glory."

She stared at him, shocked. "You insult the Allfather?"

"Believe me," he said. "If you knew him better, you

would too."

Her smile died, unsure if he was joking. "So what is it you hope for, then, in the world that follows?"

"Ah, now there's a question. I intend to live for ever, of course."

"But we're about to step through the gates of death," she said incredulously. "Do you really think we'll be returning?"

He didn't answer, looking away before she could read his face. But she didn't like the flash of something she caught in his eye – was it pity, or regret?

And then the Temple of Isis loomed in front of them, white marble lips enclosing the hungry black darkness of its open mouth, the door that led to the gateway to death. She shivered as they approached it.

Petronius hadn't imagined that the dead would follow. He'd – foolishly, he now realised – assumed they'd be incapable of mastering the chariots. But the rotting corpse behind him handled the reins with ease, and now he looked more closely, he thought he detected something familiar in the hollow curves of its face. Could that possibly be Porphyrius, the most successful charioteer ever to ride for the Greens? Petronius had a horrible feeling it was.

Nero stood clasped between his knees, wriggling to get free. The little boy had stopped crying. He was laughing and clapping his hands, as if this was all some entertainment put on for his benefit. "Faster!" he yelled in his high, clear voice. "Want to go faster!"

Petronius would have been happy to oblige, but the streets they raced through were too narrow. Their chariot was pulled by two horses abreast and there was barely room for them to pass between the high walls of the slums to either side. As he negotiated a sudden left turn the chariot tipped on its axis and the left-hand wheel scraped against the wall of a house, sending a shower of sparks into the air.

The chariot behind negotiated the turn far more gracefully, gaining ground. Nero gurgled with pleasure and slid from between Petronius's knees, forcing him to make a desperate grab that left the reins slack for a crucial second. The horses interpreted the sudden release of tension as an instruction to give it their all, and Petronius found himself thrown against the backrest as the chariot surged forward with a terrifying burst of speed.

At least the dead fell behind a little, unwilling to match their suicidal dash. Petronius could see that there were three chariots' full of them, one two-horse affair like theirs and two more that were pulled by four. If they reached anywhere wide enough to let the horses have their head, the larger chariots would easily overtake them. But these narrow streets had dangers of their own.

Petronius pulled desperately on the rein with one hand as he clung to Nero's collar with his other. The horses were slow to obey. Maybe they'd been waiting all these years for a chance to truly let loose. Or maybe they could smell the stench of decay behind them. As they galloped into a small, statue-lined square, Petronius could see a desperate white froth around their mouths and knew they couldn't keep up this pace for long.

He yanked again, harder, and this time the horses obeyed – far too enthusiastically. They reared as they drew to a complete and sudden halt, neighing their fury. Behind them, the other chariots raced on, too surprised to stop in time. The dead were closing in, milky eyes glaring malevolently and mouths stretched wide in grins that anticipated victory.

But the horses they'd commandeered had other ideas. Well used, after years of training, to avoiding the collisions that could end a rider's life, they veered to either side of Petronius's stationary chariot, like fast-flowing water diverting round a rock.

For one second, the dead were abreast. Skeletal hands reached out, fumbled and failed to connect. But one body – faster than the rest – flung itself over the gap between carriages and landed sprawled across the chariot beside Petronius.

It was one of the older corpses, brown mummified flesh stretched tight over knobbly bones. The speed of its impact had broken some of them and Petronius saw its left hand hanging from its wrist by a thread of skin. Half its ribs had been crushed to powder but it only lay still a second before it rose and rounded on him.

It was Nero who saved him. The little boy squealed in fear – or maybe excitement – and the corpse's head swung limply on its neck to locate this new prey. In the second it bought him, Petronius hooked his hands beneath its armpits and lifted. His hands cringed away from touching the decayed flesh but the corpse was far lighter than he'd imagined, all the living juices long squeezed out of it. He lifted it up then flung it away to clatter against the pavement beside the chariot.

The corpse rolled and rose, even less whole than before. Its right hand was gone entirely now, and half its skull had caved in, lending its head a leering, almost comic appearance. But the same murderous intent was evident in its empty eyes and it braced its legs and shambled back towards them.

'Skellington!' Nero said, laughing and pointing as Petronius picked up the reins again and led the horses in a tight circle. He flicked them and they were off, in the opposite direction from the chariots of dead – but not for long. Already Petronius could see that they were slowing, turning their own circles in the next square along.

The race resumed. Petronius had the lead now but his chariot wasn't steering quite true. When he looked down at the left wheel he saw that it was warped. He'd probably bent it when he brought them too close to the wall. Now he had to constantly tug the reins to the right to keep moving straight.

He barely knew this part of the city. It was where the poorest citizens lived, and immigrants or former slaves without the full rights of citizenship. The houses that whisked by on either side were tall and thin and gloomy and he knew that they were packed with people, five or more to a room. The kind of people who survived on air and corn dole.

They were also the kind of people who strung their washing on lines across the street. Petronius saw it coming but there was nothing he could do to avoid it. If he stopped the dead would be on him and the road was too narrow to turn. The strung-out toga slapped him straight in the face, wet and smelling of the piss it had been washed in. The horses snorted and neighed and he knew that they were tangled too.

With the wet cloth pressed against his face, Petronius was running blind. One hand was tangled in the reins, but he raised the other to claw at the clinging fabric.

It didn't want to move. A little light seeped through the thick cotton but nothing else and when he breathed in it stuck tight against his mouth, the smell of urine acrid in his throat. The chariot was veering from side to side, almost tipping onto its axle, and he suspected that at least one of the horses had the same problem he had.

And now, with so little control, he had to put two hands back on the reins just to slow the horses' wild flight and stop them overturning.

There was a sudden crunching sound beneath their wheels and then the desperate squawking of chickens. They must be in a market district, running through crates of the birds ready for sale. He felt one of them fly up into his face, its claws piercing the thick cloth over his cheeks to scratch the skin beneath and its beak pecking dangerously close to his eyes.

He released the reins again to flail at the bird. As if in retaliation, he felt something liquid squirt against his hand and then the strong smell of chicken shit permeated the cloth. But his reaching fingers found first a few loose feathers and then the bird's wing and when he gave it a fierce yank the creature finally flew away – its claws scraping the toga from his eyes as they passed.

He had one second to enjoy the fact that he could finally see. Then he registered what exactly it was he was seeing. Here, finally, just when it was most inconvenient, were some living people. They'd come to the market whose chicken coops he'd already destroyed and to either side they stared at his chariot through wide, shocked eyes.

The road was full of them too. It was early afternoon, well before sunset, a time of day when the pedestrians should have had the street to themselves. Petronius thought about pulling on the reins, but he couldn't afford to stop. He could hear the chariots of the dead behind him. The washing that had hit him must have missed them and they'd nearly closed the gap. If he stopped, they'd be on him – and then they'd slaughter these people too.

The terrified shoppers dived out of the way as his chariot weaved through them. The horses were as frightened as the people they almost trampled, rearing and turning their heads to nip at any who came too close. The market stalls crowded the street, too tight for the horses to fit through and they crushed them beneath their hooves. The air was thick with the smell of overripe melons and dates.

Another stall fell, this one selling spices. A brown, richly scented cloud of cinnamon enveloped them. Petronius coughed the dust of it out of his throat and wiped his streaming eyes. When they'd cleared, he saw that the people too had finally cleared the road – all but one.

The woman was very old and probably blind. From the pavement to either side of her, people were screaming at her to move, but though her head twitched from side to side in fright she didn't seem to realise where the danger was. The chariot was only twenty paces from her and closing fast. Petronius imagined it all too clearly, a vivid moment of blood as her frail old body was crushed beneath his wheels.

He'd leapt onto the horse's back before he even realised he'd done it. The creature bucked and screamed, unused to being ridden. Petronius set his teeth and clung on grimly. Behind him, alone in the chariot, Nero laughed. He'd handed the little child the reins, more to give him something to anchor himself than because he thought the three-year-old could steer. But the little boy had them in a firm hold and was pulling alternately right and left.

The horses didn't know that the person holding their reins had no idea what he was doing. They followed their orders as obediently as ever and the chariot swerved from side to side as they lurched first one way and then the other.

The old woman seemed finally to have realised the danger she was in. She was screaming, a high, thin desperate sound. But although Petronius could hear wails and sobs from the people to either side of her, no one was willing to risk their own life to save hers. She stood isolated in the centre of the road, rheumy eyes blinking up at him as the horse Petronius rode thundered towards her.

The weight of her nearly wrenched his arm out of its socket when he hooked it around her chest. He tried to lift, but his unsteady seat on the horse gave him no leverage and her sandalled feet scraped along the road as she screamed and screamed. His shoulder screamed at him to let go, but if he did she'd be lost beneath the wheels.

The horse carrying him felt the extra weight dragging it back and rebelled at this final indignity. It reared, Petronius's legs loosened round its stomach and he slid to the side, arm still dragged down by the woman he was doggedly holding. But in the moment when his mount's hooves left the road, he saw his chance.

The woman screamed even louder as he swung her, throwing her between the swift-moving legs of the horse to his right. Then he swung her back, the momentum and speed greater, towards himself, towards his own horse – and the temporary space beneath its rearing legs.

He got one final look at her shrivelled, open-mouthed face as his arms released her, and then she was flying out and away. The horse's descending hooves missed her by inches, but they did miss. And the landing must have hurt but the road was lined with people and the bodies the old woman barrelled into would have cushioned her fall.

Then she was lost to sight and Petronius was left on a furious, bucking horse, crucial paces away from the haven of the chariot. Inside it, Nero seemed to have become bored with holding the reins. As Petronius looked back, the little boy released them and began to clamber up the back, probably keen to see behind.

Petronius had a perfect view and was shocked to find that only one chariot of the dead still followed. They were close behind but not so close he needed to give them all his attention. There was a far more urgent problem – working his way back to the chariot in time to stop Nero falling off it.

The horse did everything in its power to stop him. Now that it had him on it, it seemed reluctant to let him off, and it reared and pranced every time he tried to shift himself, forcing him to cling tight with his legs around its withers.

He gave up trying to slowly wriggle his way back, and decided to opt for one desperate all-out attempt. He was running out of time, anyway. The road they followed ended ahead at a T-junction, and this place he did recognise. The left-hand fork dead-ended in a demolished tenement. If the horses, with no hand guiding them, decided to take it, they were finished.

Petronius's heart thundered in his chest, as if he was the one doing the running, not the horses. It pounded in time to their hooves as he braced his hands against the animal's neck and then – too quickly to give himself time to think about it – levered himself to his feet.

For one tottering, terrifying moment he stood there, balanced on his mount's back. Then it began to rear, he began to fall and he went with it, throwing himself towards the chariot and the little boy intent on clambering out of it.

His chest hit the chariot with enough force to drive all the air out of his lungs. Without his extra weight the horse leapt forward, the acceleration driving him even harder against the wood and he wondered if he'd ever be able to breath again.

The little boy reached the top of the chariot back at the moment Petronius reached for him. He startled to topple, yelling suddenly as he realised his danger, and Petronius grabbed his feet and pulled.

The abused muscles in his shoulder screamed their protest and so did Nero but a second later he was back in the very relative safety of the chariot –

– which was now starting to turn left into a lethal dead-end street. Petronius seized the reins and heaved, wrapping them around his own body as he'd seen the professional charioteers do.

The horses didn't want to obey. They pulled against him, determined now to have their own way. Petronius grimaced and flung himself to the right yanking the bit so hard into the horses' mouths that he saw fleck of blood among the spittle.

And finally the pain moved them. Their heads turned and their bodies followed after, down the road that led to freedom rather than death. The chariot turned too, but the circle of its path was broader and where the horses had missed the marble wall of the small temple of Aphrodite, the chariot caught it full on.

The impact flung Petronius against the shallow wooden side and Nero into his arms. It was the only thing that saved the boy's life. The chariot tipped and kept on tipping as the horses raced on. Astonishingly, it seemed to find stability at this crazy, acute angle, the right-hand wheel almost on the ground and the left-hand one high above it.

Petronius grabbed desperately for the side of the carriage with one hand and for Nero with his other. His fingers found a tenuous purchase on the thin wood, his arm a firmer grip around the little boy's waist. But he was still tangled in the reins and that saved him. Somehow he stayed in the chariot and when the horses took the next turn both wheels finally fell back to the ground.

Pain jarred all the way up Petronius's spine. Nero bounced from his knee and nearly out of the chariot before he made a desperate grab for him. The boy was still laughing, and Petronius was beginning to fear for his sanity.

And then, when he saw what was approaching, he feared for his own. Ahead lay a broad crossroads, the intersection of two of Rome's main thoroughfares. It was as deserted as the rest of the city had been, no old ladies to get in his way here. Instead Petronius could hear the clatter of approaching hooves.

The other two chariots of the dead had returned, as they must always have intended. They thundered towards him from opposite sides, meaning to trap him between them. They must have been waiting a while – they must have known a short cut – because they'd timed it just right. They'd meet in the middle at the perfect moment to crush his chariot between them. They'd be smashed to pieces in the impact too, but why should they care? There were always new bodies for them to move to.

"Race?" Nero said and Petronius choked out a laugh.

"Yes – I think we'll have to."

But he could already see that his horses were on the point of collapse. Their flanks were coated with sweat and their eyes were rolling as they galloped. The animals drawing the dead must have been equally exhausted, but as the two chariots raced towards him from either side, while the one behind continued to close the gap, he saw no evidence of them slowing. Perhaps fear of their dead passengers drove them on. And if the horses themselves died, they would simply be resurrected to continue the pursuit. If Petronius's horses died, they'd turn on their own passengers.

The dead were thirty paces and closing, and there was no way, just no way, that the chariot would make it through.

There was no way the *chariot* would make it through.

Nero yelped a protest when Petronius hoisted him onto his hip – then again when they both landed on the horse's back. The animal reared then bucked but Petronius was ready for it this time and he clung on grimly with one hand as he drew his sword with the other.

Fifteen paces. Petronius slashed down with the blade, and then again. The harness was only leather. It should have been no match for the steel of his sword. But there was no force in his blow, not twisted at that awkward angle, three-quarters of his concentration on keeping his seat.

Ten paces and the first strap parted. But the dead could see what he was doing. One of them threw a javelin, and he had to stop to pull himself and Nero out of its path. It missed them by a whisker to thump into the other horse's flank. The animal screamed and fell, dragging its harness-mate towards the ground with it.

Now Petronius had less than a second to free them or it was all over. He stopped trying to keep his balance, released his hold on Nero – trusting the boy to cling to him on his own – and brought the sword down against the remaining leather straps with all his strength.

It struck, caught and passed through. The momentum of his swing overbalanced him and the weight of the sword wanted to drag him to his death on the ground beneath his horse's hooves. He let the blade go, watching as it skittered and sparked along the pavement while his arms flung themselves desperately around the horse's middle.

Five paces, and it was up to the animal now. The reins

had flown out of reach and Petronius could concentrate on nothing but keeping himself and Nero from falling to their deaths.

A second later, the undead were upon them. Petronius looked into the mad glaring eye of the nearest horse, and knew that it had already passed away and returned. The same fate that awaited him.

And then, spurred by something – fear of its own mortality, horror at its brother, slaughtered by its side – their own horse put on one final burst of speed. The spittle and blood from its mouth flew back into Petronius's face. He blinked his eyes to clear them and when he opened them again it was over.

The chariots of the dead had timed their approach exactly. They collided in perfect synchronicity, old human flesh and fresh horse and wood crashing together in an explosion of gore and splinters. The dead screamed their rage but Petronius's horse was through, it was past, and only the fine hair of its tail was caught in the carnage behind.

Petronius stayed, twisted round to watch it for a second more, then fumbled for the loose reins and guided their horse out of the square.

Boda had one foot through the door of the temple when she heard the rising thunder of hooves behind her. She spun and ducked, sword raised – then, a moment later, she sheathed it and smiled.

Vali raised his eyebrows, not looking altogether pleased.

Petronius's horse looked on the point of collapse, and she wondered what he'd been through to get here.

The animal made a sound almost like a human groan as he dismounted and she could see that its eyes were bloodshot and its lips cut and bleeding where the bit had cut viciously into them. One of the beetles which flew through the temple doors in a steady stream settled on the horse's flank, as if sensing a body that would soon be vacant for it to occupy.

It was only when Petronius strode towards her that she saw he held a small figure in his arms.

She smiled. "You saved him."

The child turned his wide eyes on her and grinned in return. "We raced against some skellingtons!" he said.

"Did you now?" Vali looked at Petronius and not the boy. "And you still managed to get here in time."

Petronius shrugged uncomfortably. "Actually, I was mainly concerned about running away. The fact that it happened to be in this direction was just a lucky accident."

"Indeed," the other man said dryly, and strode through the open doors of the temple to forestall further conversation.

Boda pulled Petronius into a quick embrace – Nero squashed between them – then turned away from the young man's blush to follow Vali inside.

As soon as she was through the door the noise hit her, the sound of a million beetles on the wing. It was a dry rasp that sounded just a little oily, as if the insects weren't entirely clean.

The interior of the temple was dark, lit only by the bright sun piercing the doorway and, at the far end of the long chamber, the sickly green light spilling out of the gateway to death itself. None of the Cult of Isis had stayed behind to guard the place. Maybe they couldn't bear to stare into that terrible portal for too long, with the buzzing of the dead souls all around. Boda could hardly stand to look at it herself.

She found her footsteps slowing as she walked through the darkness towards the gate. Petronius followed close behind her, but he kept casting nervous glances back at the doorway to safety and the outside world, brown eyes half-hidden behind the unruly tangle of his hair. She'd wanted to spare him this, but that was before the dead had flung themselves over the walls. Now there was no safety in Rome, and she found she was glad to face this with Petronius at her side.

Nero hid his face against Petronius's side, perhaps sensing the evil lived inside the temple. Only Vali looked untroubled, his long strides drawing her on when her own would have faltered.

Then she was standing in front of the gate itself, with no further excuse for delay. The Cultists might return at any moment, and this was their only hope. She turned to Petronius, with the small, shivering boy by his side. "You can't bring him through here."

To her surprise, it was Vali who spoke. "Why not? He'll be safer inside death than facing it in the land of the living. If we succeed he'll be able to return, and if we fail, it's a pleasanter end than the one the undead will give him."

"Will we be able to return?" Petronius asked. He peered into the gateway, as if his eyes might penetrate it, but the green light hid everything behind it.

"As many as step though the gateway will be able to return through it," Vali told him. The light of death cast a ghastly pallor over his face, and dyed his red hair an unnameable colour.

Petronius looked at him out of suspicious eyes, and Nero out of round, trusting ones. "And how exactly do you know that?"

"Does it matter?" Boda asked. "My people's knowledge is different from yours. We know of the works of nature rather than those of man, but we know them deeply."

Vali smiled at her, then bowed and gestured forward. "Lead the way then, clanswoman. Your death awaits."

Boda swallowed, but she only allowed herself to hesitate a moment before stepping forward. Two paces and the green light was all she could see. She squared her shoulders and reached out her hand to feel her way blindly ahead of her –

– and when it met the gateway, it struck something solid. She frowned and pressed harder, putting her weight behind it, but nothing could move her fingers an inch past the rim of the gate.

"I'll go first, if you like," Petronius said, his voice shaking.

Boda realised that he thought she was afraid. She was, but that wasn't the problem. She turned to face the two men. "It's closed. It won't let me pass."

Petronius looked at Vali. "Is there some incantation, some ceremony we need to get through?"

Vali shook his head. "None that I know. The gates may only be closed from the inside, but it should be possible to enter them from either."

Boda took a step back towards them. "So we came all this way for nothing?"

Vali approached her, leaving Petronius and Nero behind. "Perhaps not. There are other ways to pass into death."

They were face to face now, and she saw that his was white with strain. He rested his hand against her shoulder and licked his lips.

"What other ways?" she asked him.

He pulled her closer still, and she thought for a second

that he was going to kiss her, but he just rested his forehead against hers. "Do you trust me?"

She stopped her instant, automatic response, and thought about her answer. Did she trust him? She liked him, but that was far from the same thing. And she knew he hadn't always been honest with them. She still knew so little about him. In all the time they'd been together, she'd never been able to induce him to tell her his lineage or his chieftain. She shouldn't trust him – but she did.

"Yes," she said. "With my life."

He smiled at that, pulling back only a little. "That's generally considered unwise. But I promise you this, you'll have everything you need to get to the end. Everything you need you carry within you."

At first she felt the knife in her back only as a blow against her spine. A second later and what had seemed like an impact transmuted into a piercing pain worse than any she'd ever felt. The hilt settled snug against her skin, and she felt the prick of the blade emerging through her chest to dimple her tunic.

She looked down at it stupidly for a second. It was exactly where her heart lay, huddled in its cage of ribs. Then, as she looked back into Vali's eyes, he pulled out the blade and the blood gushed free. She had one moment to watch it spatter the white marble around her, and then she could see only blackness and the agony was nothing but a memory.

PART FOUR
Cineri Gloria Sera Est

CHAPTER SEVENTEEN

The phantom sensation of a knife sliding through Boda's flesh followed her into darkness. She thought she was screaming, but she couldn't feel her mouth. She couldn't hear the sound she made. Something that was her was still thinking, but it no longer had a head with which to do it, only a cloud of thought, of anger and betrayal.

The cloud was already dissipating. There was a wind, here in this lightless, loveless no-man's-land, and it wanted to blow her apart. She felt memories drifting away from her. Was that her childhood, seeping out? She was seven and she was climbing a tree, an oak deep in the old forest, she was happy and laughing – and then it was gone. Lost in the darkness.

There was something at the core of her, something the wind couldn't touch. But with all her memories gone, what would that thing be? Nothing that was Boda. Boda... was that her name? She was already forgetting.

No. No. Boda *was* her name. She had a childhood, a good one, and she wouldn't let it go. Her life had been full, though it had been short, and it had given her courage and strength. She used them now, pulling inward on the cloud of consciousness that was dissipating outward.

Something that wasn't her hand reached out for her childhood first. It struck other things, other memories – *a morning of brilliant sunshine on Crete; the pain of childbirth in the dark of a smoke-filled hut, and I've only seen thirteen summers, only thirteen, don't let this be my last* – but they weren't Boda's memories and she batted them aside.

Then another flash, another moment. The weight of a

sword between her two chubby palms and it's so heavy, so much heavier than she'd ever imagined. Will she one day carry it in her hand, wield it in defence of her tribe? It seems impossible and she sighs and hands it back to her father, who's smiling at her through his brown beard.

This, this is hers. She pulls it in and goes to collect more. Here's the moment when she first knew a man, fourteen years old and terrified that it would hurt as much as she'd been told. Three years later and there she is, bleeding the remains of her husband's child into the dirt. They tell her she's broken inside, that there'll be no more babies for her. Two weeks later and her husband cries as she leaves him for the life of a warrior. Another year and he's found someone else. Two, and she sees his fat, red-faced child, balanced on his wife's hip. Boda feels a moment of hurt, the pulling sense of roads not taken. Six months more and she's in her first battle and she knows this is what she was born to do.

More and more memories. Her sword sliding slick through blood. Boots in the soil of the forest, leaves churning beneath in a pleasant-smelling mulch. The hot-sweet taste of mead. Fire in her gut where a pike pierced it. The long agony of fever. Darkness – and then light. The feel of chains around her wrists as she's led to Rome.

The Arena. Josephus. His poor mutilated body. The catacombs, seething with corpses. The green light. The gateway to death.

The knife in her back.

All her memories, together once again. She gathered them inside her and slammed the door shut, locking them inside. And then she thought about her body, the one she'd had and lost.

She remembered how her hand felt, gripped around the pommel of a sword. The slight slipperiness of sweat on her palm, the coolness as the metal carried her heat away from her. She thought about water, the sweet relief of it in her mouth after a hard day's work, trickling down the valley of her thighs when she bathed. She pictured her own skin, pale when she first arrived in Rome, darkening over the months she spent there, but never the olive of the city's native sons. She pictured her skin, and she imagined it wrapping around her, enclosing all these sensations of body, these feelings of physical being.

She imagined ears growing from it, the improbable whorl of her lobes. Hair, fine and fair, the exact colour of her mother's. She felt it stirring in a breeze that wasn't there, itching with dust against her scalp. And lastly she thought of her eyes, their insensitive hardness behind her lids when she blinked. She pictured the little creatures of light that lived inside them when they were shut.

And then she imagined opening them.

She lay in a field of green grass, above her head a sky that was a different blue from any she'd ever seen. Reaching high, high into it, beyond where her new-old eyes could see, a great ash tree grew. Its leaves would have blocked the sun, had there been a sun here to block.

It was Yggdrasil, the world tree, which holds up every level of the world.

And Boda lay in the lowest level of them all, the realm of the dead.

Petronius stared in horror as Boda's body slumped to the ground, sliding through the arms Vali still held loosely around her.

He'd choked a protest when the knife went in, but now he found himself without words. His fingers fumbled at his own sword belt, but anything he could do would be no more than revenge. Boda was already gone. She was gone.

When his sword was trembling in his hand, the tip pressed against Vali's chest, he thought that revenge might feel pretty good. That sending the barbarian's blood to mingle with that of the woman he'd murdered would give him the closest thing to joy he was ever likely to feel again.

"Don't be a fool," Vali said.

Petronius knew that he was crying, and wasn't ashamed. She deserved his tears. "You low-born scum," he said. "She trusted you."

Vali bowed his head. Nero slipped from Petronius's side to stand beside Boda's corpse, and the other man rested a gentle hand against his head. Petronius saw with a sickening surge of rage that Vali left a bloody handprint in the child's fair hair.

Then Vali looked up again, and there was no apology in his eyes. There was – something. Something old and a little frightening and despite himself Petronius looked away.

"She gave me her trust," Vali said. "As I required. And now you must do the same."

"Why must I?" Petronius said.

The other man smiled, looking over his shoulder. "Because you have absolutely no choice."

Petronius's sword dropped as he spun. Somewhere in the back of his head, he'd heard the footsteps all along. He'd known they weren't alone. And now when he saw Sopdet, flanked on either side by the walking dead, he wasn't terribly surprised.

Her saw her shooting a troubled glance at the gateway between realms. But when she saw that the sick green

298

light still shone through it, unbroken, she smiled. "A good plan," she said to Petronius. "What a shame that only I have the power to breach the land of death from this side."

Petronius was too shaken for bravura. He glared at her hatefully. "Then kill me. Kill me now, there's nothing left to live for."

She took a few more steps nearer, leaving her dead bodyguards behind. "I will, of course. But perhaps first I shall keep you a prisoner by my side, to share my full triumph. We'll walk the length of the earth, and where once the Pax Romana reigned, you'll see the Mortis Romana. Every person, every animal in the world will be a dead shell for the spirit living inside it. Only the trees and grass will remain as they were, green witnesses to the new world."

Her eyes were alight with a pleasure that was nowhere near sane. With her perfect rosebud mouth and fine high cheekbones and night-dark hair she should have been beautiful. But she wasn't. She was hideous.

And then, for the first time, her eyes gazed beyond Petronius, to the man she'd inadvertently stopped him from killing. Her already pale face drained of all colour and her mouth gaped open, a round black hole of shock.

"You!" she said.

Vali stepped forward until he was shoulder to shoulder with Petronius. He bowed ironically. "Fancy running into you here," he said. "What a pleasant surprise, sister."

Boda lay for a while, staring up at the sunless blue sky between the long thin stalks of grass. It must be late in the year, in this realm without time. The seed pods had released their burdens, to drift in the gentle breeze across her face. She blew them idly away, watching the non-patterns the seeds made in the air, and thought that this was very pleasant. As she'd told Vali, she had nothing to fear from death.

Vali. He'd sent her here. And – she sat up, brushing the grass out of her way – he'd sent her here for a purpose. She must close the gates of death the only way a person could, from the inside. He hadn't had the courage to come himself, so he'd stabbed her in the back to send her here by the fastest route. His betrayal hurt more than she could have imagined, but it didn't alter the job that needed to be done.

She rose to her feet, and now she could see the grass, stretching into the distance. It seemed to go on forever, without horizon. No mountain or hill or landmark marred its endless sameness. Only its colour changed a little, as a breeze blew over and through it, and the stalks bent this way and that, exposing first their soft yellow underside and then their harsher, greener outer husks.

After a while the sameness of the grass began to oppress her. Would this be it, for all eternity, the only view she'd ever see? Would she have no company but her own? She turned from the grass, back towards the monumental tree behind. Its branches were far overhead, lost to distance. But its roots lay tangled all around, their arches as high as those brick roads the Romans used to carry water throughout their lands. The very thinnest of the roots was thicker than her body.

She stood at their outer edge, and inside she saw a darkness, stretching deep and far. There, for the first time, she thought she saw something – the glimmer of a red eye. She backed away, choosing to circle the tree instead.

It was a very long way. She wasn't sure how far she walked, looking at the peaceful plain of grass when the darkness under the tree began to trouble her, and at the shadows under the roots when the emptiness of the endless land became too much.

She'd almost given up hope of seeing anything different when she found it. She saw the well first. It was a simple stone structure, no bucket dangling from a rope above, but when she came closer she saw that a curved onyx drinking horn sat on its rim. The water came almost to its top, its blue as unlike normal water as the blue of the sky was unlike any sky she'd ever seen.

Still, she realised suddenly that she was thirsty. The horn felt solid in her hand, and cooler than she would have expected. She dipped it in the water and raised the lip to hers.

"Only poison, to those who drink without permission," a deep voice said behind her.

She span, sloshing water from the horn onto the grass. But there was no one there and she stood, irresolute, looking at the dregs of water and wondering if she dared quench her thirst with them.

"You must seek my blessing first, daughter of man," the voice said again – and this time she saw its source.

His head was huge, but still only a little higher than her waist, the reason her eyes had passed over it when she first searched for the speaker. His severed neck rested against the ground, bloodless. His smile was broad and might have looked friendly if it hadn't been nearly two-feet wide.

"Mimir," she said, because now she knew him, the immortal giant traded as a hostage to the Vanir, who sent back only his severed head.

She dropped to her knees, bringing her eyes level with

his. Each was larger than her own head, but they were mismatched, the left brown and the right the most vibrant green she'd ever seen, so bright it made the grass around it seem drab.

"Do you wish to drink, child of Midgard?" Mimir asked.

Boda licked her lips. She did, but now she knew that it wouldn't be to quench her thirst. This well was the Well of Wisdom and its waters would tell her everything she wanted to know – and possibly many things she didn't. "Yes," she said eventually. "I want to drink. I need to."

The giant's severed head couldn't nod, but its huge eyes blinked in acknowledgement. "So said the Allfather himself, when the seasons turned. He needed my wisdom to save his son, but the sun was killed all the same. Is it the same business that brings you here? Do you wish to undo what even Odin himself could not?" His mismatched eyes studied her keenly.

"No," she said. "That's not what I want."

"Ah." The word was a deep rumble in a chest that wasn't there. "Then you wish for the opposite, do you? The keeping done of that which the Father of the Gods wished undone?"

She bowed her head but didn't reply. If Odin's son had perished, he might be the god Vali wished to remain dead. But she couldn't know for certain until she'd drunk the water.

Mimir seemed to understand what her non-answer meant. "And what price will you pay, for this knowledge you seek?"

"Price?" She looked down at herself, and realised for the first time that she was dressed in nothing but a simple tunic, like the lowest of Roman slaves. In all the vast empty landscape around her, there was nothing she could give for what she wanted.

The giant laughed. "There is always a price, girl, and yours will be high. The Allfather gave me his eye in return for the knowledge he sought. And you? What will you give me, that could equal the value of that?"

CHAPTER EIGHTEEN

Petronius looked between Vali and Sopdet in appalled understanding. He was red-haired and she was dark, and she was dark-skinned and he was light, but for the first time, Petronius could see the resemblance between them. It was something in their eyes, something too ancient for their young faces. And the worst thing was, Vali had told them this truth right from the start, knowing that they'd never believe him. No wonder he'd murdered Boda. He must have been working with his sister all along.

But the look Sopdet gave Vali was far from loving. "You're too late," she said. "You can't stop me undoing what you've done."

He looked down his long, narrow nose at her. "If that was all you wished, sister, I wouldn't have gone to such lengths to prevent it."

Vali's words seemed to spark a conflagration inside her. Sopdet ignited with rage. Petronius took a step back, until he was pressed against the unyielding gateway to the other side. It was less frightening than this woman's anger, which seemed far larger and more pure than any woman should be capable of.

"You've already done all in your power," she said, "every single thing to keep us apart. You've walked the ends of the earth and beyond. You've done everything you can to keep him dead – but you can't do this!"

Vali seemed supremely calm. Petronius didn't understand how he could maintain that little half-smile in the face of Sopdet's fury. It could do nothing but provoke her. "It's certainly true, sister, that I can't step through this gateway unless you open it for me. But then you're going to do that very soon, so I see no problem."

"Am I?" Petronius could see Sopdet bite back her anger, struggling to mutate it into contempt. "There's a faster way to send you to the other side. Here in the realm of man, I can give you the same fate you gave my beloved."

Vali took a step back, until he was standing beside Petronius against the gates of death. Petronius flinched away from him, but Vali didn't seem to care.

"I think you'll open the gateway," he said. "Because you need to step through it yourself. And you need to step through it yourself, because my emissary has already crossed over." His eyes drifted down to Boda's body, on the steps beneath them.

For the first time, Petronius wondered why it had remained dead, when every other corpse in Rome had risen.

Sopdet looked at Boda and frowned. "That woman? Why should I fear her?"

Vali's eyes lingered on Boda, and Petronius thought he read regret in them.

Or maybe it was just his own. "Because I've sent her to Mimir," he said. "And then I've instructed her to seek out our brother – and ensure he stays where he belongs."

Sopdet threw back her head and howled. The sound was so deep and so loud, the temple shook with it. Even the dead cringed away from their mistress, covering their decaying ears.

Petronius shrank back. His arms reached behind him, expecting the barrier of solid air that guarded the gate to death – and found nothing. Nero was pressed against his chest, the boy's wide blue eyes fixed on the howling woman. There were words in the howl, Petronius could hear that now, though he didn't know their meaning.

"Quick," Vali said. "Go through while you can – she'll

close it behind her."

Petronius spun. He saw that one of his feet had already passed through the gateway. It disappeared into absolute darkness, invisible to him, only the sensation of his calf muscles clenching in fear to tell him it was still a part of his body. The green light had blinked out, but it left nothing behind, no clue to what lay beyond.

"Do you trust me?" Vali said.

Petronius laughed, almost hysterically. "What do you think?"

"Well," Vali said. "Do you trust me more than you trust her?"

Petronius couldn't help himself. He shot a look behind him. The noise cut out the instant he did. Sopdet's hair was suddenly white, and it took him a moment to realise why. It was full of the plaster flakes which had floated down from the painted ceiling with the strength of her howl. As if to compensate, her face was red, engorged with the blood of rage. And her eyes were luminous, blazing with the same sick green light that had once shone from the gateway to death itself.

As she lowered her head and raced for the gateway, Petronius grabbed Nero and leapt across the threshold into the darkness.

Boda shook her head. "There's nothing I can give," she told Mimir. "I've already lost everything I had."

"Your life, you mean?" the giant said. She could see his huge pink tongue moving inside his mouth, each taste bud the size of a coin.

"Yes. I brought nothing with me into death, not even silver for the ferryman the Roman's believe in."

"Nothing at all?" There was a cunning note to his voice now. "What of your memories? Why did you fight so hard for them, if you hold them in no regard?"

Boda felt a heart that wasn't real pounding in her chest. "You want my memories?"

"Would you sacrifice them for this knowledge you seek?"

Would she? "No," she told him. "I need my memories to understand the knowledge. One would be useless without the other."

He chuckled. "A good answer. Then what will you give?"

She spread her hands. "What do you want?"

"I? It is the value of the sacrifice to the giver, not its worth to the recipient."

"Name any other price and I will pay it."

"So shall it be," the giant said, and his voice rang hollow with the sound of a vow given and sealed.

Boda hesitated, suddenly unsure of what she'd done.

"Drink then," Mimir said. "And you shall learn the price when you have the knowledge to understand it."

She raised the horn, watching the light sparkle on its carvings as she dipped the open mouth beneath the surface of the water.

"Fill it all," the giant said, "and drink it all. Your ignorance is far too wide, and only this can narrow it."

When the horn was full to the brim, she raised it to her lips.

"Drink," Mimir said. "Follow in the footsteps of Odin himself."

She shivered, knowing that once done, this could never be undone. That she'd made a bargain with a god, and that was never wise. Here in the realm of the dead, there was much she could suffer if it was decreed, and she'd suffer it eternally. But she'd sworn an oath as a warrior to protect her people. That oath didn't end at the gates of the otherworld.

The water felt cool as it gushed down her throat and it tasted of something she couldn't quite name. Was it rosemary? No, it was more bitter than that. Her mind chased the thought, chased the taste – and followed it out of the world of death and somewhere else entirely.

She looked down on a hall, a great hall filled with laughter and music and light, and at the table's head, a one-eyed man lifted the horn of mead to pass to the thunder-browed giant at his right-hand side. Odin and Thor and all the Aesir feasted in the halls of Asgard, and only one forehead frowned, only one mouth turned down instead of up.

Why was Vali sitting at the table of the gods? But the moment the thought was formed, Boda knew its answer. How had she confused this fierce, flaming being with the man she knew? This was Loki, god of fire and mischief and blood brother to Odin, but not brother of the heart. Not tonight.

Odin's gaze passed over Loki and didn't see the hurt in his eyes. They sought only one thing, only one man, the sun-gold face of Baldur, his beloved son.

He saw his son and didn't see the brother who scowled to see him smile. He didn't see the envy and the hate.

A wrench, a twist in time, and Boda was back at Mimir's well. For a moment she thought that it was over, that that was all she'd see. But then she realised that she was floating above the scene, a vantage point different from her body's. And she saw the Allfather standing by the water as he reached up to his face and plucked out his own eye, brilliant and green and knowing, to place inside the giant's empty socket.

Then Odin raised the horn, and as the water flowed in him and through him, so did she. She saw what he saw, the golden-haired Baldur dead, his red blood soaking the earth and his mother Frigga's face twisted in a grief that no goddess should ever know. Odin screamed with the same pain and rage and the scream carried Boda on.

Now she followed a horse, galloping the length of the earth. Frigga rode its back, tall and proud and full of love, and everywhere she rode she asked a vow of every living thing she met.

"Hazel tree," she said. "Will you swear never to harm my beloved son?" And the tree was filled with the same love she felt, and it took the oath. Next she asked a squirrel, a lion, an ant. Boda saw that there wasn't one creature in the world which didn't give its word.

But there was one beneath it, one little sprig of mistletoe. "I'll take the oath!" it said, but Frigga said it was too young.

And Loki – full of bitterness and envy – took the twig and nurtured it and grew it to a sapling. The god of fire looked on the spear he fashioned from the iron-hard mistletoe and smiled his crooked smile, beneath his long, sharp nose.

Another twitch in time, and now Boda saw the gods standing in the flower-filled fields of Asgard, with Baldur in their middle. The sun god stood and laughed as rocks and swords and hammers were thrown at him and not a single one could touch him. *We swore an oath,* the weapons cried and turned their points away.

Until, slinking and smiling at the side of the field, Loki placed a spear of mistletoe in the blind god Hodur's hands.

The spear flew, strong and true, into the sun god's heart. Laughter turned to screams and all the world gasped at the fall of this golden child. Even Hel, goddess of the underworld, cold and hard and without love, felt a moment of pity for Frigga, for a mother's pain. Hel swore that if every living thing wept for Frigga's fallen son, she'd free him from the realm of death to walk in Asgard's sunlit fields again.

Another twitch and Boda saw another horse, another journey the length and breadth of the earth. This time Frigga, tears streaming down her own face, looked for the same tears of mourning from every living thing on earth. The hazel tree wept, the lion, the ant, even the mistletoe which in its ignorant youth had killed her son.

But just one person refused – a giantess, with a face as stony as the rocks of the cave in which she lived. "I will not weep," she said. "I do not mourn him." And so Baldur was condemned to remain in the realms of death.

And when Frigga had passed on, cursing the giantess's name, the creature smiled a crooked smile beneath a sharp nose, and shape-changing Loki thought that his work was done.

Another twitch, stronger this time, and Boda found herself looking at a different scene in a different world – that she somehow knew was still the same as the one she'd witnessed before.

This time the sun-god's name was Osiris, and it was his sister-wife Isis and not his mother who mourned him so extravagantly. The god-murderer was named Set, not Loki, and sometimes he had the body of a man and the head of a beast, a composite of all the creatures that roamed the desert, the curved snout of a jackal and the long square ears of an ass. But sometimes he had a man's face, a crooked smile beneath red hair and a long, sharp nose. And here, as before, he was a stranger and outsider – a god of the foreign and the forsaken.

And then another twitch, and Boda saw that the Jews told the story a little differently, that Shaitan their red-haired desert god didn't kill the sun-god himself, but paid a living man thirty pieces of silver for his murder. And there were others – more and more images from all over the world until she thought her head would explode with them. A thousand and one stories but only one truth.

The god of mischief who was sometimes called Loki and sometimes Set and sometimes other things, murdered the sun-god out of jealousy and spite. And the goddess who had many names, of which Isis was only one, mourned the dead sun-god – sometimes as her husband and sometimes as her son, but always far too much.

She travelled the length of the earth, seeking a way to bring him back from the realms of the dead, where his mummified body sat in final judgement over the mortals who ended their short journey there. She failed, and her failure drove her mad and she hatched a final – fatal – plan.

Her husband was in the realm of death. She couldn't join him there because she was a goddess of the earth, of green and vibrant things, and her duty lay among them. The realm of death would spit her out if she stayed in it too long. And Osiris, being dead, could never cross to the living realm. But what if the two realms became one? What if the land of life became a realm of death too – not a single living man or creature still abiding there?

Then her husband could return. Then he could rule by her side.

But Isis would have to be careful – she'd have to be cunning. If the other gods knew what she was planning, they would stop her. If Set found out, he would foil her once again. And so she disguised herself as a human woman named Sopdet, and found followers among the mortals who had their own reasons to wish for the gates of death to be opened.

Sopdet, who was Isis – and also Frigga, and every other goddess who'd lost the god she loved – came to the realm of the living and opened the gateway to death. And only the trickster god Loki, who was also Set, and a red-haired man called Vali, could do anything to stop her. But he was the one who'd killed her husband-brother-son in the first place – and he was never to be trusted.

And in the world of the living, the woman called Sopdet who was also the widowed Isis and the grieving mother Frigga, plunged through the gateway to death which she had created – the gate she was forbidden to cross.

Isis was the mistress of the moon, of bread and beer and all green things. And those who worshipped her as Frigga knew that she presided over the making of new life, through love and birth.

With the goddess gone from the land of the living, everything that she ruled went with her. The moon was on the far side of the world from Rome, invisible. No one in the city, huddled terrified in their homes, saw its silver light blink from the sky.

But even inside their brick and marble they heard the distant roar of the sea, surging wildly as the force that governed its tides was taken from it. Huge waves crashed against the shore, against the grass that grew there and was dying too, without its mistress to nurture it.

All over the Empire, at the height of summer, the leaves

wilted on the trees and the flowers drooped and died, no pollen to spread on the wind and make new flowers. Without Isis in the world, there could never be new flowers again.

And in their houses in Rome, women looked at their husbands and husbands looked at their wives and where there had been love there was only indifference and where there had been indifference there was now hate, and no one remembered what it felt like to love another person, because the idea of love was gone from the world.

In Gaul, a man who'd been happily married for thirteen years passed the sixteen-year-old daughter of his best friend in the street. His cock twitched and suddenly he couldn't see why not. Why not take her right here, right in the street, if he wanted to? He covered her mouth to muffle her screams and the onlookers laughed and cheered as he had her.

In Syria, two brothers played a game of dice for coppers they could well afford. They'd played the game since they were children and they played it now to remember that happy time. But when one of them threw two ones and the other laughed, suddenly he couldn't bear it. How dare his brother laugh at him – his brother, who'd stolen his parents' attention from him when he was only four years old. The knife was only meant for cutting bread but it slid through his brother's chest like butter and he smiled to hear him scream in pain.

And in Egypt, a woman looked down in horror at this little creature suckling at her breast. What was this thing, this parasite, that was leeching the life out of her? She threw it away and stamped and stamped and stamped on it until there was nothing but a red and white mush on the floor and she could no longer remember what its little pink face had looked like.

And all around Rome, the dead raised their heads to the moonless sky and howled. Their leader was gone, and now there was no one to command them – and no one to rein them in. What had been a planned assault deteriorated into chaos, and what had been a focussed attack became a mindless slaughter.

All over the world, the green grass turned brown, the living forgot how to love each other, and the dead turned their mindless hatred on the living.

CHAPTER NINETEEN

Boda blinked her eyes open, and found that she lay on her back, a strange blue sky above her and long, thin stalks of grass all around. Had she just arrived here? Was everything she had seen and heard a dream, the last imaginings of her dying mind?

A part of her hoped so, but when she struggled to her feet she saw the well and the giant's head beside it. "Daughter of Midgard, now do you understand?" he said.

She bowed her head, because she understood all too well. Her friend Vali, who had both saved and taken her life, was also the god Loki, who might have doomed them all when he contrived to kill his fellow god out of jealousy and spite.

"And can you guess the price I demand?" Mimir asked.

She shook her head. These were matters for gods, not mortals, and she couldn't see what her part in them would be.

"Look beneath the roots of Yggdrasil," he said.

She peered into the darkness, stretching miles beneath the vast tree, and for a moment a flash of lightning illuminated some of what was hidden there. She saw a slab of rock in a dark cave, and though the distance confounded all perspective, Boda knew that the rock was huge. The metal chains that lay on it were meant to hold a being more powerful than any that had ever been bound before. Above the rock the air seemed to twist and writhe and it took her a moment to realise that it was filled with snakes, hanging from the stalactites above, twining and twisting into each other and dripping their venom onto the slab below.

"Loki's prison," Mimir said, "meant to punish him for all eternity. But the god of fire and mischief fled and now someone else must suffer in his place."

Boda shuddered at the thought of lying there, in that impenetrable darkness, and knowing there would be no escape till the world itself had ended. She shuddered because she knew now what the price was to be. "You want me to take his place. He wanted it – that's why he sent me here."

Mimir's eyes flickered in acknowledgement. There was no pity on his vast face and that made it easier to bear. "A killing demands a blood price," he said. "Someone must pay it. And the death of a god is so vastly more consequential a thing than the death of a man, it demands a vastly greater punishment."

"I will pay it then," she said. "Though it was not I who did this wrong, I gave you my word and I'll keep it. But first you must let me complete my work."

"Must I, Midgard's child?"

Boda looked beneath the roots, but the darkness was complete again. She could remember it though, and always would, the rock and the snakes above it. She looked back at Mimir. "Yes. I took a vow to protect my people, to death and beyond."

"An oath more powerful than that you made to a god?"

"Yes," she said. "Greater even that that."

The giant sighed, a large sound louder than the wind. "Go then, and find your friends. Find the dead god and face his judgement, and when it is done, your mortal spirit will return here to suffer for all eternity."

She wanted to ask him how to find her friends – she wanted to ask him a lot of things – but his smile was already fading, and with it the rest of his face, and when it was gone entirely, she was somewhere else.

Narcissus thought he'd been here a very long time, but he wasn't entirely sure. When he looked back into the past, it all seemed the same, the same wandering on the same grey and lonely river bank, and he wondered if he'd ever known anything else.

There were others here, by the shore of this underground river. Their faces would drift towards him, out of the endless mist, and he would back away. They looked so sad. He didn't think he could deal with their sadness as well as his own.

The rocky ground was uneven and he kept stumbling. His knees were raggedly cut and his hands abraded but there were no red beads of blood on his grey skin. Everything here was grey. He knew that soon he'd have forgotten what colours were. Maybe then he'd be content to stop wandering, and just sit still and wait for forever to pass.

But not yet. Not quite yet. He still remembered that his name was Narcissus. He still knew that his master had loved him. And he knew that he needed to cross the river. There was something better on the other side, if only he could reach it.

He found himself at the shore again, little wavelets lapping against the rocks at his feet. The ferryman was there too. He always was.

"I want to cross," Narcissus told him.

The man shook his head, hidden beneath his cowl. "You don't have the coin."

Narcissus felt for the purse that hung at his neck, but he

already knew that the ferryman was right. It was empty.

"I'll pay you when I reach the other side," Narcissus told him.

The ferryman laughed and Narcissus saw a brief flash of yellow teeth in the shadows. "They all say that, son. And none of them can."

"I'm different!" Narcissus said, though he wasn't sure how.

"They all say that too."

"Then I'll swim." Narcissus looked down at the water. He had a memory, a bright blue one, of being dragged through the sea to the shores of Alexandria. He hadn't known how to swim then, but he thought he could manage now.

"Unwise, boy," the ferryman said. "This river will carry away more than your body."

"What choice do I have?" Narcissus asked him, and the ferryman had no answer to that. His flat boat drifted away, lost in the mist in moments, and only the long, slow-moving river remained.

Narcissus couldn't see the far shore, but it should be possible to reach it. And, after all, what more did he have to lose?

He drew in one breath and dived beneath the ice-cold surface before his mind could supply an answer to that question.

Petronius found himself on the bank of a great river. He could hear the waters rushing past, though they were hard to see in the gloom of the world that lay through the gate. Vali stood beside him – if that was even his name – and Nero lay limp in his arms. When Petronius put the little boy down, he clung tight to his thigh, his only anchor in this strange world.

Vali frowned at the river, its far shore lost in the darkness. "We need to cross," he said. "Before she follows us through."

"Who are you?" Petronius said. "And who's she?'"

Vali smiled crookedly. "Gods and demons, beings from another realm. We're just people, Petronius, with many names and normal desires. And currently my desire is to survive. How about you?"

"Cold water!" Nero said, and Petronius saw that the child had knelt to dip his finger in the river.

Before Petronius could react, Vali swooped and lifted him back. Nero let out a little yelp of protest that faded into silence as he stared at the tip of his index finger, which he'd wetted to its middle joint. Petronius could see the middle joint. The water had withered the skin and flesh above it, ageing it a hundred years in a second.

The little boy began to cry, more from shock than pain, Petronius thought – and Vali hurriedly put him down. "This river runs with more than water," he said. "It carries the hours of the night, time passing in its ebb and flow."

"Then how can we cross it?" Petronius asked. He looked down at the water and felt a terrible temptation to dip his finger in it too – his whole hand. To feel time as a physical thing, flowing past.

Vali grimaced. "There was a day I could have swum it without fear of harm, but I've lived in the mortal realm too long. I fear time has caught my scent."

There was nothing else around them, a featureless plain stretching away from the river to a horizon that lay in darkness. Petronius suspected he could walk forever and never reach it. He could hear the gushing sound of what might be a huge waterfall, somewhere in the distance, but he couldn't see it.

"If these are the hours of night," he said, "can't we follow them into day?"

Vali laughed, a surprised and genuine sound. "How typically Roman – logic in the midst of unreason. No, the night here is endless, for all that it ticks on second by second like any other time."

Petronius found his gaze suddenly drawn behind them, back to the distant source of the dark river. "Then how about a boat? Could that carry us across?"

Vali's gaze tracked his until he saw the same thing. The barge was broad and high-sided, and it was the only thing in this gloomy land which carried its own source of illumination. The light from inside it spilled out on the water, and Petronius saw with a jolt of fear that the water itself was black. It absorbed the light that hit it and gave nothing back.

The barge sailed close to the shore, its double banks of oars sending the pitch-black water to splash against the land. The whole thing was painted in bright colours, daubed with the pictures and symbols the Egyptians used in their writing, a side-on eye and a falcon, a scarab and a bird. And there was a ladder leading up the side, Petronius could see that now. It should be possible to jump aboard it – possible, but frightening, if the aim was to avoid touching even one drop of the water beneath. The slightest stumble and they'd fall into the river and be burned to the bone by the waters of time.

Nearer still, Petronius caught his first glimpse of the oarsmen, hidden in the bowels of the barge. He flinched away from flashes of eyes slitted like those of beasts. One of the oarsmen smiled, a wide gaping in a mouth that was more of a muzzle. A pink tongue lolled over sharp white teeth.

Suddenly, climbing aboard didn't seem such an appealing prospect.

But behind them, there was another sound – a tearing in the air itself – and he guessed that Sopdet had followed them through.

"Our only chance," Vali said, and leapt aboard the barge.

His fingers caught on the rungs of the ladder, but the blue paint there must have been slicker than it looked. Petronius heard the barbarian gasp and his fingers slid until only his nails gave him any purchase. He was already leaning backwards – a second more and he'd fall into the rushing waters of the river below.

There was no reason Petronius should care. He had Nero to take care of, and himself, and Vali had lied to him from the start. But he found himself hooking an arm under Nero and flinging himself at the barge.

He aimed for the rung beneath Vali, the lowest that was still above the water. The river was smooth here but the slightest wave might splash and burn him. His feet scrabbled for their footing, finding the rungs already slick with water. The heel of his sandal saved his foot but when he risked a glance down he saw the leather rotting away.

Nero was as slippery as the wood beneath his feet, squirming in his arms. And his own hands could reach only the outer edge of the ladder, circling Vali's body between them in a loose embrace.

The initial force of the impact pushed all three of them against the side of the boat, saving Vali from falling and driving the breath out of all their lungs. Then, a second later, they all began falling back, rebounding from the slick wood of the boat. Petronius gritted his teeth and tightened his grip on the side of the ladder, hardly any power left in him after this long, strange day.

Vali was heavy, and the boat was swaying now – as if it knew it had uninvited riders, and was trying to buck them off. Vali fell back against Petronius with all his weight, and his elbow caught him beneath the ribs.

Petronius let out a harsh gasp of pain, but the pain made his hands convulse and clench and the extra strength of their grip saved him. Then the boat swayed back, they were pressed against it once again, and this time Vali didn't wait. His hands reached above him and he swarmed up the ladder towards the top of the boat and whatever awaited them there.

Petronius was only a little slower in following, hampered by the small boy clasped against his chest. The higher rungs seemed more robust, or maybe his diminishing fear made them seem that way, as he left the water below him.

As he neared the top, he began to hear a sound, a deep buzzing that was as much in his bones as in his ears. The light grew brighter too, but he was glad of that. Anything that pierced the darkness was welcome.

But when he finally entered the barge, the light was brighter than he could have imaged. He shut his eyes against it in a flinch of pain, but the light burned through his eyelids, seeming to pierce directly into his brain. He didn't dare open them again – wasn't sure that if he did, there'd be anything left behind his eyelids but burned-out black husks.

Only the image remained, almost as bright in memory as it had been of itself. He could feel the heat of it too, setting his skin smouldering – that great, burning ball of flame that he knew as the sun, carried here on a barge through the hours of night.

And Boda, too, found herself facing a river. It traced a gentle curve through the endless field of grass, its waters a pleasant tinkle to counterpoint the wind whispering through the stalks. In the far distance, she could see something black stretching into the sky, and she guessed that it was Yggdrasil. She thought the source of the river might lie beneath the tree's roots, and she was afraid to touch its waters, however pleasant they sounded, and however blue they looked.

But there was a bridge, only a few minutes' walk along its course. The light here was diffuse, no one source to sparkle from the water or the bridge itself, but as Boda drew nearer she saw that the whole thing was constructed from rich, buttery gold.

When she reached the short flight of steps leading up to the bridge, she saw the figure standing astride it, one foot at one edge and one at the other, though the structure must be twenty-paces wide.

The giantess didn't seem to sense her approach at first. The level of her gaze was high above Boda's head, and perhaps her ears were too distant to detect the sound of her tread. But when Boda placed her first foot on the bridge itself, the giantess shifted her gaze downwards, squinting as if she found it hard to focus on something so small. This close, Boda could feel the waves of cold rolling off her. Her armour had looked like silver from a distance, but now Boda could see that the whole suit was made of ice – intricately carved and near transparent, showing the blue skin beneath.

"Little mortal," the giantess said. "I am Modgudr, guardian of the bridge, and you may not pass."

Boda found herself pushed back a step by the enormous volume of her voice. The rasp as Modgudr drew her sword was louder yet, the sound of a mountain of ice breaking away to fall into the sea far below.

The blade steamed with cold and Boda fumbled at her side for her own, before remembering that in this realm she didn't wear one. She smiled at herself, because even if she had, how could she possibly have hoped to defeat this vast being?

"I must pass," Boda said. "Mimir commands it."

Modgudr huffed a breath that rolled over Boda like a freezing mist. "My bodiless brother is not my master. I chart my own course."

"Oh? Your learning must be great indeed, to exceed that of the master of the Well of Wisdom?"

"Do you mock me?"

Boda forced herself to look up and up, into Modgudr's distant eyes. "Perhaps. I've drunk from the well – have you?"

"I have no need of it! My understanding is deeper than the ocean, which Thor himself could not drain. My knowledge is broader than the plain of Vigrid, where the gods themselves shall die. How dare you question me, little ghost!"

"A contest, then," Boda said. "A test to see who's wiser."

"You challenge me?" Modgudr bellowed, the force of her words so strong, they blew Boda back to the edge of the bridge.

Boda clung on to the railing and set her teeth against the gale. "I do, riddle against riddle, and the one who can't answer must forfeit her life – or what life she has, in a place such as this."

"Hmmm..." the giantess said, a profound vibration. "But nothing must be asked that is not known by the questioner."

"Agreed," Boda said. "My word on it."

"Then mine is given too – and I shall ask my question first. Tell me this, daughter of worms, what is it that walks on four legs in the morning, two in the afternoon, and three in the evening?"

Modgudr smiled, clearly pleased with herself, but Boda smiled wider. Maybe if she hadn't spent those months in Rome, she might have been baffled, but she'd learnt their legends too. "Man crawls on four legs in the morning of his life," she said, "walks upright on two in the healthy afternoon, and stoops on two legs and a stick in the fading twilight of his years."

The giantess snorted, clouds of ice puffing from her nostrils to fall as snow on the bridge below. "Very well then – your question for me?"

Boda clenched her fists, then said: "Tell me, what did Vali whisper in my ear in the second before I died?"

There was a long silence. "This is your riddle?" Modgudr said eventually.

"Yes. Can you answer it?"

"Of course not! No one but you knows the answer."

Boda allowed herself the tiniest smile. "But I do know – which was the only condition you set."

The giantess's roar of rage seemed larger than the sky. Boda wondered if the white clouds would crack and the earth tear at the power of it. She fell to her knees, curling her arms around her head to block it out, but the noise was everywhere, in her and around her, and she thought if it went on a second longer it would melt her flesh and shake her bones apart.

When it finally ended the silence felt like a blow. Boda had a second to uncurl herself, and then Modgudr's sword began to swing. Boda flung herself to the side of the bridge, but the sword was broader than the walkway, broader than the river itself. There was no escaping it.

The point came towards her, blotting out the sky behind it, and she wondered if it would crush or pierce her. Closer still, and she could see the pits in the metal, the first huge specks of rust. It came level with her knees, her chest – and the outer reach of its swing whistled by a pace from her head, setting her blonde hair flying. Boda toppled backwards as the great blade continued to swing up, up and inward – towards the giantess's own heart.

The blade sank in without a sound, and Modgudr fell to her knees with only a low murmur of pain. Her aim was true and Boda saw the blood gush from the wound, as blue as the giantess's skin. Droplets as big as fists spattered against Boda's head. She was surprised to find that Modgudr's blood was as warm and sticky as human blood, though it smelt of wet ash.

The giantess's eyes were shielded behind lids as big as sails, but she blinked them open one last time. "Pass then, little ghost," she said. "Your wisdom is greater than mine."

He dragged himself from the water, wondering why he'd been swimming and where. The landscape around lay in darkness, the bare outlines of jagged rocks visible in the distance. Had he been here before? He couldn't remember.

He looked back at the river, and when he did he saw a boat, a flat-bottomed barge which was floating towards him. The man steering it had hidden his face beneath a deep black cowl, but he saw the ghost of a smile as he approached.

"So you crossed," the ferryman said. "Brave and stupid,

boy."

"Crossed what?" he asked. He hadn't crossed anything, he was just standing there. Except, no. He'd just come out of the water, hadn't he? He must have swum the river. This new piece of knowledge about himself excited him, and he laughed.

The ferryman shook his head, lost in shadows. "The River Lethe is unkind to mortals. Do you know why you needed to be here?"

"No," he said. "Can you tell me? Can you tell me who I am? What I want? Where I came from and where I'm going?"

"So many questions – and I have only one answer to give. Which one would you like?"

He thought about it. He'd like to know his name – he seemed to remember that people needed names – but the ferryman was perfectly happy to speak to him without one. And he'd like to know where he came from, but he'd probably left there for a reason. On the other hand, if he found out where he was going, he might find what he wanted then he got there.

The ferryman nodded, as if he'd said all that out loud. "You're going to find the god who died, and persuade him to stay dead."

He frowned, because that didn't sound familiar at all. But why would the ferryman lie to him? "And where will I find him?" he asked. "It's part of the original question!" he added hurriedly, as the ferryman shook his head.

The boat was drifting away, already fading into mist, and for a moment he thought the ferryman wouldn't answer him. But the voice floated back, almost lost beneath the splash of the waves. "The dead god sits in the hall of judgement, as far from the river's bank as forgiveness and as near as guilt."

He wasn't quite sure what that meant, but it sounded like he needed to walk away from the river. After all, why else would he have swum it? He set off across the landscape of fallen rocks, the crushed remnants of a mountain that was long gone. The sharp edges tore his feet and his knees when he stumbled, but he didn't mind. He'd forgotten how to feel pain.

For miles and maybe years the landscape didn't change. But then, finally, he saw something, a greater darkness in the distance that resolved into a gateway as he drew near. Was that where he meant to go? If not, it must lead somewhere, and somewhere was better than the endless nowhere of this land.

He was almost at the cave-mouth when he saw the creature that lived inside. He fumbled for the word and found to his delight that he remembered it: 'dog'. But weren't dogs meant to be small, no taller than his waist? And did they normally have three heads?

The three heads swung to face him as he approached, and the creature rose to its feet, lifting them far above him. The heads seemed to be smiling at him, white teeth shining, but was it really a smile? He thought there might be another word for that expression, and for the deep growl that came from the creature's barrel chest.

Saliva dripped from the pink insides of its lips to the rocks below, burning where it landed, and he discovered that fear was an emotion he hadn't yet forgotten.

Petronius had always thought that blindness would be dark, but now he knew that it was as bright as the light that had burned his eyes. He wondered if he would see the sun for the rest of eternity, blazing behind his eyelids.

Nero still clung to his hip, though he didn't know if the boy had also been blinded. Only Vali seemed entirely unharmed. He'd taken Petronius's arm and led him ashore when the barge had neared the far bank.

Stepping off into nothingness had been terrifying – knowing that the waters of time might wait to drown him beneath. But he had to trust Vali. He had no choice.

"Where's Sopdet?" Petronius asked now. "Is she close behind?"

"She's swimming," Vali said, and Petronius thought he could hear a smile in the barbarian's voice. "It looks like she's finding it harder than she expected. Like me, she's spent too long among men. But she won't be far behind. We need to hurry."

Petronius did his best, stumbling over the rocky ground beneath him. All around him he heard voices, the sound of a thousand people, but he wondered if he would have been able to see them, even with his eyes. Their whispers seemed incorporeal, the murmured complaints of spirits who'd been worn away until they were nothing but air.

He didn't know how long the journey took. Away from the river that embodied it, time seemed to have no meaning here. But after a countless succession of moments, they drew to a halt.

There was another noise now, a deep and sibilant hissing that seemed animal, not human. Petronius felt Vali's hand claw into his bicep and shrank back, terrified by anything fearsome enough to frighten even the barbarian.

"Big snake," Nero said.

Vali choked a laugh. "A very big snake – and it has two heads."

"Well," Petronius said, "and this is only a suggestion, but perhaps we should run away from it."

"We can't," Vali told him. "We need to get past. This is

the guardian of the halls of death."

"Then what do you suggest we do?" Petronius asked, and this time he couldn't stop his voice from shaking. He didn't want to face his end and not even see it. And what would it mean, anyway, for a person to die in the realms of death? Was there some deeper level, some worse hell he might be banished to?

"We hope that Boda really does trust me," Vali said, and then the hissing heads descended.

The giantess had barely finished dying when the wolf came. It looked tiny beside her vast corpse, but Boda backed away all the same, not trusting her senses in this world where nothing was quite as it seemed.

When the beast pounced, she knew that she'd been right to fear. Its back rose higher than her head and its head was the size of her whole body, each needle-sharp tooth as long as her arm. The saliva that dripped from them hissed and fizzled in the dirt.

But its size saved her. The soft hair of its belly brushed hers as she dodged underneath it, and the claw it sent raking towards her dug up a furrow of earth but missed her chest by an inch.

The beast realised she'd eluded it. Its back legs flicked up and round, trying to dance away from her, but she danced with it, keeping herself in the safe spot beneath its chest where none of its feet could reach.

A second later, the dancing ceased, and she had a sudden, upside-down view of its head as it tucked its muzzle beneath its own chest. She stumbled as she flung herself away from the wicked snap of its teeth and it saw her on the ground and knew this was its moment.

The wolf reared back on its hind legs, the great sweep of its tail raising a cloud of pollen behind it as it brushed over the heads of the grass. And then its front paws came down, claws unsheathed and slashing for a killing blow.

They caught her this time, low on the ribs, and she had a moment to wonder how a ghost could be injured, and then she found out. Her skin tore, not like flesh but something finer, the lightest silk. And when it did something leaked out of her, but it wasn't blood. She couldn't see it in the diffuse brightness of this world, but she sensed it. She was losing some essential essence, the thing that made her Boda, even when all her memories and all her life were gone.

She clamped a hand over the wound and flung herself forward to roll beneath the creature's legs. It roared its fury at her escape and slashed again, but she kept on rolling, flattening the grass beneath her and releasing a smell that was quite wrong, like sugar burning.

And then her back hit something else, something cold and hard – metal. She didn't make a conscious decision to reach for it, just incorporated it into her roll as she tumbled even further from the wolf, curling her hand around its smooth end and pulling up.

It was surprisingly heavy, wrenching at a shoulder that was somehow still tender, even in death. The wolf growled and lowered its head, hackles bristling on its back, and Boda only had one second to see what it was she'd taken. It was long and thin – sharp only at the point. It was a weapon, though like none she'd ever seen. But in this desperate fight she'd use whatever she could.

She hid it behind her as the wolf stalked forward. The creature's eyes were too wise to risk it understanding what she intended. Its tongue snaked out to wet its purple lips and she wondered what it might taste like, to eat a human soul.

Then, with no warning, the wolf leapt. Its paws descended towards her, each larger than her head, the pads like soft brown storm clouds. And, when the nearest was above her, she pulled the strange silver spear from behind and stabbed upward, into the animal's most sensitive flesh.

It yowled in agony and leapt away. The spear pulled in her hand but she clung on grimly and it came away with her and not the beast, leaving red blood to spurt from its injured paw, sticky and hot on her face and hair.

The wolf was crazed with pain and fury now, more lethal than ever. But it wasn't thinking clearly any more. It wanted to kill her, crush her – destroy this thing that had hurt it so badly. Its head snapped down towards her, snarling and spitting, and suddenly something even more vital was in her spear's reach.

And in the moment before she thrust it forward, Boda suddenly recognised the shape of her weapon – a hairpin, magnified a thousand-fold. It must have fallen from the giantess's head when she died. The realisation almost stayed Boda's arm but her will to survive was too strong.

The pin flew forward, past the wolf's snout, its snarling teeth – and straight into the great brown orb of its eye. Her arm went after, plunging into the glutinous fluid that spilled out, passing through it to pierce the orbit of the eye itself. And in the moment the spear punctured the wolf's brain, everything changed.

CHAPTER TWENTY

The first thing Boda saw was Petronius, Nero clinging to his left hip. The young man seemed oblivious to her presence, but the little boy stared at her over the corpse of something she was no longer sure was a wolf. The fur around its muzzle suddenly looked green, scale-like, and why had she thought it only had one head, when it so clearly had two?

No, not two, three – and of course those weren't scales, the fur was bristly brown. A dog's fur. The silver spear she'd used to kill it had pierced the central eye of its central head. And beyond the third head, staring at her in bafflement, was a face she'd never expected to see again.

"Narcissus!" she said, and he smiled uncertainly.

And then, as she watched, there was neither a wolf nor a serpent nor a three-headed dog lying between them all, but only a pile of freshly stripped bones, and soon even those faded from sight and the floor was just marble, black and white chequers receding down a corridor into an endless distance.

"Boda?" Petronius said, doubt and painful hope in his voice. His head swung from side to side, as if he was trying to seek her out by scent or sound alone. His eyes were as big and brown as ever, but they'd lost all expression. She realised with a shock of horror that he was blind.

"You found me– " she said, her words cutting off as he stumbled forward to fling his arms around her. She didn't know what else she would have said, anyway. How could she be pleased to see him, here?

"Are you're –" he said.

"Dead. Still dead." When she saw the sorrow on his

face, she didn't say the rest. "And you? Did Vali kill you too?"

"No. Sopdet opened the gates of death. She's very close behind." His head twisted, as if he might be able to see her.

"I'm sorry, but who are you?" Narcissus asked. His blank face was as blind in its own way as Petronius's eyes, and Boda suddenly remembered the wind which had tried to rip her apart when she first crossed over into this realm. She feared that Narcissus had felt it too, and failed to resist.

"We're your friends," she told him, and he smiled and nodded, happy to accept her word.

"Is that Narcissus?" Petronius asked.

"Am I Narcissus?" he asked and Boda answered 'yes' to both of them.

She turned to Petronius. "What happened to Vali?"

He shot a startled, blind look around him. "He was just here, a moment ago. Listen, Boda, he really is Sopdet's brother, and I don't think he's a man. I think he's—"

"A god," she said. "The god of mischief, whom the Egyptians call Set and my own people call Loki. I know. He's used us all, but he's still right. Sopdet must be stopped."

There was a sound behind them, footsteps echoing down the long corridor.

Petronius flinched, and Boda took his arm.

"She's coming," he said. "How do we stop her, if she's a goddess too?"

"We go on," Narcissus said. He spread his hands when they turned to face him. "The dead god must stay dead. It's the only thing I know."

The footsteps grew louder behind them, and Boda didn't argue, just pulled Petronius on, along the black-

and-white tiled corridor, which led only into darkness.

When she saw the figures up ahead, she thought at first that they were more of the half-real shades who drifted through this place. But her footsteps stuttered to a halt when she saw their faces, glaring at her out from the most shameful corners of her own past.

"Josephus," she said. Death hadn't made him whole again. The cavities in his chest and stomach gaped raw and red, and there was a trickle of white brain matter from his nose.

"You killed me, barbarian," he said. "You condemned me to this place."

It was only the truth and she couldn't deny it. "I didn't know," she told him. "I'd change what I did if I could."

"But you can't. You can't!" said another voice and this time it was Petronius who flinched.

She was a young girl, not much older than him, ivory-skinned and flat-faced like the people of the far east. "I died of the child you got in me," she said, "and you weren't even there to watch me bleed my life away. Your father sold me to labour in the mines, and you never raised your voice in protest."

Boda could feel the shiver in Petronius' arm through the hand she rested against it. He took a step back, and she realised she had too.

Nero huddled against his legs, whimpering, and when Boda saw the little girl with the crushed head she understood. That spirit haunted her too.

Then another figure stepped forward, an older woman, grey-haired and sad-faced. "My son," she said to Narcissus, and Boda saw the resemblance between them, the two-thin, not quite pretty faces.

His remained blank. "Are you my mother?"

A single tear tracked down her cheek. "It broke my

heart when they sold you away from me. I didn't last another year, and by then you'd already forgotten me. You loved the master who parted us more than your own flesh and blood!"

Boda winced at the pain in the woman's face, but Narcissus only frowned. "I'm sorry, I don't remember you. And I've forgotten how to feel guilt."

There were more spirits behind Narcissus, crowding back into the darkness. Boda saw faces she barely recognised but knew all the same; every Roman soldier she'd sent to his death stood beside the blue-eyed Celts she'd cut down when they tried to invade her land. Beside her, she felt Petronius begin to sob as more voices called out his name. And then she saw the smallest figure as it pushed itself to the front, the stumbling, awkward shape of a baby too young to be born. It mumbled a word that might have been 'mummy'.

Boda turned to flee, only to fall to her knees when a hand grabbed her. She didn't dare look back to see whose it was. It could be any of a hundred people. She hadn't realised she'd killed so many. So many lives unlived because of her.

But it was only Narcissus. "Close your eyes," he said. "And I'll lead you."

She didn't want to follow him. She couldn't bear the thought of passing those spirits, their dead flesh touching hers. But then she heard Petronius stumble to his feet beside her. He was already blind. If he could find the courage to face it, so could she.

Narcissus's hand was hot and dry in hers and she was reminded suddenly of their escape from the catacombs beneath Rome. Narcissus had rescued her, though it had been Petronius who led them.

There too she'd been afraid of what hid in the dark.

Here she'd seen their faces, but did that really make it worse? Wasn't the unknown always more frightening than the known? Still, when the ghostly hands reached out and touched her, she couldn't stop herself flinching away, and only Narcissus's firm grip on her hand kept her from fleeing. She heard Petronius whispering words which might have been a prayer, but the spirits he faced were less malevolent than her own. He'd killed only tangentially – by neglect or ignorance. She'd set out to take life, and only now, as she felt them plucking at her clothes and whispering in her ear did she know the value of what she'd stolen, from so very many people.

She'd looked down on Petronius, because he'd never trained as a warrior and didn't know what it was to kill a living man. Now she understood that it made him the better person.

The journey seemed to take for ever. She wondered if perhaps it would, if they'd failed and this was their punishment. Could the prison that awaited her when this mission was done be any worse?

But it did end. The whispers faded into nothing and after a while she felt no more hands reaching for her. She sensed a greater emptiness around her, as if the corridor had opened into something far more vast.

"Can I look now?" she asked.

It took a moment before Narcissus replied, and when he did his voice sounded choked, as if there were tears in it. "Yes," he said. "They've gone. Everything's gone."

She opened her eyes to utter darkness. Narcissus's hand was still in hers. She could hear Petronius's breathing beyond, and Nero's quiet sobbing beside him, but aside from that nothing. She took a step forward and round, fumbling until she could catch Petronius's other hand in her own. His was softer and warmer than Narcissus's, and he gave her a grateful squeeze. His face alone was visible in the darkness, just the barest shadowed outline of his rounded cheek.

"What is it?" he said.

"All our ghosts left," Narcissus told him, "and they took the light with them."

There was something different in his voice, and after a moment Boda realised what it was. The blank innocence was gone. "You remember," she said.

She felt his nod travel down his shoulder to her hand. "When my mother left, the memories came."

"So what do we do now?" Petronius asked.

"We go on," she said grimly, releasing his hand, and they did, into the endless darkness. They went on and on and nothing changed, no hint of light ahead of them and no murmur of voices to either side. They might have been walking in place, and maybe they were.

"Are we there yet?" Petronius asked, after an uncounted time.

"We're nowhere," Boda said and saw his mouth twist down.

She saw it, when she could see nothing else. Why was he alone visible in this world? Her footsteps slowed as she pulled the others to a halt beside her and turned to face Petronius.

He was the source of the light. She could see its faint shine from beneath his eyelids. She reached out to touch them, soft skin with the hardness of his eyeballs beneath. He flinched away in surprise before leaning longingly into the contact. And suddenly she remembered what Vali had told her, in the moment before she died – that he'd make sure she had with her everything she needed.

"Petronius," she said. "How did you lose your sight?"

"I saw the sun, burning on the barge that carries it

through the night."

"And do you see it still?"

His throat bobbed as he swallowed. "It's all I'll ever see again."

"Then let it out," she told him.

He shook his head, baffled.

"Open your eyes."

He hesitated, then flicked his eyelids open. "I'm still blind," he said after a moment. The disappointment in his voice was painful to hear, but she could see something, a golden light in the dark heart of his pupils.

"That's because you're holding the light inside you," she said. "You have to let it out. Let it go."

"How?"

"Just do it. Let the sun out. Give me the light, Petronius – please."

He looked almost wistful at that. But in his eyes the light burned brighter, and she thought she could see it now, the red-gold sphere of the sun trapped inside.

"Oh," he said. "Oh, I—"

And then the light roared out of him, blazing from his eyes and flattening his round face into blankness. Boda shielded her eyes but for an instant she was blinded too. And then she blinked them open and Petronius was in front of her, blinking back at her.

"I can see," he said. "I can see you."

And they could see everything else, too.

For a moment, Boda thought they'd somehow returned to the Temple of Isis. This marbled space shared its dimensions, its high vaulted spaces and its darkness. Behind the great, seated figure of the goddess, she could see the gateway to death, green light flickering at its rim.

But when she took a step nearer and saw the pale-faced

spirits flooding through the gate, she understood. This hall was what lay on its far side. Then the figure on its throne stirred, and she realised with a shiver of fear that it was no statue. His form was lost in shadows, but she felt the power roll off him like a cold mist, the dead god who ruled this realm.

Boda fell to her knees, and beside her she felt Petronius and Narcissus doing the same. Only Nero remained standing, his head on a level with theirs and his eyes happy and unafraid as he looked up into the hidden face of death.

"So," Osiris said, "you have come to me, mortals, as my brother foretold."

There was a shifting in the darkness at his feet and Boda realised that there was another figure there, huddled and chained.

"Hello, Vali," she said.

He bowed his head, but she saw the shadow of a smile beneath his sharp nose and knew that his plotting wasn't over yet.

"We come to seek a boon, my lord," she said to the dead god.

"A boon?" His voice was as flat as a cracked bell, dying without echo in this vast dark space. "I know what it is you seek. And you too, my beloved."

Isis stepped forward to tower beside them, as tall as the god she'd come to redeem from death. Her face was as perfect and ageless as ever, but the desperate joy in her eyes made her seem almost human.

"I've come to reunite us, my love," she said. "To bring you back to the living world."

"The living world?" Osiris said, and for a moment the gateway behind him cleared and broadened until Boda could see the entirety of Rome spread out before her. The legion of the dead had swelled, and the streets were thick with corpses, but the living still survived, barricaded inside their houses or fighting in little, desperate clusters in the street.

Narcissus cried out, and after a moment Boda saw why. Claudius had gathered the free people of Rome into the Arena while the dead congregated outside. The Praetorian Guard held the gates, the gladiators she'd trained with beside them, but their defence couldn't last long. They were too few, and too tired. She saw Marcus, the captain of the guard, cut down by the risen body of one of his own men. Adam ben Meir, who once tried to kill her, stepped in to fill the breach.

And then, beyond the walls of Rome, throughout the whole world, she saw worse. There was no greenery anywhere, only the brown of dead grass and wilting leaves, and the same grey nothingness on every face she saw.

"The living world needs you, sister," Osiris said. "It is barren and loveless without you."

"I will return," Isis said, "when you return with me. I've missed you so much. Without you, my life is barren and loveless."

"So you killed the world to give me a place in it."

"It's not quite ready yet," she said. "But soon we can be together again – and for all eternity."

"And that is your wish. You have made your way to me, sister, which grants you the right to ask one gift, if it is within my power to give. But these others have journeyed here too, through obstacles more profound than you have faced, and they also earned that right."

Boda tried to meet Vali's red-brown eyes, but they were veiled beneath his lids, and Osiris's face was lost in shadows. Was he toying with them? Legend said the judge of the dead was fair, but then legend also said that Isis was loving and kind.

Boda didn't understand how she knew it, but she sensed the dead god's attention shifting to Petronius, his regard so heavy that she saw the young man buckle beneath it.

"And you, child of Rome," Osiris said. "You wish to close the gates of death, and condemn me to this realm for ever."

"Well," Petronius said, voice shaking. "Condemning you to this realm is really only a side effect of saving the world. It's nothing personal, if that makes any difference."

She felt a dank wind blow over them as the dead god shook his head. "And would you still wish it, if you knew what closing the gate entailed? For you live, and the woman you love has died, and if the world is restored she may not join you in it. But if you allow my sister to have her way, you and she may remain united for as long as you both desire."

The hope on Petronius's face was so naked that Boda had to look away from it. She understood suddenly that Osiris was both playing entirely fair and cheating horribly.

She tried to tell Petronius not to take the bait, but found her voice sticking in her throat. It seemed this was his decision alone to make, and she wouldn't be allowed to interfere.

The silence stretched on for a long time as he knelt with his head bowed. But when he looked up there were tears in his brown eyes. "The thing is," he said. "If I did that, she couldn't love me – so what would be the point?"

Osiris's laugh was as dry as autumn leaves. "A paradox indeed. And what of you, boy?"

Now Narcissus cringed under his unseen scrutiny. "The

dead god must stay dead," he said. "Charon himself told me that, my lord."

"And is the ferryman's power greater than mine? If I go through to the living land, this realm requires a judge to take my place. Would you do it, slave? I could place you above every man and woman on earth. You would have the power to punish those who wronged you."

"Why me?" Narcissus asked, and Boda winced. He was tempted, she could tell.

"Because a ruler should know what it is to be ruled," Osiris said. "And who better to judge the sins of Rome than one who was their victim? Caligula is already in my kingdom, awaiting judgement. Would you like to deliver it? You could give him back a thousandfold the torment he gave you. It is in your power to make him suffer the pain of crucifixion every day for eternity."

Narcissus swallowed. "But not every Roman was cruel. My master…"

The dead god shifted in his throne with a sound like rock crumbling. "Yours would be the power to reward, too. You could bring as much pleasure to the pure as suffering to the guilty. What do you say, Narcissus?"

He stood up, looking as if he had to press against a great weight to do it. "But I'd have to choose, wouldn't I, who suffered and who didn't? I was born poor and powerless. I never had the ability to hurt anyone, so I never did. But how can I be sure that if I'd been raised high, and not low, I'd have been any better than them?"

"Do you not know yourself, boy?" Osiris asked in his strange, flat voice.

Narcissus shrugged, but he didn't drop his gaze. "I don't think anyone can know that. And I won't stand in judgement on people for crimes I might have committed in their place."

There was a moment's frozen stillness, then Boda felt the dead god's attention shifting to her. It pressed against her mind, a power so strange and ancient that she could barely comprehend it. She knew that it was looking inside her, and that it saw everything.

"Woman of the north," Osiris said, "you have made a terrible bargain, but I can spare you its consequences."

Petronius's head swung to face her. "What bargain?"

She didn't reply, but the dead god said: "In exchange for the knowledge to complete her quest, she agreed to suffer for all eternity upon its completion. A vow to a god that may not be broken."

"It's true, Petronius," she said when she saw the denial in his face. "I had no choice."

"But what if your mission is never completed?" Osiris asked. "Then your vow need never be honoured. While the doors of death remain open, you remain free. What say you, daughter of Midgard?"

Now she understood the terrible temptation that had been placed in front of Petronius and Narcissus. The image of that prison hovered in the back of her mind, like a nagging pain that couldn't be ignored. She'd suffered enough in her life to be able to imagine what eternal torment might feel like. She could imagine it all too well.

And now, instead of that, she could be free – without breaking her word. The world would die, but why should she suffer to save it? She hadn't led a blame-free life, but she didn't deserve that. No one did, not even Vali.

She was shaking as she pushed herself to her feet, and she couldn't meet Petronius's eyes. She knew he'd want her to take the dead god's bargain, but the Boda he loved wasn't the woman who could accept what Osiris offered – another of the dead god's twisted paradoxes.

"No," she said. "I will keep my word. Let the gates of death be closed."

"Ah," he said, a bass note she felt in her bones. "Then it seems we have met an impasse, where I cannot grant one wish without frustrating another."

"Wait," Vali said suddenly. "Wait. Let me suffer the punishment, it's not Boda's to endure. The crime wasn't hers."

He crawled forward a little, chains rattling, until his face was in the light. He wasn't smiling now. His red-brown eyes looked wide and shocked, as if he couldn't quite believe his own words.

"Why?" she asked him, a desperate hope blooming inside her.

He shrugged. "Because I let a little girl die, and I can't forget her face. Because I spent too long as a mortal and forgot how to be a god, and if I let you suffer for my sins, your face will haunt me for all eternity and even that prison might be easier to bear."

"Brother, your bargain is accepted," Osiris said. "The one who is responsible for this shall pay for it, in full."

In front of him, Isis smiled, a chilling expression.

"Sister," Osiris said, "you see that my killer is repentant. Will you forgive him?"

"Forgive him?" she hissed. "Never." While her love had looked human, her hate was larger and more terrible than that.

"Will you not remit one year of his sentence? Not even one day?"

"Not one hour," she said. "Not one second. Let him suffer the way he made me suffer."

"You?" Osiris said. "Yes, I see. It is your suffering you wish to end, not mine. So then beloved, is this your final word? Shall we be reunited at last?"

There was a sound like fingernails grating against glass as he rose to his feet. Vali skittered out of the way, awkward in his chains, and then Osiris stepped into the light.

Isis gasped as she recoiled. Boda shielded her face from the sight but it was seared on her memory. He was hideous, decayed and rotting. He was dead, and more monstrous in death than any mortal man could be.

"What happened to you?" Isis whispered.

"I died, beloved," he said, his shrivelled tongue visible through the holes in his gaunt cheeks.

"But... but you can be whole again! You can live!"

Osiris shook his head. "That can never be. But this world you mean to create, this world of death, there I can have a place and we may be reunited."

He took a step towards her, and she took one back. Boda might almost have pitied the horror in her face.

"No," Isis said. "I want you back as you were. Not this shadow, this mockery!"

Boda thought she read sadness on his rotting face. "The shadow is all that remains." He reached out a hand, swathed in bandages like the Egyptian dead. "Can you not love me as I am?"

She stared at his hand but didn't take it, and after a moment he let it drop.

"Then it has all been for nothing," he said. "And you must reverse what you have done."

Her mouth set in a mulish line. "Why should I? What care I for the world now?"

"The living world is your realm," Osiris said, "and you must return to it. Heal it, sister. It is your duty. Summon back the spirits of the dead to where they belong."

She stared at him a moment longer, but his decaying face was set in a severe frown, and after a moment she raised her hand. "Come then," she said, facing the gate. "It's over. It's all over."

Boda watched the gateway, waiting for the spirits to flood back through, but nothing happened. The green light buzzed at the edges and the dead only passed out.

After a moment, Isis stepped back. "I don't understand. They're not listening to me."

"Because you speak with hate, sister. They must be called with love."

She raised her arm again, then dropped it. "I can't. I don't love them. Now you're dead, I'll never love again."

"Ah," Osiris said, and Boda heard the same finality in his voice that had been in Mimir's when she made her vow to him. The dead god's milky eyes turned to her. "Then you must summon them, daughter of man. Or the world will remain a realm of death and your quest will have been for nothing."

It seemed impossible. How could she do what a goddess couldn't? But Osiris said they needed to be called with love and Boda thought that maybe she understood. When she'd found herself confronted by the spirits of those she'd killed, she'd tried to run from them. It hadn't been because she feared them. She'd run because she understood that all the people she'd killed were people who in another world might have been her friends. Someone had loved them, even if it hadn't been her.

And someone had loved all those spirits out there too. Isis had filled them with hate when she summoned them, with resentment against the living who had carried on when they had stopped. She understood that. Death was hard to accept. It wasn't meant to be easy. But it was necessary, because the living required it, and the dead were all people who had once loved the living.

She felt her mind, pressing outwards, expanding in

ways she didn't understand. It travelled through the gate and into the outside world. Out there she could sense them, all the lost dead spirits, and she called their names. She knew them all, though there were a million of them. She knew them all individually, and though some of them had been terrible people, she found something in them that had loved or been loved, and she used it to call them back.

It was Petronius's voice which summoned her back to her body, crying out in fear as the spirits of the dead howled through the gateway, returning from the land of the living. A blue fire flickered around their peaceful faces as they flew past.

Beside him, Isis screamed. "No! What have you done? You've given her my power!"

Surrounded by the ghosts of the dead, Osiris shook his head. "I did not take it, you gave it up. You renounced it, and your right to it, when you sacrificed the world for yourself. But the world needs a goddess of love and life, and my brother has found a replacement."

"What?" Boda said. She shook her head, but the denial was pointless. She could feel the power inside her, too large for her small mortal frame. She felt it burning the mortality out of her, until she was something very different from what she'd always been. "But I'm a warrior," she said. "I know duty, and honour and war – not love."

"There is duty in love," Osiris said, "and honour too. Or there should be. Now –" He looked down at Vali, and the chains fell from him. Boda heard his joints pop as he straightened and when he had, he'd grown to the size of Osiris. She realised that she had too. But Isis had shrunk. She shivered beside Petronius. She looked human now because she was, everything godly stripped from her.

"Please, beloved," she said.

Boda did pity her then, but she could see in his face that the dead god felt nothing. There was only a cold, unyielding judgment in his eyes. "There must be a goddess of love," he said, "but it need not be you. And there must be someone to suffer in Vali's prison, but it need not be him. You said that the one responsible for this should be punished eternally, and so it shall be, not one day, not one second of the sentence remitted."

Isis screamed as the floor opened beneath her. The distance below seemed to stretch into infinity, but Boda knew what prison lay at the bottom, and she closed her eyes against it.

When she opened them again she found herself looking at Vali. "You knew," she said. "When you offered to take my punishment, you knew you wouldn't have to do it. You planned this all along."

His crooked smile was exactly the same whether he was a man or a god. "And if I did, you lived up to my expectations admirably. Or perhaps it wasn't like that at all. Perhaps it was my brother's scheming which lay behind all this. Maybe he planned everything, even his own death, because he knew that perfect order has no place in the living world, but the afterlife needs a judge who is fair and final."

She looked at Osiris, but his rotting face was unreadable, and Vali was never to be trusted.

"And the living world is the place for the chaos you bring, brother," Osiris said. "You must return to it now."

Vali bowed, seeming to shrink as he did. He sauntered to the gateway, but turned round to face them before he entered it, and his gaze found Petronius. "A word to the wise. If you value the new life you've been given, leave the child behind." Then he stepped through the gate.

"What?" Petronius said. He turned to Boda, craning his

neck to look up at her, but the sight of her face seemed to pain him and he looked away.

"He speaks the truth," Osiris said. "This child is one of his, an agent of chaos. If he returns to the living world, he will grow to be the man who kills you. You may leave him in death if you choose, and I will not punish you for it. The world will be more orderly without him."

Nero seemed to understand something of what this meant. He looked up at Petronius with trusting eyes, and Petronius rested a gentle hand against his head. Then he looked at Osiris and shrugged. "I've still got time to change his mind, haven't I?"

Osiris didn't say anything, and Petronius seemed to take that as an affirmative. He smiled at Nero, then hoisted him onto his hip.

"And what of me?" Narcissus asked. "I'm dead. I belong here."

"It lies in my power to grant you reprieve, since you have earned it by voyaging to me," the dead god said. "Do you wish to live again? There is always more pain in life than the dead remember."

"I do remember," Narcissus said. "But yes, I want it. There's more I want to do, no matter what it costs me."

"Go then," Osiris said. "All of you. And Boda will close the gates of death behind you." He sank down into his throne, hiding his face in shadows once again, so that his last words floated out of darkness. "Farewell, sister. We shall not meet again until the final battle, when all the gods will fall."

Boda nodded, but didn't say anything. She knew that in that battle, Osiris and Vali would fight on different sides, and she wondered now whose she'd choose.

Then the gate stood before her and she realised that she was the size of a mortal woman again, though her skin contained a thousand times what it once had.

Petronius stood to one side of her, and she smiled when she looked at him. "So," she said, "we're not to be parted after all."

"Not by the gates of death," he whispered, then followed her into life.

They'd arrived back where they started, in the Temple of Isis. The moment the gate snapped shut, the marble beneath them shook and tore. For a moment Boda was just a woman, and then she felt her power stirring within her and flung it outward. The temple roof shattered and fell and she lifted her hands and brushed it aside, keeping the two men and the small boy by her side safe.

A cloud of white dust floated down around them, and when it had settled she saw that the sky was pale blue with the start of a new day. Around them, the streets of Rome were littered with corpses, but the corpses didn't move. And as Boda felt the world with senses she didn't used to possess, and the world felt her, the brown grass poking through a crack in the wall turned green, and everywhere people remembered what it was to love, and some of them screamed when they saw what they'd done in the hours her power had been gone from the land of the living.

She turned to Petronius, wanting to share these new feelings with someone, but his eyes looked straight through her and she realised what he already had. Though death didn't separate them, his mortality did. He occupied the land of the living, and she was part of a different realm.

"Well," he said to Narcissus. "That was memorable." His voice shook, but not too much.

Narcissus nodded. "We should find Claudius. He'll need help to clean up – rebuild."

Petronius looked around him, at the wreckage in the streets. "But first, we should find a bar." He walked away, stepping nimbly over corpses with Narcissus at his side and Nero slung high on his shoulders. The little boy giggled and pointed at the mutilated remains and Petronius shifted him till he was facing away from them, towards the rising sun.

Boda watched them till they turned the corner. There was much she needed to do, a burden she hadn't asked for and wasn't sure she could shoulder. She took one last second to enjoy the dawn on the streets of Rome, then closed her eyes and went elsewhere.

EPILOGUE

She was glad to find him surrounded by his friends. There was a feast laid out on the tables and though he didn't seem to have the strength to eat, he made sure that everyone else did. She lingered at the back of the crowd for a while, watching him.

"Well, Petronius," one of the men said, a fair-haired youth who might have been of her own birth people. "She was very tall."

"Just the right height," Petronius told him, "for what I had in mind," and the men and women around him laughed.

He'd changed, of course. He was a man now, the soft lines of his face sharpened, with threads of grey in his long black curls. His eyes were the same brown, though, and after a moment they picked her out in the crowd. Shock transmuted into a moment of unguarded pleasure. Then his gaze dropped and he quirked a private smile.

"My friends," he said. "I fear it's time for you to go."

There were expressions of regret, some genuine, some fake. Some of them looked embarrassed as they brushed past her, and glad of the reprieve. They didn't know what to say to a man on the day of his death.

When they were alone, she went to sit beside him. His arms hung limply over the sides of his chair, the blood draining slowly from his wrists to the bowls beneath them.

"Boda," he said. "Or is that no longer your name?"

"It's still one of them," she told him. Close to, the signs of age were clearer on him, the fine network of wrinkles just beginning around his eyes. And his smile was more cautious than it had been, though still not bitter. He'd chosen to spend his last day with company and in laughter, and she thought that he couldn't have changed that much.

"I wondered if you'd come," he said. "I hoped I'd see you again – at least this one last time."

"I would have stopped it if I could," she told him.

He laughed. "I tried to. I don't think you would have approved. I made myself Nero's closest friend, the one he could always rely on – who never questioned him. Even Seneca showed more backbone than I did, in the end. Did you know that Claudius called the old bastard back from exile to tutor Nero when he adopted him as his son?"

Boda nodded. "I heard Seneca had time to consider the error of his ways while he was away. That he wrote some thoughts on how to face your mortality. I always wondered why Claudius didn't just have him killed."

Petronius shrugged, then winced, as the motion jarred the wounds in his wrists. "I think he was so pleased to see Narcissus in the land of the living again, it put him in a forgiving mood. Narcissus rose very high, but I expect you know that too."

"Claudius freed him," Boda said, "and named him praetor. Gave him more power than almost any man in Rome. But Narcissus picked the wrong side in the battle for the succession, and Nero killed him – he killed them both."

"The boy's sanity snapped in the underworld. I should never have taken him there. But Seneca, he had some control over him. Nero wasn't a bad Caesar, while that old bore held sway."

"And then Nero killed him too," Boda said.

Petronius laughed weakly. "Last year. While I – the court favourite, Nero's Arbiter of Elegance – lived on. I thought I could cheat fate, but... Well, you know best of all how impossible that is. And now here I am, opening my veins on Caesar's orders. I've seen my last summer, and it was only my thirty-ninth."

His eyes glazed for a moment and she knew that his death was near. Then the bright light that had always shone from them switched back on and his hand twitched, gesturing towards the table. "I've written my last words too, a letter to Nero telling him just exactly what I think of him – and reminding him of all the fun we had together, most of which I suspect he'd rather forget."

Boda smiled. "I'm sure it's a masterpiece. I read your book too, you know."

"Did you? And what did you think of it?" He barely had the energy to lift his eyelids now, but she saw that he really cared about her answer.

"You turned our story into a comedy. A sex comedy."

"A boy can dream," he said. "Besides, who wants to read about the undead?"

"But you captured the voice of the people. The ordinary people, whom no one has written of before."

"You taught me to listen to them." He sighed, and she knew that it was almost over. "I've bedded a thousand men, Boda, and a thousand women. But in all these years, I've loved only you."

"I know," she said. "I felt it."

And now the man she spoke to stood beside her, the empty shell of his body still and silent on the chair in front.

"Is that me?" he asked. "I really am as handsome as I thought."

She laughed, but the sound died when she saw the expression on his face. "It was a short life," she told him, "but a full one. Like mine."

"And unlike most people, I've already been where I'm

now going. But..." He looked away. "You can't join me there."

"That's true," she said. "The gates of death remain closed to me. So perhaps it would be best if you stayed here."

She smiled, as his head snapped round to face her. "I can do that?"

She shrugged. "Osiris owes me a favour. He's said that as long as your words live in this world, so may you."

"As long as my words live..." He looked into the distance, then switched his gaze to watch her from the corner of his eye. "That seems fair. And what shall we do, Boda, with all this time we have?"

"We should visit Vali. You're as much his as mine, after all."

"You speak to him?"

"Our paths cross. Love is a force for chaos too – I'm not sure Sopdet or Osiris ever really understood that."

He turned to face her completely, and now his expression was entirely serious. His spirit looked a little younger than his corporeal remains, but still a man, with a man's knowledge behind his eyes. "Why?"

She took his hand. "You've bound me to the mortal plane, and my mortal self – your memories of me, and your feelings. You help me to remember how it felt to be a living woman, and I don't want to forget. I don't want to become like Sopdet. You've earned a part of my godhead if you want it."

"I can be the demigod of pornography," he said.

"Of passion and pleasure."

"Why?" he said again.

She looked at his dead body one last time, then turned to leave. "Because the world's a more cheerful place with you in it."

THE END

REBECCA LEVENE has been a writer and editor for sixteen years. In that time she has storylined *Emmerdale*, written a children's book about *Captain Cook*, several science fiction and horror novels, a novelisation and making-of book for Rebellion's *Rogue Trooper* video game, and a *Beginner's Guide to Poker*. She has also edited a range of media tie-in books. She was associate producer on the *ITV1* drama *Wild at Heart*, story consultant on the Chinese soap opera *Joy Luck Street*, script writer on *Family Affairs* and *Is Harry on the Boat?* and is part of the writing team for Channel 5's *Swinging*. She has had two sitcoms optioned, one by the *BBC* and one by *Talkback*, and currently has a detective drama in development with *Granada Television*.

Out Now!

Now read a chapter from another blood drenched
title in the Tomes of The Dead collection...

TOMES OF THE DEAD

I, Zombie

Al Ewing

ISBN: 978-1-905437-72-6

£6.99/ $7.99

"The *Tomes of The Dead* series is on the top of its game with a thoroughly enjoyable romp in which those brain munching zombies we have come to love take centre stage."

– Peter Tennant, *Black Static*

CHAPTER ONE

Time slows to a crawl.

The broken glass around me hangs in the air like mountains of ice, floating in space in the Science-Fiction movie of my life. Like healing crystals in a New Age junk shop, hanging on threads, spinning slowly. Beautiful little diamond fragments.

For five minutes – or less than a second, depending on your viewpoint – I drift slowly downwards, watching the glass shimmer and spin. It's moments like this that make this strange life-not-life of mine seem almost worthwhile.

Moments of beauty in a sea of horror and blood.

I'd like to just hang here forever, drifting downwards, watching the shards of glass spin and turn in the air around me, but eventually I have to relax my grip or get bored. And I'd rather not get bored of a moment like this one.

I let go.

Time snaps back like a rubber band.

The moment passes.

Time perception is a trick of the human mind. The average human perceives events at a rate of one second per second, so to speak, but that doesn't make it the standard. Hummingbirds and mayflies perceive time differently. It's much slower for them, to match their metabolism – I'm pretty sure that's the case. I read it somewhere. In a magazine.

New Scientist, I think. Or *Laboratory News*. Maybe

Discover.

I read a lot of scientific magazines.

It might have been *Scientific American*. Or *Popular Science*. Or just plain *Science*. I go through them all.

I look for articles about decomposition, about autolysis and cell fractionation, about the retardation of putrefaction. About the factors that affect skin temperature or blood clotting.

Things that might explain my situation.

I know it wasn't the *Fortean Times*. Unless it was talking about an alien hummingbird kept under a pyramid. Or possibly building the pyramids. I read that one for the cartoons.

Anyway. Time perception is a trick of the human mind. It's possible to slow down the perception of time in humans, to perceive things in slow motion, experience more in a shorter time. Shorten reaction time to zero. Anybody can do it with the right drugs, or the right kind of hypnosis.

I can do it at will.

I concentrate.

Time slows.

The glass hangs in the air.

I look for articles about the basal ganglia and the superchiasmatic nucleus, about neurotransmitters and the subconscious. I've done research when I can. Heightened time perception burns a lot of adrenaline, apparently. A lot of energy stores. You can't keep it up for long periods without needing plenty of sleep.

But I don't need to sleep.

I don't need to eat either.

Or breathe.

Time rushes back in, like air into an empty lung that's never used.

The moment passes...

...and then the soles of the converse trainers I wear to look cool slap loudly onto the concrete floor of a disused warehouse in Hackney and four big men in badly-fitted suits are pointing guns at me. But that's okay. I've got a gun too. And if they shoot me, I won't bleed.

My heart doesn't beat, so the blood doesn't pump around my body. My skin is cold and clammy and so pale as to be almost blue, or green, depending on the light. My hair is white, like an old man's. My eyes are red and bloodshot and I keep them hidden when I can.

Let's see, what else do you need to know before we get started?

Oh yes.

I've been dead for the last ten years.

I don't have any memory of not being dead. The earliest thing I can remember is waking up in a cheap bed-and-breakfast in Stamford Hill. The room was registered in the name John Doe – the name generally used for an unidentified corpse. I'm sure somebody somewhere thought that was hilarious.

Still, it was the only name I had, so I stuck with it. To all intents and purposes, it was mine.

To all intents and purposes, the gun sitting by the sink was mine as well.

It's strange. I don't have any memory of feeling different, of anything being out of the ordinary. I got up, brushed my teeth even though they never need it, took a shower even though I never smell of anything. People hate that more than B.O., I've noticed. That smell of nothing at all, that olfactory absence. Cologne can't cover it, because there's just the cologne on its own, with that huge blank void beneath that rings all the subconscious alarm bells. Even your best friend won't tell you.

I don't remember being surprised that I was dead. I'm actually more surprised now than I was then, surprised at not being surprised. What sort of person was I, that I woke up dead and took it in my stride?

I remember that the first thing I did that day was shoot a man in the back room of a dingy pub in the Stoke Newington area.

Why did I do that? What sort of person was I then?

Obviously, I had a reason. I mean, I must have. I just can't remember quite what it was.

I had a reason. I had a gun. I had a mobile phone that was a bit clunky and crap and didn't even have games on it, never mind anything useful, and occasionally it rang and then I had a job to do that fit someone who was dead but still moving around. I had a bank account, and I had plenty of money sitting in it for a rainy day. I had a low profile.

No matter what, I always had a low profile. I always knew how to fit in, even though I was dead. Even though I killed people.

Even though I have occasionally...

Just occasionally... I may have...

I may have eaten...

You know what? I have better things to do right now than think about that.

For a start, the bad men are pulling their guns.

They're pulling their guns. My legs uncoil and I sail up, arcing forward, the first bullet passing through the space I've left behind me. I hold time in my mind, keeping it running at a reasonable speed, not too slow, not too fast. Behind me, the last shards of glass from the window hit the floor. At this speed, it sounds like wind chimes clanging softly in the breeze. The gunshots sound like the bellows of prehistoric monsters. The shells clang against the stone like church bells.

Did you ever see *The Matrix*?

Bit of a busman's holiday, I thought.

My own gun roars and I'm almost surprised. The bullet drills slowly into the head of the nearest man, already fragmenting, leaving a bloody caste-mark in the very centre of his forehead, the flesh rippling slightly under the pull of an obscene tide. I watch the exact moment when the look of surprise freezes on his face, goes slack, and then the back of his skull swings open slowly like multi-faceted cathedral doors, and the pulsing chunks of white-pink matter float out, carnival-day balloons for a charnel-house Mardi Gras.

Slow it down enough, and everything fascinates. Everything is beautiful.

Little chunks of brain, flying through the air. Scudding like clouds. Floating like jellyfish. I'm casting about for a better simile here because I don't want to admit what they really look like to me.

Tasty little hors d'ouvres. Canapes.

The trouble with being able to slow down time for yourself is that it gives you far too much time to think. And I have better things to do right now than think about that.

I speed things up a little, force myself back on the job as the bullets move faster, one cutting the air next to my left ear, another whispering against the leg of my jeans. My empty hand slaps on the concrete ahead of me and pushes my body up through space, somersaulting until I land on my feet behind a wall of stacked crates. I'm not sure what's in them, but hopefully it's something like dumbbells or lead sinkers or metal sheeting or just big blocks of concrete. Something that'll stop small arms fire. I don't want to patch up any more holes in myself.

There's a sound coming from close by. It's not wind chimes or church bells or a prehistoric monster. It sounds like some kind of guttural moaning, like a monster lost in an ancient dungeon.

I let go of time and it folds back around me like bad origami. The moment passes.

The sound makes some sense now.

It's a child. Sobbing. From inside the crate I'm hiding behind.

That's where they put Katie, then.

At least it wasn't paedophiles. At least it wasn't 'SAY A PRAYER FOR LITTLE KATIE SAYS OUR PAGE 3 STUNNER'. That's something in today's world, isn't it?

It was an old-fashioned kidnap. Scrambled voice mp3 file, two days after she went missing, nestled in amongst the inbox spam with the fake designer watches and the heartfelt pleas from exiled Nigerian royalty. 'Give us the money, Mr. Bellows, or we give you the finger. Do you see what we did there? It's a pun.' Then a time and a place and an amount to leave and no funny business, please.

Mr. Bellows runs a company called Ritenow Educational Solutions. He's the one who prints the certificates when you do the adult courses.

'This is to certify that MARJORIE PHELPS has achieved PASS in the study of INTERMEDIATE POTTERY.'

Marjorie won't get any kind of job with the certificate, even if she achieves DISTINCTION in the study of ADVANCED SHORTHAND. It's worthless, but she'll pay up to a couple of hundred pounds to have it on her wall and point it out to the neighbours.

Mr. Bellows doesn't run any of the courses. He doesn't make the sheets of china blue card with the silvery trim and 'This is to certify has achieved in the study of' written in the middle, with gaps. He just has a list of who's passed and what they got, and he runs that through a computer and then his big printer churns out ten or twenty thousand useless certificates a day. He has a staff of three single mothers and a temp who's just discovered The Specials and thinks that makes him unique, and all they do is collate the list of the gold, silver and bronze medal winners in these Housewife Olympics and then print them onto china blue with silver edging and sell them on for exorbitant amounts of money.

Mr. Bellows runs a company that does essentially nothing to make essentially nothing. He's the middleman for a useless end product. He's living the British Dream.

And now, the British Nightmare.

Doing nothing to make nothing is a profitable line of work. Mr. Bellows has two houses and two cars, neither of which have more than two seats. He also has a flat in Central London which he's working up the courage to install a mistress in. Little Katie Bellows is going to Roedean as soon as she's old enough. If she gets old enough. Mrs Bellows collects antique furniture as a hobby. And Mr. Bellows has my mobile number.

That doesn't come cheap.

"Find them, John," he said.

He had whisky on his breath and his voice came from somewhere deep in his throat, rough and hollow, choked with bile. "Find them and kill them. Bring her back safe." There were tears in his eyes that didn't want to come out. A big, gruff man who could solve things with his fists if he had to, but not this. Standing in the drawing room he'd earned with graft and grift and holding my dead hand and trying not to cry. The echo of his wife's soft sobbing drifting down from an upstairs bedroom. An antique clock on the mantelpiece that hadn't been wound, silent next to a photo turned face down because it couldn't be looked at.

Frank Bellows had my number because he'd used me in the past to do things that weren't strictly legal. He hadn't always had the monopoly on doing nothing to make nothing. He'd needed someone who didn't strictly exist to break into a competitor's office and burn it to the ground. Because if the perpetrator doesn't strictly exist, then it isn't arson, is it? Not strictly.

I smiled gently behind my shades, a non-committal little reassurance. Then I stepped back and nodded gently. He only sagged.

"Get them. Kill them. Get out." His voice was choked as though something was crawling up from inside him, some monster of grief that had made its nest in the pit of his stomach. I felt sorry, but what could I do? They only make promises in films.

But then, they only make this kind of kidnap in films. If they'd been real crooks, well, she'd be vanished still. 'HUNT FOR MISSING KATIE CONTINUES PAGE EIGHT. Saucy Sabrina, 17, holds back the tears as she keeps abreast of the news of Little Katie – and speaking of keeping a breast! MISSING KATIE BINGO IN THE STAR TODAY.'

These weren't 'real' crooks. They were fictional. The script-written ransom note. The suits from Tarantino, the bickering and sniping at each other with perfect quips that they'd spent months thinking up, while I stood on the warehouse skylight, the one they hadn't even bothered to check, picking my moment to crash through the glass and kill them all because the customer is always right. The lack of any covering of tracks, because they were too busy being 'professional' to actually be professional.

There's nothing more dangerous than a man who's seen a film.

The police would have found them eventually, but by that time Katie, age six, probably would have been killed.

They're keeping her in a crate and shooting at her, for God's sake.

It can't be healthy.

Bullets smashing wood, sending splinters and fragments into the air, puffs of shredded paper. The crates are full of catalogues, thick directories of day-glo plastic for schools. 'Teach your child about disabilities. Neon wheelchairs help kids learn.' Most of the bullets thump into those, gouging tunnels and trenches until their energy is spent.

One comes right through the crate I'm hiding behind. Right through, and there's a little yelp. A little girl's half-scream, too frightened to come all the way out.

The silly bastards have hit her.

Instinctively, I grab time and squeeze it until it breaks. Dead stop.

This is the slowest I can go. I look at the bullet, crawling from the hole. Slightly squashed but unfragmented. No blood on it. It missed.

Oh, thank God.

I'd never have managed to explain that.

Time rushes past me like a tube train and my legs hurl me backwards, firing over the top of the crates at them. Follow me. Shoot at the catalogues. No father's going to mourn a listing of expensive fluorescent dolls with only one leg. Shoot the crates over here, you silly bastards, you wannabe film-stars.

And they do.

I squeeze off a couple of shots at them, but they've found their own cover. More crates, more catalogues. Right now they seem to just be blazing away with their guns held sideways like in a music video. When they run out of bullets they'll probably chuck them at me. The trouble is, they're such rubbish shots, because of their crappy sideways gun shooting and their stupid unprofessional Tarantino mindset that thinks all they have to do is blaze away and the bullet will magically find its way into my face if they can only look cool enough doing it, that they're going to blow Katie's head off long before they put a hole in me.

It's time I got a little bit creative.

One of the advantages of being dead is that you can do things that people who aren't dead can't do. Actually, most people who are dead can't do them either, but never mind that for now. The important thing is that I can do them.

For example, my left hand – the one not sporadically pointing the gun over the crates and keeping them busy – is severed. It's held on with surgical wire.

I have no idea when this happened.

I mean, it must have been done after I woke up ten years ago. Surely. Nobody living has their hand chopped off and stuck back on the stump with surgical wire.

I mean, you'd have to be insane.

What sort of person was I?

My memory is a little fuzzy on things like that – whether I'm insane or not. I do kill a lot of people.

And I do eat... occasionally, I do eat people's...

But I have better things to do right now than think about that.

I shoot off three or four rounds to keep them busy, then put the gun to one side and grip my left hand in my right. And I pull. I'm a lot stronger than the average person, even the alive ones. Since I feel no pain and never need to rest, my muscles can work much harder, strain much longer. The wire snaps easily, link by link, and my hand pops right off in a couple of seconds, like a limb off a Ken doll.

Now I'm holding my left hand in my right, feeling the dead weight of it. Only it's not dead. Well, it is, but it's still wriggling. Twitching. Flexing.

I can still move it.

I wiggle the fingers on my severed hand. I snap them, and the sound is like a dry twig snapping. Then I toss it over the wall of crates like a grenade – a hand grenade, ha ha. The fingers hit the floor first and skitter like the legs of a giant beetle. I can feel them tapping the concrete. And then – it's off. Racing across the concrete floor as the wannabe filmstar boys widen their eyes and make little gagging sounds in their throats. They know what kind of film they're in now. Oh yes.

I can feel it moving. I can feel the fingers tapping. I'm reaching to pick up my gun, but I know exactly where my other hand is. Moving quickly across the floor, skittering and dancing, a dead finger ballet. I can see it in my mind's eye. Is it me, drumming my fingers, that's propelling it along? Or is it my hand, moving further away from me now, a separate entity crawling and creeping on its own stumpy little legs?

The further away from me it gets, the more I think it's the latter.

The more it moves on its own.

That's pretty weird, if you think about it.

What sort of person was I?

I can still feel the fingers tapping, but I'm not directing it any more. It's close now. Skittering around the crates as they lower their guns and stare in horrified fascination. I can't help but hum to myself at moments like these.

Their house is a museum... when people come to see 'em... they really are a scree-um... the Addams Fam-i-ly.

Ba da da DUM.

It leaps.

I mentioned how strong I am. And when my hand is this far away from me... there's really no human impulses to hold it back. The fingers flex and push against the concrete and launch it forward like a grasshopper, onto the face of the nearest cinema tough-guy. He's in a film now, all right. He's in *Alien*.

Where's your Tarantino now, you tosser?

Fingers clutch, sinking into cheeks. I can feel his lips against my palm, squashed, pleading desperately, trying to form words. I have no control over my hand, my evil hand. But I still enjoy feeling it squeeze... and squeeze... and squeeze... until the fingers plunge through the flesh and crack the bone, crushing the jaw, the thumb and the forefinger alone mustering enough pressure to punch through the temples, cracking the skull, sending ruptured brain matter seeping out of it.

Brain matter.

I've got better things to do than think about that.

My hand drops away, sticky with blood and juice, as the last one starts blazing away at it, shrieking like a little girl. He misses every shot. It's a hard thing to hit, a scuttling hand, and besides he's probably still holding his gun sideways. I'm trying not to laugh, I really am.

Does that make me a bad person? Does that make me a monster?

What sort of person am I?

Crushing a man's face with my severed hand that crawls around on its own when I let it off the leash, that probably makes me a monster, I'll admit that. But I can be forgiven for the occasional chuckle at the death of a would-be child murderer. *The News Of The World* would canonise me.

His gun clicks out. He's fumbling for ammo now. He's in a whole other world now, the silly bastard. There's nothing so important to him as killing that thing that's come scuttling around the corner of his little school-catalogue fort and broken everything he thinks is real into little pieces. He's forgotten everything else in the world, which is stupid, because I'm in the world.

And I'm coming for him.

Grab time. Slow it down. Gunshots flatten and stretch into whale songs and I'm floating, somersaulting over the crates, converse trainers smacking the ground, propelling me forward as the gun comes round...

And there aren't any bullets in the gun.

How did I miss that? The slide's all the way back.

Do I even have any ammo on me?

How could I possibly miss something like that?

What sort of person am I?

He's seen me. He turns like a cloud formation revolving in a light breeze. The gun lifts like the thermometer in an unsuccessful TV telethon, one atom at a time. So slow. But so am I.

That's the trouble with compressing time. It looks great, but there's no use in slowing time down if you're already too late.

The gun goes off, slow and beautiful as sunrise, and here comes the bullet. Cross-cut head this time. I throw my weight off, but he's too close...

You need a bit of space to dodge bullets.

I don't feel pain, but still, it hurts. It hurts because there's no real way to patch the holes up when I get shot. I've been shot a fair bit, although not as much as I should have with the life I lead. In my arms and legs there are little tunnels and trenches where I've been shot with 9mm ammunition, a couple of nasty exit wounds packed up with clay. In my left breast, there's a big ragged hole from where some crack shot tore my heart open with a well-placed sniper round. I stitched up the hole as best I could, packed it with gauze... but my heart is sitting in my chest, not beating and torn apart. And that does hurt.

Because I do try to know what sort of person I am.

I do try to be normal.

I really do, with my severed hand and my time senses and my strength and my speed. I try and be a normal guy, as much as I can. I drink. I eat. I go to the bathroom, though it's just to sit and think for a while – there's no pressing need for me to be there, if you get my meaning. I go to the cinema and watch the popular films. I get popcorn. I used to watch *Big Brother* but now I've stopped, like everyone else. I buy *The Sun* but I get my actual news from the Internet. I listen to Radio 2. I make up opinions about religion and music and television and political parties and I try to stick to them even if they aren't very logical or intelligent. I want to be like everyone else.

I want to fit in.

I try.

I can feel the bullet press against my gut, then pierce the skin, boring into me, fragmenting, splitting, shrapnel shredding my intestines, cutting and tearing. Slowly and carefully, like surgeons' scalpels in a random operation, the surgery dictated by the roll of dice.

My arm moves forward, pushing against time. It's like I'm underwater. The gun begins to arc slowly through the air, my empty, heavy gun. Rolling and tumbling through space.

Chunks of tattered, bloody meat drift out of the ragged hole in my lower back. My T-shirt has 'The Dude Has Got No Mercy' written across it, and it's brown with kind of seventies lettering in orange and white. It's my favourite shirt and it's ruined. My shirt's ruined. My belly's ruined, because I was stupid and this silly filmstar wannabe bastard got off his lucky shot...

I watch the gun tumble through space, turning over and over, like a space station on a collision course with a nameless, forbidding planet.

I threw it very hard. The sound of his skull fracturing is like a great slab of granite, big as the world, being snapped in half by cosmic giants. It's a good sound. It makes me feel better about my shirt.

Stitch that, bastard.

I let go, and time closes over me like the case for an old pair of spectacles. The moment passes, and I stumble for a couple of steps, feeling more meat slop out of my belly and back, more scraps on the floor. There's a hard thud as a hundred and fifty pounds of flesh that used to be a human being crashes onto the concrete.

I walk gingerly around the stacked crates and have a look. His legs and arms are thrashing, his eyes rolled back in the sockets. His skull is cracked and bleeding. His fragile, fractured eggshell skull.

And the tasty yolk within.

And all of a sudden –

– all of a sudden my head is pounding and there's a hot metal taste in my mouth and I don't have anything better to do than think about –

– *Brains* –

– and now it's later.

How much later? How much time has passed?

It feels like a long time.

Mr Tarantino, the filmstar, the silly bastard, he's still lying at my feet. His position's changed. Like he's been shaken about like a rag doll.

His head is... empty.

Hollowed out. The top of it missing, cranium tossed across the room, and there's something... something is clinging to my lips. To my tongue.

Something I've been eating.

The taste is still in my mouth.

And it tastes so good.

Time is still slow, still in my grip. I look to the left, and I see a small, terrified eye staring at me through a bullet hole in the side of a packing crate. The eye slowly closes, like a curtain majestically falling, then rising, opening again. Blinking.

There's a sound in my ears like lowing cattle. It's Katie's sobbing. I wonder how much she saw?

I try to be normal. I really do. I try so hard.

But I just can't seem to stop eating brains.

And that's the sort of person I am.

I let go.

Time wraps around me like a funeral shroud.

And the moment passes.

For more information on this
and other titles visit...

Abaddon
Books

WWW.ABADDONBOOKS.COM

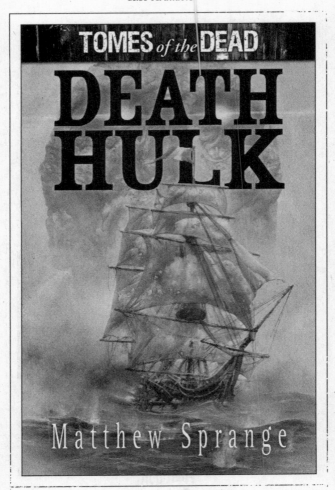

TOMES *of the* DEAD

DEATH HULK

Matthew Sprange

Price: £6.99 ★ ISBN: 978-1-905437-03-0

Price: $7.99 ★ ISBN: 978-1-905437-03-0

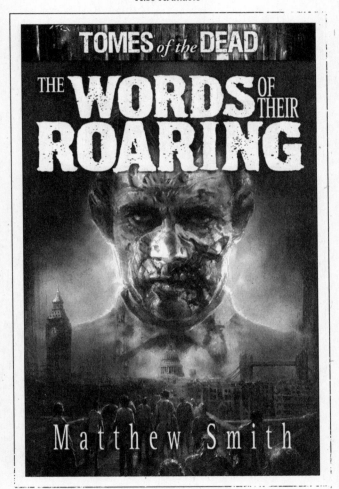

THE AFTERBLIGHT CHRONICLES

The CULLED

Simon Spurrier

Price: £6.99 ★ ISBN: 978-1-905437-01-6

Price: $7.99 ★ ISBN: 978-1-905437-01-6

THE AFTERBLIGHT CHRONICLES

KILL or CURE

Rebecca Levene

Price: £6.99 ★ ISBN: 978-1-905437-32-0

Price: $7.99 ★ ISBN: 978-1-905437-32-0

THE AFTERBLIGHT CHRONICLES

SCHOOL'S OUT

Scott Andrews

Price: £6.99 ★ ISBN: 978-1-905437-40-5

Price: $7.99 ★ ISBN: 978-1-905437-40-5

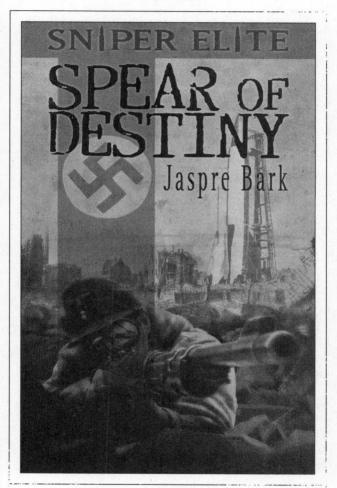

Price: £6.99 ★ ISBN: 978-1-905437-04-7

Price: $7.99 ★ ISBN: 978-1-905437-04-7

Abaddon Books

WWW.ABADDONBOOKS.COM